The D'Karon Apprentice

Joseph R. Lallo

ISBN: 1523933992
ISBN-13: 978-1523933990

Dedication

This story is dedicated to all of the fans who, with their enthusiasm and support, have made the writing of this and future stories in the *Book of Deacon Saga* possible.

Table of Contents

Acknowledgements

I would like to acknowledge my editor Tammy Salyer and my cover artist Nick Deligaris.

Prologue

Peace is a fragile thing. A long war drives a people. It works its way into the minds and souls of a nation, giving them something to live for, and something to die for. When the fighting ends, the prospect of what comes after—the rebuilding and the healing—can be terrifying. The horrors of war are too often more comfortable and familiar than the challenges of peace.

What had come to be known as the Perpetual War had scoured the lands of the Northern Alliance and Tressor for as long as any could remember. Dark figures, the D'Karon, had risen to positions of power within the Alliance Army. Through this influence they had stoked the war like a furnace, burning away generations of the best men and women of both nations and weakening the world as a whole. It was only through the efforts of the divinely anointed warriors known as the Chosen that the D'Karon were finally defeated, but in many ways it was then that the greatest challenge began.

After more than a century of fighting, peace was tenuous. Heroes once called upon to vanquish evil were now tasked with holding together the ragged edges of their world until the healing could begin. Too much blood had been shed and too many lives lost to allow war to return. But in a dark place long forgotten, a spark stands ready to ignite the war anew.

#

Somewhere deep in the arid wastes of the southern shore of Tressor, a woman lay sleeping. Hers was a deep, dreamless slumber, a slumber unbroken for years. The woman was frail and forgotten, a motionless bundle of ragged cloth and withered flesh. If undisturbed, she might never have awoken, sleeping blissfully until the end of time without troubling the world or its people. But this was not to be.

Piece by piece her body flickered to life, like soggy bits of firewood sluggishly taking to flame. Her lungs took the initiative, deciding that shallow breaths were simply not sufficient. And so she breathed deep, quickly releasing it as a painful cough. Next her eyes grew weary of the darkness and slid open, feeding her mind images that it was not quite ready to comprehend. Her fingers twitched, her cracked lips parted, her dry tongue smacked, and slowly a word formed in her mind. It took several minutes of effort before it worked its way to her lips.

"Thirsty," she croaked in a voice from the wrong side of a grave, startling a nest of mice that had made a home in her hair.

She slowly scraped together enough of her wits to sit up, stiff joints crackling with every motion. The light was dim, filtering in from the mouth of a low-roofed cave. She swept her eyes around until she found beside her a small cup caked with sand and dust. Beside it was a cork-topped wine bottle. It took three poorly guided grasps before she was able to close her bony hand about the bottle's neck, and four tries to manage the complex maneuver of pulling its cork free, but persistence earned her a long swig of vinegary swill.

One need dealt with, her body quickly alerted her of another.

"Hungry," she stated, her voice a shade closer to human now.

Again she scanned her surroundings. There were empty bags chewed through by rodents and the bones of a dozen assorted animals that had been picked clean and bleached white. Nothing even resembling a meal had been in the cave for years. For a moment she contemplated climbing to her feet and seeking out some provisions, but having only just managed to work out how to use both arms at the same time, she felt the task of walking was one that would be easier to tackle on a full stomach.

She picked through the mound of bones nearest her. Though it was an uphill struggle to determine the proper sequence of opening and closing her fingers that was necessary to grasp them, oddly she found identifying them to be utterly effortless.

"Skull of a jackal. Where is the jaw? Here. Good, good. One of its legs too. Don't need the toes. A few rat spines, yes. Ah, perfect, a serpent skeleton. Intact, save the head. That will do nicely."

Like a child with a new set of building blocks, she merrily began to fit the bits of carcass together. Under her breath she uttered arcane words, conjuring black tendrils that fused the bones to one another. After a few minutes she had assembled a creature that could only have been born of madness.

The jackal skull sat atop the long, narrow spine of a snake. Ribs, femurs, and claws linked together into a set of six spidery legs that connected to the curving spine a third of the way down its length. The rest of the serpent's spine formed a curled tail. She dangled the horrid concoction by the spine, eying it critically.

"A motley bit of odds and ends, but it will have to do... Now, *live*."

Inside the hollow skull, darkness began to swirl and coil. The edge of the tail twitched, and the mismatched legs quivered. Two points of violet light sparked to life in the jackal's eye sockets. She lowered it to the ground and watched it shudder, quake, and finally hoist itself to its feet, twisting its oversize head toward her and sweeping its tail in expectation.

"Good. Now listen closely, Motley. You will fetch me food. Meat. Something large, lots of blood, lots of skin, lots of bone. Bring it quickly and I'll be sure to give you the bits I don't need."

The abomination pranced in place for a moment, radiating delight at the chance to serve, then rattled off toward the mouth of the cave. When it was out of sight, the woman ran her fingers through her scraggly white hair, combing away any other creatures that might have taken up residence.

"Now then... to work. I suspect there's much to be done."

She looked beside her and found a tall ivory staff. It was intricately carved with runes and sigils, and the top was set with a deep violet gem. She pulled the head of the staff to her lap and worked a simple spell. Inside the gem a muddy red glow pulsed, and she felt her thoughts grow sharper, if not more orderly. Yes... her name. She was Turiel. Her task. She was to prepare the second keyhole. Her masters... why had they not woken her? And why did something feel lost, something missing? She reached out, seeking guidance, but there was no answer.

"Something has happened... I've slept too long... Need answers... Something must be done..."

Chapter 1

Six months after the city of Verril was freed and the Perpetual War had failed to live up to its name, life was progressing as usual in an icy little town called Frosnell. A thoroughly unremarkable city, it contained little more than a few cobbled streets crisscrossing a city center dominated by a thriving marketplace and a sturdily built inn called Merrimead's Hearth. Though a part of the frost-bound Northern Alliance, Frosnell was far enough south to enjoy a growing season that could support more than just the hardy cabbages and potatoes of the more northerly farms. The market bustled with farmers selling their wares. With the end of the war, the slowly opening borders to the south allowed traders' wagons to appear. They were a welcome sight to locals, none of whom had yet been born when the fruits of the southern pastures had last rolled through town. On a normal day these wagons, heaped as they were with exotic goods, would be the talk of the town. Today they were the last things on the minds of the townsfolk. Far more interesting was the ornate carriage drawn by four gleaming white horses that was approaching the town from the north.

If there had been any doubt that the majestic carriage belonged to someone of great importance and influence, the escort of no less than six heavily armored men would have set it to rest. The largest of the escorts—a beast of a man who by rights ought to count as two—had taken a place of honor beside the carriage's door. Children and curious onlookers gathered around the carriage as it reached Merrimead's, but the guards kept them at a safe distance. When all was calm, the hulking guard opened the door, and out stepped a young woman layered in furs and dripping with jewels. She was the new queen and empress of the Northern Alliance, a woman named Caya. From the moment she showed her face, it was all her escorts could do to keep the locals at bay, a task made considerably more difficult by the social proclivities of the new queen.

"Hello! Yes, hello! Is this your child? Such a fine, strong boy. I'm *certain* we'll have a place for him at the palace some day!" Caya called, singling out villagers to greet. She turned to her largest guard. "Really, Tus. Need you keep them *so* far back? What good is it to be queen if I can't interact with my public?"

Tus didn't reply. He was far too busy squeezing the grip of his weapon and staring down a man who he had decided was less than trustworthy. This opinion was based primarily on proximity. Anyone near enough to fire an arrow at the queen was someone he would prefer to see move along. It was his great fortune, then, that something even more noteworthy had appeared, steadily drawing the attention of the crowd.

One by one eyes turned to the sky as a dark form drifted out of the bright clouds of midday. It was a dragon. The beast was massive, its body easily the size of an elephant and its wings wide enough to cast a shadow on half the market. Some of the townspeople reacted with fear, but more roared with excitement and wonder. This far from the mountains, there was only one dragon who would venture so near the city. Soon her crimson and gold scales were visible. The magnificent creature carried two passengers on her back, each dressed in fine, thick cloaks and huddled against the wind.

Caya grinned as the form wheeled closer to the ground. It set down just outside the city. The queen set off toward the beast without a word to her guards, but in the few months they had been guarding her, they had come to know the queen better than to expect her to give them warning of her intentions. The best they could manage was to keep up with her. Tus caught up in two easy strides, then stepped in front to serve as a plow through the thickening crowd clustered about the dragon. The creature seemed to have much the same attitude of strangers as Tus, and a hard gaze from a mighty creature served as remarkably effective crowd control. Therefore, though quite curious about the dragon and its passengers, no one in the town was bold enough to approach it too closely. The queen, on the other hand, had no such concerns. Tus elbowed his way through the ring of spectators, and the queen slipped gracefully through the wake in time to greet the first of the passengers with open arms. She was a young woman, her hair deep red and her gaze warm and compassionate.

"Myranda!" Caya said happily, wrapping her friend and ally in a firm embrace. "Don't you know it is poor manners to upstage your queen?"

"Always a pleasure, Your Majesty," Myranda said when the hug was through, stepping back to offer a respectful curtsy.

"Oh enough with that 'Your Majesty' nonsense. If you're being *accurate*, it is 'Your Royal and Imperial Majesty,' but if you start calling me that, I'll start calling you 'Your Highness.' And Deacon, my boy. How has the regal life been treating you?" She clasped his hand in a vigorous shake. "I'll wager you've barely got time to scribble in that book of yours."

"Hello, Caya," answered a young, studious man. He was somewhat disheveled from the flight, and he didn't seem quite as at ease in his finery as Myranda. "As a matter of fact, I *haven't* been able to record matters as thoroughly as I'd like."

7

"I doubt *anyone* could record matters as thoroughly as *you'd* like. But where are my manners? I mustn't forget your steed! Welcome, Myn! Let us give you a scratch!"

The dragon lowered her head until her chin rested firmly on the ground, offering up her brow for one-half of the customary reward for a job well done. Caya gave the creature a good firm rub over the eyes and a pat on the head for good measure. When she stopped, Myn's beautiful golden eyes slid open with an accusing look, wordlessly suggesting that a few more rubs might be in order. Myranda happily supplied them as the queen turned toward the inn.

"I must compliment you on your punctuality. I trust your journey was pleasant enough," Caya said, stepping briskly through the parted crowd.

Townspeople, still more intrigued by the arrival of the dragon than their monarch, attempted to close in again, trapping Myranda in the process. They quickly changed their minds when Myn released a satisfied sigh from Myranda's vigorous affections. One tends to treat the breath of a creature with great respect when there is a better than average chance it could burn one to a crisp. When Myranda was through, Myn raised her head. The motion was more than enough to finally convince those lingering around them to view the spectacle from a safer distance. Myranda took advantage of the dispersing crowd to catch up with Caya, who had continued speaking as though there was no doubt her guests had remained beside her.

"The trip was glorious, Caya. You really ought to let Myn give you a ride," Myranda said.

"Ah ha, no. Once on the back of a winged beast was more than enough for me. These feet stay on the ground."

"Is Croyden not with you?" Myranda asked, glancing to the carriage.

The queen, as was to be expected, had quite an entourage, but the elf she had taken as an informal consort was notably absent.

"Someone needs to see to the affairs of the palace. He's really rather skilled at the assorted drudgery of leadership. That's a military man for you. He did, however, handpick a keeper to look after me, see to my affairs, and see to it that I don't do *too* much to embarrass the crown. Myranda, Deacon, meet Khryss."

She gestured to a gentleman emerging from the carriage. He had an uneasy look on his face, the expression of a man who had been tasked with "handling" a woman who was simultaneously the most politically powerful and most headstrong individual in half a continent. He was portly, exceedingly neat, and dressed in a manner calculated to be precisely proper for an individual in his role. This included a fine robe that hung almost to the ground and an exquisitely made satchel hanging by his side.

"Khryss, see to it that Myn is cared for while Myranda, Deacon, and I work through some matters of state. I presume that a meeting room has been prepared for us?"

"The room, of course, has been waiting for our arrival, Your Majesty. The, err, the dragon…"

"She is quite easy to care for, as I recall. Plenty of meat, plenty of water, and as many potatoes as you can get your hands on," Caya said dismissively.

Khryss looked uneasily at the beast, who had been staring hungrily in his direction since the mention of the words "meat" and "potatoes." Myranda placed a steadying hand on his shoulder.

"Myn, this man will show you where to wait for us. Behave yourself. I'll be out just as soon as I can," Myranda said. She turned to Khryss. "She's quite sweet. You needn't worry."

"But… do mind her tail," Deacon added quietly.

Caya and her associates slipped inside, followed by Tus and four other guards. The carriage was guided to the stables, and the locals decided there was very little to be gained by standing outside an inn while a hungry dragon was about. This left Khryss and a single guard alone with the beast. He looked up at Myn. Her head towered above him at the end of a powerful, serpentine neck. There was nothing *threatening* about her gaze… but it was most certainly locked on Khryss. He reluctantly turned from the creature and scanned the market, spotting a butcher shop not far from the inn. He turned back to Myn to find she'd lowered her head, meeting him eye to eye and rumbling hungrily.

Khryss abandoned dignity, lifting the hems of his long robe to practically sprint to the butcher. He slipped inside to find the proprietor hard at work dividing an elk into steaks.

"I need meat, good sir," Khryss said quickly.

"Certainly," remarked the butcher without looking up. "How much?"

Khryss pushed the door open to find that Myn had followed him. She peered inside with interest. Khryss eyed her shakily.

"Rather a lot of it, I would imagine."

#

Inside Merrimead's, after Caya's arrival and enthusiasm for an audience had finished whipping the clientele into a frenzy, the group was led to a small, comfortable room with a table and a few chairs. Oil lanterns filled the windowless room with a warm glow, and a secure brace hung on the door. The guards took up positions outside the door, with the exception of Tus, who joined them inside. A pair of servers set a tray of dried meat and cheese before them as well as a bottle of wine, a few plates, and a few tankards. With that, they were left to their business, the door firmly secured from the inside.

"I don't know that I'll ever become accustomed to this," Myranda said, taking a piece of cheese. "For so long I hadn't a clue where my next meal would come from. Now I needn't even ask."

"One of the few benefits of the title that lives up to its expectations," Caya said after filling a tankard and draining it. "Though their spirits do tend to be a bit spineless. So Myranda, tell me, how are things in Kenvard?"

"They are moving, albeit slowly," she said. "My father is overseeing the reconstruction of the old capital. We both feel the people deserve a city to call their own once again."

"A good, strong fortified city near the Tresson border wouldn't hurt either," Caya said.

"Peace takes work, and it takes trust," Myranda said. "The Tressons don't want to lose another generation to war any more than we do."

"I'll concede that, but the facts of the matter are that the Tressons won't *need* to lose a generation if they decide to go to war with us again. As wonderful as it is to be free of the D'Karon, they *were* rather effective at keeping the Tresson troops at bay. We wouldn't last long in another offensive without their help."

"Another offensive?" Deacon said. "Have things truly degraded so far so quickly that there might be another war? The Battle of Verril was barely half a year ago."

The Battle of Verril was the name given to the crescendo of the Perpetual War, an assault on the Northern Alliance's capital and northernmost city. Myranda, Myn, and the rest of the Chosen had joined with Caya and her band of rebels to take the capital from the D'Karon generals. With them defeated, their troops quickly fell and the control of the kingdom returned to its people.

"A long war makes for a short armistice," Caya muttered.

"Things were going so well at the discussions just a few weeks ago," Myranda said.

"Much can happen in a few weeks," Caya said, filling her tankard again. She took a sip and sighed. "Much *did* happen, or so they say. Listen carefully; what I am about to say is *not* for common knowledge. There are concerns, concerns from quite high in the Tresson government, that this peace is a ruse. They have accused us of at *least* not being in control of our units, and at *worst* outright assaulting them in defiance of the truce."

"That's absurd," Myranda said. "The troops on both sides have been ordered to stand down. The borders are *open* again, at least near the larger cities. Outside of a few skirmishes between excitable soldiers, there hasn't been a blade wielded in anger since we reclaimed Verril."

Caya gestured for something from Tus. "Soldiers aren't the problem." Tus handed her a bundle of parchments. "These come directly from the Tresson contingent, assembled by them from a few scattered reports in the deep southern portions of their kingdom."

Myranda took the parchments and began to read through them, Deacon doing the same with a second set. "'It was a creature, like a dragon, but not. A mockery of one. It breathed stinking black mist that burned all it touched.'"

"'It looked to be a cape or robe, but no one wore it. It drifted about, slashing at things with bony claws...'" Deacon said.

"Sound familiar?" Caya said, topping off her tankard and leaning back in her chair.

"Dragoyles, cloaks," Myranda said, "D'Karon creations."

"And more of the same," said Deacon, leafing through the pages.

"Mmm. As I said, these come from the deep south. Far from the front. None of these people have *seen* dragoyles and cloaks. They've heard stories, rumors, but they can't be certain that it wasn't some other creature, or perhaps something imagined. But the Tresson military is not pleased and doesn't intend to take any risks. Tell me. Is it possible some of the D'Karon creatures survived the last few months?"

"It is possible, certainly. Ether spent *months* exterminating them, but she could have missed some. But the D'Karon creatures have only ever been found in the Northern Alliance. Why would they be in Tressor but not here?"

"Such was my question to the Tresson army. If these demons were ours to command, and we could sneak them past the border and strike at the *flanks* of their kingdom, why wouldn't we have done so a century ago? Why now, when the war has ended? Unfortunately the simple answer is difficult to argue. As you've said, the borders are open. Debate aside, there remains the more troubling question. Is it possible that the D'Karon *themselves* might have survived. Might they still be here? It had been in their interest to start the war. It would *certainly* be in their interest to start it anew."

"It is possible..." Myranda said. "There's only one way to be sure. We need to go to Tressor. We need to learn for ourselves the nature of these attacks and the creatures responsible."

Caya nodded. "Agreed. That is why I called you here." She took back the pages and placed them on a plate, then touched the flame of an oil lamp to them and watched them burn. "For the moment the Tressons are as interested in foregoing war as we are. They have their doubts about our stories of the D'Karon. Most still believe the nearmen, dragoyles, and other monstrosities that held our front and ravaged their soldiers were the work of powerful Northern sorcerers. As a result, they believe if the war were to begin again, they would be once again faced with an endless horde of the things. They don't realize we are effectively helpless right now. This is a rare instance where distrust is the only thing keeping us from ruin. To keep the swords in their sheaths, the Tressons are keeping these attacks as quiet as they can. I've arranged for a diplomatic tour of Tressor for you, Deacon, and Myn. You'll be escorted, naturally, and very closely watched. While you are there, you must do everything in your power to preserve peace and to find the source of these attacks. For the next few weeks at the *very* least, I will be at the temporary hall down at Five Point discussing the details of the relations between our kingdoms. If anything goes wrong, I will do my best to keep the world from catching flame. But unlike you, I do not work miracles."

"Caya, I cannot work miracles either," Myranda said.

"Bah! Save the humility for behind the podium and in front of the crowd. With drink on the table and friends at your side, that's the time to be boastful," Caya said. "I need to see you confident, Myranda. Like so many other things you've been tasked with, we can't afford failure."

"I'll do everything I can," Myranda said.

"As ever, we can only hope that will be enough. I'll be heading to the front tomorrow… or rather, the *border*. I'd best avoid more slips like *that* if I'll be speaking in the interest of peace. If the weather is with me, I'll reach Five Point in a week. Do you believe you can be ready and to the border at that time?"

"It depends, the border is still in flux a bit near Kenvard. Would we be crossing at that new settlement, Crestview? That's just a few hours south of Kenvard."

Queen Caya scowled slightly. "I know… but no, you'll be heading for the Loom River. Farther east, where the border dips down."

"Ah. Yes, I believe we can be ready in a week's time. We'll need to stop back at New Kenvard to gather some things and ready our affairs to be handled in our absence, and there are some matters farther north that will need to be seen to, but with Myn, if we leave today, it shouldn't take long. Pardon me for asking, but if it is your intention to present this as a diplomatic tour, why have you arranged for Myn to join us?"

"Officially because she is a Heroine of the Battle of Verril and a Guardian of the Realm. As such she is a symbol of our people and a representative of the throne just as the two of you are. The Tressons are going to have to accept that."

"And unofficially?" Myranda asked.

Caya took a sip of wine. "Unofficially, it never hurts to remind a former foe that you've got a dragon and you're willing to use it."

"Well, I can't argue the fact that having her along will help enormously if we need to travel or fight, but don't you think she'll cause a bit of a stir in Tressor?"

"She causes a bit of a stir *here*. Tressor's got their own dragons. I understand to keep things even they'll actually be assigning one of their famed Dragon Riders to your escort. The matter has been settled. However… there is one more complicating factor."

"If the matter of Myn has been settled, I can't imagine what remains can be *too* troublesome."

"Then you underestimate just how confounding the nuances of diplomacy can be. Naturally they will not simply allow us to come traipsing through their kingdom without an envoy of their own coming to the Northern Alliance. It is something of an exchange."

"That's a fine idea," Deacon said. "The more we understand each other, the better our relations will be in the future."

Caya grinned. "I'm *sure* that's their thinking as well. There will be three of them, and as we have three kingdoms that make up our alliance, they intend to send one representative to each."

"Excellent," Myranda said.

"And they have requested the honor of being escorted in their journey by *our* most honored subjects, the Guardians of the Realm and Heroes of the Battle of Verril."

Myranda tried to suppress a smirk. "I see."

"Yes… With you, Deacon, and Myn in Tressor, I'll personally be hosting the envoy to what was Vulcrest, as it won't require us to venture far from the site of the talks. That leaves only two Guardians of the Realm to go around."

"Ivy and Ether…" Deacon said. "I'm not *entirely* certain Ether has the proper skills to be a diplomat."

"And while Ivy will no doubt be a wonderful host, she…" Myranda began.

"Is a malthrope, and they don't like them any better in Tressor than we like them up here. They are *quite* aware, and insist it will not be an issue." She took another drink. "It'll be interesting, and it won't be without incident. But if this world could survive one hundred and fifty years of war, we'll have to hope it can survive at least a year of peace." She set her cup down and clapped her hands. "Well then. With business settled, let's get a proper meal on the table and a proper brandy in our cups."

Caya turned to call for service, but Deacon hesitantly raised his hand. "If I may?"

The queen turned to him flatly. "You annihilated a horde of abominations to protect the city that I now call my home. You needn't ask for permission to raise a subject. Speak up!"

"How will communication be handled during this journey?" Deacon asked.

Myranda smiled and leaned back. "I'd nearly forgotten!"

"I imagine the same way we always do. Each envoy will have runners, and messages will be relayed. I understand they use messenger falcons in Tressor."

"Might I suggest an alternative?" he asked, digging through his bag.

He produced a small, unassuming notebook. The covers were made from thin leather without any noticeable markings. The binding was at the top, and it was barely the size of Caya's open hand. Affixed to the binding was a length of string. Midway along the string was a tiny silver bell, and at the end was a smooth gray stylus. Caya flipped through the pages to find it empty.

"I've prepared seven of these. One each for myself, Myranda, Ivy, Ether, and you, plus some spares to be left in central locations. I sent another via messenger to the capital a few weeks ago, which should have arrived by now," he said. There was pride in his voice.

"I don't imagine you are merely suggesting we pass these pads between us with the messengers."

"No, of course not. There would be no need! These are much more convenient. Watch." He arrayed the remaining six on the table. "Write the word 'all' and underline it twice."

Caya looked at Myranda with a raised eyebrow and received an encouraging look in return. With a few crisp swipes of the stylus, she scrawled the word. Despite the lack of ink, a clear black line followed the tool. When she'd drawn the final line, the covers of the other books flipped open and the styli rose, ringing their bells as they did.

"Now write something," he said.

Caya scribbled her name. The other styli quickly duplicated it exactly.

"It is the same enchantment I've used to transcribe my notes, modified somewhat. You can address a message to anyone or everyone that has one of these books. Simply write their name, underline it twice, and write the message."

The queen nodded in appreciation, though her attitude was more like that of a parent humoring a child. "Clever. I see there are only eight pages."

"The book will never fill. There will always be at least four blank pages, and the note you are searching for will always be on the second page."

She nodded again, this time a bit more genuine in her interest. "We'll certainly put it to the test with this mission. Enough business. Let us dine!"

#

Not long after their meeting with Caya, Myn soared through the icy skies nearing New Kenvard. Myranda's mind was heavy with the task ahead, but even so she couldn't help but marvel at the view. The magic of flight, of traveling so far, and seeing so much all at once, had never truly worn off. From above, things were simple, beautiful. Patches of white snow striped with gray roads and mottled frosty green forest painted the landscape. Cities were mosaics, intricate and unique. Even her own home, the devastated ruins of a place once known as the city of Kenvard, seemed almost elegant from the skies.

The illusion faded as she circled lower and more details became clear. The palace was little more than rubble. Whole streets and quarters lay abandoned and decaying. The walls were hastily patched in some places and wholly missing in others. What few buildings still stood were cold, lifeless structures constructed by the forces that had occupied the city after its collapse. New Kenvard, the capital of the region of the same name, was a broken city. The fact was made all the more tragic for those who remembered what it had been.

Kenvard was once a grand place, at its peak rivaling even Verril in size and importance. That was long ago, before the Kenvard Massacre. There was some question of who was responsible for the deeds of that day. Most believed it was the Tressons, though in her battles Myranda had learned it was—as was the case with so many tragedies in recent history—the work of the D'Karon. Regardless of how it happened, the massacre had cost Myranda her home and her family and claimed the lives of nearly everyone she cared about. She was among the few residents of the city who escaped. Now it was her task to put the pieces back together, a process that had so far produced a neat and orderly fringe on an otherwise decrepit ruin.

Myranda looked down at her city, smiling at the activity and life that was returning, even if it was coming slowly. At the southern edge, the city crews of workers bustled about clearing streets and rebuilding shops and homes. Myranda and Deacon were Duchess and Duke of the region—a revival of the old title granted as a reward for their role in shaking off the yoke of the D'Karon. As such they were obliged to live in the capital, something Myranda eagerly agreed to. The first building completed was a cozy little home not so different than the one she had grown up in. It was just past the southern gate, the first gate to fall on the day of the massacre. It seemed only right that the healing should begin there.

Myn touched down, her graceful glide turning into a trot. Before she'd taken three strides toward the city, a figure was sprinting gleefully through the gate to greet them. It was a malthrope, though at this point it might be fair to say that she was *the* malthrope. Her face was like that of a fox, covered in snow-white fur, her lips twisted into a happy grin. Peering out from that face were the warmest, most expressive eyes one could ever hope to see, their irises pink and lively. She was dressed in a slate-blue tunic and shawl with tan trousers, a magnificent white tail swishing behind her. Even if she wasn't already the most visually distinctive resident of the entire Northern Alliance, the prancing rhythm to her step and undeniable joy in her every motion would have dispelled any doubt as to who she was.

"You're home!" Ivy shouted, bounding up to Myn and throwing her arms around the dragon's neck. Myn rumbled happily in response. If she'd been a cat, it would have been a purr.

"Ivy, we were only gone for a few days." Myranda laughed as she climbed to the ground.

Ivy quickly wrapped her in a tight hug. "I know, but I missed you. There's a lot to do, and my head is spinning. Also, it hasn't been easy making friends with the workers. They're all so busy and… well, they don't know me like you do. They're still stumbling over what I am and not giving *who* I am a try."

"Give them time, Ivy," Deacon said.

"I know," she said, giving Deacon his hug. "The man setting up the tavern seems nice. He says he may let me play the violin for the patrons, once he's ready to open the doors."

"That's an excellent idea," Myranda said.

Servants rushed out to meet them now. It was telling that unlike those of Frosnell, the people of New Kenvard did not seem at all bothered or impressed by the arrival of a dragon. Indeed, like all other things in the recovering city, it had quickly been boiled down to a simple procedure so that it could be dealt with easily and efficiently.

Two stout men wheeled out a sturdy barrow of potatoes, stopping when Myn spotted them and quickly retreating. As commonplace as Myn had become in New Kenvard, a dragon advancing hungrily is the sort of sight that tends to convince one to err on the side of caution. When they were clear of the food cart, Myn opened her jaws and gently bit down on it just enough to clutch it in her teeth. She then curled her neck up, tipping the tool back and dumping its contents onto her waiting tongue, which curled around them as she carefully replaced the barrow. She crunched away happily at the treat while the servants took back the barrow.

Myranda waved off a man attempting to take her bag, and Deacon did the same. They set off toward the gate to New Kenvard. Though much of the wall still showed scars of the massacre, the gateway had been restored, carved stone forming a sturdy arch. All that remained was to replace the iron gate itself and the workings to raise it.

"Have you seen my father?" Myranda asked.

"The last I saw he was talking to the crew trying to clear the main road to the castle. I think they sent people to fetch him when we spotted you coming," Ivy said, pacing along beside them. "How was the trip? What did Caya have to say?"

"Big news. We'll be heading out again, possibly as early as tomorrow," Myranda said.

Ivy stopped and slouched. "*Already!* But you just got back!"

"It's important. Once we get warmed up and father is here, I'll tell you all at once. Have you seen Ether? But there's good news. You won't be lonely. Did Ether show up at all while we were gone?"

"No. … *She's* not the reason I won't be lonely, is she?"

Myranda smiled. "No. But we do need to contact her. This involves her as well."

Ivy looked to Myn. "I don't know if I'm going to like this…"

Myn lowered her head down beside Ivy and huffed a contented breath, smacking her tongue a bit. Ivy gave her a scratch.

"I guess we'll see. Oh!" Ivy said, suddenly realizing something she'd forgotten. "Come on, Myn. Follow me. We finished your stable!"

Ivy rushed past Myranda and Deacon, the long easy strides of the dragon easily keeping pace with her. "You too, Myranda. And you, Deacon. It'll only take a minute."

She hurried along, Myranda and Deacon in tow. Myranda smiled as Ivy waved a cheerful hello to a pair of carpenters hauling some long planks.

"Look at her," Myranda said. "A dragon and a malthrope on the streets of a city in broad daylight. I was worried the day would never come, that Ivy would always have to disguise herself."

16

"It would appear that a hero is a hero, regardless of race," Deacon said. "Though I understand she didn't fare so well in her visit to Bydell a few weeks ago."

Myranda's expression hardened a bit. "What happened?"

"She didn't tell you?"

"She said she enjoyed herself."

"I'm sure she did, but she did it at night, and behind closed doors. There was an… incident."

"I *asked* you not to tell her," Ivy called back sternly.

"What happened? And why didn't you want me to know?"

"It was nothing. Some people yelled some things. Some people threw some things. Most of them were children. They didn't know any better. Or old folks, and they're too stubborn to change. But never mind that. Look! We just finished this morning!"

Ivy was standing beside Myranda and Deacon's home. Before the massacre, it belonged to a carriage driver who delivered mail and supplies from Kenvard to the surrounding cities. As such, attached to it was a rather large coach house. When Myranda had left not three days ago, the front wall was still missing and they had only just raised the struts to repair the roof. Now it was complete, the air still strong with the smell of fresh thatch and wet paint. The door was a bright, cheery red and the walls were gray stone.

"It's just the way I remember it," Myranda said, her eyes getting misty at the sight of an image from her youth. "We would pass this coach house every time we entered the city."

"Look inside," Ivy said, grasping the latch and pulling it aside.

The inside of the coach house had never been much to look at. It kept the carriage from the weather, sheltered the horses, and gave the coachman a place to store his tools and tack. The walls had been unpainted wood and stone, hung with equipment or left to gather dust and flies. Such was no longer the case. Much of the interior had been cleared. There was no longer any sign of the stables or the workshop for fixing the carriage. Now it was open and clear. Ivy had clearly been busy in their absence, as a magnificent mural was painted on the rear wall depicting Myn herself in various poses. The artwork was gorgeous and stylized, like something from a storybook. Indeed it told a story, showing her first as a hatchling curled in Myranda's lap, then standing bravely with her wings outstretched, much as she appeared today, and finally asleep atop a pile of gold eggs nestled beneath her.

"What was, what is, and what will be," Ivy said proudly. "What do you think?"

Myn stepped inside, finding she barely had to duck to get through the large doorway, and looked over the mural. Almost immediately she became more interested in the loft directly above it, craning her neck to peek at the dusty cloth sacks piled there. She sniffed at one and licked it.

Joseph R. Lallo

"Oh no you don't," Ivy said with a giggle. She climbed onto Myn's back and scrambled up her neck to reach the loft, hopping off to push the dragon's head away. "Yes they are potatoes, and yes they are for you, but not *now*. You already had some."

"They did fine work, didn't they?" came a voice from the door.

Myranda turned quickly to the source, a thin, tall man, his hair nearly white and a beard to match. He wore a fur-lined coat of rough but sturdy tailoring. There was something about his stance that suggested, despite his slight build, he was tough as oak, and something about his eyes that suggested he'd seen far more than anyone would ever wish to see.

"Father," Myranda said happily, hugging him.

"My little girl," he said, squeezing her tightly.

Myranda held him for a long time. Each time she saw him, the gratitude and relief in having reunited with him washed over her as if for the first time. She hoped it always would. She had spent far too much of her life wondering if her father was still alive to ever take him for granted again.

Her father was only in his late forties, but to look at him, you might think him to be twenty years older. A short but remarkable military career, followed by a tour in the legendary Elites, and then more than a decade in the dungeon beneath Castle Verril had taken its toll. Nevertheless, his mind was as sharp now as it had ever been, and once his feet touched the ruined soil of his former home, his drive to resurrect the place had been relentless. In all of the Northern Alliance, none wished to see Kenvard live again more than Greydon Celeste. It was a blessing, in that the city badly needed him, but a curse in that it as often as not kept him and Myranda from one another.

"I didn't expect you back so soon. The men nearly didn't finish."

"I thought you were focusing on clearing the road to the palace," Myranda said.

"That is the focus, but with the workers we've got and the state it's in, it'll be months before that happens. Before it can be a city again, it should be a home again. And any good soldier takes the time to care for his steed." He turned to Myn, who had stepped up and was now making her presence known with an ominous rumble in her throat. "No matter how large that steed might be."

Myn settled down comfortably and rested her chin on the ground, subtly sliding it forward until Myranda and her father had to step apart to allow it between them.

"Curious creature," he said. There was a rigidity to his posture and expression.

It was clear he had not yet become comfortable being so near a dragon. Myn angled her head slightly toward Myranda and slid open an eye to look over Greydon, causing him to tense a bit further. When she released a sigh that

18

was near enough to a hiss, Greydon reflexively took another step back. The look of satisfaction on Myn's face made it clear what she was up to.

"This is my father, Myn. If you can learn to tolerate Deacon, you can learn to tolerate him."

It took a trained eye to read the expressions of a dragon, but once one had the knack, one could read volumes into their feelings by a twist of a lip or a shift of a brow. At the moment, Myn may as well have been muttering under her breath about how crowded her little circle had gotten and how much better she'd liked it when it was just herself and Myranda. She relented, though, curling her head aside to yawn and then tucking it under her wing for a nap.

Greydon cast a wary eye at the dragon. "I trust your meeting with the queen went well?"

She looked to him doubtfully. "Come with me, Father. There is much that needs to be discussed."

#

At the edge of a yawning chasm stood a figure of unnatural beauty. It looked to be the form of a woman shaped from the stone of the mountain itself, and her unblinking eyes gazed down into the blackness of the abyss below. The place was known as Lain's End, and the figure was Ether. She was a guardian of her world, crafted by the gods themselves for the sole purpose of turning back the dark menace of the D'Karon. Now that task was complete, and she was faced, for the first time in eternity, with a future without purpose. Her path from this point was hers to choose, but freedom was uncomfortable to her. So she chose not to look forward. Instead, she looked back, lingering here at the site of her final meaningful act, and her greatest failure.

For those lucky enough to have seen it, Lain's End was a wonder to behold. It was a gouge in the earth, many miles across and with sides perfectly straight and extending farther down than the eye could see. The pit was circular, save where it curved in upon itself to a narrow point sticking up from the southern side. It was at this point that the Chosen had taken their stand, joining their strength to push back the cataclysm that had swallowed nearly all in its path. What escaped destruction was perhaps even more awe-inspiring than the pit. Great sections of land remained suspended in the air, some shifting and spinning, others stationary. No two of these floating bits of debris seemed to be the same. Some were lush and green, sprouting with junglelike plants despite the icy cold. Others looked to have been formed entirely from precious metals. It was a spectacle unmatched anywhere in Ether's world, but it did not interest her. All she saw when she came to this place was one simple bit of stone, just beyond the edge of the outcropping. The patch of rock was stained black with the shadowy remains of a terrible being known as Bagu. From the center of the silhouette stood a masterfully crafted sword. And on either side of the remains was a pair of footprints, etched into the stone itself. It was all that remained of the mighty warrior known as Lain. He had given his name to this tragic place, and his life to protect this world.

Ether would linger here for days at a time, gazing down into the darkness or staring at the sword. Her mind fixated on what she saw. None of it made sense to her. She was Chosen. A product of the gods. Unlike Myranda, Myn, or Ivy, she had taken her place in history as she was *intended* to. She had not been changed, and she was no replacement. The only one who could say the same was Lain. The two of them were unequaled in their world. They belonged together, even if Lain hadn't yet realized it. She had allowed him time to come to the proper conclusion. Both were immortal, after all. They had the luxury of time… but then he had fallen. He who should have lasted until the end of time by her side had been taken. There was no sense to it. It wasn't fair. It wasn't right. And if he could fall, then what of her? What did her future hold? Until now she had been an immortal protector of her world, but if she was not immortal, and her world no longer required her protection… then what was she?

As the sun circled the sky again and her mind spiraled ever deeper into this confounding riddle, she felt a flutter in the back of her consciousness. It was difficult to know how long it had been there. She struggled a bit to identify it. Lately pulling her mind to order was more difficult than it had been. After a few moments she heard the flutter become a voice. It was one of the others… Myranda. The human was calling out to her, requesting her presence. Ether's stony eyes narrowed. It was likely nothing, a ceremony or a celebration or some other mortal foolishness. Myranda seemed to feel some obligation to involve Ether in such trivialities. Twice she had been summoned for no reason other than to be present at a meal shared between Deacon, Myranda, Ivy, and Myn. Still, this beckoning was rather insistent, and the interruptions thus far had been mercifully brief. The sooner she addressed whatever simple task the human had for her, the sooner she could return to her pondering.

She shut her eyes and allowed her substance to shift, forgoing the solidity of stone for the fluidity of air. Her consciousness bound together a loose form of churning winds and allowed the rest of the mass that had been her body to whisk away as a powerful gust. Now mixing with the frigid breeze around her, she drifted skyward and set off to the lands to the south. It was perhaps not accurate to state that she *enjoyed* traveling as wind, as for her it was simply one of her many states of being, but after spending any reasonable amount of time solid, there was a feeling of connection to immersing herself in an element that cloaked the whole of her world. She was completely unrestrained, her body merely a point of focus, a small part of something that reached the ends of the globe. If she allowed her focus to slip enough, she could feel the coolness of the clouds and the prickle of the dry grass, the solid mountains and the lapping ocean all at once. She was one, she was all. It was the very definition of freedom, and it at times was a difficult temptation to resist.

The D'Karon Apprentice

The land rushed by beneath her, cities coming and going in the time it would have taken to blink an eye. First was the bustling capital of Verril, nearly recovered from the damage done during its liberation. Then came the Rachis Mountains. She swept over fields and tundra, roads and lakes. In the time it took the sun to cross half the sky, she left most of the Northern Alliance behind her and approached the broken city of New Kenvard, where she could feel what remained of her fellow Chosen awaiting her. Her windy form touched down, scattering the dusting of snow on the city streets, and began to draw in sufficient substance to craft something more suitable for interacting with mortals. Bit by bit she tightened her focus on the air that made up her body, and it shifted to bone and tissue, each tiny component held in form through sheer will. Though this too was more of a struggle than it had been, it was still the work of moments to slip into the shape that had become almost second nature to her: that of a beautiful woman. To finish her transition, she conjured a few layers of fine garments and topped them with a thick robe.

Ether glanced around the streets to see a handful of people staring in awe at the woman who had appeared from thin air. She gave them a nod of acknowledgment and stepped up to the door of a building she felt certain contained her associates.

"Are you Ether?" asked a tiny voice beside her.

The shapeshifter looked down to a young boy, his face positively aglow with excitement.

"Obviously," Ether said wearily.

"Dana, come here," warned a young woman, no doubt the boy's mother, as she rushed to his side. "Leave Guardian Ether be." She looked at Ether. "He's heard the stories about you."

"Can you *really* turn into *anything*?" he asked, bopping up and down and trying to squirm away from his mother's grip.

"Given the time and the strength, most things are within my power," Ether said.

"Can you turn into a griffin?" he asked.

"If I can turn into nearly anything, then it should be clear that I can turn into a griffin. I have been one on more than one occasion." She looked at the boy's mother. "Is there a reason for these questions?"

"He's curious. When I told him we would be coming to help rebuild New Kenvard, he said he wanted to meet all of the Guardians of the Realm. He's spoken to Myranda and Ivy many times, and Myranda even let him scratch Myn. But he's been hoping to see you most of all." She looked at her son. "You've seen her now. Leave the Guardian to her work. I'm sure she is very busy."

"Can I see you turn into something?" the boy asked.

Ether looked from the boy to his mother and back again. "You've seen me take form. I've shifted from wind to flesh. Is that not sufficient?"

21

"But I've *seen* humans. Can't you be something else?"

"I do not exist to entertain children. Now this *is* Myranda's home, correct? She is expecting me," Ether said.

"Yes," said Dana, disappointed.

"Very well," Ether said, making ready once again to push open the door.

"Will you be coming here often?" Dana asked.

Ether shut her eyes in frustration. "It is my sincere hope that I will not…"

#

Inside her home, Myranda was seated at the dinner table with Deacon, Ivy, and her father. Through the wall shared with the coach house, the distinctive steady breathing of a slumbering dragon could be heard. Myn, weary from her journey, had eaten a heavy meal and slipped quickly off to sleep. Now the others were preparing for their own meal.

Myranda's present home was not the sort of thing one might envision as the estate of a duke and duchess. It was warm, clean, and sturdy, but it was hardly the lap of luxury. The dining room shared a wall—and thus the heat of the fireplace—with the kitchen. There were six seats at the table, and when fully occupied, there was little room for much else. To one side a staircase led to a second floor, which boasted four rooms. In the days before its fall, three of these rooms were provided for coach drivers staying the night during longer journeys, with the largest for the owner of the home. Now Myranda and Deacon had claimed the largest of them. Greydon Celeste slept in another. The third was for the servants that the queen had quite firmly insisted they take on, and the final room was intended for guests. As often as not, that room belonged to Ivy, who had a home of her own elsewhere in the city but had been reluctant to embrace the idea of living alone.

The first plates of their meal, prepared by a plump and motherly servant named Eliza, were being set on the table when the door pushed open and Ether entered.

"Ether," Myranda said, rising to greet her. "I'm glad to see you. Thank you for coming so quickly."

"Hi, Ether!" Ivy said, excited in spite of herself to see her fellow Chosen. She pushed out her chair and bounded over to the shapeshifter, pulling her into a tight and thoroughly unwanted embrace. When she was through, she stepped back and gestured around her. "What do you think of Myranda's home? Isn't it beautiful?"

"I assume I was summoned for a reason?" Ether said, ignoring the pleasantries.

"You *could* visit first," Ivy reprimanded, hands on her hips. She paced back to her seat.

"I'm afraid there is a problem that concerns you," Myranda said, motioning to a chair. "Please, have a seat."

"I would prefer to stand," Ether said.

22

"Don't be rude," Ivy scolded. A plate was set down before her. "*Thank you, Eliza.*" Ivy eagerly picked up the sumptuous mutton chop from her dish and tore away a mouthful. She continued to speak while chewing. "Eliza is the *best* cook. I hope you stay for dessert. She's making a peach cake."

"Now Guardian Ivy, that was to be a surprise," Eliza mock scolded.

"You can't surprise this nose," Ivy said. "I just hope—"

"May we *please* see to the matter at hand?" Ether said, her patience at its end.

Ivy narrowed her eyes. "I already remember why I didn't miss you."

"We had a word with Caya, Ether," Myranda said. "She's been in discussions with the Tressons, and there are stories of creatures appearing in Tressor that sound very much like D'Karon creations. There have been cloaks and dragoyles at the very least, or things of similar description."

"That is impossible. I spent months tracking down anywhere the D'Karon blighted our world with their treachery. I found and destroyed the last of their living creations six weeks ago. And *none* had made their way any farther south than this very city."

"Yes," Deacon nodded. "I've been focusing on the task of detecting anything that has the feel of D'Karon handiwork, and there is nothing that would suggest any new spells or conjurings are at work."

"Nevertheless, the Tressons see the D'Karon creatures and the Alliance Army as one and the same. Their military and leadership have been doing their best to keep the news of the creatures a secret, but it is only a matter of time until word spreads, and that could mean a new start to the war."

"This does not concern me. It was never my goal to end the war. I was created to rid this world of outsiders, and I have done so."

"Would you agree that if there is even a chance that some D'Karon have been missed, then we cannot afford to ignore them?"

"If there was a chance, then certainly it would be our obligation to seek them out no matter where they might hide. But there is *not* a chance. I am certain I have done my diligence. No D'Karon or D'Karon creation lives. Is that your only reason for summoning me?"

"No. Regardless of your feelings on the subject, the rest of us are dedicated to preventing a new war if at all possible. To that end, Deacon and I will be touring Tressor as part of a diplomatic mission. The purpose of this tour will be to locate and identify the cause of these attacks. If they are D'Karon, we must eliminate them and make it clear they were not our doing. If they are not, we should do our best to help our neighbors to the south to be rid of them. In exchange for allowing us into their kingdom, the Tressons would like permission to tour our land, and they have requested the most honored among us to be their guides. You specifically were requested to escort them on their tour of the Ulvard region."

"I cannot imagine a greater waste of time. What possible reason would I have to agree to such a thing?" Ether asked.

"Your queen has made this request of you. As a subject and defender of her kingdom, your solemn duty is to honor that request," Myranda's father said. His voice was steady, but the rumble of anger hid behind his words.

"I am not a subject of this kingdom. I existed long before your kind arose and began drawing lines and carving away land for yourselves. I owe no loyalty or allegiance to your queen or any other. If that is all, I shall be on my way," Ether said, turning to leave.

"I told you she couldn't do it," Ivy said with a smirk. She tossed a boiled potato in her mouth, stuffing it into one cheek to speak. "She can't handle this sort of thing."

Ether turned back to Ivy, shooting her a vicious look. "Do not think me too foolish to realize that you are trying to manipulate me."

Ivy sipped at a tankard of water. "Doesn't matter if I'm manipulating you or not. It's still true. To do this tour you'd have to deal with people. You'd have to treat them with dignity and respect. Answer questions and be patient if they didn't understand. You'd have to be *nice*. And you can't do that."

Myranda leaned back and tried to stifle a smile. There were always sparks when Ivy and Ether got together, but the malthrope had a special knack of pulling Ether's strings in the right directions.

"Don't you *dare* presume to tell me what I cannot do," Ether fumed.

"I'm looking forward to being a diplomat. It's all about chatting with people and trying to win them over, right? Who has more experience at that than *I* do?"

"They have asked you to engage in this folly?" Ether said.

"Yep! They asked for me *specifically*."

Ether practically sizzled with anger while the rest of the plates were set out. Finally she sat at the table and, as though doing so caused her physical pain, said, "What precisely would you have me do?"

Ivy made a musical little hum of satisfaction as she tore away another bite of mutton.

"In a few days a group of Tresson representatives will arrive at a small, recently built border crossing directly south of Territal. A group of Alliance soldiers, a handful of servants, and a pair of ambassadors will be there as well. You are to be host to the Tresson delegation. A short list of points of interest has been selected, which the ambassadors and soldiers will ferry you between. During the trip the delegation will speak to you. You should treat them well and answer any questions they might have that will not endanger the safety of the Alliance," Myranda said.

"I am to play nursemaid to a gathering of self-important humans," Ether said. "This is a task so thoroughly beneath my status and abilities it baffles me that I am expected to perform it. But if it will silence Ivy, then I will endure it."

"Thank you, Ether," Myranda said, sincere relief in her voice. "I cannot express how important this is for the Alliance and its people. If war sparks between our lands, there will be much bloodshed and little hope for the Northern Alliance. Deacon has prepared some notes for you." At Myranda's mention, Deacon leaned aside to his bag and pulled free one of the small communication books, handing it to Ether. Myranda continued, "Your tour will take you up to the edge of Ravenwood, across the Low Lands, and into the Melorn Woods as far as the mouth of the Cave of the Beast."

"Would you require that I lead them as far as Entwell as well? What are the lengths of this foolishness?"

"That won't be necessary," Myranda said.

"In fact, we would ask that you not tell them of Entwell unless pressed," Deacon added.

"Why?" Ivy asked, tearing free a hunk of bread that had been set on the table.

"With the war at an end, it is entirely possible that the legend of the beast of the cave will bring new wizards and warriors, hungry for glory, heading to the cave to battle the beast again," Deacon explained. "If near certain death with the tiny chance of a legendary reputation is enough to send people to their doom in the cave, imagine what might happen if people knew that it held a paradise filled with the best trained and most motivated fighters and spell casters in the world? The lack of a beast does not make the cave any less dangerous. There exists no map to reach the other side safely. Dozens could be killed, even hundreds. To have that happen on Alliance soil so soon after the war would be unacceptable. In time we can work to reintroduce Entwell to the rest of the world, but such a thing must be done carefully. Until then I must reluctantly agree that the legend of the cave should stand as is."

"And there is also the more practical concern," Myranda said, cutting into her own meal as it was set before her. "It is likely that the Tressons would be highly displeased to learn that a secret village of astonishingly potent warriors is nestled within the mountains of the Alliance. Knowing a recent enemy may have access to centuries of accumulated mystic knowledge and an army of legendary fighters is not something apt to settle an already stormy political climate."

"I defer to your expertise on such matters," Ether said. "The logic of such squabbles and their motivations escape me."

"What about me? What should I be doing?" Ivy said. She swabbed some gravy from her dish with bread, glancing to Ether. "They made me wait until you showed up before they told me any details, so we could learn together."

"Your task would be much the same as Ether's. Deacon has some notes for you as well. Treat the visitors well, ask them questions. Because the queen is going to be at a rather important gathering at the border and conducting her own tour, there are precious few trained diplomats remaining to handle these tours. Given Ether's… history of friction when it comes to delicate matters such as these, she will be joined by the two nobles best versed in Tresson affairs. My father will be helping you, Ivy."

"He will?" Ivy squealed, leaning aside to place a hand on the man's arm. "I can't wait! We've been in the city together for so long, and we've shared so many meals, but you hardly talk. I hardly know you. This will be a lovely way to get to know each other." She eagerly snatched up the notes regarding her tour when Deacon offered them. "The distillery and brewery from Caya's family?" She bounced happily. "I've never been there! Do you think they'll let me sample some more wine when I'm there? I'd *love* to try some of their ice cider. And we'll be spending time along the coast. It is *so* beautiful there! Oh! The first day is right here in New Kenvard. Can we have a big dinner? A banquet?"

"I believe it would be expected of us," Myranda said.

"Eliza!" Ivy called out, just as the cook emerged with a final plate.

"Calm yourself, Ivy. You needn't shout," she said, setting the plate down before Ether.

"I do not eat," Ether said, pushing the plate forward.

"Nonsense. Everyone eats," Eliza said, tipping her head to the side. "Now what did you want, Ivy?"

"We're going to throw a banquet for Tressons! And you need to make pies and cakes…"

"I do *not eat*," Ether repeated, pushing the plate away again.

"You are a guest in this home, Guardian Ether. It would be rude not to feed you. And you look just this side of death," Eliza said, pushing the plate back. "A good meal will do you good."

"… and cobblers!" Ivy continued in excitement. "Apple and blueberry and strawberry…"

"Slow down, Ivy. What's this, the Tressons? Coming here? Did we invite them?"

"They invited themselves," Greydon said sternly.

"I think it is an excellent sign," Deacon said, turning to him. "Opening communication and sharing knowledge is always a fine way to build a lasting peace."

Ether's face was becoming increasingly stern as the conversation grew louder and more vigorous.

"I suppose I'd best make a list of ingredients I'll need then," Eliza said. She turned back to Ether, nudging the plate forward again. "Surely you could at least try it. If you don't like it, I would be glad to prepare something else. I refuse to let a guest go hungry in this house."

Ether stood, a flare of wind accompanying her motion, causing the flames of the lamps to flicker. "*I do not eat!* Listen to my words, human! I do not require, nor do I desire, the seared flesh and softened plants that you seem insistent in foisting upon me." The rest of the conversation silenced as all eyes turned to her. She snatched up the book from the table. "I will perform this demeaning task for you, but only on the condition that upon its completion you promise not to summon me again unless you are certain the D'Karon or some other threat *worthy* of my attention has arisen!"

She turned to the door and threw her hand down, prompting a gale that heaved it open, then stormed outside. A second gust pulled it shut behind her.

For a moment silence lingered in the room.

"And meat pies, too," Ivy said, turning back to Eliza. "Those ones with the beef and the onions and the carrots…"

"If you'll excuse me," Myranda said, looking to the door with concern.

She stood, leaving Ivy to continue to plan out the rest of the menu.

When Myranda stepped outside, Ether was still walking along as a human, fist clenched tightly about the book.

"Ether," Myranda called, hurrying to her and bearing down a bit against the sharp drop in temperature from inside to out. "You are… shorter of temper than normal. And Eliza is right, you *do* look exhausted. Is there something wrong?"

"*Is there…*" the shapeshifter began sharply. She paused to gather herself, then continued somewhat more calmly. "How do you do this, human? The noise and commotion? The tiny space, the smells of fires and other creatures. All of these little details and pointless problems. How do you *tolerate* that place? How do you tolerate being so set upon by such drudgery and triviality?"

"How do I tolerate it?" Myranda said. "That's my home, Ether. That's what a home is. It is supposed to be filled with commotion, crowded with family and warm with the smell of food. I've only had it back for a few months, and I'm already dreading leaving it to go on this mission. I don't know how I lived without it for so long."

"But you are *Chosen*! You are like me, or as near like me as all but a handful of creatures could ever be. You were meant for more than this! Even this 'mission' is little more than a chore to mend the lingering symptoms of the disease that we cured! Our job is done. Why devote yourself to this? It doesn't matter. Nothing matters anymore."

"It matters to me. And to a great many others," Myranda said. She placed a hand on Ether's shoulder. "Desmeres once said to me that a short life was a blessing because it would end before we'd seen and done all we cared to do. For the immortals, he said, a purpose must be found to maintain the drive to go on."

"I *had* a purpose, human. The grandest purpose that could possibly exist. I was the guardian of this world. And now that purpose is fulfilled. The world no longer needs a guardian. And I watched my equal *die*, human. If Lain could…" She stopped herself. "I shall be at the appointed place at the appointed time. Contact me if you discover the taint of the D'Karon in the south."

Without another word, her form dissolved away, leaving only the notebook hanging in the center of a churning female form. She burst skyward. Myranda watched her soar away. She'd just slipped from sight when Deacon joined Myranda, throwing a cloak about her shoulders.

"What was wrong?" Deacon asked.

Myranda shook her head, eyes still on the sky. "A few months ago she was the eternal defender of a world. Then, in the same moment, her world suddenly no longer needed her defense and she learned she might not be eternal," Myranda said. "I don't envy her for the path she's got ahead. I only hope she can find her way."

Chapter 2

Deep in Tressor, on the eastern edge of the Tresson desert, a well-fortified estate was tucked away in a sparsely treed plain. Though utterly surrounded by troops, smiths, and other elements of a strong military, the estate was nonetheless luxurious.

A pair of men on horses, one in the red and tan uniform of the army and the other in the rather shabby clothes of a farmer, approached the ivy-clad trellis covering the cobbled entry path. Four guards questioned the soldier, then showed him and his guest inside.

As they walked through the halls of the estate, the poorly dressed man seemed stricken with both awe and anxiety. As he paced through the well-built and better-adorned halls, he clutched his hands anxiously in front of him. Paintings and tapestries covered the walls, each of them quite likely as valuable as his whole farm to the south.

"Listen carefully. The man you are speaking with is a military patron. You shall refer to him as Esteemed Patron. Any question he asks, you will answer. Answer with all of the detail you can manage and speak only the truth, is that understood?"

"Of course," the farmer said quickly.

"Good," said the soldier. "Then this should go smoothly."

They approached a heavy door carved with an intricate depiction of a great battle early in the Perpetual War, the Battle of Five Point. The soldier knocked on the door.

"Esteemed Patron Sallim," he announced.

"Speak," came a voice from within, managing in a single syllable to sound profoundly arrogant and entitled.

"I have here the man you asked to see."

"Send him in."

The soldier opened the door and ushered the shabby man inside, shutting the door behind him.

Inside was an office that may as well have been a museum. Finished wood shelves lined each wall. Leather tomes, intricate figurines, and antique weapons were on display. Seated at a massive wood desk at the far side of the room, a glass window behind him open to the grandeur of the desert, was his host. He was a man a few years the farmer's senior, neatly dressed in the formal equivalent of the lesser soldier's uniform. He had black, tightly curly hair trimmed short and a relentlessly superior expression on his face.

"Sit, sir," he said.

The farmer did so, treating the request as an order.

"In the interest of saving time, I hope you don't mind if I skip the pleasantries. I assume you have better things to do, and I know I do. I understand you've recently had a traumatic and unexplained experience on your land?"

"I have."

"And how long ago was this?"

"I… uh… about four months."

"About? You aren't certain?"

"It's been… I've had to handle the funeral. Things have been…" he said, flustered.

"It's fine, sir. Would you say it is safe to say it is at least four months, or at most four months?"

"At least."

"Very well. What exactly happened?"

"I…" he began uncertainly. "I was warned not to tell anyone."

"Yes, sir. That warning came from my immediate superiors, through me. I assure you, I am the one to whom you may recount the events." He opened a drawer and retrieved a stack of parchment, then dipped a quill in an inkwell. "Now please do so."

The farmer took a breath. "Like I said, it was about four months ago…"

#

Several Months Prior…

It was nearly dusk and a weary pair of farmers was pacing back from the fields. They were brothers, and each was looking forward to a good meal and a long night's rest. This far south in Tressor, there wasn't much that would grow without a tremendous amount of work. Most fields were left to grow coarse grass and then were grazed by goats and sheep, but their family had made a good living growing hazelnuts for some years, and they were determined to keep the land producing. It simply took a bit more effort each year.

A rustle in the fallow field to the side of the road drew their attention. Something small and fast was disturbing the wiry blades of grass that grew there, causing a wave of motion streaking south.

"Hmph. Wildcat. Or maybe a jackal," muttered the first man, the older of the two brothers.

They watched the disturbance retreat into the distance.

"At least that's something we can be thankful for," said the younger brother.

"What, wildcats?"

"That's right. Maraal and Temmir have been complaining about all sorts of curious losses lately, particularly when they bring their flocks and herds to the open fields to graze. Maraal claims he lost half his flock overnight. Plenty of things to worry about with an orchard, but there is little fear of a pack of wildcats preying on the crop."

"There's that, I suppose."

As they reached the turn that would take them around the southern corner of the property, the older brother glanced to the south and noticed a figure approaching. That in and of itself was rather odd. Their field was just about as far south as anyone in their right mind would have any interest traveling on foot. There was nothing between it and the sea but dry grass, barren fields, and a few mountains. He stood, pulling his coat a bit closer about his shoulders, and watched the figure as it drew nearer. With little else to do, his brother lingered beside him. Sure enough, *someone* was coming.

"Suppose the goatherds are getting desperate for grazing land," the older brother reasoned. "No sense heading home with the mystery hanging in the air. A few more minutes and we'll say a friendly hello and 'What brings you to the hind end of Tressor?', eh?"

They leaned against the fence, and the stranger crept closer. After a few minutes the figure was near enough for them to make out a few more details.

"Looks like he's wearing some pretty rough skins. You figure him for a nomad?" asked the younger brother.

"There wouldn't be any nomads this far south. They stay to the deserts or the plains. They *might* linger near the shore, but the shore is clear on the other side of the mountains," countered the older brother, squinting. "Is that... is that an old woman!?"

Without thinking, the pair rushed into the tall grass. An old woman, alone in the Southern Wastes. They couldn't imagine how it might have happened, but it was a wonder she was still alive. She was quite a distance away, and as such they were badly winded when they reached her, but one look was all it took to know she was... not right. She was a frail thing with long, scraggly white hair. In one hand was a white ivory walking stick. In the other was a curved knife. Her feet were bare yet somehow undamaged by what must have been a lengthy trek through rough terrain. Despite no doubt being alone in the Wastes for quite some time, the old woman didn't seem to be in poor spirits. Indeed, a wild grin came to her face as they approached.

"I offer greetings to you, pair of men who are not yet of middle age!" she crowed, gesturing vigorously with her knife and stick.

Her voice and diction were bizarre, but she spoke with great certainty, as though she had no doubt that she was communicating properly.

"Do you need help, old woman? Are you ill? What is your name?"

"In a manner more slowly. You desire that I inform you of the name that belongs to me?"

"Yes, and how did you—"

"*In a manner more slowly!* I shall tell to you the name that belongs to me. This information I am quite certain of, and it is an action that will give me great pleasure to perform for you on this day. The name that belongs to me is Turiel."

"She speaks like those old prayers they used to make us say," the younger brother muttered.

"You seem healthy enough," said the older brother, speaking loudly and slowly. "Those furs you've got are strange. They look fresh. Well-tanned, too. It is the wrong season to be tanning hides." He turned to his brother and added quietly, "But then I suppose the nomads don't keep to the same schedules as the rest of us."

"You sure she's a nomad?"

"Absolutely. You can always tell a nomad. They look out of place no matter where they are."

"But look at that skin! She's pale as a ghost. That's a Northerner."

"I'll buy that she's a pale nomad before I buy that she's a Northerner this far south." He turned back to the woman. "Do you need help? Something to eat?"

"After some amount of thinking, my mind has presented to me the suggestion that I do require help. And a thing for me to eat would be quite useful in addition."

"If you'll just follow me to the house…" the older brother began, but his word trailed away when the tip of her walking stick touched his chest.

There was a dull blue glow, and the color quickly began to drain from his face.

"What are you doing? Get away from him, you witch!" he cried.

He attempted to rush toward her, but before he could even move a foot, something clawed its way up his back from behind, while at the same time something wrapped tightly around his legs and constricted them. Both brothers fell to the ground, the first stricken by whatever magic she had conjured and the other tangling with some manner of beast he'd not yet been able to see.

As the younger of the two desperately tried to free himself of the grip of whatever had attacked him, the old woman began to reap the benefits of her spell. The years began to peel away from her face. Her craggy skin became smoother, her white hair earning streaks of black. Withered muscles became firm and healthy again. In the space of a few minutes she went from a hag at death's door to a woman perhaps old enough to be the mother of either of these young men.

"That's enough, Mott," she said, clucking her tongue.

Instantly the beast that had immobilized the younger of the two brothers released him and scrabbled around her to cling eagerly to the head of the staff. It was the same beast she had hastily constructed in the cave some weeks prior upon awaking, though since then it had been… improved. The jackal skull now had flesh again, though the lower jaw hung a bit further open than nature had intended and lacked a tongue. The flesh and fur of the head faded gradually into the serpent body, which was covered with dark green scales, but rust-colored jackal fur jutted out from between the scales like weeds on a cobbled street. Bony flesh, like the legs of a stork, covered the six spidery legs, and a pair of undersized leathery wings fluttered madly on its back. Notably absent was a pair of eyes. Instead it had horrid empty sockets with embers of violet light within.

Now free of his attacker, the younger brother scrambled through the grass to see to his sibling, but it was no use. He was gone, just as shriveled and decayed as the old woman had been moments before, and somehow already cold to the touch.

"He's dead."

"Yes! He's quite dead. It couldn't be helped, boy. I'm a necromancer. I speak to the dead. Once it became clear my mastery of the Tresson language had become obsolete, I had to learn the newest inflections. Forgive me, but a lifetime of communing with the dead has made it much more efficient for me to absorb knowledge along with life force. And since I was going to drain him *anyway*, I may as well put the energy to good use."

"But… but you…" he said, nearly sobbing in anguish and fury.

"I must say, the language has become so much less *formal*. I quite like it," she said, disregarding his emotional state. "Odd it would have changed so *much* since I last spoke to a Tresson. I suppose it has been a while. What's the year, boy?"

The man spat at her and hurled a barrage of expletives.

"Yes," she said excitedly. "*Much* less formal language these days. And so much more colorful as well. But really now, the year."

"Why should I answer you?"

"That's true, there *is* the easier way. If I'd been thinking, I'd have gotten that out of your brother before I let him wander off, but there's always another person about…"

She lowered her staff, bringing the bizarre creature riding it unnervingly close.

"No! No, I'll tell you! I'll tell you anything, just don't touch me with that! It's 157."

"That doesn't make any sense. No monarch rules for that long."

"Monarch?"

"Yes. Surely you mean one hundred fifty-seven years since the coronation of the sitting monarch. If not, then one hundred fifty-seven years since *what*?"

"Since the start of the war!"

"Which war?"

"There's only been one war!"

"And it lasted one hundred and fifty years? That's absurd. Perhaps the easy way *is* best, eh, Mott?"

"No! Please!"

The creature clutching Turiel's staff released a throaty churring noise.

"Yes… I suppose you're right, Mott. Someone's got to bury his brother. I hate to see the dead dishonored unless they are being put to good use. I've wasted enough of your time, young man. I'll get my information elsewhere. Good day to you," she said. She started to walk away, but another churr from her companion stopped her. "Oh, yes. You are right, of course." She turned back to the survivor. "I'm afraid I'll have to ask that you keep this encounter to yourself. Until I feel otherwise inclined, I would much prefer to move discreetly. If you tell others what happened here, I'll have to return, and there will be very little reason for me to let you live."

He nodded, terrified.

"Excellent, once again, good day to you."

Mott chittered again.

"… What? … No, I've *told* you, *we* are going to find *Teht*. … Because she is late for her visit and I'm concerned. … I'm sure she's in the north. She always had snow on her cloak when she visited. … Yes, we could open a portal, but we are saving our power for the *keyhole,* remember? … Oh, learn some patience. The walk will do us good. It will be nice to see what's become of the world while we were away. … Oh, you can *so* see. Don't be so dramatic. If you want some eyes, I'll get you some eyes, but I'm waiting for green ones. … Because you'd look so *precious* with green eyes."

She sighed and lowered her staff slightly. The body of the stricken brother shuddered and glowed, then ponderously sat up, breath sliding from it in a voiceless moan. His lifeless eyes slid open. She crouched and looked into them, then nodded and raised her staff, dropping him limply to the ground again.

"*There*. You see? Brown. You don't want brown eyes, do you? So common. …" She looked to the grief-stricken younger brother. "His are brown too."

She paced off to the north, chatting idly with her pet.

"… Yes, I'll get you some proper wings too. Perhaps we can swing west. That's where those riders come from, yes? Some nice baby dragon wings and some green eyes, my little patchwork pet. You'll be darling."

#

"And that's it. That's what happened," he said. "She killed my brother… that *witch*… And she told me not to tell anyone. And then your men came and asked me, and then *they* told me not to tell anyone, and I…"

"That's fine, sir," Sallim said without looking up from his parchment. "I have what I need from you."

He sat silently for a few minutes, flipping between the fresh parchment and some older ones, comparing details between them.

The D'Karon Apprentice

"May I leave now?" the farmer asked.

"One moment… Yes… Yes, this would appear to match other accounts. I would say we are through here."

"Other accounts? This… this woman has done more?"

"That really isn't any of your concern, sir."

"But… if it was known that she was dangerous… if we'd been warned…"

"You'll be happy to know that based on the description, yours is the *earliest* encounter—which means it is more likely five months than four. There could have been no warning in your case. Now, if you would be good enough, just head back through that door and inform the soldier that his orders stand."

"Um… yes, sir."

"Esteemed Patron," Sallim corrected.

"Err, yes, Esteemed Patron. I'll be on my way," he said, standing and pacing toward the door.

When the farmer left, Sallim pulled out a fresh parchment, this one a thin ribbon, and inscribed a message in small, precise writing.

Another credible account, he wrote, the first. Most detailed yet. As with the others, he will be held to prevent further spread of information. As I write this, Northern diplomats are crossing the border. Your time with the subject is limited. I will be visiting personally in one week's time. I expect answers.

He completed the message and rolled it into a tube, labeling it with the intended recipient, Commander Brustuum.

#

"We must be getting close now, Myn. Dip down and let's get our bearings," Myranda suggested.

Myranda was in her usual position astride the base of Myn's neck, holding tightly to the broad scales on either side. Deacon sat behind her, his legs hooked over the base of Myn's wings and his arms about Myranda's waist. Behind them, held in place with a sturdy leather harness, was a small bundle of supplies and equipment. Overall the load was somewhat heavier than Myn typically carried, but not nearly enough to cause a problem.

At Myranda's request Myn tipped her wings and dropped down through the thinning clouds beneath her. The last five days had held a tremendous amount of travel, but the journey was a pleasant one. Repairing Kenvard was a monumental task, and one that required their constant attention. With the mission to the south requiring their presence, Myranda and the others had been forced to journey north to meet with those who provided the stone and lumber for the repairs, providing payment and explaining how the tour would change matters. They'd also dropped off messages to prepare some of the diplomatic stops for their requirements. Then it was back south and to the front. There had been two snowstorms in the days they had been flying, but above the clouds they were of little concern. Flying so high made for a frigid journey, but a blast of dragon fire, a good, heavy cloak, and a few whispered spells kept everyone comfortable. Unfortunately, over most of the Northern Alliance the clouds were thick enough to make it difficult to see the ground even without a storm, so dropping through from time to time was necessary.

"If you like, I can navigate. Last night I looked through my primer to refresh my memory regarding the necessary spells," Deacon offered, raising his voice against the rushing wind.

"No. I think it is important Myn learns to navigate on her own. We can't always be guiding her. I'm not sure how dragons do it naturally, but the least I can do is help her along. Show her how I do it until she can find her own way."

"Yes. It is something of a mystery how they find their way in the absence of more traditionally human means," Deacon said. "Worthy of study."

Myranda leaned forward to address Myn more directly. "You see how much more green and lush the land is there near the horizon? We're getting close to Tressor. Those peaks there are the southern fringe of the Rachis Mountains. That silvery thread is the Loom River. We are to cross the border where the Loom crosses it. The border is where the ground … darkens for a bit. That's the Crimson Band… where all of the fighting was happening."

Myranda paused for a moment, looking sadly at the subtle but undeniable stripe of landscape that stretched as far as the eye could see in both directions. It was darker in some places than others, but even six months after the last major offensive the land had not healed. Perhaps it never would. It was said that so much blood had been spilled on that soil—both the red blood of humans and the black blood of nearmen—that it had permanently darkened to a rusty, sickly color. The war had lasted so long it had left scars not only on the people but also on the land itself.

She tried to push the thoughts away. "Make sure to land well before that. They have requested that we cross the border on foot. They will be waiting at a checkpoint on the road just east of the Loom. Keep a look out for it, and land to the north of it. Understand?"

There was a rumble through Myn, felt more than heard, in response.

"You know something, Myn? Perhaps when you learn to navigate, you will explain it to me. And sooner rather than later," Deacon called out to her, giving her a pat on the side. "Don't think I haven't noticed you've been more vocal lately. Perhaps not verbal, but vocal. And you've always been enthralled by Myranda's voice."

"She'll talk when she's ready," Myranda said, giving Myn a pat of her own.

Myn tucked her wings and dove more quickly toward the ground, prompting Myranda and Deacon to hold tighter and lean closer. The young dragon had a bit of a tendency to show off, particularly regarding her landings, and it wouldn't be the first time she'd lost one of her riders and had to fetch them before something tragic happened. As a matter of fact, it had happened no less than six times to Deacon. It was enough to make Myranda suspect that this was simply a new way of toying with him. When they held tight and leaned low, though, the wind swept over them with barely a flutter of their clothes. It was like they were one with her, cutting through the sky as though they belonged nowhere else. As the ground approached, Myn stretched her wings once more and they caught the wind, swooping her upward and slowing her descent. Myranda felt herself pressed firmly against the dragon's back with the force of the maneuver, and just as the pressure began to ease, she felt the smoothness of flight turn to the gentle rhythm of a trot.

"I think you might take that a little more slowly in the future, Myn," Deacon suggested, sitting up straight and checking to be sure he hadn't dropped anything.

"This is right where we need to be, though. Excellent work," Myranda said.

Myn stopped and crouched so that both wizards could dismount, and the trio continued on foot. Without the chill of the skies, the warmer southern climate became quite apparent. This strip of the Northern Alliance just above the border was the only part of the empire to truly experience all four seasons. The sharpness of the change from the cold of the north to the warm of the south was almost supernatural. Even a few days travel by foot north and there would often be snow on the ground in the dead of summer. Here, there was hardly a nip to the air, and green fields filled the landscape behind and ahead of them. Bees buzzed in the air, birds sang. There was life here, thriving. It was beautiful... though one didn't need to look far to see evidence of what had happened here. Farmers had done their best to reclaim land on either side of the border, but where their hoes and plows had not been put to work, the ground was still churned up by hooves and boots. Here and there the broken shaft of an arrow or a rusted plate of armor jutted from the soil. Mixed with the scent of blooming flowers and tilled fields, a sour, acrid smell tinged the air. Life was trying its best to take this land back from the death that had made its home here, but it would take time.

The crossing was just a few hundred paces ahead of them along a packed-earth road, and already the serenity of the sky was giving way to the tension of the surface. The border was, for the moment, marked with waist-high stakes driven into the ground every twenty paces or so. At some point in history walls might have separated the two kingdoms, at least between some of those cities nearest to one another, but the war had demolished them, and both sides agreed it would not show confidence in the continuing peace efforts if the first order of business was erecting new walls. There was, however, a set of tree-trunk-sized posts on either side of the wide road, and a heavy gate had been mounted on both the northern and southern sides. With soft soil on either side, no vehicle would pass here without the knowledge and permission of the half-dozen soldiers on either side. The same went for the nearby Loom River. The sharpened trunks of trees had been driven into the riverbed, some quite fresh, others rotted by decades in the water. The only difference between those placed by the north or the south was the direction the points were angled. It was worrying that after six months no efforts had been made to remove them and make water passable by river traffic once more.

The other significant addition to the crossing was a set of guard posts, small but sturdy buildings erected on either side of the border to provide lodging and supplies for those stationed here. The northern post was like any other building Myranda had seen erected in the last fifty years: thick planks cut from pine, solidly assembled and topped with thatch. The construction was simple but strong and built to last. The Tresson counterpart was subtly different. It was more ornate, painted a warm red color and bearing carved doors and curved accents on the corner posts. The roof had a shallower peak as well and an unusual combination of thatch at the top and shingles at the edge.

"Oh, my goodness," Myranda said, stopping suddenly.

"Is something wrong?" Deacon asked, he and Myn stopping as well.

"I've just realized—I'm supposed to be a representative of the throne and an ambassador for my people, and I've been flying on the back of a dragon." She shed her cloak and tucked it under one of the straps of Myn's harness. "I must be a mess."

She smoothed down her blouse and leggings, both a great deal more formal than she was accustomed to. By rights, on an occasion such as this she should have been wearing a gown, but such clothes were not designed with travel by dragon in mind. Instead she selected the finest alternative she could, each a shade of Alliance or Kenvard blue. After half a lifetime of wandering from town to town struggling to survive, the concept of dressing for grace and elegance rather than practicality was one she was slow to warm to, and the idea that someone might require her hair or face to look a certain way tended to slip her mind.

"You look lovely as ever," Deacon said. "Though I suppose a bit windswept."

Myranda pulled a blue ribbon from one of her bags and conjured a simple whisper of magic to smooth the tangles from her hair before she tied it back. When Deacon had stowed his cloak, she helped him put himself in order as well.

"I'm not entirely certain I'm suited for this aspect of diplomacy," she said. "It's never been something I've had to concern myself with."

"If appearance has any more than a cursory impact on matters of state, then I would suggest the entire process is badly in need of reassessment," Deacon said.

Thus prepared, they continued on their way, though with each step, Myn seemed more distracted. She sniffed the air, her eyes wide with interest and curiosity. Ahead, the Alliance Army soldiers on the north side of the border were assembling themselves for the approach of three ambassadors, and a small group stepped out of the Tresson guard post. Unlike Myranda, they had arrived by carriage and therefore were outfitted in the full regalia of their position. Each of the three emissaries wore flowing, airy robes made from fine, thin cloth the same yellow-orange of ripe peaches. The trim of each was a shade of red, though Tressor was a single kingdom rather than an alliance of them, so the shade here indicated rank. The deepest red was worn by a tall, portly man with short salt-and-pepper hair and a full beard that was more silver than black. He wore a tall, round hat made from some sort of stiff cloth. His face was stern—not cruel or angry, but serious and steadfast—and his skin the dark color of a native Tresson. A step behind him on each side stood similarly dressed men, also with short dark hair, but lacking the hat and bearing trim closer to yellow than red. There was something about them that Myranda couldn't quite identify. Their presence was… significant in some way.

As the Tresson diplomats approached, their soldiers lifted aside the Tresson gate. The Alliance soldier did the same. Myranda stepped forward to greet her equal. He lifted his right hand, she did the same, and they clasped one another's left shoulder. With the gesture complete, Myranda held her right hand out and he did the same, clasping it in a firm shake across the border.

Myranda cleared her throat and, in her best Tresson, stated, "It is my honor and privilege to meet you as a representative of my people, and it is my profound hope that this is merely the first step toward a lasting peace between our lands."

"May our children know only peace, but may they never forget this war," he said in response, in excellent Varden. "I am Ambassador Valaamus. And you are the mythic Duchess Myranda Celeste. It is truly humbling to know that the lives of countless thousands of soldiers on my side and yours could have been plucked from the jaws of endless war by someone so young, and so lovely."

He had an avuncular disposition that seemed at odds with his serious expression, but nonetheless his words seemed as sincere as they were impeccably pronounced. If his pleasant and welcoming demeanor was an affectation, it was a masterful one.

"You flatter me, Ambassador. I was but one of those responsible. As much thanks can be given to my fellow ambassadors. May I introduce Deacon?"

"The scholar! We have heard of you as well," he said, exchanging the shoulder clasp and handshake with him too. "And this is the mighty dragon, Mine."

Myn glanced briefly at the ambassador but quickly resumed her curious sampling of the air. She had her forepaw raised, as though ready to bound across the border to investigate whatever it was that had caught her interest, but she held her ground faithfully beside Myranda.

"It's Myn, actually, but yes," Myranda said.

"Ah, my apologies. I have only seen it written. A fine specimen, and expertly trained."

"Not trained. Just observant and eager to please," Myranda said. "If you don't mind the observation, I've seldom met a group who so gracefully handled their first introduction to Myn."

"Like many in service to the Tresson throne, I am no stranger to the company of dragons. To that end, I suppose it is best that I introduce our protector for this tour." He turned and clapped his hands, barking a sharp order in Tresson that was a much better match for his expression. "Grustim, to my side!"

The hiss of heavy breath and the sound of rustling grass came as a reply. The ground shook lightly as a long shadow separated itself from that of the Tresson guard post. A stout full-grown dragon slid from behind the post. It must have been curled up behind the building, because now that it was visible, it was astounding that the little structure could have hidden it so completely. The beast was a bit larger than Myn overall, but also of a *much* thicker build. Rather than the red of Myn's scales, this beast's were a deep forest-green along its back, and its belly scales were a similar but lighter gold color to hers. Its snout was shorter and broader, its lower jaw jutting just a bit further than its upper one and featuring a bristly "beard" of downward-pointing horns. Its eyes were smaller than Myn's and set slightly deeper in its head. The two forelegs had a wide, almost bulldog-like build, and the horns and spines of its head were longer, more numerous, and more vicious. The same could be said of the spikes running down its spine and along the back of its long neck. Its most peculiar features, though, were the accessories on its head and back. Strapped over its face was a sculpted metal plate, something between a mask and a helmet. The armor was covered with green enamel that was a precise match for its natural color, and here and there silver scrapes and gouges gleamed through the coating. A second bundle of metal nestled between its neatly folded wings, this time made of a strange assortment of overlapping plates of the same green color. When the dragon had taken its position just behind the diplomats, this metal bundle moved.

Gradually the form of an armored human seemed to coalesce on the creature's back, though it was quickly clear that his armor was simply designed to match the hide of the dragon so closely it had been difficult to tell where one ended and the other began. The human smoothly dismounted with a jingle of plates. For anyone who had never ridden a dragon in flight, the armor would have seemed nonsensical. The helmet was rounded and flared out at the neck, and the back plates shared a similar flared and overlapping shape. The tops of the shoulders came to a pointed ridge, and the belly was lightly armored with smooth plates and thin mail. When standing, the plates jutted awkwardly out behind him and seemed to offer little protection, but when riding low against the dragon's back the gaps closed and he may as well have been an extension of the beast.

At the first glimpse of the beast, Myn froze in place. She then took a cautious step forward, subtly placing one huge paw slightly in front of Myranda. She craned her neck, stretching it forward as far as she could without leaving her spot, and drew long, slow whiffs of the beast's scent. Every muscle in her body seemed tense, and her eyes were wide and locked on the other dragon.

"You may be the first Northerners in two hundred years to see a Tresson Dragon Rider without his lance in hand. This is Grustim Terrim, the fourth Rider of Mikkalla and Shaal's Terrible Green Gristle," said the ambassador.

"It is an honor and a pleasure to meet you, Grustim, and you as well... I'm sorry, how should I address the dragon?"

"You address dragon and Rider as one. I refer to them as Grustim, you may do the same. Though for the purposes of this tour, they serve as our escorts only and need not be addressed at all. Similarly my attendants are merely record keepers and servants for this journey. Consider me your host. But please, we have reached across this line in the earth for long enough. Please allow me to formally invite you to my land so that we can begin this tour properly."

He stood aside and spread his arm magisterially to the land beyond. Myranda stepped forward and onto the soil of Tressor. Deacon followed. Myn remained where she was for a moment, eyes still locked on the green dragon. When she glanced down and noticed Myranda stepping past the ambassador and toward the beast, she quickly strode forward and placed herself between them. With her forepaw planted firmly in front of Myranda to keep her from getting any closer, she extended her neck again, sniffing at the foreign dragon.

"Myn, relax. No one here means us any harm," Myranda said.

The ambassador chuckled, somehow managing to sound mirthful while the humor barely registered on his face, and paced onward. Myranda tried to follow but had to step further and further aside as Myn angled herself to separate her and Deacon from the Dragon Rider and his mount. For their part, both the green dragon and the Rider stood impassively, keeping an eye on the newcomers but otherwise offering no indication of interest or concern. When the others were far enough ahead, the Dragon Rider made a barely audible sound in his throat, and his steed slightly raised the forepaw nearest to him. The Rider stepped on and, with a smooth motion of both man and beast, vaulted into place on the dragon's back. Myn kept careful pace beside them, never taking her eyes from the pair.

"Our carriage will return for us shortly. Horses, if well trained, will ride beside a dragon, but try as we might we could not get them to calm when *standing* near one. I sent them ahead," Valaamus said.

"Yes, it usually takes a few days before any new horses will ease themselves around Myn," Myranda said.

"I hope you don't mind a bit of walking while we await their return."

"Of course not. May I ask what has been planned for this tour? We were not given many details. This all was organized quite swiftly."

"Yes, I'm quite curious as well. I've heard of many wonders of this land," Deacon said, pulling out his book and stylus. "I attempted to find literature concerning your land to prepare for this journey, but there was little to be found."

"Is it any wonder?" Valaamus said. "If you found any, might I politely suggest you disregard it. Those things written of one's enemies during war tend not to paint a flattering picture. I hesitate to think what the common folk have read of you and your people. It is that sort of thing that we hope to change. But I ramble. When the carriage arrives, we shall set off immediately to the first point of interest. With luck we will reach it by nightfall. There we shall see the Memorial for Fallen Officers and spend the night. The following morning we shall discuss the remainder of the itinerary, as it is currently somewhat... fluid. In two weeks time you will make an official appearance at the capital for a banquet in your honor. From there any further stops will be discussed and planned for. I apologize for the lack of specificity but... well, the circumstances prohibit it."

"I very much look forward to the sights and knowledge your people have to offer. I'm already most impressed with your mystics," Deacon said.

Valaamus glanced to him, his expression unchanged. "Oh? Have you observed them in some way?"

"Only since my arrival, obviously," Deacon said simply. He turned to the ambassador's two attendants. "I'm particularly impressed with your suppression techniques."

Myranda kept her expression steady, but with Deacon's words came a flash of realization. Now that he'd drawn attention to it, it seemed obvious in retrospect. Everyone, whether mystically inclined or not, had an aura of power about them. Sensing this was among the first lessons a wizard would learn, and shortly thereafter it became second nature. Both attendants at first blush seemed to have the same subtle power to them that any human might. But it was wrong somehow... like the shifting subtle energy was an illusion covering something else.

Deacon turned back to Valaamus. "For a moment I wasn't certain your men were trained mystics at all. Quite effective. It wasn't an area of focus for me, but I would be happy to discuss my own—"

Myranda touched his shoulder, quieting him. "I think such matters can wait for our next visit."

"Yes. Time is short," Valaamus said quickly. "Let us be sharp in our focus."

"Yes. Of course," Deacon said.

Valaamus gave his men a brief but significant glance and they retreated a few steps behind the rest of the group. In the distance, a form appeared on the road, turning the bend around a small stand of trees.

"Ah!" said the ambassador. "The exquisitely timed return of our coach. Let us be properly on our way."

The ambassador quickened his step to greet the carriage. Deacon stepped a bit closer to Myranda.

"I feel as though my compliment was not taken in the spirit in which it was offered," Deacon said.

"Under the circumstances, I think the observation served its purpose. There was never any doubt they'd be taking precautions, but it never hurts to let them know we're aware of them…"

#

Ivy stood anxiously in the foyer of a small church a short distance down the main street from the southern gate of New Kenvard. As the largest and most formal of the buildings that had finished their restoration, it was chosen as the meeting place for the diplomatic envoy. Efforts had been made to decorate it in a manner befitting so historic a moment. The colors of both Kenvard as a kingdom and the Northern Alliance as a whole were hung as banners and pennants, swathing the walls and tall ceiling of the church in two shades of blue and an icy white. At some point long in the past, the northern kingdoms had agreed that blue should be the color of the north. Ostensibly it was to invoke the frigid temperatures that hardened the populace. More likely it had been a means to illustrate the wealth the mountains provided, as blue dye had been and remained highly expensive. Thus the mere ability to swaddle their meeting place in blue was evidence of the Kenvard's steady recovery. Seven months prior, during the small ceremony in which Myranda and Deacon had been wed, this church was nearly bare and still badly in need of repair. It had come a long way in a short time.

Chandeliers and torchères loaded with tallow candles filled the space with warm yellow light. The pews were pushed to the walls, and a long banquet table was placed in the center of the room, set with all of the delights the Northern Alliance could provide. There were fine wines, roasted meats, fresh breads, and rich desserts. It was as grand a welcome as any dignitary could hope to receive, but that did little to set Ivy's mind at ease.

She was dressed elegantly. Her gown was Alliance blue with Kenvard blue accents. The skirt fell to just above her ankles to reveal tasteful blue slippers with low heels. The sleeves were short, just long enough to meet the full-length blue gloves she wore. Her long white hair had been tamed, woven into an intricate braid and topped with a silver chain headpiece. To her left, standing carefully away from Ivy, was a young woman in similar but lesser attire. To Ivy's right was Greydon Celeste, dressed in formal but, again, lesser attire.

"I'm excited," Ivy said, offering a nervous smile to her lady-in-waiting. "Aren't you?"

She replied with a demure grin and nod.

"I'm nervous too. Are you nervous?" Ivy asked.

Another smile was her only reply.

"Why aren't you answering?" Ivy asked.

"Because her role is to see to secretarial matters and those of etiquette. She isn't to address any members of the delegation directly. That is the role of the diplomats and ambassadors," Celeste quietly instructed.

"Oh… yes, yes. That's right. You told me that." She fidgeted. "I don't know what to do with my hands."

"Fold them in front of you. And stand still," he said gently. "Do you remember the Tresson greeting?"

"I hold out my right hand and clasp their left shoulder, and they do the same to me."

"Correct. But do not touch their shoulder until they raise their hand to do the same."

Ivy nodded and took a steadying breath. Almost immediately she started fidgeting again.

"These slippers don't fit properly. Women's shoes just don't fit my feet right. Can I do this barefoot?"

"I would advise against it."

"I wish they would have let me cut a hole for my tail. The dress is bulgy in the back." She ran her hands down the dress in a failed attempt to flatten it.

Her breathing became faster, and she began wringing her hands. When the horns sounded, heralding the arrival of the dignitaries at the city gates, she nearly leaped out of her skin.

"This… this was a mistake. I shouldn't be the one doing this." Her eyes darted, and though somewhat concealed by the similarly colored dress, a blue aura flared faintly around her.

"It wasn't your decision. They requested you. It is your duty to serve."

She looked to him, desperation in her eyes. "You should do this. You're an ambassador. You can do this!"

"They requested you. It would be an insult to refuse."

"But what if they don't like me?"

"They *won't* like you. You are a malthrope and a Northerner. You are everything they have been taught since birth to despise. But they are diplomats. If they are well trained, they will behave with respect and decorum."

"Th-this is going to be a disaster! I'm going to ruin things! I'm going to make all of Kenvard look bad. I-I can't do this."

The blue aura was intensifying, flickering and flashing around her as she struggled to control it. Her lady-in-waiting took two startled steps back, gasping.

"I have to go! I have to go away *right now!*"

She grasped her skirt and hiked it up to keep from tripping over it, then turned toward the back of the church, eying a door she knew led to the alley behind it.

"Ivy."

Greydon did not bellow the name. He merely spoke it, but somehow it had all of the force and authority of a command called down from the mountaintops. She stopped and snapped her head to him. He placed his hand on her shoulder and looked her evenly in the eyes.

"Listen carefully. This meeting, this visit, exists because of you. You are a warrior and this is your land. You helped end the war. You are *responsible* for the peace we now enjoy. The people who will walk through that door are diplomats. They and a thousand like them were appointed by their king to negotiate an end to the war and they failed. *You* succeeded. You and the others have done more for the cause of peace than anyone else in either kingdom for more than a century. They should feel honored to stand in your presence. They came here to see *you*. They *selected* you because they *knew* there was no greater honor than to meet you. All you need to do is greet them and let them see the sort of person it takes to change the world. Just be you."

The aura faded and she slowly caught her breath, taking his hand from her shoulder and clasping it briefly.

"Now I see where Myranda gets it," Ivy said gratefully.

She released his hand and took her position, smoothing her skirt again and standing straight. "If I do something wrong, or forget to do something, just whisper it under your breath," she said, tapping her pointed ear. "If you make any sound at all, I'll hear it."

"They are nearly here. Are you ready for them?" he asked.

"Yes... No, wait!"

Ivy turned and stepped quickly to the table, selecting one of the carving knives and twisting to reach the back of her dress. With a deft poke she pierced a small hole, then hooked her tail with a finger and pulled it through, fluffing it and swishing it until it was back to shape. She then replaced the knife and kicked her slippers off, padding back to her position and releasing a sigh of relief. Celeste gave her a measuring look. She glanced at him and smirked.

"If I'm going to be me, I'm going to be *me*," she said.

A servant quickly snatched the knife and substituted a fresh one, then gathered her slippers and returned to his position. Moments later the door opened, and the small delegation stepped inside.

The ambassador assigned to Ivy was a woman, perhaps forty years of age. She was stately and proper from the tip of her tightly wrapped bun of black hair to the point of her fine leather shoes. Like Ivy she was clad in the colors of her land, a tawny fur cloak layered atop a red-orange gown with peach-colored embroidery. If there was one flourish to her appearance that seemed to be more of an appeal to fashion than tradition, it was her jewelry. There wasn't an overabundance of it, but each piece she wore was notable for its size and quality. A ruby and gold ring on two fingers of her right hand, a silver and garnet necklace gleaming proudly against her dress, and a topaz earing in each ear.

The woman paced toward Ivy, flanked by two subordinates, who took her coat and handed it to one of the servants waiting beside the door. Though the ambassador's face was even and neutral, there was something in her eyes and her posture that made Ivy feel as though she was being judged, and that the initial assessment was not good.

Ivy shifted her weight to step forward and greet the visitor, but Celeste touched her leg, reminding her that she was to wait until greeted. The dignitary approached her. Ivy lifted her arm until the ambassador matched her gesture, then gripped the shoulder of her visitor lightly. The ambassador mirrored her, though Ivy couldn't help but notice she didn't so much grasp her shoulder as touch it gingerly with her fingertips.

"On behalf of Queen and Empress Caya, I welcome you to New Kenvard," Ivy said, taking her hand away and offering it for a shake.

"On behalf of King Aamuul, I am honored to visit your fair city," she said, accepting the offered hand in a dainty shake. "My name is Ambassador Amorria Krettis."

"I'm Ivy." Her ear flitted toward Celeste. "That is to say, I am Guardian of the Realm, Heroine of the Battle of Verril, and Ambassador Ivy. And may I introduce Ambassador Greydon Celeste?"

Ambassador Krettis exchanged the traditional greetings with Celeste, then cast her eyes up and down Ivy slowly, lingering at her feet before sweeping her gaze up again. Ivy felt a flutter of anxiety at first, then a blush of pride.

"Oh! My dress," Ivy said, turning in a circle. "Do you like it? It was made specially for me, and just for this occasion. Your gown is *gorgeous* by the way."

"Thank you," the ambassador said, her eyes drifting briefly to Ivy's tail.

Ivy's ear flicked. "Please, take a seat, make yourself comfortable."

The lady-in-waiting stepped forward to lead the ambassador to her seat, and Ivy sat opposite her. Celeste sat to her right. The rest of the servants and attendants remained standing.

"Please, all of you, sit down, dig in!" Her ear flicked. "Err... after we, the diplomats, are through eating, of course. As is custom. We'll try to hurry up for you."

The ambassador turned to Celeste. "Is this all the first course?"

He glanced to Ivy.

"No! No, this is everything," Ivy said. "I know usually they bring out things one at a time, but I like it better this way. Now you know everything we're going to eat, so you can save room for—" Her ear flicked. She cleared her throat and took on a more serious tone. "If you like, the chef will describe the dishes and their origins."

"I'm sure that will be most enlightening," the ambassador said, again addressing Celeste.

One by one, those responsible for the meal stepped up to the table and described in detail the dish, its significance to the Northern Alliance, and the manner in which it was traditionally served and eaten. When the process was through, serving spoons and forks were set out and the meal began.

"I hope you enjoy it," Ivy said. "I am *starving*."

She reached to load her plate, flicked her ear, and then leaned back and allowed herself to be served.

"So your name is Amorria. That's a lovely name. Is it common in Tressor..." she flicked her ear again, "Ambassador Krettis?"

"It is quite common, Ambassador..." She looked at Celeste. "I apologize, but is Ivy her family name?"

Ivy looked in confusion to Celeste as well.

"Madam Ambassador, while I would be happy to answer any questions you might have, Ambassador Ivy is the designated representative," he said. "Both protocol and the will of your king would direct you to address her rather than me. Particularly on matters relating to her specifically."

"Yes, of course." She turned back to Ivy. "Is Ivy your family name?"

"No. I'm just Ivy. I don't have a family name. ... Well, there was a time when my family name would have been Melodia, but that was before..." She paused, trying to find the proper words. Finding none that seemed appropriate for the occasion, she simply repeated, "That was before."

"Yes... they say that you were once human."

"It's more complicated than that, but I'd really rather not—"

"They also say that the duke and duchess of this region are great wizards."

"Oh, that they are! Myranda and Deacon are truly amazing."

"Is it not within their power to change you back?"

"As I said, it's more complicated than that. This body is a malthrope. It has only ever *been* a malthrope. It can't be changed back."

"Perhaps if we broker a lasting peace, you might find your way to our land. We have some of the finest wizards in the world. I'm quite sure one of them could treat your condition."

"I... I don't have a condition, Ambassador. This is what I am. I like what I am. I don't want to change." Ivy swished her tail twice, as if for emphasis, then put her mouth to work on a bite of food before she slipped and said something she might regret.

"May I say, you eat quite daintily."

Ivy furrowed her brow. "Thank you, I suppose... So do you. It isn't easy though, with this feast."

"I must agree. The meal has only just begun and its quality has vastly exceeded my expectations," she said, sipping at a spoonful of soup.

"And wait until you try the desserts! Eliza cooked them. She's the personal cook for Myranda and Deacon." Her ear flicked. "The duke and duchess of Kenvard."

"The duke and duchess," Krettis said. "It is a shame I couldn't meet them during this journey. I would have liked to conduct my first formal diplomatic reception with a more traditional representative of the north."

Ivy's eyes narrowed briefly, then her ear flicked. "Guardian of the Realm is one of the oldest and most honored titles in the long history of the Alliance, and is regarded by tradition as one of its most valued diplomatic positions."

"Of course. My apologies," Krettis said, without a drop of sincerity.

Ivy gripped her fork more tightly and speared some meat. She'd prepared herself to keep her fear in check. She'd not expected to have to cope with anger.

"You say this is your first formal diplomatic reception," Ivy said, now not quite able to keep the irritation from her voice. "I wouldn't have known it to look at you."

"In Tressor our diplomats are selected and educated based upon the region to which we are to serve as representative. Owing to your empire's disinterest in diplomacy until recently, I was not given any opportunities to ply my trade."

"Now that the D'Karon are gone, I think you'll find our people more than eager to mend the relationship between our nations."

"Ah, yes. The D'Karon. I wonder if during our tour of your land I might meet any of these D'Karon. Perhaps in a prison?" she asked.

"I'm happy to say that there aren't any D'Karon left."

"I see. Rather convenient that you would blame all of the atrocities committed by your nation on a group whom you claim to have entirely eradicated in a matter of months. And this coming from a nation that couldn't even rid itself of..." She paused, for the first time offering a flicker of regret for her wording.

Ivy's lip twitched and her fist clenched tightly around her fork. Celeste put a hand on her arm. The temperature in the room suddenly felt considerably warmer, but through some miracle the red aura of anger did not flare. "Say it. Say 'malthropes.' Brag to me about killing my kind."

The ambassador sat quietly, her face still steady, but her eyes betraying more than a bit of concern. Ivy placed her fork on the table. It had been bent effortlessly by her grip.

"I know that you hate me. You hate me because I am a malthrope and you hate me because I am from the north. I'm used to hate. I deal with it all the time. Hating someone comes from not knowing them well enough, and you are here so that we can fix that. But I think we both underestimated just how much needs to be fixed. Mr. Celeste told me you'd treat me with respect and decorum because that's what diplomats do. You said this is your first time, and I'm sure it shows that it is my first time, too. Mistakes were bound to happen. I'm willing to set this one aside. Peace is much too important to be shattered by a few angry words, right?"

"Yes. Yes, of course I agree," Krettis said, taking a rather large sip of wine.

"But! Since we already broke the respect-and-decorum rule, I don't see any reason to adhere to some of the other silly little bits of protocol. Everyone. Servants, cooks, everyone. Pull up a chair. Eat. This is a feast after all. Let's enjoy it properly."

Ivy tugged off her gloves and reached across the table to heap her plate as the servants and underlings reluctantly joined their superiors. Ivy took the leg from a turkey and tore into it, chewing happily as she turned to Celeste. He had an uncertain look on his face.

Ivy shrugged. "No sense being dainty anymore."

#

Across the continent, at a border crossing south of Territal similar to the Loom River crossing, a pair of diplomats and a sizable entourage of servants and soldiers were waiting with increasing anxiety for Ether to arrive. They had been informed of her agreement to attend, but owing to her unusual lack of travel requirements, they didn't know precisely when she would arrive. All involved had assumed she would arrive a day or more ahead of time in order to be briefed and properly prepared for the introduction. Now the carriages of the visiting dignitaries were visible on the road to the south, and the Guardian who was to greet them had still not arrived.

Of those present, the most concerned were the two diplomats, an old man named Gregol and a somewhat younger woman named Zuzanna. Gregol was a rail-thin, hunched-over man who would have looked fit to collapse under the weight of his ceremonial robes even under the best of circumstances. In the face of the looming political disaster, he was shuffling back and forth, wringing his hands and stroking his beard.

"Perhaps… perhaps she has been killed!" Gregol fretted.

"She is an elemental, and a shapeshifter. I am not certain she can *be* killed," reasoned Zuzanna.

She was young enough to still have a few strands of blond amid her head of gray hair. She supported her weight on an oak and copper cane and, though equally concerned, was a bit better at maintaining her composure.

"Yes. Yes! She can take on any form! Perhaps she is already here! If any of you is Guardian of the Realm Ether, please speak up!"

"Gregol, I believe she is approaching," Zuzanna said, pointing.

He turned his eyes to the western sky, where the wail of wind was growing steadily sharper. There was a barely discernible form approaching, but it grew more distinct with each moment, coming as a tight rush of air wrapped about a small brown book. When it reached them, all eyes watched in fascination as Ether's human form coalesced out of the swirling gale

"Guardian Ether, it is an honor," Zuzanna said, bowing her head reverently.

"An honor and a privilege," added Gregol, offering the same sign of respect. "We wish only that we might have had the privilege sooner."

"Oh? This is the time indicated for the beginning of this tiresome errand, is it not?"

"Yes, but you have never performed a task of this sort," Gregol said. "There is style, protocol. There are things you must do, and things you must not!"

"Then speak. Tell me the rules for this insipid game," Ether said.

"Might I suggest you begin by avoiding 'insipid,' 'game,' and other words of that sort when speaking of diplomacy to other diplomats, great Guardian."

"There simply isn't time for either of us to tell you all you should know. The carriages will be here in minutes."

"Then both of you speak at once," Ether said simply.

"How can you listen to both of us?"

"I am quite capable of splitting my attentions sufficiently."

"There are interactions we must rehearse, things which will require your undivided attention," Zuzanna said.

Ether looked wearily from one of the advisers to the other.

"Hold this," she said irritably, handing the book to Zuzanna.

When the woman accepted it, Ether stepped away and, in blast of brilliant light and searing heat, shifted to flame. The advisers stumbled backward, mouths agape, as the figure of flames separated into two, then shifted back to flesh. Standing before them was a pair of Ethers, each looking expectantly to one of the advisers.

"Speak," they said simultaneously.

Gregol looked to Zuzanna, then to the approaching carriages. Given the choice between taking the time to cope with what had just occurred and seizing the opportunity to potentially give this mission a chance at success, he eagerly chose the latter.

"You tell her what not to do; I shall tell her what to do," he said.

"Very well," Zuzanna agreed.

For the others observing, what followed was a bizarre and rather entertaining performance. Gregol, with a frantic energy that increased as the Tresson delegation drew nearer, spouted volumes of information about Tresson customs and beliefs. He illustrated the traditional greetings, briefly gave points of historic importance, and suggested fruitful topics of discussion. Zuzanna laid out cultural taboos to be avoided, points of etiquette to be emphasized, and sensitive information about the Northern Alliance that should be politely declined for discussion lest the defense of the Alliance be endangered. At nearly the same time, the pair began to run dry of topics that could be covered quickly. It was just as well, as the carriages were now near enough for the rattling of their wheels to be heard.

"Simple enough," each Ether said.

Again there was a burst of flame. A few moments later a single figure stood before them. Ether took back her book.

"I shall take your words into advisement," she said, walking forward to take her place at the border.

"Into advisement?" Gregol said.

"With all due respect, oh honored Guardian, we must insist that you behave precisely as we have instructed," Zuzanna said.

"If you were treating me with all due respect, you would not presume to insist upon anything. Much of what you have described requires me to supplicate and demean myself to an intolerable degree for no reason but to forestall an inevitable squabble between arbitrarily divided members of your own kind. It is a pointless exercise in futility, and I engage in it only because it has been suggested that it is somehow beyond my capabilities to do so. *Nothing* is beyond my capabilities. So I have listened to your words, but I shall take from them only what I choose."

"Of course, oh Guardian," Zuzanna said.

"Thank you, Guardian Ether," Gregol said with a bow of his head.

With that, Ether turned and awaited the arrival of the delegation.

"This is an inauspicious start to very delicate proceedings," Zuzanna said quietly to her partner.

"To put it *very* lightly," Gregol agreed.

Ether stood, stone still and utterly quiet, until the carriages reached the crossing and the delegation stepped out for the formal greeting. As before, Tressor had sent an ambassador and a pair of aides to represent their kingdom. Joining them was a reasonable accompaniment of guards and individuals fulfilling a half-dozen other minor roles necessary for a successful diplomatic tour.

The shapeshifter stepped forward, toeing the line of the border, and looked her counterpart in this exchange in the eye evenly. The Tresson ambassador was elderly, older even than Gregol. He had steel-gray hair contrasting with dark, almost black, craggy skin. There were thin, intricate tattoos visible at his wrists, and while his garb was similar to that worn by those hosting Myranda and Deacon on their own mission, his was adorned with a complex pattern of beads and embroidery.

Gregol sighed in relief as Ether initiated the interaction as instructed, flawlessly executing both the Tresson and Northern greetings and utilizing the proper style of address.

"Ambassador Maka, may I formally invite you and your delegation to enter the Ulvard region of the Northern Alliance," Ether said, stepping aside and sweeping her arm in a mechanical imitation of Gregol's suggested gesture.

The ambassador nodded and he and his people filed through. Gregol stepped up and offered his own welcome.

"We are very pleased to have you here. It is our hope that you will enjoy what little of Ulvard you will have time to see during your journey, and may we all learn much of one another. As per our prior communications, for the duration of this journey we shall be using Alliance carriages, as the climate and conditions of the road have rather special requirements for both horse and carriage. You shall be joining Guardian Ether in the first carriage, along with Ambassador Zuzanna and myself and two of your aides. The rest—"

"No," Ether said.

All eyes turned to her.

"No?" asked Gregol.

"The ambassador and I shall ride alone in the carriage. The rest of you may divide yourselves as you please among the remaining carriages."

"Guardian Ether, this was discussed at length prior to arrival of the delegation," Gregol began.

"It was not discussed with me. Ambassador Maka is my equal for the purposes of this tour. I fail to see the value in crowding the carriage with subordinates and cluttering the conversation with additional voices."

Gregol stammered somewhat in searching for the proper words to convince the headstrong elemental of the crucial nature of protocol. He'd not yet found the appropriate phrasing when the Tresson ambassador spoke.

"That is most agreeable," said Maka. His voice was more heavily accented than the other representatives, but he spoke slowly and with great clarity.

"Ah! Ah, well then, splendid," Gregol quickly proclaimed.

A flurry of discussions and activity arose as the individuals responsible for the smooth execution of this journey clambered to adjust to this unanticipated change of plans. Ether simply stepped up to the carriage, opened the door, and climbed inside. When it became clear that he would require it, she offered a hand to Maka and pulled him inside with ease.

"Driver, you may depart," Ether instructed in a raised voice.

"I am supposed to—" the unfortunate driver began to reply, his voice muffled by the thick walls of the carriage.

"Those individuals for which this tour was designed and arranged are presently in your carriage. The other drivers are aware of your itinerary. They shall meet us. Depart," she ordered.

The carriage jerked into motion.

"I admire your directness and pragmatism," Maka said, easing back into the overstuffed seats of the carriage. "I have never understood why it is believed that great understanding can only come from great numbers of people. Many voices lead only to more confusion. This, two representatives speaking as equals, this is the essence of diplomacy."

"I am pleased that we agree on this matter," Ether said. "I was instructed to inform you that this carriage is a fine example of the many trades and materials that have brought the Northern Alliance great pride in the years since the war began. The copper of the hardware is from the historic Grossmer Mines, the leather is worked and dyed Alliance blue by skilled artisans, and the wood is rock-pine felled from the base of the Dagger Gale Mountains. At your feet is a basket of food, each a Northern delicacy. You may partake as your appetite requires. It may also be of value to you to know that this is my first and quite likely my last instance as an ambassador."

"This, may I say, does not come as a surprise."

"No?"

"There is a… a certain language a diplomat uses. It is softened, smoothed. It has no edge, padded with bluster and pomp. Many words are used, but little is said. You speak like a blade hacking to the core. Also, what you have done, breaking with arrangements agreed upon? This is something an ambassador would never do."

"I see. Then this is a profession defined by rigid adherence to arbitrary customs."

"Most definitely. Another man might have refused the new arrangements, or perhaps terminated the whole of the tour in outrage."

"You feel no such outrage."

"I am old, I am cold, and I am hungry," he said, opening the basket and looking over the contents. He selected a small cloth pouch of dried fruit. "They will say their empty words and come to their agreements in the other carriages. A pleasant ride with a lovely woman sounds like a far preferable way to spend this journey. Now, please, tell me about your land…"

#

Most of Myranda and Deacon's first day in Tressor was spent traveling. The first half of the day's travels had been through towns and fields that at one time or another had been at the center of the fighting. While a century of warfare had kept the front line remarkably consistent, this stretch of it still wandered north and south a dozen miles or so depending on the intensity and outcome of the battles. As a result, some towns they'd passed through were being rebuilt for the dozenth time. The same thing had happened all across the northern side of the border as well, but Myranda had had a lifetime to adjust to it, and the Northern Alliance was far less populous than Tressor. After it became clear to the people that a city could not be reliably defended, it was simply abandoned, even if it was a capital like Kenvard. It said something about these people that they continued, decade after decade, to take back the land and return to the life they wanted to live.

The sun was setting by the time they were beyond the reach of the war, and the tone of the landscape changed. Buildings were older and more ornate. Indeed, if there was one thing to be said about the people and the architecture of Tressor at a glance, it was that much more time and effort were put into expression. Clothing was more colorful and vibrant. Buildings were more than just shelter; they were nuanced and accented, often to an almost sculptural degree.

And then there were the fields. All of the Northern Alliance's greenest land was also closest to the border. The same shifts in the front that had chased away the cities could easily wipe out the farms. Therefore they were kept small so that if one was destroyed, it was not so great a loss. Even those fields safe from battle tended to be small because any land far enough from the front to avoid combat was also cold and rocky enough to need tremendous care to bear any crop at all. For that reason farmers could only manage small plots. Here the farms and plantations seemed endless, literally covering the whole of the landscape in both directions at times. Just one such farm could probably feed half of Kenvard.

Myranda looked out the window of their coach at the green expanse, workers still toiling in the fields as the light faded. They were tending to thorny bushes Myranda had never seen before.

"Excuse me, Valaamus, but what is this farm growing?" Myranda asked.

"Ah! This is a rakka plantation. They are rare so far north. Surely you have heard of rakka?"

"Yes... yes, I think so. Your provisions. The berry you bake into your bread."

"Yes indeed. Very hard to grow. Closely kept secret. Most of our plantations are much farther south, but where the soil is right, our enterprising farmers are always willing to give a rakka crop a try."

"I understand the plants are quite finicky," Deacon said. "Surely the climate here would be too volatile for them."

"Again, it is the soil that is most important. If the soil is good enough, it is well worth the effort to have the slaves dig up saplings down south and bring them here to bear fruit."

Myranda looked to the window again, eyes scanning the workers.

"Slaves..." she said.

"Of course. Rakka requires much work. It would not be possible to grow it in quantity without slave labor."

"We abolished slavery in our kingdom," she said.

Valaamus nodded. "A recent decision, I understand. Bold, in the aftermath of war, to make so sweeping a change. Surely more strong hands would be preferable, particularly when rebuilding is necessary."

"We now believe that freedom takes precedence," Myranda said.

"A fine philosophy. I wish you luck in putting it into practice."

"We've done well enough so far," Myranda said.

As evening slid into night, they approached the place where they would take their meal and sleep. It was a small, comfortable cabin overlooking a lake and nestled in a dense forest. The carriage pulled to a stop not far from the cabin, where a small shrine stood by the lakeside. Myranda and Deacon gazed at the shrine. It was tall and carved of stone. Like most Tresson creations it was elaborate without being gaudy, and even without understanding the symbolism, there was a solemness about it. The top of the shrine was a carving of a lantern. A flame burned inside. The rest of the shrine was an obelisk carved

54

with the likeness of ivy and accented with copper inlays tinged green with the passage of time. On either side of the shrine, each rising only as high as the hub of the carriage wheel, was a line of stone slabs. The sweeping, curling script of the Tresson language formed the names and ranks of hundreds of Tresson officers in total.

An attendant opened the door to the carriage. Before Myranda could step out, the thumping of heavy footsteps caused the attendant at the door to quickly retreat. A moment later Myn's head filled the doorway, looking somewhat reproachfully at the diplomats who had tucked Myranda away with them for so long.

"Myn," Myranda scolded, "don't forget your manners."

The dragon backed away and sat on her haunches, eying the attendants, who were reluctant to return to their tasks. Eventually they got their nerve and saw to the delegation, helping each down and seeing to the bags of the Tresson nobles.

"You speak to her as if to a child," Valaamus observed, "and yet she obeys."

"I've been with her since she was born," Myranda said, walking over to the impatiently waiting dragon and giving her some long-awaited attention as Deacon unloaded their things from her back and handed them to the attendants.

Grustim, for the first time since Myranda had been introduced to him, made a sound that might have been intended for human ears. It was muttered beneath his breath, a Tresson word Myranda didn't recognize.

"Hold your tongue," hissed Valaamus.

"What did he say?" Myranda asked.

"It is a very old word," Deacon said. "It means fertile soil. Or the material used to fertilize it. I believe, in context, he was suggesting that something you'd said was untrue."

"My apologies, Duchess. Grustim is a soldier. He is not as refined in his interactions as the rest of the delegation," Valaamus said.

"I'm not offended, Ambassador. But I *am* curious. What prompted such a remark?" Myranda asked.

"Answer the duchess," Valaamus ordered.

The Dragon Rider stepped down from his mount. "You say your dragon has been with you since her birth," he said. He spoke Varden, but with a less practiced diction than the ambassador. "A female mountain dragon of that size would be at least ninety years old. She's nearly as large as Garr, and Garr was hatched before the war."

"Garr is your dragon?" Deacon said. "It thought it was named—"

"The breeders have their name and I have mine. He is Garr, and he is one hundred and sixty years old."

"Myn is only about two years old," Myranda said.

Grustim barely managed to prevent himself from repeating his earlier outburst. "She is *not* two years old, Madam Duchess. You are mistaken."

55

Myn cast a hard glare in his direction. She clearly did not appreciate what he had to say or the tone with which he was saying it.

Grustim continued, "I will prove it to you." He turned to his mount, uttering a guttural command. The dragon lowered its head, tipping its horns toward him. "Here, on the horns. Dragons shed their skin once per growth season. The scales leave a mark and stain the horn a bit. Come, look. Learn something about the beast you ride."

Myranda and Deacon stepped closer, Garr not even acknowledging them. Grustim pointed to a very faint dip in the surface of the deep-green horn, and a slight discoloration. It ran around the circumference, and Myranda never would have spotted it if not directed, but once she knew what to look for, she found dozens more along the length of the horn.

"Now go find them on your mount and learn how old she really is," Grustim said.

"Come here Myn, let's see your horns," Myranda said.

"Fascinating…" Deacon said, looking over Garr's horns. "In all of my dealings with dragons I've never noticed this…"

Grustim issued another order, and the dragon raised his head again. Myn marched over and tried to lower her head for inspection without taking her eyes off Grustim or Garr. Myranda ran her fingers along the length, but she found no hint of the rings until she reached the very tip, where there was a pair of them about a finger's width apart.

"Here, you see?" Myranda said. "There are two."

The Dragon Rider stepped doubtfully forward, but Myn pulled her head back by the same amount. He made a sound of irritation and stepped forward again, and again she pulled away. When he stepped forward again, there was a sudden flurry of motion and an angry rumble from both dragons. The humans turned to find Myn's tail trapped under Garr's forepaw. Based on the awkward position of the tail, it seemed clear now that she'd been luring Grustim into position for a good, hard lash with her tail and Garr had put a stop to it.

"Myn, what's gotten into you?" Myranda said.

She tried to tug her tail free, but Garr refused to release it, and the pair once again rumbled a threat to one another. The Dragon Rider grunted an order, and after a moment more, Garr shifted his weight to release Myn's tail.

"Now behave yourself and let him see," Myn said sternly.

The dragon huffed in annoyance but held still. Grustim stepped forward and gazed at the horn. Not satisfied with what he saw, he ran his fingers over it with increasing confusion and disbelief.

"I don't understand it. Even if you had sanded the horn there would be *some* sign… And it certainly hasn't been sanded… These two at the end are proper. Perhaps a bit close to one another, but proper. Where are the rest?"

Myn pulled her head back and thumped it to the ground beside Myranda.

"No, Myn. No scratches. You didn't behave yourself," Myranda said, crossing her arms. She turned to Grustim. "We thought we lost her once. She was still smaller than me at the time. In a battle with some of the D'Karon creatures, she fell through the ice. I tried to save her but I was too late. We had to flee, and much as it pained me we couldn't take her remains with us. Some time later I was to fight a terrible beast as punishment for my refusal to submit to the D'Karon after being captured by them. *Myn* turned out to be the beast. She was alive, and she had grown. I don't know if it was the work of the D'Karon or some other force, but that's how she came to be this size."

"Grustim, I want you to apologize to the duchess immediately," Valaamus ordered. "And after the completion of your duties, you shall receive a formal reprimand."

"That really isn't necessary. It is hardly the sort of circumstance he could have predicted," Myranda said.

"It doesn't matter. The goal of this tour is to foster trust between our people, and Grustim is a soldier. He should have discipline and the capacity to follow orders." Valaamus allowed himself a single irritated sigh. "Duke, Duchess, may I present to you the officers' memorial. The flame within this shrine represents the resolve we have to carry with us the memory of these fine men. The ivy represents the tenacity of the Tresson spirit, clinging even to sheer stone and in time breaking it to dust. The copper symbols are invocations for luck, strength, wisdom, and courage. Each stone is carved with the names of thirty-six officers who served at least five years before falling."

Myranda bowed her head in quiet observance of the lives lost. "We have a similar monument in my city. It lists the names of those who fell in the Kenvard Massacre. The fallen deserve to be remembered."

"I hope one day that you might grant me the honor of a visit, and may no new names be added to either in our lifetimes. Now please, let us retire to the cabin for a meal and some business before we rest for tomorrow."

"Wait," Myranda said. "Myn will need to be fed. Normally she would hunt, but I imagine it might not be appropriate to release her into your woods unattended."

"Garr needs to feed as well. I will escort her for the hunt," Grustim said. "It is only proper that I make amends for my prior indiscretion."

"Does that suit you, Myn?" Myranda asked.

Myn and Garr looked distrustfully at one another for a moment before she stood and stalked off toward the nearby woods.

"Excellent. To business then?" Valaamus asked.

Myranda and Deacon watched Myn trot into the woods, followed closely by Grustim and Garr. Satisfied that she could care for herself, and hopefully show enough restraint to avoid causing an incident, they followed Valaamus into the cabin.

#

Myn stepped lightly through the underbrush, moving with slow care. The air was heavy with the scent of prey, far more so than all but the best forests back home. This was fortunate because, if not for the bountiful hunting, she might have gone hungry. It wasn't that the creatures were particularly elusive. Far from it. They were as plump and clumsy as she'd ever encountered. But today she was not alone. Today she had another dragon to contend with. And that *man* on his back… She found herself spending as much time watching them as she did searching for a meal.

Not since Entwell had she had the chance to observe another dragon. She caught their scent sometimes, in the sky or in the mountains, but she'd never sought them out. It was enthralling to watch Garr move. His movements were smooth and confident, each step placed where the last had fallen. When prey was distant, he raised his nose high, sniffing and tasting the breeze, then dropped it low to sample the ground. When prey was near he moved low to the ground, tail straight, wings flat and tucked. It was all as Solomon had taught her. But there was more. At times the human on his back would make a very un-human noise, and he would hold. The human would then gaze about in the dim light, glancing at a broken branch or a nibbled-upon bush, then another grunt from the human would send Garr in a new direction. Often it wouldn't be long after that a new scent would grow stronger. The human was helping him hunt. Myn didn't know humans could do that.

Other times Myn would step on a felled branch or dry patch of grass and Garr's head would whip in her direction. And there were times when she'd made no such sound, yet she would still notice him watching her, just as she had been watching him.

The pair wove their own way through the forest, snapping up a bird here or a rabbit there. Enough to make for enough of a meal, but nothing truly satisfying. Not when there was so much more appetizing prey to be found. It soon became clear that each of them had the same quarry in mind. There were deer about. Five of them. It would be a fine meal for whichever of them could catch a few. Alas, as always seemed to be the case, the most succulent prey was the most elusive. Myn tried and failed to catch one or two, and Garr did the same. After a third attempt she decided to make do with a few more of the easier targets when she noticed Garr catch her gaze. He was far across the forest, barely visible even to Myn's keen eyes. He stalked slowly forward, his eyes on Myn rather than the prey. Deeper in the woods between them Myn heard the rustle of the deer moving away from Garr and toward her. Myn moved forward, taking a bit less care with each step. The prey now turned back toward Garr. Step by step, gradually, Myn and Garr drove the group of deer tighter together. It wasn't until both dragons were nearly within striking distance that the deer finally panicked and bolted.

Moving as one, Myn hooked left and Garr hooked right. Thundering through the forest, they quickly gained on the herd. Garr struck first, capturing two and startling the others directly into Myn's waiting claws. When each had dealt with their prize properly, they snatched them up and padded toward each other. Garr dropped his catch on the forest floor and crouched, allowing Grustim to dismount. With a few quick slices of an ornate dagger from his belt, he carved away a slice or two for himself, then uttered a short command. Garr eagerly crunched up the rest of his kill. As Myn ate the first two of her catches happily, Grustim sat atop Garr, watching her.

"I'll say this for that Northerner… if she did raise you, at least she didn't ruin you."

#

Myranda and Deacon sat at a small table in an extremely private room within the cabin. They awaited the return of their host as he had a rather animated discussion with the two mystics who had accompanied them. A light meal had been set out on the table, and Myranda and Deacon had been instructed to start without the others. The food was tasty, but quite different from what they'd been accustomed to in the north. Rather than the rich, hearty meals that could sustain one throughout the day and warmed one from the inside out, the food before them was comparatively focused on taste. Much of it was extremely spicy, and all of it was intensely flavorful.

"This truly is a beautiful nation. It is remarkable how sharply the land shifts in just a day's travel," Deacon said, dousing the lingering burn of one of the more potent entrees with a bit of wine. "And I'm truly intrigued by Grustim's knowledge of dragons. Such a subtle thing, faint rings on a horn, can tell you so much. I imagine it could tell you not only how many years the dragon has lived, but how quickly it grew! At least in relative terms…"

"They haven't had us stop anywhere with citizens yet," Myranda said. "I wonder if they are afraid of how the people will react to us…"

Valaamus paced inside, a bit red-faced and, despite the table settings for his associates, alone. Under his arm was something rather substantial bundled in thick cloth. He lowered it to the floor with care and took his place at the table.

"I apologize for the delay. Are you enjoying the meal? Have you sampled the wellindo? Delicious, made from stewed minced venison and seasonings. It goes brilliantly with the fig bread."

"Was there something wrong?" Myranda asked.

Valaamus sat and grabbed a piece of the bread, spreading a dollop of spicy-smelling meaty paste onto it. "Another reprimand, I'm afraid. Please, if you would, shut the door behind you."

Myranda did so. The instant they had complete privacy, Valaamus's demeanor changed. Suddenly his body language and tone of voice were a match for his stern expression.

"Let me begin by assuring you most vigorously that you have the deepest apologies of myself and my kingdom for any perceived deception regarding my aides. As I'm sure you can understand, there was some… concern about inviting three of the most powerful warriors of our generations-old enemy into our kingdom. We did not want to appear distrustful, but at the same time we needed to be certain that no spells were worked without our knowledge. It was an act of poor judgment on our parts to attempt to conceal our mystics, and I hope you will take me at my word that no harm was meant."

"I'm sure before this tour is through we'll each have made our share of mistakes," Myranda said. "In the future, let us err on the side of openness."

"Agreed… And it is for that reason, and again forgive me, I must ask about some enchantments my associates have detected."

"I am perfectly willing to discuss them," Deacon said. "I tend to rely somewhat heavily on enchantments. I often forget the concerns some may have for such things."

"The first is…" he reached into a pocket within his robes to fetch a scrawled note, "some manner of connection, reaching outward in many directions."

"My stylus and the books I've fashioned. They are really quite useful. They operate by—" Deacon began eagerly.

"My apologies but any words you might spend describing their workings would be wasted on me. You can discuss them with my associates after our business here is through. Now, something pertaining to protection of some sort?"

"That would be my ring," Myranda said. "Enchanted by Deacon upon our engagement."

One by one they worked their way through the list of enchantments and active spells that the pair had been using. Most Valaamus disregarded as harmless, but one was strange enough that he simply could not bring himself to understand.

"I'm sorry, but how can a hand be 'unpredictable' as you say, and how can such a problem be solved by a ring?" Valaamus mused.

Deacon looked uncertainly to Myranda. "I believe the simplest path to understanding would be to show him."

"Very well, but be careful," Myranda said.

Deacon grasped the ring and began to slide it off. "Please prepare yourself. This may be… unsettling, but it is entirely under control."

Valaamus watched with interest as Deacon removed the ring from his finger. For a moment there was no result. Then, slowly, the skin began to shift. It marbled with red, veins of discoloration widening until the whole of his hand was a mottled crimson. Wide, stiff scales burst forth, and his fingers lengthened. Just as it seemed to stabilize into the claw of some horrid creature, it shifted again, returning to a roughly human shape but changing in substance to something between metal and stone. He allowed it to shift twice more before shutting his eyes and willing it back to normality. The demonstration completed, he slipped the ring back on.

The diplomat's face retained the rocky, stoic expression that never seemed to leave it, but his eyes were wide with shock and barely concealed disgust.

"What in this world or any other was *that*?" he said.

"It's an affliction, the result of an imprudently cast spell. The details are complex, even by my standards, but suffice it to say my hand is not as stable as it might be. The ring is an adequate treatment."

"I believe… I believe you will have much to discuss with my aides. But that sets my mind at ease. As you've seen, we are quite adept at detecting magic. And as we have seen, you are quite adept at casting it. I hope you will understand but… we *are* recently enemies. The military has requested that you limit any usage of mystic power, and completely forgo anything that might give you insight further into our nation than we choose to show. I, of course, would never accuse you of espionage, but if the military were to feel the influence of your mind probing the land…"

"I understand. Of course we agree," Myranda said.

"And what of passive magics?"

"We thank you for your cooperation. Now, poorly timed as this may be in the face of our recent agreement to forgo any further deception, I must now request a degree of discretion on your part for the matter we are about to discuss. You are, I hope, aware of the incidents that prompted our hasty assembly of this diplomatic exchange."

"The supposed D'Karon attacks," Myranda said.

"Precisely. Now, I know that neither your kingdom nor mine is eager to begin again what has so recently been ended. But if we determine that someone within your empire, or allied with it, has been attacking our people, then we will have no choice but to defend ourselves, and to do what is necessary to prevent further attack."

"Of course," Myranda said. "And speaking as a citizen of a land that has been held prisoner by their dark whims since the start of the war, there is no one more interested than I in making certain that any seed of the D'Karon is snuffed out before it can blossom."

"It is heartening to hear that. Every attempt has been made to prevent the word of the attacks from spreading. Even my aides do not know the full details of what we now discuss." He held up the item he'd brought with him. "Contained within this bundle is a small sample of two of the D'Karon creatures that attacked one of our most southerly cities. You may wish to complete your meal before we continue—I understand they are somewhat gruesome."

"I don't believe we can justify further delay," Myranda said.

"Very well," he said.

61

They moved the food to the side of the table and placed the bundle of cloth down. Myranda carefully pulled the layer of cloth away. The bundle contained a few scraps of leathery flesh and some bone fragments, a skull and a vial of black liquid. A small stack of pages described the contents and included sketches based on the accounts of those who had personally encountered the creatures from which the samples had been taken. Deacon picked up the stack of pages and began to read.

"'The fact there are remains at all suggests these are at the very least not the beasts we have faced in our own kingdom. Many vanished into dust when defeated. Those that did leave remains didn't leave behind anything that looks like this.'" Myranda leaned close to inspect the leather. It had a strong aroma, like something one would find in an alchemist's shop. "Have these been treated in some way?"

"'Those who discovered them were forced to preserve them, as they were swiftly rotting,'" Deacon read. "That swatch is from this creature."

He slid a page over to Myranda with a simple sketch of a billowing form. It could easily be one of the cloak creatures that had so often plagued the Chosen, though there were subtle differences even in the sketch.

"This flesh… the page says it came from the 'cloak' of the creature, but it looks to be leather. The cloaks we knew were certainly cloth," Myranda said. "And this sketch shows claws along the edge of the cloak. It could be simply a misremembered detail, but the cloaks typically had no such things. When claws did flash into being, they were ghostly and faded to nothingness before reaching the empty void within the cloak."

"And the cloaks we battled did not rot. If they vanished, they vanished into dust, and if they remained, they remained as shreds of simple cloth. The page indicates that these fragments of bone come from the cloak-creature's claws, and the beings we fought had no bones," Deacon added. "We shall set it aside for study through mystic means when the cursory assessment is through." He selected another page. "Now this, to all appearances, is indeed what we would call a dragoyle."

He shared the sketch with Myranda. At a glimpse it might first have seemed to be a dragon, but even drawn as it was based on descriptions, there were telltale signs of its unnatural characteristics. There were no eyes in the sketch, only dark sockets with gleaming points of light within them. The head lacked flesh and scales, appearing as little more than a skull. The sketch showed seams running along the monster's hide, making it resemble a doll sewn together from scraps of cloth too small to form it individually.

Myranda grasped the skull and raised it, turning it about in the light. It was white, or at least it might have been if it was clean. In its present state it was stained with brown and smeared with black. Ribbed horns curled down from the skull's temples with a smooth, natural curve. They were joined by other irregular spikes that seemed to have erupted at random from the top, back, and sides of the skull. The jaws were lined with jagged bone. It looked broken, but the more intact portions formed cavities where teeth might once have been.

"It is small for a dragoyle's head, though we found beasts of many sizes... The color is wrong, too. The dragoyles we knew were black, or at their lightest a deep purple. The colors could have varied as well, though. This here... this looks to be dried red blood. That is wrong too. Dragoyles had black blood. And this seems to have once been teeth. The dragoyles had only serrated beaks. I cannot be certain, but this looks more like a ram's skull that has been twisted into a new form," Myranda observed.

Deacon picked up the vial. "This, the page says, is the beast's breath." He tipped it side to side, watching the viscous substance ooze down the vial. "Look how it has pitted the glass. The page says this is not the first vessel the stuff has been poured into. It eats at everything it touches."

He eased the cork from the end, only for it to crumble away in his fingers. The scent that filled the room was sharp and acrid, and it conjured dark memories.

"That is the miasma..." Myranda said, no hint of doubt in her voice. "I know it all too well."

"Have you known anything but these... *dragoyles* to produce such a substance?" Valaamus asked.

"Nothing," Myranda said.

"And have you known anything but the D'Karon to utilize such creatures?"

"They are a product of the D'Karon," Deacon said.

"In all of the years that history records, we have encountered these D'Karon and their creatures *only* at or near the battlefront and *only* operating on behalf of your people. If you are certain that this substance is genuine and a result of their influence, then to our military it will be seen as damning evidence that you have resumed hostilities despite the ceasefire," Valaamus said steadily.

"Let us not jump to conclusions. I suggest we begin the mystic analysis," Deacon said.

Myranda nodded, but she scarcely needed to open her mind's eye to know that the spells that tainted these bits of flesh and bone had the shape and color of D'Karon workings. It wasn't the same ghastly perfection that seemed to define most D'Karon magic, but it was certainly drawn from the same roots, grown from the same seeds. Deacon's face made it all too clear he had come to the same conclusion. Valaamus saw it as well.

"What does your magic tell you?" Valaamus asked.

"There is unmistakable D'Karon influence in the residual enchantment of these samples... But I can say with certainty that this is not the work of a true D'Karon."

"A true D'Karon?" Valaamus asked.

Joseph R. Lallo

"These spells are imperfect, incomplete," Deacon said. "This skull was certainly that of a sheep, and these bones and that hide are from a goat. The D'Karon conjure the substance of their creations. They are entirely constructed with no element of what we would call nature."

"This means little, does it not? Even the most experienced mystic can miscast a spell or take liberties in the interest of speed or ease," Valaamus said.

"You don't understand. Spell craft is sacred to the D'Karon. To miscast them would be tantamount to blasphemy."

"They have been committing war atrocities for generations. Blasphemy would not be beyond them, I'm sure," Valaamus said.

"While I agree with Deacon's assessment, it does not change the fact that D'Karon knowledge is at work here. I would not liken this to an attack by an enemy. With the evidence we have, we can at best make the claim that we know for certain that an enemy's weapons have been used," Myranda said.

"Which in any case would be an act of war," Valaamus said.

His carefully measured diplomatic tone had not faltered, but his words were increasingly carrying the threat that the damage had been done.

"I realize that my assurance on this matter carries little weight, but no force within the Northern Alliance would ever rely upon D'Karon spells," Myranda said. "Not after what very nearly happened to us while we were under their thumbs. Before you make your final determination, I implore you to allow us to continue the investigation. Again, these are merely the weapons. Until we find who has been wielding them, we must not assume that the Northern Alliance is behind the attacks."

"Of course I agree. Anything is preferable to an unnecessary war. But as diplomats you must realize that the investigation can only continue with the blessing of the military, and I am obligated to present these findings to them," Valaamus said. "They may not agree that war is unnecessary."

"When do you present your findings?"

"We are all expected in the capital for a banquet in your honor in two weeks. My first formal briefing of the military is expected on the evening of my arrival, some days earlier. As I will be traveling by carriage, I do not expect to reach the capital in less than five days. I may be able to suggest some alternate routes that would extend that journey to a full week. Anything beyond that and a military representative will be dispatched to meet us en route. With the evidence currently available, it is very likely that they will call for an immediate termination of the diplomatic exchange, and they could very well close the border in preparation for troop deployment. You *must* find something compelling to suggest that it is not the work of a Northern Alliance ally that has blighted our lands with such treachery, if such evidence exists, and return it to me before I deliver my briefing."

"Then there is no time to waste. Where were these creatures encountered?" Myranda asked.

"At the most northerly fringe of the Southern Wastes. I don't pretend to know how quickly your dragon can carry you, but given a guess I would say it would take every bit of six days for you to reach it. That would leave you no time at all to seek out any evidence, let alone deliver it to me. It was my great concern that such would be the case, and you must believe me that I fought for every moment of time I could for this mission, but... a nation so long at war, allowing figures such as you to pace its lands..."

"I understand. But for the return of the information, at least, I have a solution. I will leave a messenger pad with you," Deacon said.

"A... messenger pad?" Valaamus asked, his tone indicating he believed he had misheard.

"It is really quite simple, you see—"

"While you explain it to him, I'll have a word with Myn, Grustim, and Garr about our plans," Myranda said.

"That is wise," Valaamus said.

Deacon, Myranda, and Valaamus gathered and stowed the samples, hiding them once more in their bundle before Myranda opened the door to seek out the dragons and Rider.

#

Outside the cabin, Myn sat patiently, eyes on the door. She had the remaining deer from her hunt clutched beneath her claws. Garr lay across from her, eyes shut but still alert. Grustim had shed his armor and reclined in the curl of his mount's tail. He whittled idly at a piece of wood, ostensibly sculpting it but mostly just making it smaller and passing the time.

The group had only just returned from the hunt, the kill still warm beneath her claws, but Myn couldn't help but let her gaze wander from time to time to the other dragon. She sniffed the air as the breeze carried his scent to her. It was strange. The scent of the man was present on the dragon, not just from the ride, but from days and weeks earlier. Likewise the man seemed steeped in the scent of the dragon. It was clear at a single whiff that the two were together, always. She felt the flutter of envy in her chest at the thought.

In part the envy was for the togetherness. She and Myranda had been inseparable at one time, but Myranda had others in her life. Many depended on her. Myn understood. The others would be helpless without Myranda, while she could handle herself if required. But at times she longed for the old times. Yes, the nights had been long and cold. Yes, the danger had been ever-present. There had been little food and much traveling to be done. But Myranda had been with her, warm and safe beneath Myn in her early days and folded beneath her claws in the days that followed. Seeing a dragon and his human sharing such togetherness made those days seem so far away.

A whisper of the envy, though, was for the dragon himself. Myn may not have been able to spend as much time with Myranda as she would have liked— if she did, they would never be apart—but she did get to spend plenty of time with her. In all of her life she'd had only a few months during which she'd had the opportunity to spend time with another dragon. It didn't seem fair that a human should be allowed to spend so much time with one when she did not.

Her thoughts vanished in a puff of excitement when she heard the door open and saw Myranda walking toward her. The dragon hopped to her feet and snatched up the deer, taking two steps forward to meet Myranda and dropping the deer at her feet.

"For me?" Myranda said with a smile. "Still my little hunter. Come here."

Myn lowered her head and received a good, hard scratch.

"I think you should keep this one for yourself, though. We've got a great deal of travel ahead of us, and I don't want you pushing yourself too hard without a full belly."

Always happy for another morsel, Myn snapped up and gulped down the remaining deer.

"Grustim, Garr, may I ask something of you?"

The Rider looked at her. "I have been instructed to treat you with deference and respect. What do you require?"

"You are more familiar with your land than I. There is a place in the Southern Wastes that we must reach as soon as possible. How quickly do you think you can guide us there by dragon-back?" she asked.

"The Southern Wastes are a big place, Duchess. Garr could reach the nearest of it in four days. The farthest in seven. But you will not be able to reach it so quickly."

"Why not?"

He paused for a moment. "I don't know that I can answer that question with deference and respect."

"Then answer it with honesty. We don't always have the luxury of gentility."

"You're a duchess, Duchess. And he is a duke. When I travel, I travel with my lance, my armor, my dragon, and the dagger of command that affords me the right to issue orders to troops when the need arises. Though I've never known nobility to travel by dragon, look at the bags you've brought. You bring civilization with you where you go, and that slows travel."

"Nobility is a recent development, Grustim. I'm quite accustomed to traveling light. To be honest, I'm not accustomed to having any other choice."

Grustim did Myranda the courtesy of not voicing the doubt that was clear in his expression. "Even so. The dragon will need to carry you and the duke both. Garr is bigger, faster, and will have to carry only me. Even without a passenger, your dragon would lag behind. She is an able hunter, that much I have seen, but she lacks the training and conditioning of a dragon worthy of a Rider."

Garr's eyes slid open, peering through the iron mask he wore.

"You will slow us," Grustim continued. "I think eight days will be enough."

The low roll of what might have been thunder rattled in the air, though there were no clouds. Myranda smiled and looked to Myn. Her tail was scything back and forth, her eyes locked on Grustim with a burning intensity.

"I think Myn respectfully disagrees with your assessment."

"Then tomorrow we shall see."

Chapter 3

In a desert stronghold in Tressor, Commander Brustuum returned to his primary task. He was an older man, his black hair slowly succumbing to gray. He marched with purpose through the airy halls. Like most Tresson creations, artful expression had been sprinkled into every detail. The walls were white clay with green leaves and vines painted around doors and windows. The doors themselves, though sturdy and wooden, were carved with scenes depicting great battles and honored warriors. The man himself was no different. His chin bore a beard nature had striped with gray. He'd trimmed it with care and sculpted it into subtle flares to each side. To cope with the often intense heat and beating sun of his homeland, his robe and trousers were light and billowy, made from a thin tan cloth and tied about the waist by a red sash. The edges of the robe were embroidered with patches and emblems labeling him a commander of some reputation in the Tresson army.

His journey through the stronghold took him down from the brightly sunlit upper levels to the dank, flickering holding cells below. The last of them, buried deep enough in the bowels of the place that the heat of the beating summer day was replaced by the coolness of the earth, was the only occupied cell on the entire floor. Whereas the other doors on the floor were simple iron grates, this one was made of thick planks and reinforced with iron bands, offering openings only in the form of a small metal grill at eye level and a slot at ground level. Four fully equipped soldiers guarded it. Two of them held curving swords and wore thick leather armor. The other two were dressed in thick embroidered robes and wore jeweled rings on three fingers of each hand. These were the casters, trained mystics who made up barely a fraction of the Tresson army. Most regiments had only a single caster. To have two guarding the same room spoke volumes for the threat that awaited within.

"Esteemed Commander Brustuum," greeted the first of the swordsmen with a respectful bow of his head.

"Soldier," the older man said with a stiff nod. "She's awake?"

"Yes, sir."

"Has she caused any trouble?"

"No, sir. She has continued to be very cooperative, though she will not eat."

"And the secrecy of her presence has been maintained?"

"All in the stronghold believe that the cell is still being used to hold the accused traitor, Trimik."

Maintaining the secrecy of his prisoner had been difficult. Only seven of his men within the facility knew. Beyond them, only the military patron who provided the food, funding, and equipment was aware. The word had gone no further. It hadn't even gone to the high command. Some things were simply too important to be left to those in charge. They were too often dedicated to diplomacy, willing to give away too much. But ensuring they didn't discover his prisoner until he was satisfied meant he had to expend a tremendous amount of resources to maintain the charade that she'd not yet been caught.

It had taken a fair amount of time to plot out troop assignments that kept enough men in the field to appease any superiors who might look in on him while keeping enough of his men on hand to be certain that their prisoner remained secure. Of the two, the security of the prisoner was the most crucial. The woman didn't appear to be dangerous, but neither did a viper until it brought its fangs to bear, and by then it would be too late. Therefore, he'd sent as many troops as he could spare out to search for a woman whom he'd already found so that he could be left to the task of questioning her.

He paced down the hall toward the cell, watching as a rat skittered from one empty cell to another, and wordlessly motioned for the appropriate steps to be taken to allow him access to the prisoner.

The mystic conferred briefly with his partner, then each stepped beside their commanding officer and folded their hands, interlocking the gems of their rings. They uttered a few throaty chanting syllables. Brustuum grimaced as he felt the crackle of arcane energies run over the surface of his body. He detested magic. If he'd not been so skillful a commander he might have gone so far as to ban it from any units under his command. As it was, he knew all too well the value and even necessity of a mystic defense against the troops of the north, so he allowed and fostered the necessary evil of wizards within his army. He watched as the magical warding was removed from the door and it was unlocked.

The inside lay in utter darkness, save for where the dancing lantern light of the hall spilled, but even that seemed to enter only reluctantly, pushing weakly against an overpowering pitch-blackness within.

Brustuum snapped his fingers. "A lantern. Now."

The soldiers quickly supplied him with a polished-copper oil lamp, which he held out before him. The light fell upon a figure seated on a straw-stuffed bedroll and leaning against the clay wall.

It was a woman dressed in standard prison attire: a simple sleeveless tunic and a pair of trousers that ended just below the knee. The clothes were, by design, poorly suited to travel in Tressor. They would offer little protection from the punishing sun. Thick iron chains lay coiled neatly beside her, connecting shackles at her wrists and ankles to thick rings driven into the stone of the walls.

Such defenses seemed to be far more than were necessary for such a prisoner. The shackles were nearly too large for the delicate ankles and wrists to which they were affixed. Her skin was so white it almost seemed to glow in the light of the lantern, and her hair was black but for a single streak of gray. As she raised her head to look upon her visitor, she showed a face of middle age or younger. She was not unattractive, her face bearing a crisp, almost angular beauty. At this moment, the most distinctive feature of that face was its utter lack of concern. If anything, she viewed her visitor with vague disinterest, as though his visit had pulled her from more interesting thoughts. Brustuum scanned the floor around her. A plate of thick porridge with a wooden spoon sat to her left, largely untouched. To her right was a handful of dead rats. They'd been piled with apparent care, and they seemed desiccated as if by years of dry desert air.

"On your feet," Brustuum commanded.

The prisoner obeyed, though with a casualness that would have been more appropriate for a request than an order.

"I am told you've not been eating your food. Be aware that starving yourself will do no good. If necessary, I shall have my men force food down your worthless gullet rather than lose you before I'm through with you."

"I wouldn't dream of starving myself, sir," replied the woman, her voice oddly chilling. She sounded unimpressed by both her keepers and their prison. "It is simply that your *recent* offerings do not suit my tastes. Fortunately I've found a passable substitute."

She gestured with one hand toward the pile of rats, causing the shackle to slide noisily down. The sudden sound caused the guards outside to stir.

"I do wish you would provide a *proper* meal, as you did a few weeks ago. You were a far better host then."

"You'll have no more of that. Until my mystics can make sense of what you've demonstrated and further demonstrations are called for."

"That hardly seems polite…"

"For now, I have more questions. Do you recall what we last discussed?"

"Oh, you. Yes, I believe you were telling me where to find Mott?"

"I was telling you no such thing. You were telling me all that you'd done since arriving. I have been able to corroborate your recollection thus far, so you shall continue."

"Yes, right. I recall now. Yes. I suppose we can continue if you wish, but might you know when I shall be allowed to be on my way? I appreciate the steps you've taken to keep my dealings from the others, as it has helped me to remain in compliance with the wishes of my masters, but there comes a point when the delay will do more harm than good. I am, after all, out of place. If

Teht were to arrive and find me missing, I'm quite certain she would be just as displeased as if she found I'd made a spectacle of myself against her wishes."

"And you, of course, wish only to please your masters."

"Don't you?"

"If their plans are wise and their methods just, then I do."

"So we are of one mind. When shall I be allowed to leave?"

"You will leave this place when I am satisfied you have shared all that there is to share."

"Lovely. I shall continue then. Remind me, where were we when we were interrupted?"

"You had confessed to murdering a farmer on the northern edge of the Southern Wastes."

"A farmer… a farmer… Oh, yes. I recall. Let us continue…"

#

Several Months Earlier…

In a sparsely treed field, somewhere in the southern half of Tressor, Turiel sat on a stone surrounded by the skillfully butchered remains of animals. Though the sight was inarguably a gruesome one, it was not nearly as hideous as it might have been. Some gazelles, a wildcat, and a bear lay dissected on the ground around her, but they had been separated with such care it looked less like the scene of a slaughter and more like a taxidermist's shop. She had laid out intact skeletons, the bones unnaturally white as though bleached. Muscle groups were arranged with care on the dusty ground, and skins were somehow removed in one piece. If such a thing were possible, it would almost seem that Turiel had taken the animals apart with the intention of putting them back together when she was through.

Mott was by her side, and his appearance had once again changed. He'd grown somewhat, not only thanks to an overall increase in size, but with the replacement of some of his scrawnier pieces with burlier parts. The spidery legs were stouter now, still insect in structure but mammal in appearance, and numbering eight rather than six. They had shaggy brown fur and ended in bony two-toed claws. On the serpentine body, in addition to the already unnatural presence of scattered tufts of hair, the scaly skin had taken on the horny thickness of a crocodile's hide. Its jackal mouth—the head being the one part that had remained unchanged—opened and it chittered.

"You *must* learn patience, Mott. Yes, we are to find Teht and learn why she has left us for so long without instructions, but what is our *purpose* if not to hone our skills? We came so swiftly to the Wastes to begin work on the second keyhole we missed the opportunity to see what the beasts of this land had to offer. And they have *much* to offer. Look at the wonders we have found in just a short time wandering the land."

She tapped her staff twice on the ground, and tendrils of black traced its length and peeled away from it, swirling along the skeleton of the bear. Like a beast waking from a long slumber, it climbed to its feet and stood before her. She turned her fingers in a slow circle, and the skeleton obediently turned about.

"Good, strong jaws on this bear…" She reached out and plucked its head away, hefting it. "Perhaps a bear's skull next time?"

She dropped the skull, its body still standing and awaiting new orders. Before the skull hit the ground Mott caught it with a coiled tail, flipped to its back, and rolled the skull about like a kitten with a knot of string.

"Let me see, let me see," she said. She opened her fur wrap, made from harvested skins earlier in her travels, and reached into the tattered black robes beneath. From within she pulled out a small bundle of old, well-used but well-kept pages and leafed through them. They were scrawled with an unnatural foreign script and detailed sketches of beasts never meant to exist. "Here. The dragoyle… no, no. This skull isn't right at all. It is so very difficult to find a match for his designs…" She turned to Mott. "Do you suppose Demont did so on purpose? Crafting creatures too different from those of nature to be simply duplicated? Bah! I'll get it right one of these days. I simply need something closer. A beak. The thing has a beak. I wonder… a detour to the seaside cliffs to the west? I seem to remember something about great birds there. Roks, I believe they were called. That would give us a fine skull for a dragoyle. And wings as well. A griffin would work well, and I know that those can be found in the mountains. First to the cliffs, *then* to the mountains, you think?"

Mott churred and began to gnaw on the skull.

"Yes, of course you are correct. We stay to the west coast. If we do not find a rok, then we can continue to that place with the dragons. The blasted dragoyles are based on them. They *must* be near enough to be used. Then we can get you that set of wings I promised, too."

Mott chittered and dropped the skull.

"… Because I feel it would be an excellent illustration of my skill and initiative if I was able to craft a dragoyle of my own. It should be simple enough with the correct resources. I want the D'Karon to know that I've learned their teachings well." She looked about and stroked her chin. "Much as it pains me to do a poor approximation of their fine work, it would pain me further to waste so many wonderful pieces."

Turiel picked up the discarded skull in one hand and her staff in the other. She shut her eyes, and many bones scattered about her began to jerk and twitch. More strands of black coalesced about her staff and peeled away, coiling about the bones and seeming to thread into the muscles and organs. When every last scrap was under her influence, Turiel opened her eyes and willed them into the air. Skeletons reformed, mixed and matched from all of those that had donated their bodies. They came together to create what might have been the bones of a misshapen dragon. Then came the flesh, stretched thin around the monstrous frame. The skin came after that, sealing with a surge of dark energy but leaving the skull bare.

With the form complete, she curled her fingers into a fist and the tendrils of dark energy bled through to the surface, staining the skin black and causing the hair to embrittle and fall away. The final product was a fair approximation of the monstrosity known as the dragoyle, though anyone who had clashed with one would see the faults immediately. It was only the size of a horse, or a bit larger. The hide was more leathery than rocky as well, and vicious teeth were mounted where a beak should have been.

"There. Good practice if nothing else," she said, eying her creation critically.

Mott churred.

"There was not nearly enough material to make a pair of wings, and I haven't the strength to render them functional right now besides. Just two more things to be done."

She stooped and plucked the wildcat's tongue from the ground, one of the handful of anatomical spare parts left behind when she completed the dragoyle.

"Open, Mott," she said.

Her familiar skittered to the ground at her feet and gaped its mouth like a starving baby bird. She lowered the tongue carefully down, and when it was near Mott's throat it leaped into place.

"There. Now once I find a nice set of green eyes and some suitably sized wings, you'll be complete. ... Well, yes, I *could* shift the color of a pair of these leftover eyes, but that would be disingenuous. ... Well *I* would know, my pet. Now hush, I've still got the most difficult part to see to."

She planted the tip of her staff into the sandy earth at her feet. The gem in its tip took on a deep glow, and once again tendrils of black began to spiral down its length. When they reached the ground they spiraled outward, splitting into strands finer than threads. Each blade of grass or scrap of unused flesh the tendrils touched blackened and shriveled. A speck of white formed above the head of the staff, pulses of black surging up through the tendrils and feeding the gem. The trees all the around them twisted and darkened, their energy leeched away to feed the growing speck.

Turiel shook with the effort of her invocation. The countryside for a hundred paces in all directions looked as though it had been scorched by wildfire, drained utterly of life before the ball of white began to darken. It shifted to red, then to deep purple before condensing into a murky violet gem the size of a walnut. She held out a trembling hand, and the gem dropped into her palm.

"There," she said with a weary sigh. "Not nearly as difficult as I'd feared. Here, open wide, my darling."

The would-be dragoyle opened its mouth, and with the sickening sizzle of searing flesh, Turiel installed the gem in the back of its throat, then stepped back once more.

"Well? I didn't give you the miasma stone for nothing. Let us see it put to work. There."

The pseudo-dragoyle shifted its unnatural head and coughed a cloud of black at the brittle remains of a bush. The plant sizzled, its thin bark and dry branches quickly eroding under the influence of the horrid substance.

"You see? If there is one spell I've learned properly, it is the conjuring of the miasma stone. Here, Mott. We'll be on our way."

The creature scurried up to its place at the head of her staff. Her familiar was now so large that his serpentine tail coiled all the way to the ground, and after the energy she'd put into summoning the gem, she barely had the strength to steady it.

"Hah… I am not as young as I once was, Mott," she said. "Do you suppose we might find some people along the way who would offer their aid in correcting my unfortunate physical state? The people of Tressor have been so obliging thus far." She took a few wavering steps forward, then turned to her latest creation. "You know… I had intended to set this one off to seek its own way in the world… but the D'Karon ride them, don't they? We would be remiss if we did not test this aspect as well."

Turiel mounted the creature.

"Onward, beast. To the coast, and then to the city. Let us once more sample the fine hospitality of this land."

#

Brustuum fumed as he listened to the madwoman's recollection, weighing her words against the facts he already had available. His instincts were to distrust her. Surely no one could survive in the Wastes as she claimed or sculpt monstrosities from the flesh of dead beasts as she described. Yet the descriptions she'd given matched the monster he and his men had been forced to subdue, and the timing would appear to match. Combined with the confirmation from Sallim, there was reason to believe her story had at least the kernel of truth.

"If you can craft deadly beasts with such ease, and if you have been within our borders for as long as you claim, why have you not been unleashing them upon us for decades?"

"Because until very recently I was fully devoted to the opening of the keyhole. It was not until Teht failed to meet me and answer my calls that I felt the need to stray from that task. And unleashing these creatures was not my intention. I seem to have some trouble maintaining control. It is nothing that practice won't solve."

"So you would willingly and purposely continue to manufacture these abominations if you had your way."

74

"You *have* asked for demonstrations. And one cannot hope to improve without practice... Tell me, how exactly do you *know* that I unleashed the creature if I did not yet tell you that I'd done so?"

"Because my men were the ones who eventually destroyed the beast in defense of our people. You have been told this repeatedly."

"Oh? My memory truly is ailing these days. Was it at least a struggle for them? I'm curious how successful my creation was. Did it take any of their lives? How did you eventually vanquish it?"

"Must I continually inform you that you are here to answer my questions and not the opposite? Now continue."

"Very well..."

#

Turiel's journey had been a long one, but she seemed untouched by the elements. Her pale white skin had ignored days of pounding sun, and though she'd had no water she was not parched in the least. Now she was drawing near the first town that had piqued her interest along the way. She'd kept mostly to the edge of the Wastes. Her mind, like her body, had felt the ravages of the years, but she still had some of her wits about her. She knew that as weak as she was, even with the aid of her creations she couldn't afford to venture into just *any* town. It would have to be a relatively defenseless place. Someplace with a handful of people, but lacking a proper city watch or something similar.

It took time, but she'd finally happened upon the perfect place. Ahead lay a small nomadic settlement. The huts, a dozen in total, all had the simple wood and cloth construction that betrayed their eventual fate of being packed up into the back of a carriage when the time came to move on. Some lean jet-black horses were tied near a small spring around which the settlement had formed. Joining them were a half-dozen mules, two camels, and three lanky dogs with short sandy-yellow coats and docked tails. At the edge of the settlement a small herd of goats was gathered within a makeshift fence.

"Ah, Mott," Turiel said with a smile. "This shall serve our purposes nicely." She dismounted the dragoyle she had fashioned and paced unsteadily toward the town.

Most of the residents had taken shelter within their simple homes, but three stood watch, each heaped with linen robes that hung to the ground. Deep, billowing hoods hid their heads and cloth scarves wrapped their faces. Their gazes had drifted toward Turiel as she'd approached, but once she was near enough for the horrific nature of her mount to be seen, they stood and drew their weapons. Two carried stout, cleaver-like swords. The third swung a sling.

"Hold! Hold there!" warned the first man. Though his build and face were entirely hidden beneath his robes, his voice was that of an older man.

"I have come too far to stand at the edge of so inviting a settlement, good nomad. I am just a simple woman seeking food and shelter."

"It is not you, old woman, but the beasts that accompany you," he said. "Come no closer."

Turiel turned to Mott, still situated atop her staff.

"Oh, but Mott here is a darling, good nomad. As harmless as a lamb. And my steed is a humble beast, a mere echo of the thing that should truly frighten you."

"What you have is frightening enough. Either tie them far from here or keep moving."

"You would sentence a poor old woman and her simple pets to the ravages of the wilderness?"

"We do not know you, we do not know your beasts, and we will not risk our safety for someone such as you."

"*Well*, and to think I'd believed the tales of unparalleled kindness from the people of Tressor. You injure me. Now I feel quite justified in doing the same in return. Mott, disarm them. Of their weapons at least, but also their arms if you feel the inclination."

In a flash of fur and scales, her familiar dove from her staff and cut across the ground in a sweeping, serpentine path. The sling-wielder let a stone fly and struck Mott square on the jaw. It popped aside, then hung loose. Mott did not lose a single step, his legs skittering and scrambling across the dusty ground with an insane frenzy of motion.

Finally Mott was upon them. He attempted to bite the sling-wielder, hacking down with his upper jaw and seeming to notice for the first time that his lower jaw was not where it ought to be. He paused to click his errant mandible into place, but the delay was more than enough to allow both swordsmen to put their weapons to work. One blow cost Mott a leg, the other bit into his tail, but neither seemed to bother the beast in the slightest. He whipped his tail aside, disarming one attacker, then snapped the sling in his teeth and tore it away. The final lookout to retain his weapon chopped again, this time cleanly separating Mott's head from his body. Hideously, the attack still did no good. Both body and head continued to move, the former lashing its tail at the swordsman to tear his weapon away. The disembodied head snapped and gnashed its teeth, but didn't seem to have the necessary coordination to make itself a threat.

The lookouts called for help, and people flooded from the huts. Few were armed, but once they had determined what was happening and organized themselves accordingly, Mott, the dragoyle, and Turiel were outnumbered seven to one. The patchwork familiar, his displaced head seeing the rush of reinforcements, decided discretion was the better part of valor. He snatched his head up in his tail, then grabbed his missing leg in his mouth and dashed away.

"Now, Mott, really. Do you call that devotion? I'm very disappointed," Turiel said, placing one hand on her hip.

76

The lookouts rearmed themselves, and several of the other nomads found weapons as well, but none were willing to approach Turiel and her as yet motionless dragoyle.

"Leave this place, woman," warned the elder lookout. Based upon the authority with which he spoke and the fact he was the only one yet to speak beyond the general call for aid, he was almost certainly the chieftain.

"Goodness, no. I've not yet eaten. I did not come all this way to leave hungry."

"I care not if you starve. You will take your abominations and leave this place, or my slinger will bury a lump of lead in your skull."

"Well that is simply unacceptable," she said.

The chieftain turned to the rearmed slinger, who was already swinging her weapon up to speed. "Do it."

Before the words were said, the lead sling-bullet was on its way to its target. In the blink of an eye the sorceress's staff blackened and a web of tendrils darted from it, ensnaring the heavy projectile and swinging it aside of Turiel's unflinching face. It continued its swing and returned from whence it came, though lacking the same power and accuracy. The slinger *just* managed to dodge the counterattack, and the swordsmen charged.

Turiel turned casually to her dragoyle. "Try to keep them reasonably intact. I'll fetch Mott."

She paced toward her familiar, who was stumbling along in a manner only a beast holding its own head can manage. Behind her, the nomads and her creation clashed. The beast heaved them about, lashing its tail and swiping its claws. It seemed more dedicated to the task of breaking them than killing them, but any motion toward Turiel was met with its full wrath. Twenty nomads were more than a match for the beast, and before long it took all the beast's efforts and attentions to keep them from its creator.

Slicing swords came within inches of reaching Turiel, but she paid them no mind. It did not appear to be something so virtuous as courage, or as confident as trust in her creation's ability to protect her. She simply did not seem to be aware that the commotion was something that should concern her. She moved with slow ease, kneeling to see to the skittish Mott.

"Let me see that," she said, taking the leg. "Now hold still."

She drove the end of her staff into the ground and ran her fingers across it, summoning more of the black threads. Like a tailor repairing a simple garment, she aligned the leg and coaxed away tendrils to coil and apply to the cut until it eased away, a thin black vein the only evidence that it had ever been removed. Once the leg was restored, she conjured more threads but frowned as the last of them took more effort than she was willing to spare.

With a light sigh she stood and turned. The chieftain himself had gotten past the dragoyle. His robes were stained and sizzling with the fetid black miasma, and his eyes were filled with righteous rage. Turiel raised her withered

77

hand and grasped his wrist. Instantly he dropped to his knees, eyes now wide with fear and his hidden mouth wheezing with a stifled cry of pain. A midnight-blue ripple of power fluttered against his skin as she gripped him. The two visibly seemed to trade years. What youth he had left was flowing into her. His skin became papery and drawn, its color draining. Her own skin smoothed, her bony fingers plumping up and gaining a youthful, delicate luster.

Desperate to save his leader, a younger swordsman thundered forward, but his throat found its way into her grasp before his sword could taste flesh. The sight of two of their own being drained of life while their foe seemed to sweep backward from her sixties was enough to convince the remaining nomads that there was no more to be gained from attacking this woman or her monsters. They pulled back, weapons held defensively.

When she was through they looked upon a woman who might have been forty years old. She released their countrymen, but the afflicted men did not collapse. They merely turned, each with flesh seared black where her skin had met theirs. Their eyes were milky and glazed, staring at without seeing the other members of their tribe.

"Ah," Turiel said, finally acknowledging the other nomads. "I am pleased to see you are ready to be proper hosts. Since neither of these men will need to sleep any longer, I must assume that at least one of these huts has got a vacancy, so I'll be staying for the night. A good, hearty meal would be nice too. I haven't eaten in… well, it *must* be years by now. And I do hope none of you were planning to travel deeper into civilization anytime soon, because I'm afraid I've been asked to be discrete in my dealings here, and I'm not certain any of you can be trusted to remain silent on the details of my visit."

"What have you done to our chief?" asked a voice from the gathered crowd.

"Nothing. Well, nothing that *time* wouldn't have done eventually. I simply pushed it along a bit and gathered the runoff. Like crushing grapes to make wine. I'm sure if they had been willing to be reasonable, they would have been more than willing to offer themselves. You see, I've got a very important and noble purpose. I cannot *share* it, of course, but when I succeed you shall all reap the benefits. That is to say, you all *may* reap the benefits. Some of you may need to make a sacrifice similar to theirs before I move on. I have some tasks that could prove taxing."

The surviving nomads stood motionless, uncertain of what to do.

"I *thought* I'd been clear. Prepare a hut, some food, and some water." No one moved. She turned back to Mott, who was fumbling to align his own head with his neck. With a dismissive gesture, she said, "Bring them to order. And you come here."

Her dragoyle responded to the second command, and the withered remnants of her two victims responded to the first, shuffling forward.

"Do as she says…" said what remained of the chieftain. His voice had no intelligence behind it, no soul. It was hollow, empty.

"That is not our chief," said a voice from the crowd. "We must kill that... thing. We must kill them *all* and..."

"Really, sir," Turiel called without looking, her tone that of a parent disappointed in a child who had not learned its lesson. "You cannot kill him. He is already dead. The blood is cold in his veins, he breathes only to speak, and he speaks only to say what *I* tell him. The best you can do is slice him rather pointlessly into pieces as you did my poor little Mott." She finished repairing the familiar and stood to address the crowd. "But since your chief isn't *nearly* the masterpiece Mott is, it would be far simpler just to replace him."

She paced fearlessly forward, and the spokesman did the same.

"She is just one woman, and her largest monster is weakened. She cannot defeat *all* of us..."

Turiel leaned close, squinting at the voice of the opposition. "How delightful! You see, Mott! I *knew* it wouldn't take long."

She drove her staff into the ground and shifting vines of black split the earth at their feet, coiling up the legs of the nomads and locking them in place. She grasped the spokesman by the chin, released her staff, and drew her knife. "Hold still. Your eyes are the *perfect* color..."

#

Brustuum, in spite of himself, turned aside in disgust at the words he was hearing.

"Is something wrong?" Turiel asked innocently.

"You... you would *kill* a man to harvest his eyes?"

"Heavens no. He was still alive when I removed them. And besides, he was quite rude. His body and soul could be put to much better use elsewhere. Did you *see* how wonderful his eyes looked in Mott's head before you stuffed him in that trunk? And really, keeping my darling in an equipment room like a piece of luggage. I contend that *you* are the one who doesn't respect the sanctity of life."

"You are not in a position to judge anyone, Turiel... And how is it that you seem to know the location of what *remains* of your little pet?"

"As you've observed, I am something of a collector when it comes to eyes. I hate to see them go to waste, so I scatter them about."

He backed to the door and rapped on it. "Swordsman, go to the supply room and see that the monstrosity is still safely stowed. And search the room for anything out of the ordinary." He returned his attention to Turiel. "Speak. Complete your confession so that I can be done with you. Your very presence is beginning to make my flesh crawl."

"There's precious little that remains to be told."

#

Several days had passed and Turiel stood at the edge of the nomad camp gazing downward and beaming with pride. Anyone who had seen the woeful creature who had awakened in a cave to the south just weeks before would scarcely have believed that she was the same creature, let alone the same woman. Her clothes were now fresh and clean, ragged skins abandoned in favor of black robes found among the things of her hosts. More impressively, she now looked *almost* to be in the full flower of youth again, though here and there she seemed to have picked and chosen elements of maturity to retain. A single shock of gray hair remained, threaded through the rest like a vein of silver in a block of obsidian. The corners of her eyes and mouth retained some fine lines, almost artful in the way they made her look more distinguished. Her cheeks, rather than showing plump, childish roundness, remained somewhat drawn, allowing her face an angularity that bordered on sculptural. She was a woman who had recognized and embraced some of the gifts of age, and had reinvented herself as a figure with all of the assets of youth yet all of the badges of wisdom.

At her feet lay a work of grim brilliance. To all outward observations, it was a simple leather cloak. Save for the fact it was freshly tanned and a bit thicker than a normal garment, one might never have suspected anything sinister of it.

"There. *Much* better. I must say it was quite a fortunate happenstance to have stumbled upon this lovely settlement, eh, Mott?" Turiel said, wiping her hands on a few discarded shreds of linen. "So many fine materials to work with, and so many helpful people to assist and nourish us along the way. Arise, my cloak."

A ripple fluttered across the form. It shuddered and rose, odd angular folds appearing and disappearing as it shifted and twisted. A few moments of writhing and squirming allowed it to rise to its scalloped edge and stand erect, empty yet with its form bulging as though occupied. A sharp eye might notice that its motions came with the twitch of muscle and the rigidity of bone layered beneath its surface, but as it stood, rolling itself in imitation of a breezy flutter, it almost seemed lighter than air. The creation was some horrid combination of dark magic and sleight of hand.

"Entirely unlike their enchantment, yet with a virtually identical result. The lack of flight is a limitation, I grant you, but the efficiency is *far* greater. It takes little effort at all to craft one of these, and one needs only the flesh of two goats. I would dearly love to see it put to use in battle, but the only possible targets are my courteous hosts, and I would hate to appear ungrateful for their kindness. Come, my cloak. Let the others see how brilliantly you've come along."

She turned on her heel and paced toward the camp. The nomads who called it home seemed to be standing at attention outside their tents, waiting for her. As she drew near, the colorless flesh and milky-white eyes of each made it clear that they were no more than shells of what they had been, drained of their life and will. Each husk stood limply upright, looking as though held aloft by unseen strings and ready to collapse at any moment.

"There, you see, Marraam? I told you I would do it," she said happily, addressing what had formerly been the matriarch of the tribe.

The figure who once had been called Marraam stood, unseeing, unhearing, and unheeding. Nonetheless, Turiel spoke to her as though she were pleasantly interested in what the sorceress had to say.

"You have my endless gratitude for keeping as many goats in your herd as you did. It took every last one of them to perfect my design! … Well, yes, I realize it isn't *perfect*. Theirs can fly and mine can't, but I'm not convinced flight is *necessary*."

She turned suddenly to what had been a young man. His eyes were hidden behind a tied rag. Or, more accurately, the place where his eyes had *been* was so hidden.

"Now that is uncalled for, Poormaa. This is not self-indulgent tinkering! I *must* illustrate my worth to the D'Karon. They only share their most potent secrets with those they deem worthy, and I must know those secrets."

Her head whipped around, and she jabbed a finger at the husk of Marraam's husband.

"I *heard* that! I am *not* power hungry. My motivation couldn't be nobler. This is a matter of vengeance. It is my duty! A noble soul deserves to have her stirring put to rest, and I cannot do that until I am strong enough to finish her task."

She turned back to Marraam and placed a hand on her shoulder.

"It is kind of you to say, but what you've seen here is only a fraction of the wonders she could do. She chose a different path than I, so it is hardly a comparison of like for like, but I know my strength and I know hers. I still feel the chill of her shadow. Until I step into the light and grow beyond her strength, then I cannot hope to avenge her. And I know that I cannot reach those heights without the aid of the D'Karon."

Her head turned to Poormaa again.

"*Your* deaths… What do you mean, who will avenge *your* deaths? You did not *die*. You gave of yourself freely. You helped me to grow and to hone my skills. That is no cause for vengeance." She paused for a moment, then charged up to him, bringing her face within inches of his. "I am *not* a monster! You take that back! I am doing what I *need* to do. You would do the same if you could! … Be silent! *Be silent damn you! Be silent or I will silence you!* That's enough. Cloak, you have your target.*"

The leathery concoction coiled and sprang forward. In its leap it unfurled itself, catching the breeze and gliding toward the standing remains of Poormaa. Bony claws emerged from the seams closest to where the arms of a wearer might have been, and more slipped from the scalloped edge. It wrapped about the unresisting form of Poormaa and put the claws to work.

With grim efficiency the animated remains of the nomad were reduced to shreds. It was not as gruesome as it might have been. Slices and gashes in the lifeless flesh did not bleed, and there were no screams of pain, but the sight and sound of the attack should have been more than enough to turn even the steadiest stomach. Yet Turiel simply watched, a look of vindication on her face.

"There! You see? Every bit as effective as the cloaks conjured by the D'Karon. And though they can't properly fly, they aren't nearly as vulnerable to flame as the D'Karon version. If ever they allow me to meet face to face with Demont again, I feel quite certain he will find my innovations valuable. Isn't that right, Mott?" She turned and looked at her staff. It was vacant. "Mott? Blast it, where did that rascal get off to? And come to think of it, where has the dragoyle gotten off to?"

She took the staff in her hand, raised it up, and thrust it down. "To me, my creations!"

In reply, a strangled cry of a stricken bird echoed across the fields. She squinted through the shifting haze of heat and spotted the misshapen form of her familiar skitter out from behind some prickly shrubs. It was dragging something limply along, but it wasn't until it was nearly upon her that Turiel was able recognize the form of a sizable buzzard that Mott had pulled from the air.

"Well what have you got there?" she asked.

Mott flopped its prey down and chittered, prancing about.

Turiel smiled and shook her head, cooing as though she'd just seen a puppy overturn its water dish. "Oh, you naughty little beast. I have *told* you, these birds haven't got the wings to keep you aloft, and I haven't got the power to spare to make up for the shortcomings. We'll get you some fine wings soon enough."

Her creature whined pathetically.

"Oh very well, we shall give it a try if you *must* see for yourself how poorly suited they are, but after this we must be on our way." She pulled out her knife and began to carefully remove the relevant parts of the buzzard. "If their loose tongues are any indication, my welcome with these nomads has largely worn out. Fortunately they have served their purpose. I feel quite healthy once more, and I'm satisfied that I've made adequate progress to make proper use of the resources a larger city can provide. Once my dragoyle returns, we will find our way to those dragon breeders on the west coast. Where *has* that beast gotten off to?"

Mott chittered, then yelped as she sliced away the skeletal wings on his back in preparation for the fresh ones.

"Wandered *off*? Again? That's what happened to each of the prior cloaks as well! Blast it all. Why do they keep doing that?" She mused to herself as she aligned the first wing and began to stitch it in place with arcane threads drawn from her staff. The horrific act of flesh-crafting seemed as mundane as darning a sock to her. "I never would have imagined that the most difficult part of manufacturing the cursed things would be maintaining control of them.

That's a secret I would *dearly* love for Demont to share with me. I know there's a trick to it. There must be. Based on what Teht said, he was able to control *armies* if he so chose. Bah. When we find Teht, we will request an audience with Demont. If only they'd seen fit to make *him* the trainer instead. He and I have so much more in common…" She wiped her hands and stood. "There. You have your wings. Go ahead and try them."

Mott stood on his spidery legs and spread his new wings. They were a bit scraggly after the brief struggle with their previous owner and didn't seem to be nearly in proportion with the rest of the familiar's body, but he nonetheless seemed delighted with the new addition. He skittered along, flapping desperately and springing into the air. The best he could manage was a few prodigious jumps and a handful of short glides before he scrambled back to her, tongue lolling out and breath heaving.

"I *did* tell you, didn't I?" she said, scratching the creature under the chin. "You'll get used to them, my little concoction. At least until we get some proper ones. Something from a baby dragon will be just right. Green scales to go with your own scales and your eyes, I think." She clutched her hands in excitement. "Oh, you will be *perfect*. Come, Mott, I believe I can cobble together a horse out of scraps. Let us be on our way."

#

"You know the rest," Turiel said simply. "I'd overestimated my own capacity to craft a suitable steed from the parts available, and therefore I'd made little progress along the shore before your men encountered me. Rather than draw any undue attention to myself, I surrendered to you, and I've thus been treated to your less than admirable hospitality since then."

"Our intention is to keep our land safe from your treachery, not to make you comfortable. I would like to clarify a few matters of your account. You speak of your intention to open something you call a 'keyhole.'"

"A second one, yes."

"What precisely is this, and to what end do you seek to do so?"

"A keyhole is a portal. It is a gateway to another world, but a very special sort of gateway. It isn't so grand and remarkable as the full gateway the D'Karon have been seeking to open since their arrival. In a thousand lifetimes I couldn't hope to craft such a portal on my own. It takes more strength than I could ever hope to gather. A keyhole, on the other hand, is very limited. A physical creature cannot pass through it, but spirits can. Beings of pure magic as well. That's how the D'Karon reached this world. And upon completing the first keyhole and allowing the first of the D'Karon through, I was swiftly assigned the opening of a second. It was to be a contingency, a means for drawing in additional support in the event of difficulty. The first took me *ages* to open. This one is coming along even more slowly. Nonetheless, I believe I have gathered and sequestered perhaps four-fifths of the strength I need to cast the spell. A few more decades and it shall be ready."

"Your claims seem to support those of your countrymen, that these D'Karon creatures are beasts of another world. You are the first to admit what I have surmised since the first such claim. These D'Karon were summoned by your own hand. You recruited them to aid in the war effort, in hopes that through their might you would turn the tides of the war."

"What? No. That is madness. If the D'Karon were inclined to wage war with us, they would wipe out any army they encountered in weeks at most. You cannot comprehend the depths of their mastery. And though I freely and proudly admit to summoning them, there was no war at the time, and I've *yet* to see any evidence of this so-called endless conflict against this so-called Northern Alliance."

"You've spoken of Teht and Demont. We know these to be the names of Alliance generals, in addition to Bagu, Epidime, and Trigorah."

"Trigorah? I'm afraid I don't know the name. The others are D'Karon, though. And I'll thank you to speak their names with reverence. I must say it is a tremendous relief that you know of them all already. I'm quite sure if I had been the one to make their presence known, they would have been cross with me. But if you know of them, then they must have revealed themselves."

"Following their defeat, there has been considerable information of dubious reliability spread about their—"

"Defeat?" Turiel said, eyebrows rising as she suddenly realized what had been said. "Surely you are mistaken. The D'Karon cannot possibly have been defeated."

"If your own people are to be believed, some six months ago they were banished or destroyed by a group who claim to be the prophesied Chosen."

"No… No, no, no, that is absurd," Turiel said, her voice rising. "I refuse to believe that the D'Karon have been defeated."

"I'm growing weary of your feigned ignorance on the matter," Brustuum growled.

"And I'm growing weary of your attempts at deception. I don't know what your game is, sir, but you'll get nowhere by attempting to convince me that the godlike entities that I have devoted *centuries* to calling forth and serving—entities that have promised to bring our world to order under their wisdom and guidance—could have been so much as *hindered* by creatures of this world. No, sir. They live. They must. You could sooner destroy the night itself than destroy the D'Karon, to say nothing of the things that would follow."

"You claim to have ventured out of this cave of yours—which, I assure you, I'll be sending troops to investigate once we determine its location—specifically because your masters had not answered your calls. Did it not occur to you that they have been silent because they were defeated?"

Turiel shook with fury, tilting her head down slightly but keeping her eyes locked on Brustuum's. "These words are blasphemy and sacrilege." She twitched and beside her several of the desiccated rat carcasses shuddered.

"Caster, are your protective spells in place?" Brustuum asked.

The caster's voice was steady, but his posture stiffened. The rats were beginning to stir.

"She's... she's overpowering me, sir."

Turiel spoke again, her voice seeming deeper not in tone but in intensity, as though it was booming from the bottom of a yawning cavern. "I have focused my mind, gathered my spirit almost to the point of death, since a time before your grandfather was born. Do you believe your fledgling hedge wizard could hope to hinder me in any meaningful way? This is *precisely* why it shows nothing less than contempt to suggest that the D'Karon would make war with us for more than a month, let alone this multidecade *fiction* of a war."

Brustuum backed to the door and threw it open.

"I don't care what you must do, short of incinerating her. I want her toothless. I want her helpless."

"It will take everything I have," the caster said, placing his hands together. His rings took on a brilliant glow.

Brustuum slammed the door shut, though Turiel had barely moved let alone made any attempt to escape. Her gaze remained locked on Brustuum, but she seemed to be unconcerned, or perhaps unaware that the cell was meant to hold her.

Scuttling and scratching began to filter through the door. A dozen rats, or what remained of them, scurried out from the slot beneath it.

"I told you to *contain* her!" Brustuum barked, stomping on three of them. The rest were able to evade him and pour down the hall.

"There is no active spell. They are *alive* now," the caster said.

He shut his eyes and began to chant ancient, potent incantations until the air seemed almost *thick* with magic, shield upon wall upon barrier conjured from his mind to counter the thrumming energy that radiated from the cell.

"She's... beginning to... push through..." the caster said. "I... may be able to hold her... but her focus is terrifying. If she were to get her staff..."

"Just keep her here!" Brustuum said. "I need her mind and her voice. The staff can be destroyed."

Having sent the other guard away, and with precious few to spare after deploying the others for their fruitless search, he dashed through the halls personally. The staff was kept in an equipment room several floors above. He climbed the stairs shouting for aid.

"Anyone near weapon storage, destroy the staff! Grind it to dust!" he bellowed.

In reply, he heard the cries of the nearest men. One stumbled out into the hall, reanimated rats tearing at him. Brustuum charged by, shouldering his way through the slightly ajar door to the equipment rooms. To one side a fortified door was open, the guard he'd sent to see to the crated beast motionless on the ground as more rats emerged from chewed-through holes in his armor and returned to the task the man had tried and failed to stop. Their chisel-like teeth had carved deep gouges into the gray planks of a once-sturdy chest. The contents of the case were rattling and scratching viciously, all the while releasing a familiar chitter.

Brustuum dashed past the doorway and continued to another one, an ominous violet glow already lighting the interior. Heaving the brace aside, he tore open the door. Inside was the staff, with Turiel's black robes tied about it. He pulled a dagger from his belt and raised its thick pommel to shatter the gem. The rattling and chattering in the room behind him was replaced by the sound of splintered wood and scrabbling feet. In a heartbeat the piecemeal creature that had accompanied the witch bounded over Brustuum, snapping up the staff and robes in its jaws. He slashed at the monster, hacking into two of its legs, but it ignored the dire wound and worked its remaining legs and its wings to scramble along the hallway back toward the stairs to the cells below.

The air within the hallway was beginning to darken, as though the light was being drawn away. The depth and reverberation of Turiel's voice intensified further. No longer was she speaking Tresson. Now she spoke Varden, a Northern dialect, and one that seemed archaic to Brustuum's ears. Though there were walls and floors separating them, the Tresson could hear the voice as though she stood beside him.

"Answer my call. I need guidance. I need knowledge," she chanted. Now the air seemed to grow warmer. "Why will you not *answer*? Why can I not feel your presence?"

Though the mismatched beast seemed like it should be ungainly, it moved with astonishing speed. By the time he'd reached the hall, it was already disappearing down the steps. When he stumbled back into the hallway with the witch's cell, the monster had reached her door and was scratching madly at it. The Tresson caster was standing aside, sweat pouring from his brow as he muttered his incantations in tighter and tighter sequence.

Brustuum hurled himself at the witch's familiar, slashing and stabbing. He was trying to kill the monster, to shatter the gem, splinter the handle. He wanted to do *anything* to disarm the sorceress, but the monster eagerly and expertly clambered out of harm's way. It lashed at his feet with its tail, buffeted him with its wings, and did everything else necessary to keep its grip and force him to keep his distance.

"Damn it, man, help me!" Brustuum ordered the caster.

"I am trying, sir. The spells she's throwing off... if I do not concentrate... she... she isn't *trying* to escape. She's breaking through the best I have... and she's merely attempting to *communicate*. ... I will not be strong enough to hold her."

"*Answer me!*" Turiel cried, the very walls trembling with her voice. "Something is wrong... They cannot have been defeated. They *cannot* have been banished. ... I must know... I must *see*."

She looked to Brustuum again, gazing through the barred grill at eye level on the door. She had stared him down before, all through the interrogation. It was not until that moment, when her gray eyes locked on to his again, that he realized the degree to which she had been restraining herself. Her gaze cut through him. The eyes seized his mind, seemed to sear at it like embers kicked up from a long-burning fire on a dry, windy night. He couldn't move, couldn't breathe. His whole being was skewered by her stare like a pig on a spit.

A dozen spells had been cast upon the door, the whole of the will and wisdom of his caster rendered down into supernatural bonds keeping the brace in place and the locks secure. With a sequence of crimson flashes she shattered them all, and the door hurled open, narrowly missing the caster.

The familiar had sprung back, perhaps on instinct or perhaps heeding an unspoken command, and when the door was open, it leaped inside, delivering her staff to her. When her flesh met the bony grip of her casting-rod, Brustuum felt something inside him and all around him recoil. It was as if the very fabric of his being was sickened by what had been allowed to occur.

"Listen to me, Tresson. If the D'Karon live, and you have forced me to squander some of my precious gathered strength to expose your lies, I will be displeased. And if what you say is true, and the D'Karon have fallen or been chased from this world after all I did to summon them… I will be *very* displeased. And there will be consequences. To say nothing of the consequences of what you've done to Mott. My sweet little beast. I am sorry to say I do not have the time and materials to repair you properly. It shall have to be a patch."

Turiel curled her fingers, scooping at the air and gathering up from nothing a handful of pure night. She then flicked it at her pet. Where it struck the beast, its flesh blackened, then the stain crawled along and found the wounds and bits that were hacked away, filling them in with tarry scar tissue.

With her pet repaired, she turned to the far wall. This exposed her back to the soldiers without fear or regard, something that burned Brustuum all the more as his body refused to allow him to capitalize on the opportunity. Slowly she stirred the air and muttered words that seemed ill-suited to a human tongue. From a single circle, she shifted to a figure eight. At the center of each loop, a black point formed. They widened until they filled the loops traced by the staff's head. When twin black circles hung in the air, at their centers a point of light appeared. More than that, from each point of light came a piercing cold breeze, brisk and bracing in the baked air of the Tresson facility.

Satisfied, Turiel stepped back and watched as two windows opened in the air. Combined, they were nearly large enough to fill the cell. Each opened into the interior of a stone structure. One was lit only by what light spilled through the portal itself, offering barely a glimpse of the shadowy shapes within. The other was lit with the cold blue-tinged light that could only be reflected from snow and filtered through distant windows.

"Mott, you will seek Demont. If I recall correctly, Teht claims that is one of his workshops. Search the facility for him and remain with him if you find him. If you don't, attempt to awaken some of his creatures. He will certainly seek them out if they awaken. I shall find you when the time comes. I shall seek Bagu."

Mott chittered something. Turiel shuddered.

"No... not Epidime. We will never find him, and I dare not speak to him regardless. He of all of them, I would prefer not to find... Now off with you. I shall see you soon."

Her familiar bounded through his portal and off into the dimly lit facility. She stepped carefully through her own portal and turned back.

"And you, sir," she grinned as the portals began to close, "do remain nearby." She wavered slightly, her eyelids fluttering as though she had been struck with an intense wave of fatigue. She managed to hold the wavering sensation at bay long enough to deliver a final, ominous statement. "I look forward to seeing what sort of scars you shall have when I return..."

Chapter 4

Early the following morning, back in Kenvard, Ivy was preparing to once again face the Tresson delegate. Her first impression hadn't been a victory, but it certainly could have gone worse. Once the servants and staff had joined the meal, Krettis at the very least had been as off balance as Ivy. A bit of wine and some good food had coaxed several of the servants and staff into conversation, and she was quite sure she'd earned a few friends among them. The same could not be said of Krettis, who said less and less as the night wore on.

She pulled on her traveling cloak and looked at herself in the mirror. As glamorous as it felt to be wearing a beautiful dress the night before, her simple gray cloak, comfortable boots, and warm clothes made her feel strangely at ease, as though the night before she'd been playing a character on stage and now she was finally herself again.

A gentle knock at her door came as she was pulling her white hair back into a ponytail.

"Are you nearly ready?" asked Celeste.

"Nearly. Come in, please," Ivy said.

He opened the door and stepped inside.

"Is the *ambassador* ready yet?" Ivy asked, spitting the title as though it was a loathsome insult.

"She will be shortly. It would be best if she was not kept waiting."

"My bags are packed. I'm just making sure I'm decent. Not that it matters. Something tells me it doesn't matter how I look; Krettis isn't going to want to have anything to do with me."

"You both had your share of diplomatic black eyes last night, and of them, I believe yours were more forgivable."

"But this mission is already going in the wrong direction, and we've got *weeks* to go yet."

"Then there is plenty of time to turn it around," he said. "The rest is very straightforward. You and I will ride in a carriage with Ambassador Krettis and one of her aides. She will—or, based upon her attitude thus far—will *not* ask questions about our kingdom and its history. You will answer or defer to me if you are uncertain. Pleasant conversation and a greater understanding of one another are the intended goal, but I believe that we shall call this mission a success if at no point it descends into name-calling and violence."

"We'll see…" Ivy said. She picked up two cases. "Let's go."

"What are you taking with you?"

"My secret weapons. If all else fails, they'll be a lifeline for me."

The pair walked downstairs to find that their timing at least was right on target. Ambassador Krettis was just stepping out of her quarters, one of the most recent Kenvard homes to be fully restored. She was wearing her fur cloak, though the rest of her clothing was more understated than it had been for the banquet the night before. A woman several years younger aided her, dressed simply in a rougher fur coat.

Each ambassador climbed inside, Ivy sitting beside Celeste and Ambassador Krettis beside her aide. Ivy slid her cases under her seat and smiled.

"Hello!" Ivy said brightly, holding out a hand of greeting to the aide as the carriage lurched into motion. "Marraata, right? You were the one who loved the ice cider and the stuffed cabbage leaves. You really should have saved room for the snow candy."

Marraata nodded sheepishly and shook Ivy's hand without a word.

"Yes… we will discuss her behavior at the banquet when we return to Tressor," Krettis said. "I'm told the itinerary for this trip was still in transition prior to my departure. What sights of this fair land do you plan to share?"

Celeste unfolded a parchment and handed it to Ivy.

"Oh, wonderful!" Ivy said, glancing over the list. "I'm only just learning the final details of the journey myself, but it is going to be lovely. We will be heading along the coast, stopping at many of our most quaint and comfortable inns. In three days we will reach our first stop, which will be the Azure Saltern, a centuries-old source of salt for much of the Northern Alliance. Then we'll continue to the hot springs four days later…"

Ivy continued to list off the most interesting sights that the north had to offer. Ambassador Krettis feigned interest for a time, and her aide dutifully recorded the descriptions, but it became clear to all that Ivy may as well have been talking to herself. Because she knew that it was part of her role to finish reading through the list, she did so, but her own genuine enthusiasm for the exciting new sights they would visit faded swiftly in the face of Krettis's obvious disinterest.

She looked the ambassador in the eyes. Krettis looked back, but Ivy felt uncomfortably as though the Tresson was looking through her.

"I'm particularly looking forward to the orchestral performance in Martinsford," Ivy said, hoping in vain to initiate discussion.

"Mmm…" the ambassador murmured.

Ivy crossed her arms. "You do not seem terribly impressed with the planned events."

"I'm sure they will be quite acceptable."

"If in the future you were to host a tour of Tressor, what sort of things would you like to show me?"

"I would not be in a position to make those selections. It would be done by a tribunal. I would not hazard a guess, for fear of raising your hopes of seeing them in the unli... in the event of a Tresson diplomatic tour."

Ivy tried to push away the flutter of irritation she felt. Clearly the sting of Krettis's prior behavior had faded. She was back to her less than diplomatic mindset.

Ivy furrowed her brow and turned to Marraata. "It is your job to write things down during this trip, right?"

Marraata looked uncertainly to Ambassador Krettis.

"She is the record keeper, yes," Krettis said.

Ivy kept her eyes on Marraata. "As you saw last night, Ambassador Krettis and I are both new to this, and we're likely to say and do things that won't be in keeping with the spirit of this tour." Ivy turned to Krettis. "We can sit here and woodenly quote back to one another the civil little fibs and white lies that we know we are meant to, but I don't think that will do any good, do you? We'll just go home knowing that the other side can follow the same rules as we can, which I think we already know. Marraata could probably write down every little flavorless comment and empty observation we would have said for this whole trip without us even saying them. I say we should let her do that. Let her write down what *would* have happened. Meanwhile you and I can say what's *really* on our minds. That way at least the people in this carriage will walk away with a genuine understanding of one another."

"You are suggesting my aide falsify her report?" Krettis said, raising an eyebrow.

"This whole journey was destined to be pushed through a sieve to remove anything too dangerous or too honest. All I'm suggesting is we move the sieve to between our mouths and her quill rather than between our minds and our mouths. We both know the sorts of things that might be *dangerous*, and we won't say any of that. But you speak your mind, I speak mine, Marraata translates it into something the rest of the delegation will tolerate, and no one is any the wiser."

"This is highly irregular," Krettis said.

"Your people selected a malthrope to be your host. It was never going to be anything *but* irregular. So what do you say? Shall we secretly turn this carriage into a place of honesty? Or shall we chat about," she glanced at her pages, "the fine quality of Alliance pine for the next few weeks."

"This is not wise," Celeste said.

"Maybe not, but at least it won't be dull," Ivy said.

Krettis blinked once, then turned. "Marraata, I will personally review your records each night to ensure that they are suitable to be presented. Ambassador Ivy, your offer is acceptable."

"Excellent!" Ivy said. "So what's wrong with the stops we've got lined up for you?"

"They are toothless," Krettis said. "You are showing us places of what you perceive to be beautiful or of cultural relevance, but they leave unspoken and unexplored the one thing that has dominated both of our cultures for generations. They ignore the war. To look at your itinerary, you would think that the war had never happened. And so long as we are being *frank*, your land is icy and windswept. There is little more to be learned of it. You could drag me about for a *year* and I would see little more than snow, rock, trees, and huddled people trying to keep warm. What you are showing me teaches me nothing. The one thing I'd hoped to learn is the truth behind the D'Karon, a group whom you dubiously blame for every life lost in the entirety of the conflict. Not once in your banquet did you offer evidence of them. Not once in your itinerary are they even mentioned. I see very little value at *all* in any of it."

Ivy raised her eyebrows and looked at Celeste. "It's nice she's taken so enthusiastically to the suggestion." Her eyes shifted to Krettis. "Let me begin by saying that no one who sees the crystal lakes, frost-dusted forests, and majestic mountains of my home would ever for a moment suggest that the sights are not worth seeing. And those huddled people have scratched out a life for themselves in conditions that those of you in the warm, bountiful south could hardly imagine. We are iron hard, all of us. As for the D'Karon, I will gladly tell you of their treachery. I'll tell you of the cage they kept me in, the experiments they subjected me to. I'll tell you of the way they hoped to turn me against those who were destined to be my friends. They took our healers and sent them to die at the front so that those left behind would wither and weaken. You believe that we will not show you things of the D'Karon? Look around you! The ruin of this capital? That is their doing. My body, the whole of the war. The stories I can tell you, Krettis. You'll learn *plenty.*" She huffed a breath. "Care to read that back to us, Marraata?"

The aide scratched down a few final words. "'Ambassador Krettis praised the landscape and expressed interest in the many sites described. Ambassador Ivy agreed to answer many questions and spoke highly of her own people and those of Tressor, noting the southern land's bounty.'"

Ivy grinned. "This is going to work out just fine…"

#

Myranda and Deacon loaded the last of their bags into the carriages used by the rest of the delegation. In the interest of lessening the load for Myn, they would be carrying only the essentials. They kept one shoulder satchel each, as well as Myranda's staff. Grustim had a word with Valaamus, then approached the edge of the lake. He knelt to fill his water skin at the water's edge, dictating over his shoulder to Myranda and the others.

"To reach our destination will take no less than six days," he said. "Garr will set the pace. Follow closely. We shall fly near the clouds. Dragon Riders over the heart of Tressor are a rare sight, particularly in pairs, but nothing the people will fret about. You will go nowhere without me as an escort. You will enter no place without my permission, interact with no one without my knowledge. To most of our land you are still the enemy. Your dragon and your items of wizardry are weapons of war. No diplomatic parties have been sent ahead to prepare the people. There will be no warm welcomes."

"Understood," Myranda said. "Let us be on our way."

"One moment," Deacon said, scribbling something in one of his pads.

"What are you up to?" Myranda asked.

"It strikes me that while we've been forbidden active spells to aid our search, perhaps *passive* magic would be acceptable. Simply opening our minds to the signs left by D'Karon magic. I've passed the question to Valaamus," he said, stowing the book again.

"Will he understand the question?"

"His mystics seem capable. They will understand," he said. "I apologize for the delay. When you are ready."

Grustim nodded once, mounted Garr, and pushed his helmet into place. Myranda and Deacon climbed onto Myn's back as the Tresson dragon and Rider began to strut forward.

Myranda was no stranger to soldiers and military discipline. There was undeniably something different about how a soldier moved. The same could even be said for warhorses, but until now Myranda had never seen a war dragon take to the sky. The training was apparent from the first glance. Garr moved with sharpness and precision. He had an economy of motion that could only have been the result of endless repetition. He brought himself to speed with short, swift steps. His wings snapped open and caught the wind. Two crisp flaps were all it took to get the creature airborne, and from there a long, slow flap began the rhythm that would pull him skyward.

Myn watched the demonstration evenly, eyes narrow and neck rigid.

"Remarkable what a difference some training can make," Deacon said, appreciating the technique.

Myn huffed a breath through her nose and bounded forward, her steps long and spirited. She unfurled her wings and held them out, catching the wind and taking to the air with a leap. Whether it was her intention to show off or not, she certainly took to the sky with a grace and confidence that was every bit the match for Garr's precision. Once in the air, Myn worked her wings to close the gap. The two dragons rose high into the sky. Once they'd reached the proper height, they each caught the same breeze and settled into a soar.

Myranda leaned back slightly, and Deacon went so far as to open his bag to fetch a book. Travel by dragon-back, at least as far as Myranda had experienced it, was mostly soaring. Myn's great wings caught the air, and with the aid of a few warm updrafts she could fly for hours without once flapping. Normally the journey from this point on would be a leisurely glide through the sky, leaving dragon and rider alike to enjoy the spectacular view and brisk air. This time, however, Myn had different plans. Unsatisfied with trailing Garr, she swooped aside, then worked her wings until she was beside him.

Garr turned his head slightly, eying Myn. The female dragon returned his gaze, then shifted it to Grustim. The Rider was watching through the eye slits of his helmet, almost matching Garr's own helmet-obscured gaze perfectly. He leaned low and grunted an unheard order. Garr looked ahead and put his wings to work, increasing his speed. Myn accelerated to match him. Myranda and Deacon leaned low, the wind rushing by forcefully as the dragon gained speed.

So began a very memorable flight. Myn and Garr went motion for motion, matching each other's speed despite Myn's slightly smaller size and much greater load. Garr dove and surged forward, but Myn mirrored the maneuver and inched ahead. Then came the swoops and rolls. Through intuition, training, or perhaps instruction from his Rider, Garr seemed to be innately aware of where the strongest updrafts and most useful tailwinds would occur. He dipped here, rose there, darted aside, and tucked his wings, always to maneuver into a better wind and thus ahead of Myn. She wouldn't have it, finding her way to the same breeze through imitation when possible and through sheer effort when that failed. It made for a rough journey for Myranda and Deacon.

"I had... not anticipated this degree of maneuvering..." Deacon said, speaking between swoops. He had one arm tight around Myranda's waist and the other hand clutching his casting gem in case his grip proved insufficient.

Myranda adopted the same speaking patterns, holding her breath and bearing down when Myn decided a dive or turn was in order. "I think she... might be showing off." She leaned a bit closer and gave Myn a firm pat on the neck. "Don't push yourself too hard. We've got a long way to go!"

"Perhaps not for today. Grustim seems to be motioning for a landing," Deacon said, more than a bit relieved.

Garr did indeed seem to be pulling into a spiraling descent. Myranda and Deacon had spent so much time focusing on keeping themselves seated they hadn't had a chance to observe the changing landscape beneath them. The lush green fields of Tressor, which had been spreading out as far as the eye could see when they started, now looked a good deal sparser. The green of the land was a shade closer to yellow, and a vast expanse of sand and stone loomed in the distance.

A field sprawled below them near a wide stream. It would be a fine place to spend the night, and Grustim had likely selected it for just that purpose. Myn saw the potential as well and decided it was one last chance to show what she could do. As Garr approached the ground in an easy spiral, Myn tucked her wings and dove, darting toward the ground as quickly as a falling stone. At the last possible moment, she spread her wings again and turned her fall into a speeding glide, then from a glide into a run. She dug her claws into the dusty ground and slid to a stop a few strides from the river.

"I hope you're proud of yourself," Myranda said as she dismounted and stepped back to observe her friend.

Myn was heaving breath, visibly exhausted, but had a defiant gleam in her eye as she watched her rival draw nearer. He landed with the same crisp precision as his takeoff nearly a full minute after Myn touched down. The female strutted up to him, head held high, and swished her tail. Though she spoke no words, her body language made it clear that it had been a race, and she had won. Though a dragon's expressions are difficult to read, Myranda had become something of an expert. Even with his helmet to hide all but his eyes, Garr was visibly irritated. It was worth noting that he was not winded in the slightest, his breathing as slow and steady as it had been when they left that morning. He stepped slowly to the riverbank and lowered his head to drink. Myn did the same, gulping almost desperately at the water.

Grustim jumped from his dragon's back and stormed up to Myranda.

"Is that... did you... is that what you..." he stammered, hands shaking. "My superiors have asked me to speak with care, but care be damned. How *dare* you treat your dragon that way?"

"I don't understand," Myranda said.

"Look at her! She is exhausted! If you feel the need to illustrate the supposed superiority of your precious Alliance over my people, then that is to be expected, but to do so at the expense of your dragon is unacceptable!"

"Grustim, I assure you, I required *nothing* of Myn. I asked her to save her strength, but she chose to do otherwise. Myn *loves* to fly, and I've always left the task to her to do as she sees fit," Myranda said. "She didn't do anything that Garr didn't."

"Garr was carrying but one rider and has been conditioned for aerial maneuvers. I was *attempting* to keep him ahead of you, as I am expected to be your *escort*."

Myranda stepped up to Myn's side. "Myn, look at me for a moment," she said, worried.

The red dragon raised her head from the river, licking the water from her chin with a curl of her tongue.

"Are you all right? You didn't overtax yourself, did you?"

Her breathing was still heavy, but it was beginning to return to normal. She gave Myranda a nudge with her nose and dropped her head to the ground, angling for the usual affection.

"You promise me you'll behave tomorrow. Garr is an ally, not a rival. Understand?"

Myn rumbled in her throat and gave a subtle nod.

"Good," Myranda said, scratching her on the brow. She turned to Grustim. "What shall be done for food?"

Grustim glared at her for a moment, judgment in his expression. "The Dragon Riders are granted hunting rights in all of Tressor, but the same cannot be said of Myn. Accompanied, she might be permitted to hunt, but in light of her lack of restraint in the air I believe it best if she remains here. Grustim and I will fetch a proper meal. When I return I will ready a fire."

"I'll see to the fire. Thank you," Myranda said.

The Dragon Rider tapped his mount. Garr raised his head from the river and huffed a breath of flame to sizzle the moisture from his helmet. He then helped Grustim to his back. Once the Rider was in place, Garr looked to Myn and Grustim to Myranda, then the pair dashed off into the fields. Myn stood rigidly and watched them go, her muscles tensed with the desire to spring after them.

"No, Myn. We are in their land. We must honor their laws. If you must help, help me gather some wood for the fire."

Myn watched reproachfully as Garr bounded off into the distance, then padded along beside Myranda and Deacon toward a small stand of trees. With a slow rake of her claws, she stripped a large tree of several of its smaller branches, then clutched them in her teeth to carry them. By the time they had returned to the riverside, she'd caught her breath, though the occasional huff of anger still hissed from her nose.

"I must say," Deacon remarked. "Having been the object of Myn's ire in the past, it comes as a bit of a relief to see her angry at someone else."

"I thought she was through with this jealousy," Myranda said. She turned to the dragon. "You get along so well with the people of Kenvard, Myn. You'll have to learn to do the same with the people of Tressor as well. Here, this is an excellent place. You can drop the wood and break it up a bit," Myranda instructed.

Myn let what was probably Myranda's weight in lumber fall from her jaws and dragged her claws across it twice, easily shredding it. Deacon and Myranda went to work finding stones the proper size to ring the fire.

"There, scoop out a bit of a hollow," Myranda said.

The dragon clawed away the stubby plains grass and then plopped down on the ground, lying on her side with her head upright and alert.

Myranda released a contented sigh. "You know something? The circumstances are trying, but… I do believe I missed this. There is something so peaceful, so serene about readying a camp for the night."

"The weight you carry upon your shoulders is a great one. Any respite must be precious." Deacon patted Myn on her neck. "And the task *is* made easier with Myn's help."

Myranda pile the wood into a suitable arrangement while Deacon placed the stones. "I suppose the simplicity is a part of it. But… for so many years I roamed the north looking for a place that I could call my home and dreaming that I'd finally have a family to share it with."

She stepped back and nodded to Myn, who puffed a jet of flame until the wood began to burn.

"Then I found Myn. Suddenly those little icy clearings or frigid alcoves weren't places of solitude. In a way, before I was finally able to return to Kenvard, *this* was my home. Not any one place. Just a warm fire, dear friends, and the firm knowledge that there were important things to be done the next day. What more could anyone *want*?"

She eased herself down and leaned against Myn's chest. The dragon curled her head around to rest at Myranda's side. Deacon approached and sat by Myranda's other side. Myn quickly shifted to push her head between them. Thus situated, the three waited, each of their minds turned to the tasks and riddles of the day.

#

The sun sagged in the sky as Ether's delegation approached its first major stop. Their journey had taken them through a very carefully selected strip of the Low Lands, following the former border between Vulcrest and Ulvard toward one of the north's most notable features: the seemingly endless Ravenwood Forest. It was a frosted green ocean of pines, scattered with the occasional hearty oak, maple, or ash. Their destination was a large, well-supplied inn called The Eagle's Terrace in a town known as Highpoint. As the name would suggest, Highpoint was located upon a large hill in the otherwise flat expanse of the Low Lands. This gave the town in general and the inn in particular a fine view of Ravenwood in all of its glory.

"We have arrived," Ether said.

"So I see," Maka replied.

The pair had chatted for the duration of the trip, though Ether's asocial manner left Maka with the burden of keeping the words flowing. He'd been quite up to the challenge, asking questions, enjoying the answers, and offering his own observations in exchange. Ether's replies were flavorless, bordering upon clinical. Invariably she spoke of the nation and its society as though she were well outside of it, an observer and nothing more. Nonetheless, her answers were thorough, accurate, and offered a scope of perspective stretching centuries into the past.

Ether stepped out of the carriage into the street outside when they reached their destination. The town was built in such a way that all roads seemed to lead to the inn, with the main street sloping downward and angled for a clear view of the forest in the distance. Maka stepped down from the carriage behind her.

"Ravenwood," Ether said. "The largest forest in all of the Alliance."

"Impressive. A rival for our own Great Forest," Maka said.

"Ravenwood supplies most of the wood for the Low Lands, which spans the border between the Vulcrest and Ulvard regions. It continues to grow, and has done so for many thousands of years in spite of the harvesting. It could easily supply the needs of a land many times the size of the Alliance without decreasing in size. Several potent mystical leylines meet at many points, fueling the energies of the place and making it a fine home for wildlife and mystic entities alike. No human knows its interior fully, with large swathes completely untouched by man.

"Highpoint is the oldest and largest town in the area. Built as a fort when the kingdoms were separate, it has since stripped away its walls and grown far beyond its original limits. The Eagle's Terrace is the centerpiece to the town, one of the finest inns in half the kingdom. It was considered as a possible host for the queen's summit prior to the decision to temporarily restore Five Point."

Maka nodded and watched as the crowd, which had gathered as the carriage approached, was held at a distance by the imposing presence of a dozen guards. Most eyes were turned to the Tresson ambassador and his delegation, some with curiosity, most with far more vicious emotions.

"Again I see your countrymen are not pleased by our visit," Maka said.

"With the exception of those who attended the queen's coronation, you are the first Tressons to travel this far north in more than one hundred and fifty years. You are the first Tresson most of these have ever seen outside of a battlefield. Human emotions are stubborn and foolish. They linger long after their source has departed."

"Perhaps we should step inside then. I would not want to disrupt the peace of this fine town," Maka said.

"Agreed," Ether said. "I believe there is some manner of formal greeting planned."

"Ambassadors!" Gregol said, unable to forgo the anxious hand-wringing that seemed always to rear its head when he had to deal with Ether. "I trust your ride has been a pleasant one?"

"Yes, Ambassador Gregol. Thank you," said Maka.

"You need not ask that each time we leave the carriage. I am capable of conducting myself in the manner you have advised," Ether said, the rumble of impatience in her voice.

"Yes, oh Guardian, thank you. If you will step inside, we will begin our evening meal and offer Ambassador Maka the traditional—"

"Very well," Ether interrupted, striding toward the doorway.

Maka followed, a strangely amused grin on his face. He stepped close to Ether as they approached the door. "You are aging your assistants by many years. They perhaps were not prepared for someone so willful."

"Then they were fools," Ether said. "I am Chosen. The safety of this world owes itself to the strength of my will."

They entered the inn to find it, as would be the case for all formal meeting places during the trip, emptied of all but the staff who maintained it and the local officials who greeted them. Knowing the lingering hatred fueled by so long a war would be difficult to quell, the tour's organizers chose to take no chances, minimizing contact with the public. Upon entering, there was a brief ceremony. A simple woven wreath of pine boughs was presented to each of the delegates.

"These wreaths are an ancient gift of acceptance and hospitality. Woven from boughs cut from young trees deep within Ravenwood, they are symbolic of the embrace of the land and its people, welcoming you into our hearts. Take them with our blessings," Ether said, the words spoken without spirit or sincerity.

"Thank you," Maka said with a bow of his head.

The delegation continued inside to the dining hall of the inn. It was a grand place, three stories tall and built from stout wooden beams. The walls were white plaster, decorated with wood carvings and the mounted heads of deer, elk, bears, and moose. Five tables had been arranged in a semicircle before a fireplace large enough to heat the whole of the room with plenty of warmth to spare for guest rooms. Many such rooms wrapped around the chimney on the other side of the wall. The mantle was so tall one had to crane one's neck to look at the great carving of the Ulvard crest mounted there, and the fire within the hearth was nearly as tall as Maka.

Ether and Maka were seated alone at a four-person table in the center of the arrangement. The table to the left hosted Gregol and his counterparts among the delegation. To the right sat Zuzanna and her portion of the entourage. The outermost tables hosted the lesser members of the group, various assistants, servants, and record keepers.

"Another fine meal," Maka said appreciatively as soup and bread were set before him. He noted that none were placed before Ether. "I've not seen you take a meal since my arrival. Does this food not suit your tastes?"

"I do not require food."

"No? Surely you must require some form of sustenance."

"I draw my strength directly from the elements, and at present I have no need to replenish myself."

"Remarkable," Maka said, with genuine interest. He sampled the soup. "Delicious. I have not eaten so well in a great while." He shifted in his seat, facing her a bit more. "We have spoken much of your land as we traveled, and I have spoken much of mine, but we have not yet discussed each other."

"It did not appear to be a relevant diplomatic matter, and I am taken to understand that diplomacy is—as often as not—about avoiding those things which need not be said."

"On this matter, I believe there can be no harm from gaining a greater insight."

"All the same. I have no interest in discussing such things."

"Very well. I wish only to do you the courtesy of sharing my interest."

Ether watched as he ate, the enjoyment clear in his wizened expression. Her mind began to drift in all-too-familiar directions. A thought arose.

"You are old," she observed.

"Quite old, yes," he said, again his lips turning up in a grin at the novelty of the statement.

"Death is near for you," Ether said.

"Hah! I try to avoid thinking in such terms, but it is fair to say that more years are behind me than ahead."

"How do you do this? Why do you spend your time in this way if it is so precious for you?"

"It is my duty to my land."

"Will this duty ever be fulfilled for you? Does it have an end?"

"When I feel I lack the strength or will to represent my land, then I shall retire from diplomacy, but that time has not come yet."

"And what then? What will you do when your purpose is gone?"

"My purpose will not be gone. It will simply change. I shall devote myself to such things as matter most to me. To my family."

"Your family."

"Yes. I have three sons and four daughters, all married. Thirty grandchildren and twenty great-grandchildren, to say nothing of my nieces and nephews."

"Do these offspring require your aid and support any longer? Your protection?"

"Oh no. My children are fine men and women. Quite able to meet their own needs."

"Then your task is done. There is no purpose for you to serve."

"When one has a family, one always has a purpose to serve. Sometimes it is enough simply to be near, to share wisdom, and share strength."

"Life is so insignificant, so fleeting. How do you continue on when you know that nothing you do, nothing you leave behind, will ever truly be important in the widest scheme? How do you cope with the knowledge that at any moment your life might end?"

"How do we cope knowing that life may end soon?" He laughed. "What other choice do we have? And perhaps we are but drops in a great river, but we all contribute to the flow. Whatever the 'widest scheme' may be, it arrives at its destination in part because of us. That is enough. These are questions far beyond the depth of a simple diplomat. But it seems to me that such questions are asked of others only when they have first been asked of ourselves without a proper answer. Tell me, what brings you to ask them now?"

"Nothing… It was foolish to ask."

"Nonsense. Why are we here if not to share of ourselves?"

"Your answers will be of no use to me. You speak of family. I have none."

"We all have a family, Ambassador Ether."

"Not I. I was crafted by the gods, no mother or father. I have no siblings, save the lesser elementals who are to me what insects are to you. And I have no children."

"There are other types of family than those who share our blood. There is the family we choose for ourselves. Are there any you would call friends?"

"There are those who I would call allies. I have no need for friends."

"Another phrasing then. Are there any who would call *you* friend?"

"There are some."

"Then these are your family."

"But you spoke of family as those who need one another. They do not need me beyond tasks such as this, and I do not need them at all."

"I think on that the second point you are mistaken. Someone who speaks as you do of life and death, someone who asks the questions you ask? That is a person who needs family, now more than ever. Of these who would call you friend and who you call allies, is there one who is special to you?"

"There was one who was my equal, one who, unlike me, seemed to *seek* these connections of friendship and family that you insist are so crucial… or at least one who would accept them. But he did not seek them from me."

"He spurned you."

"I offered myself as a target for his affections, and he chose not to do so. It is just as well. In time he would have seen that affection had no place in what we were. He and I were unique in the world, creatures crafted by the same forces that sculpted the very firmament, joined by a higher purpose and undiluted by impurity or mortality."

"Mmm… And you say he would have, and he was… is this special one no longer with us?"

"It was foreseen that to defeat the D'Karon, our world would have to sacrifice one of the Chosen. He was the one to fall."

Maka nodded. "Then I understand. Ambassador Ether, it is a fine thing for you to host me in this journey, and I look forward to what remains of it, but may I suggest that when you are through, you return to these allies for a time."

"For what reason? My task with them is through."

"Perhaps, but I think if you were to speak to them as you have spoken to me, they would learn that their task with you is just beginning."

#

Some time after they set out, Grustim and Garr returned with the fruits of their hunt. At the campsite they found Myn with her eyes shut, a purr of contentment rumbling in her chest as the wizards leaned against her belly and enjoyed the warmth of the fire in the coolness of night. Garr clutched three large gazelles in his teeth. Myn opened her eyes and watched him as he dropped them beside the fire, then Grustim hopped down to inspect the camp.

"You build a proper fire," Grustim stated.

"We wouldn't last long in the north if we didn't know how to build a good fire quickly," Myranda said. "Though Myn gets most of the credit for the hard work. Should I help prepare the meat to be cooked?"

"I will see to it," Grustim said, drawing his knife and getting to work.

His skill with the knife was every bit a match for Garr's mastery of the skies. Grustim sliced a share for each, fashioned spits to prepare them, and set others aside to cook and smoke more slowly. Garr sat patiently, his catch at his feet, until Grustim finished prepping the food to be cooked. When the Rider gave a low command to his mount, Garr snatched and swallowed his meal.

"This one is for Myn?" Myranda said, indicating the prey that had been placed nearest to her.

He gave a single nod.

"Eat, Myn. You'll need your strength for tomorrow."

Myn looked at the meal, then looked to Garr. With a sniff and flick of her tongue, she pushed it away with her nose.

"Oh, don't be stubborn," Myranda said. "I know a big meal can last you days, but after the flying you did today I'm sure you're starving. You'll have plenty of chances to hunt for yourself and for me when we get back to Kenvard."

Myn flipped the tip of her tail back and forth and acted as though the meal was not there.

"Grustim, what can you tell us about where we're headed? The Southern Wastes?"

"Little to be said. Myn's *enthusiasm* has brought us half a day closer than I'd expected. The Wastes are a region near the southern coast. Colder than the rest of Tressor. Little rain, and nothing grows there."

"Is there anything sensitive there? Something that might attract the D'Karon? Any resources? Perhaps temples or artifacts?"

"Most years there is little at all. This season there may be some shepherds or goatherds."

"There may be?"

"The Wastes grow and recede. For years they will seem to recover, the fertility of the land returning slowly. Inevitably it comes to an end. The life drains from the soil and the cycle begins again."

"Why would the D'Karon strike there?" Myranda wondered aloud. "If it is truly the D'Karon, then to focus on a lifeless place is unlike them. Above all else they seek power. If these attacks are their doing and are intended to restart the war, surely they would have struck somewhere in the heart of Tressor, or even the border where the war burned for so long. Attacks there would have left no doubt in the minds of your people that hostilities had begun anew. To strike on the fringe of your kingdom would only make sense if there was something of great value there."

"Of course, such thinking only holds if it *is* the D'Karon themselves," Deacon observed.

Myranda nodded. "Even if the evidence suggests the contrary, we can't afford to take this situation lightly. We must be prepared for the D'Karon." She looked at the Dragon Rider. "Grustim, if we find dragoyles, whether they are true works of the D'Karon or merely something like them, there are some things you should know about them and how to face them. They are massive creatures; their—"

"You need not describe them, Duchess. I know them well. They are meant to be dragons, though they come as near the true creatures as a shadow comes to the man who casts it. They share their form, but little else. It is as though you made weapons of the great creatures we ride, keeping the claws, the wings, the strength, but stripping away the grace, the nobility, the soul…"

"They are not our doing, Grustim. They are the work of the D'Karon."

He looked at Myranda, his expression unchanged. "Of course. A slip of the tongue."

"How do you know of them?"

"The Dragon Riders have had many a clash with those twisted mockeries of our mounts."

"You fought them?" Deacon said. "From what we've found, and what we've learned from soldiers stationed at the front, dragoyles were not deployed at the front lines. And I admit I may have misunderstood, but it seemed to me that the Dragon Riders were not frontline fighters either."

"Not now, and never was it the intention. But once. It was decades ago, long before my time. The war was raging as hot as it ever had. Our king, the father of the man who now holds the throne, believed if the front line could only be broken, the tide could be turned. He demanded that the Dragon Riders be deployed en masse, targeting the weakest defense point. A dozen Riders descended and made a crucible of the battlefield. Our soldiers claimed more of your land on that day than they had in the months that preceded it. But then the sky blackened with your… with the D'Karon creations. They did not breathe anything so clean and pure as flame. They spat a choking black mist. We lost nine Riders that day, and four mounts… We *still* haven't recovered our full numbers. It was decided that no matter the gains that might be had, the Dragon Riders were too precious to be squandered at the battlefront, but the stories of that battle, and of the hideous foes they fought, remain a part of our training."

"Well, know that we've done all we can to rid our world of them, and if we find that they have done any harm to your people, we shall do all in our power to repair the damage and find those responsible," Myranda said.

"And if those responsible are indeed operating under the orders of your crown?"

"I assure you such is not the case."

"Your army then? You've already admitted that the military was in the clutches of the D'Karon for much of the war. What if your soldiers were less reluctant to abandon their former masters than you?"

"If they are the allies of the D'Karon, they are no allies of ours. They will be brought to justice," Myranda said with resolve.

Grustim watched the meat roast, and a heavy silence sat over the campsite. When the leaden quiet was broken, it was not with a word, but a growl. Myranda turned to find that despite Myn's clear reluctance to eat the food offered by Garr, the rumbling of her stomach betrayed her.

"Are you ready to swallow your pride and eat what they've given? Or will you continue to act like a child?" Myranda said.

Myn thumped her tail angrily at the ground once. Garr stood, looking to his Rider, then padded forward and picked up the meal intended for Myn. She watched him warily. He took a step closer and dropped it again, practically placing it between her paws. A conversation began, one that was more felt than heard. Deep, throaty vibrations Myranda hadn't heard since her time in Entwell when Myn and Solomon "spoke." At that time both dragons were much smaller. To experience such a conversation at full scale was almost enough to rattle one's bones.

When the conversation was through, a final growl from Myn's gut served as punctuation. She reluctantly curled her head down and snapped up the meal.

"There, at least *someone* was able to talk some sense into you," Myranda said. She turned to Deacon. "Did you understand any of that?"

"The language dragons speak to one another isn't quite like the languages you or I might speak, or even to the one they might use to speak to a human listener," Deacon said. "The thrust of the argument was that there will be bad hunting where we land next, and she would be still hungrier when we reach that place. It is better to eat now than risk waiting. Myn felt certain she would be able to seek out enough food and took some convincing otherwise."

Grustim raised an eyebrow. "You understand Draconic?"

"I should hope so. I apprenticed in flame magic under a dragon," he said.

"Tell me, Grustim. Does Garr speak at all? Any human languages?" Myranda asked.

"A Dragon Rider's mount is meant to understand him and to be understood by him. He needs no other language besides that of his kind," he said.

"Though I've done my best to do right by Myn, I admit I don't know much about dragons. Deacon knows a bit and has assured me I've done her no harm in raising her as I have, but I still worry. Should I be teaching her to speak? Should I wait for her to learn on her own?"

"When things are not in a dragon's nature, they are best learned when the dragon *chooses* to learn. A good dragon mount is rare because few take to the training necessary."

"I'm curious about your training, and breeding. Though he spoke little of his past, I believe that my fire master may have been brought from the same place that the Dragon Riders—"

"Enough. I have agreed to escort you, not share the secrets of my kingdom," Grustim said brusquely.

"Yes… of course," Deacon said. "My apologies for overstepping my bounds."

"Your meal will be finished soon. I suggest we eat and get to sleep. The sooner we are rested, the sooner we can continue south."

"A fine idea," Myranda said with a nod.

While each of the humans stared quietly at the shifting flames of the campfire, Myn swallowed and licked the remnants of her meal from her lips. She gazed at the remaining portion of the gazelle that had provided the meat for the human meals and licked her chops once more. Garr, lying beside his Rider, watched her for a moment, then grumbled something. Grustim's eyes darted from the fire to his dragon. He gave a stiff nod and turned back to the flames.

Garr stood and snatched up the remaining meat. Myn released a heavy breath and turned away, then turned back at the sound of the meal dropping to the ground at her feet. She looked quickly upward and cast a measuring look at Garr as he stood looking down at her. Finally she stretched her neck until their noses nearly touched and flicked her tongue across his snout before accepting the gift.

"Well," Myranda whispered to Deacon, "at least some of us are starting to get along."

#

A wet, dismal snow had begun to fall in Kenvard as Ivy and her guest continued northward. Strangely, awful weather like this always made Ivy happy. Perhaps it was because she was more often than not warm, dry, and safe. Wretched weather outside reminded her of how wonderful it was to be so. The pleasant state of mind brought by the dismal weather was pushed far to the back of her mind, however, as it had produced some unpleasant side effects. The weather made the roads treacherous and put them far behind schedule. It was deep in the night before Ivy and Ambassador Krettis approached what would be their shelter. The lengthy journey had been enough to take the fight out of both of them, which was a welcome relief for the malthrope. Her many spats with Ether had been nothing compared to the venom Krettis could sling when she had a mind to, though the ambassador took care to make most of her aggression passive, and all of it political. Thanks to their agreement to speak their minds, Krettis had done little to veil her theories of deception regarding the D'Karon.

"I must say, any people who could thrive in the face of weather like this are worthy of *some* praise," Krettis said.

"This is nothing. I've seen storms that left us knee deep in snow after just a few hours," Ivy said, looking out the window at the dim lights of the approaching city.

"You seem distracted," Krettis said.

"I'm excited… and a little nervous," Ivy said.

"Why?"

"I've never been to Strom. I'm not always well received the first time I come to a new town."

"I imagine in this case you'll be seen as the lesser of two evils. A delegation of Tressons will surely draw more scorn than you."

"You're talking to a malthrope, remember. Not everyone has gotten the message that we aren't to be killed on sight anymore. And in this case I'm not just a malthrope. I'm a malthrope who *brought* a bunch of Tressons to their town."

They rolled into town, and guards climbed down from one of the other carriages, approaching the doors of the primary carriage to escort the delegation to the small inn that would host them for the night. The cold snow had done them the favor of keeping the people off the streets, at least initially. A procession of luxurious carriages entering a town peopled mostly by port workers, fishermen, and salt-rakers was a curious enough sight to coax a small crowd out to watch from the shelter of their eaves.

"Let me disembark first," Celeste said. "I'll try to keep order."

Ivy sighed shakily. "It'll be fine. I've been through this a bunch of times."

Celeste stepped into the horrid weather and assessed the crowd.

"I don't understand," Krettis said, pulling a thick rain cloak over her outfit. "You are a Guardian of the Realm. Surely despite your species you would be revered."

"When people tell stories, they tend to leave out the parts they don't like. They don't always remember that there was a dragon or malthropes or shapeshifters involved." Ivy donned a thinner shawl and slipped a wide-brimmed hat over her ears. "One of these days I'll have to have someone tell that version to me. I'm curious who they replace, and how. Plus, most people are slow to accept that the five generals were evil. It's caused some confusion, and when people are confused they don't always embrace newcomers like me."

Celeste motioned for Ivy and the others to follow. One by one they stepped out into the streets. Through the impatient shuffling of the carriage horses, the sloppy trudge of a dozen boots, and the steady plop and patter of snow Ivy knew that the humans in her group couldn't hear the reaction of the crowd, but *she* could. Even with her ears squished beneath her rain hat, she could hear the distant conversations hush, then the voices turn harsh with whispers. And one didn't need her acute hearing to see scattered faces scowl in the light of their lanterns. Her heart dropped a bit.

"Could you please grab the two cases under my seat in the carriage?" Ivy called to one of the servants unloading the bags for them. "I think I'm going to need them."

Ambassador Krettis was by her side. Ivy cast a look to the crowd and tried to judge their gaze.

"Well… good news for you. I think they're more upset about me than they are about you." She sighed. "You might want to walk a few steps farther back."

"Why?" Krettis asked.

Ivy moved suddenly, pivoting around behind the ambassador and snatching something from the air. It was a stone.

"They don't always have very good aim," Ivy said.

Two guards descended angrily upon the man who threw the stone, but Ivy called out to them.

"Leave him be. It didn't do any harm," Ivy said.

The guards were less forgiving, barking reprimands and threats as the delegation continued forward along the packed gravel streets.

"How did you know to catch the stone?" Krettis asked.

"You start to learn what to listen for after you've been hit a few times," Ivy said, disappointment in her voice. "It's been a few weeks since I had to do that."

The city was one of the larger along the Kenvard coast. This far north it had never been struck by direct Tresson attack, though as the war had worn on it had seen its strongest citizens lost to battle. That left the place with barely half the population one would expect for a city of its size. Most houses on the main street were stout, comfortable homes, but peering down the side streets into the darkness of the night revealed more than a few homes left empty for years. Some had begun to succumb to the elements.

Celeste led the way into the inn. Not nearly as grand as the one in Highpoint, it was nonetheless warm and dry, which was a curse and a blessing. It was certainly a welcome respite from the weather, but for those members of the populace without proper heat in their homes it was a nightly gathering place. Ideally the keepers would have cleared it in preparation of the diplomatic procession as they had elsewhere. On a night such as this it would have been cruel to turn the people away, and an enterprising innkeeper is disinclined to turn away eager customers on the best of nights. There was room enough for the guards, servants, diplomats, and drivers, but only just. The inn would be packed to capacity, and the Tressons would be rubbing elbows with the locals.

All eyes turned to the newcomers as slush was stomped from boots and wet coats were taken by the staff. Some looked at the malthrope and the dark-skinned strangers with curiosity. Most looked with distrust or distaste. Celeste shared some words with a well-dressed man near the doorway, then addressed the others.

"This man is the operator of the saltern. He has assured us that tomorrow morning, when the weather has improved, he will provide the promised tour. I recommend we take our meal and retire early," he said.

"I've been cooped up in that carriage all day," Ivy said, taking off her hat and flicking her ears. "I need to do something to get the blood flowing a bit, or dinner will never sit right, and I surely won't sleep."

"What did you have in mind?" he asked warily.

"Who has the cases I asked for? Ah! There! Give them here!" She turned to Celeste. "I smell good, fresh bread. Make sure to save some for me. And a nice warm glass of cider for after."

She grabbed both of her cases and gracefully navigated the obstacle course of tables and bodies, working toward the large, warm fireplace that was inevitably the focus of any inn in the north.

"Attention!" Ivy called out.

The rare eye that hadn't been turned in her direction now darted to her. Fifty or more people inhabited the establishment, many well on their way to deep inebriation, and none of them seemed happy. Ivy swept her eyes across the crowd and saw everything from fear to fascination.

"People of Strom, I thank you for your hospitality. For those of you who do not know, my name is Ivy. Some call me Guardian of the Realm, and there are other titles that have been layered on top of that, but I want you all to call me Ivy. Today we are joined by our friends from the south. And they *are* our friends. I want you to treat them as such. I can see that some of you aren't thrilled about what's going on right now. Probably I'm the first malthrope you've ever seen, and those are the first Tressons you've seen in a time of peace. I know that most of you don't know what to make of us. Well, if there's one thing I've learned since this all started, it is that things get a lot easier once you know a bit more about each other. I've been telling Ambassador Krettis and her people all about us, so now I'd like to share a bit of them with you."

Voices were beginning to rise, most gruff, and rude words were beginning to flow. Ivy tried to ignore them, stepping onto a spare chair to get her head up above the crowd. She dropped a case onto the mantle.

"If you learn one thing about me, let it be that I *love* art. Art of all sorts. That's why I made certain I got my hands on this before Krettis and her people arrived. It is a work of art, and the best kind, because it helps to create *other* things of beauty."

She unfastened the clasp and opened the case, retrieving the contents. The crowd hushed a bit as she revealed a curious and attractively made instrument. It was stringed, but larger than a fiddle, rounder in the body and longer.

"This is called a lute. It is the official instrument of Tressor. It wasn't easy, but I was able to learn a little something of theirs, and I will play it for you now. I hope I can do it justice."

Ivy was already having to raise her voice to be heard and didn't dare put off the performance any longer. She slipped her hands from her gloves and began to pluck the strings of the instrument with her claws. At first the unruliness of the crowd completely drowned out the soft, tinkling tone of the strings, but like a slow wave rolling out from her, the crowd began to silence.

The song she played began as a simple one, the tempo slow and the notes distinct. As the notes penetrated into the crowd, her playing deepened. More notes joined in, complex chords and rolling scales. Her fingers danced flawlessly across the strings. Her face wore a look of concentration. The song grew faster, and the audience's attention solidified. As the tempo and complexity of the tune both built, the spirit of the song subtly changed. Whereas it had begun almost solemnly, it was growing more vigorous, more jubilant.

Another change came about as well. As her playing became more confident, and her audience more enraptured, Ivy's face brightened, a deep spiritual bliss coming over her. The sounds coming from her instrument didn't seem as though they could possibly be coming from a single player. When she wasn't strumming or plucking, she was thumping and drumming at the body of the instrument. Her foot kept a steady rhythm, tapping on the chair. And then there was the glow. It was dim at first, barely noticeable, but as the audience began to forget where the music was coming from and instead embraced it, the golden aura began to become more apparent. It was pure, triumphant joy. Bone deep and utterly infectious. By the time the song rolled toward its crescendo, the clientele and staff alike were enraptured by the music.

A furious flourish of notes threatened to shake the instrument apart, Ivy's claws at times plucking all strings at once. Then, like a wave crashing against the shore, it was over. The silence of the audience was complete, such that the buzzing of the strings was all that remained. When it, too, dropped away, the crowd erupted into applause. Ivy jumped down and thanked the crowd—shaking hands, getting slapped on the back, and nodding her way through compliments until she reached her table.

"Yes! Thank you! It was my pleasure, really. I'm glad you liked it. Certainly I'll play more. I've got a fiddle, so if you've got any local favorites, I'll do my best. Just have to get something in my stomach." She looked at her table. "I hope I did okay with it, Ambassador… Ambassador?" Ivy said.

Krettis had her hands over her mouth, her eyes wet with tears.

"Is something wrong?" Ivy asked.

"I've… I've never heard it played so beautifully," she uttered, moved almost beyond words. "That was… oh, how is it translated? 'The Ascension to the Stars.' It was played at my wedding."

"It was? Well, I'm so pleased you enjoyed it."

"How did you learn to play it? And alone? The song is meant for three."

"I'm not much of an ambassador, I know that. But art, any sort of art, comes to me like breathing."

"What was that light that surrounded you?"

"It's complicated. That's what happens when I'm truly happy. Other emotions have different effects. I try to keep them down, but joy is one I can share."

"I've never seen anyone win over a hostile group so easily."

Ivy took a seat and tore herself some bread.

"I didn't win them over. Maybe one or two of them, but those were the ones who weren't really against me, they just didn't know what to do with me. What I did mostly was distract them, entertain them. They thought I was a wild animal before. Now they think I'm a trained animal. It isn't much, but if it helps us get through the night without anger and hate, that's enough. First I convince people I'm not a menace. After that I can start working on being equal."

Krettis wiped some of her tears away. "You may one day make a better diplomat than you realize."

Chapter 5

Myranda awoke just before dawn to the familiar feeling of a dragon's paws folded over her and Deacon sleeping by her side. Myn had barely made it through the meal the previous night before scooping Myranda and Deacon close and dropping off to sleep. Sleeping clutched to the chest of an overprotective dragon might not have been the most regal way to spend a night, but for Myranda it brought back some of the only pleasant memories of her time battling the D'Karon. She tried to ease herself from Myn's grip without waking her, but the dragon pulled herself groggily to her feet only a few moments after Myranda did, rousing Deacon in the process.

The air was already warming with the rising sun. With a river beside her and a climate that wouldn't make such a thing a death sentence, Myranda had the rare luxury of at least a cursory bath while traveling, something that had been all too infrequent when living off the land in the frigid north. Myn stood guard, her extended wings offering a degree of privacy, then reluctantly offered the same favor to Deacon.

Grustim, in an act Myranda could scarcely conceive of becoming accustomed to, had slept silently in the same position he'd flown, lying on his dragon's back. Through the whole of the morning ablutions he'd remained asleep, though Garr woke shortly after Myn did and observed the morning routine, motionless. The Rider didn't awake until Myn gave the remnants of the previous night's fire a huff of breath to reignite it, and Myranda put the set-aside portion of the previous night's meal over it to warm.

"Good morning," Myranda said. "Will you be having some before we leave?"

"Yes," Grustim said. He stifled a yawn. "I… didn't expect to be able to sleep so soundly."

"Why not?" Deacon asked.

"Garr seldom allows it when other humans are about. He becomes watchful of them, over-aware of them. Distrustful."

"Well I'm pleased that he does not feel distrustful of us," Myranda said. "Myn is the same way, but I think last night she was simply too exhausted to do anything but sleep."

"Perhaps it was the presence of other dragons. Or perhaps Garr has judged us to be of trustworthy character. Solomon was always a quick and very accurate judge of character," Deacon suggested.

"Perhaps… Listen. When we've eaten and resupplied our stock of water, we will set off. Based on Myn's performance yesterday, if she can follow without attempting to pass, I think we can set a swifter pace today. We may be able to reach our destination in four more days, perhaps a bit less."

"Do you hear that, Myn?" Myranda asked. "Stay close, but let Garr and Grustim lead the way. This is important."

Myn straightened up and padded over to the wizards, looking steadily at her Tresson counterpart. The air of challenge and rivalry between them seemed to have faded quite a bit. Whereas previously there had always been tension in their gaze when they regarded one another, each seemed far more at ease with the other now.

The meal went quickly, and less than an hour later they were in the air. Fields and towns swept by quickly below them. At first it seemed that Myn was up to her previous antics, as she seemed unwilling to trail behind Garr, but once she was able to maneuver beside him, she fell into a steady, swift rhythm. Though they were moving nearly as fast as the day before, the lack of unnecessary jockeying and general misbehavior made it far less taxing on both dragons. This permitted Myranda and Deacon to enjoy the journey a bit more. More importantly, it let them discuss matters.

"I'm concerned, Deacon," Myranda said, calling over the sound of rushing wind.

"Many things of late are worthy of concern. What specifically is troubling you?" Deacon replied.

"Even if we were to reach the site of the attack this evening, weeks have still passed since it happened. A trail that is even a few hours old is difficult to follow. And we don't have much time to get new information to Valaamus."

"Perhaps, but we may well find evidence, or witnesses, who can tell us what we need to know, and if not, we are no strangers to tracking the D'Karon. If the D'Karon are there to be found, we shall find them."

"And if they aren't? It is one thing to find something quickly, but how does one prove quickly that there is nothing to find?"

"The truth will be revealed in time," Deacon said.

"But time is something we don't have. If war begins again…"

"It is a pity we've not yet heard from Valaamus regarding… wait… one moment." Deacon carefully loosened his grip with one hand and rummaged through his bag. "We've been so distracted, it strikes me I've not had a moment to check our pad. It's been tightly closed in the bag; if it were to receive a message the stylus wouldn't be able to move to alert us."

He unearthed the pad in question. The very moment it was free of the confines of the pack it snapped open, nearly flipping itself from his grip. The stylus then swiftly traced out a series of messages, most minor notes from Ivy and of little consequence. Buried among them, however, was a message from Valaamus.

"'You may use passive magic sparingly, but only to track. Genuine evidence must be found to allay our concerns,'" Deacon read aloud. He cleared his throat. "The message looks to have been written some time ago. It seems the pad is not without its shortcomings. Perhaps…"

"Later, Deacon. Let us… oh heavens…"

She felt a chill rush through her. Though this far into Tressor the air was growing almost uncomfortably warm for those accustomed to the north, here among the clouds it was still brisk. The shiver that shook the young wizard had nothing to do with the cool breeze, however. She'd only just begun to open her mind, to allow the flow of magic around her to instead flow through her. And what it brought was something she'd simultaneously hoped for and dreaded.

"Deacon…" she said.

"I know… I feel it too. D'Karon magic. Freshly worked… not more than a day ago," Deacon said. "Portals…" He shut his eyes. "One entrance point… two exits…"

Without opening his eyes he began to rummage through his bag, pulling out a thick leather tome and flipping it open. The whipping wind tore at the pages, fluttering them wildly. He sliced the air with his hand, and it parted around him. His book calmed, and he willed a stylus into his fingers, blindly scribbling notes and tracing shapes.

"Grustim!" Myranda called out over the howling wind. "Grustim! We need to talk. It is very important!"

Her voice couldn't cut through the howling of the wind. She shut her eyes briefly and reached out with her mind to the gem of her staff, focusing her will through it and weaving it into the air around them. Like a hot iron dragged across some wrinkled linen, her mind smoothed away the flutters and whirls of the wind around them, quieting the howl such that it fell into near silence.

"Grustim!" she called again.

"You were not to work your magics within our land, Madam Duchess," he called gruffly.

"At this moment I believe the others who are working magics within your land are the greater concern. Deacon and I are certain a D'Karon spell has been cast. If there *are* D'Karon within your borders, they must be found and stopped immediately," she said.

"Through what means have you determined this?" he said sternly.

"We can discuss that later, but please believe me that there can be no doubt."

"He, she, or they are no longer within your borders… at least, not *solely* within your borders," Deacon said, eyes still shut and the formerly blank page now virtually black with his hasty notes. "D'Karon magic has created two portals, and there have been two incursions into the Northern Alliance. I am still determining their exits, but one is certainly in the Kenvard region, and the other certainly in the Vulcrest region."

"We *need* to land and plot a course to wherever these portals originated," Myranda said.

"I'll have it for you momentarily," Deacon said.

"It would not be wise to land now. We are passing over the Mistraal. Many people call this place their home. It may be difficult to find a place where we will not be seen."

"I cannot impress upon you how important it is to act quickly. These portals are not gentle spells, and they are unmistakably D'Karon. If there was anyone nearby when the spell was completed, I assure you, they are hurt."

"How can you be certain this is a D'Karon spell?" Grustim asked. "We have powerful sorcerers within our land. You could simply be feeling some of their workings, could you not?"

"Grustim, we have nearly lost our lives to the D'Karon too many times. We are intimately aware of the texture of their magics."

"And this spell could only have been cast by a person who had been steeped in D'Karon teachings," Deacon said. "With the defeat or departure of the D'Karon we knew of, it is fair to say that *I* am at least *one* of the foremost experts in their teachings. Or so I'd believed until now. Though I have tried, I haven't been able to master one of these spells accurately enough to cast it, but this wizard has done so twice. This spell is rougher than those cast by the D'Karon, but functionally complete in a way that I have never been able to achieve. This is the result of guided instruction, I know it. And I can only hope that we are facing a group because, if this is an individual, we are dealing with someone of frightening focus and power."

"This is the very threat your military summoned us to help locate. We must waste no more time," Myranda urged. "The nature of this spell allows the D'Karon to travel from place to place instantaneously. If they truly have access to this level of mysticism, it will take more than me and Deacon to track them."

"You realize that if you are as certain as you seem to be that we are facing a trained D'Karon, you have as much as confirmed that an act of war has been committed against our people," Grustim said.

"Grustim, if there must be war, there must be war. But in this moment, there may be people here and in our homeland who need our help. If you feel the need to take us prisoner after this, so be it, we will go willingly. This *must* be dealt with *now*."

Grustim rode his beast in silence for a moment.

"Very well," he said. "You will follow me closely. You will land where I land. If any Tresson people approach, you will not engage or interact with them. When you have made your determination of where you believe this spell to have been cast, we will change our destination at my discretion. Now, follow."

114

And cease your spell craft. I cannot be expected to fly properly without the wind in my ears!"

Myranda released her will, and howling wind washed away their hearing. Grustim leaned low, and not long after, Garr cut his wings and dove toward a stand of trees a short distance from a road. Myn followed suit, keeping near enough to Garr to nearly touch him. Myranda was no stranger to flight on a dragon's back, and Myn was quite a skillful flier, but when it came to the union of human and dragon working as one, Garr and Grustim were truly on another level. It genuinely appeared that every shift and lean Grustim made was done to help Garr slice through the air more effectively. Truly the two were better, more precise, and more maneuverable together than they were apart. They were effectively a single being.

Nowhere was this more apparent than when they were landing. Grustim practically stood on Garr's back as they neared they ground, setting his feet wide and rocking side to side as Garr honed his angle between the trees. When the beast touched down, Grustim absorbed the shock with a roll of his legs, keeping him comfortably atop Garr despite a landing that brought him from flight to a standstill in little more than a step. It would have been simple enough to dismiss the act as taking an opportunity to show off, but in this case it was necessary. They'd chosen a clearing barely large enough for a dragon to slip through the canopy, let alone for it to slow itself to a stop in the traditional way.

Myn attempted to imitate the feat. With two riders, each untrained, even if she'd been flawless in her execution, it would have been problematic. She was far from flawless. The result was a somewhat graceless stutter step and skidding grind that nearly caused the dragon to fall to her side. Myranda held tight and managed to remain seated. Deacon, still consumed by the task of identifying the three points of magic that lingered in his mind's eye, was not so lucky. He was sent tumbling from her back and rolled across the ground into a bush. In a less dire circumstance, Myranda would have had to stifle a laugh. As it was she simply hopped down and helped him to his feet.

"Are you all right?" she asked.

Myn swung her head around, breath still heaving from the effort of flying, and looked Deacon up and down, flicking her tongue at a raw patch on his cheek where his face had met the ground.

"Yes. Yes, I'm fine," he said, ignoring the trickle of blood from the scrape in favor of collecting his notes and stylus and swiftly mending any tears in the pages.

Myranda stroked her hand across his cheek, wiping away the injury as effortlessly as one might brush away some dust. She looked to their escort.

Grustim was still atop Garr, having stepped up the stout dragon's neck to the top of his head, and rumbled a command. Garr craned his neck, allowing his Rider to rise up above the cover of the trees to scan the horizon.

"Listen closely," he called down, "we have certainly been seen. A Dragon Rider so far south is a rare sight. No one seems to be coming yet, but the locals will be concerned and will likely investigate. Whatever needs to be done needs to be done before they arrive."

"Yes, yes. I agree entirely," Deacon said with the frazzled tone of someone frantically attempting to hang tight to the last lingering details of a fast-fading dream.

He held a book out before him and then took both hands away from it, leaving it to drift before him while he sought out a second from his bag and pulled it open. As he riffled the pages, first countless volumes of notes swept past, then sketches of every shape and size. Finally maps fluttered by. He slapped a hand down on a rather crude rendering of the land of Tressor.

The map, though occupying both pages of the book, was rather sparsely labeled. The mountains, forests, and other features of the land were rendered in very broad strokes, and the names of rivers and cities were largely absent. Only the regions nearest to the northern border had any real detail. It was clearly a map drawn up by a military with little recent knowledge of their enemy.

"Grustim, where precisely are we?" Deacon said, stepping quickly to Garr's feet. "Can you show me on this map?"

When he drew near, Garr released a rattling warning within his throat, tensing his muscles and digging his claws into the earth. Almost in reflex Myn released a rumble of her own, casting a sharp look at her counterpart and taking a protective step toward Deacon.

Grustim slid down and placed a calming hand on the neck of his mount. "How can you claim to know where this spell was cast if you do not know where you are?"

"I know how far it is from here, and in what direction," Deacon said.

The Dragon Rider gazed down at the map. "This is pitiful."

"We've not been able to get a more recent map of your land yet."

"Let me see it."

He ran his gauntleted finger across the rough page, tracing the edge of a river, then drawing it eastward. "Here. This is where we are."

Deacon nodded and marked the map, then dug into his bag and came up with his egg-shaped casting stone. A blue-white glow was conjured from within, and the black lines of the page began to glow a brilliant amber. They traced themselves beyond the pages of the book, weaving and painting themselves out into the air to fill out the more familiar mountains and plains of the land to the north. The map continued to weave itself in light, until as near an accurate depiction of a full map of the continent as he could manage hung before them. When he was through crafting the illustrative illusion, he closed the book and stowed it, leaving only the conjured image.

"I am quite certain of the distances and directions. These points are the positions of the portals." As he spoke, he dabbed the tip of his stylus in the air above the map, leaving two points of green light and one point of red. "Red is the entrance, green are the exits." He added a final white point, nearer to the red one. "And this is where we are."

He shifted his hand and the points dropped down onto the map, the white one aligning with the position Grustim had indicated.

"If this spell was the same sort that the D'Karon had cast, then they cannot simply exit anywhere," Myranda said, looking over the map. "They would probably have traveled to one of the major D'Karon strongholds."

"It seems likely. Here..." Deacon pointed. "This point is quite near one of the forts Ether cleared." He stirred his fingers, causing the points of light to shift until the nearest of them rested upon the location of the stronghold. "With those points known, then this other exit..." His eyes widened.

The point was resting squarely upon Castle Verril.

"We've got to get a message to them," Deacon said.

"You left one of your pads in the capital, didn't you?" Myranda said.

"Yes! Yes of course," he said, scrambling for his bag.

"No. I'll handle it. Work with Grustim. Find out where these portals originated," Myranda said.

She reached into his bag and came up with the pad. Deacon turned to Grustim.

"Grustim, here. This red point. Is there anything sensitive or distinct there? Anyone who might need help or who might have something of mystical value? The D'Karon value nothing more than mana. They harvest it in any way they can."

Grustim looked over the conjured map. For the first time since they had met him, his face hinted at something more than disinterest and contempt. The wonder of gazing at a precisely rendered map hanging in the air was not lost on him.

"This would be near the northern edge of the desert. Not more than a day from here. Well north of our intended destination." He gazed at what few landmarks were present on the near regions of the map. "A small military prison and training barracks may be there."

"Better that than a village. We need to get there as soon as possible. People could be badly hurt. Even if the D'Karon did not become hostile, the portal closing at the origin point can be terribly destructive."

"Can you offer me any evidence of what you say?"

"If you will take us to this prison..."

"No. I am your escort. My task was to protect you from my people, and to protect my people from you until such a time as you had determined if the threat to our land was indeed the D'Karon. My superiors have left it to my discretion where and how you are to be taken for the purpose of your investigation. If you are truly certain that it was the D'Karon, then by rights your purpose in our land is fulfilled. You have through your own methods determined that a group of warriors allied with your kingdom has unleashed weapons upon our land. That is an act of war. If I were truly permitted to act upon my best judgment, I would take each of you as prisoners of war."

Myn thumped her tail against the ground and huffed a searing breath through her nose, challenging Grustim to attempt such a thing. Garr adopted a similar posture, going so far as to hiss actual flame through the nostrils of his helmet.

Grustim grunted an order and Garr hissed again, now flameless.

"I am not eager to clash with you. Your beast is clearly devoted to you, and your mystic capacity is evident. And if blood is to once again be spilled on the field of battle, I do not wish to be the first to put blade to flesh. I will continue my mission as assigned for as long as is reasonable. But what you are asking is that I take you to a facility that we utilize to train our soldiers. Given your frightening capacity to observe, and to make much of very little information, that would give you an incredible opportunity to attain extremely sensitive information. Unless I can be given a compelling reason to change our course beyond your intuition, you will not see this place. I shall take you to a place which I know to be the beginning of a trail, however cold it may be, and we will follow it through means I can verify."

"Grustim, the proof is mystic in nature. It is evident to us and would be evident to you as well if you had the expertise to detect it. We were summoned to this task precisely because of this expertise. If you cannot take our word on this issue... what would convince you?"

"Show me a boot print. Show me a drop of blood, a scrap of writing. Show me something I can see, that I can touch. Give me something to trust besides your word."

"My word and my thoughts are all that I have. Why is that not enough for you?"

Grustim's voice became more rigid, his expression held firm only through extreme discipline. "Because your people have been killing mine, and mine have been killing yours, for longer than either of us have been alive. A dragon sheds its skin. At times it is dull and hard. At times it is shiny and soft. But it is born with its teeth and it dies with them. It will always be ready to blacken you, tear you, devour you if you fail to treat it with the proper respect for even a moment. A centuries-long distrust is not repaired in six months of diplomacy. Trust is earned, and you've done nothing to earn mine."

Myranda handed the open pad to Deacon, her message scrawled upon the page, and finally raised her voice. "What if you do it without us?"

"I do not understand."

"See to the facility without bringing us along."

"That would require you to be left unattended while I was doing so, an even greater abandonment of my duties."

"Then what if you contacted anyone else? Send someone in your stead. What we know is that someone with D'Karon teachings was in that place, whatever that place might be, and that one or more of them left that place for our own kingdom. We have sent word to all of the keepers of these pads, warning them of the consequences, and that includes your superiors and mine. At any moment, this pad could provide us with fresh orders—"

"Orders that I have no way of knowing are genuine," Grustim said.

"Granted, but our people will be sending anyone they can spare to contain the threat that may have arisen within our borders. Please do not let something as simple as lingering distrust rob your own people of help they might badly need. I give you my word, we will do anything in our power, follow any order, grant any request if it will make you comfortable enough to see to your people now."

"Our people can see to ourselves. We have fought D'Karon for the duration of this war."

"Not like these," Deacon said. "You have fought nearmen, cloaks, and dragoyles. Even the spell casters they deploy do not approach the level of prowess that fueled the spells we have detected. I have only known the generals to cast spells such as these. The generals *created* and *fueled* the D'Karon you faced. They manufactured the army that held you at bay for all of these years. And they did it all while keeping control of the entire Northern Alliance."

"The generals manipulated my people," Myranda said. "They robbed me of my home. Every drop of blood is on their hands, and I would rather see myself shackled and locked away in your land than see another life taken by them if I could stop it."

Grustim measured Deacon and Myranda, each looking back with sincerity and urgency. In Deacon's hand, the message was still visible on the page of the pad. *D'Karon portal opened to the south. Exits in Castle Verril and coastal Demont fortress. Take immediate action.*

As he held it, the stylus pulled itself from his hand and rattled the bell tied to its tether, then scrawled in a sweeping and elegant hand: *I am close to Demont's fort. I'll go there right away. - IV*

A moment later a more precise and formal lettering read: *Acknowledged. Capital watch is on high alert. - CL*

And after that, this time in the careful hand of a non-native writer, simply one word: *Investigate.*

When Deacon was through reading, he looked up to find Myranda still looking Grustim in the eye.

"Everyone else knows the danger, Grustim. I leave it in your hands because I must. I implore you. Do what is right for your people."

The Dragon Rider again measured the others. Just as had been the case during the landing, and during the flight, and during every step along the way, Grustim's connection to his dragon was more than evident. A dragon was a remarkable beast. In one glance it looked upon others with the eye of a predator, puzzling out weakness and intention with instinctive precision honed by the simple fact that it was too often the difference between life and death. In the next glance, there was the wisdom and clarity that would be the envy of the finest thinkers in the kingdom. In this moment, Grustim seemed to have the same qualities to his gaze.

His eyes flitted to the map, still hanging crisply in the air.

"You would have me believe that some calamity has happened here," he said, pointing to the red mark. "And I was intended to deliver you here." He pointed to a location farther south and west. "It will take us a day to reach the prison, and doing so will take us half a day off course. We've gained more than that much back through young Myn's dedication. We shall pass over the place. If I see evidence of what you say, we shall act. But not before."

"Then let us not waste a single moment," Myranda said, climbing to Myn's back.

Deacon dispelled the map and joined her. Garr took two strong strides and leaped into the air. Half a heartbeat later Myn was beside him.

\#

At the same moment, in a carriage far to the north, Ivy carefully closed the pad and stowed it.

"I'm really very sorry about this," she said, her motions suddenly stiff and her eyes darting. "I... there's something happening. There's something... I can't..." She took a steadying breath. "I have to leave you at the nearest town. I'm sure Ambassador Celeste will do a far better job of continuing the tour..."

"What is happening?" asked Krettis.

"There's a... the D'Karon have this way of moving from here to there. Only they know how to do it. They can go from anywhere to one of their strongholds like *that*," she said, snapping her fingers. "And Myranda says it just happened, and not so far from here. I *need* to find out what's happening and what I can do about it."

"So you will be visiting a D'Karon stronghold?"

"I must, I really must. I'm sorry, but as I said—"

"I shall join you," Krettis said.

"Join? No. No, no, no."

"I must strongly advise against it, Madam Ambassador," Greydon said.

"I said I shall join you, and so I intend to," Krettis affirmed.

"You can't. You don't understand, the D'Karon—" Ivy stammered.

"Oh, I understand perfectly. As *charming* as you've made yourself, as *harmless* as you've made pains to illustrate yourself to be, you've clearly done everything you can to keep me from seeing any hint of the legacy of war that we both know has *stained* your land and mine. And, in a moment when you have not only the opportunity but the obligation to visit a piece of this legacy, you are scrambling to leave me behind. You want to ensure that this mask you've crafted for yourselves as a nation remains firmly in place, even if it means abandoning the very act of diplomacy devised to maintain it."

Ivy tightened her fists for a moment before she noticed and eased them loose again. "It isn't that. It is the danger. You could be badly hurt or killed if this is one of the D'Karon. Have you been *listening* to me as I described their atrocities?"

"I have. I've also been listening as you insisted that all that could be done to wipe them away *had* been done. So there should be no danger at all."

"Clearly we missed some! Who knows what we'll find up there!"

"You have your guards, I have mine, and I have been told you are a warrior of historic renown, something that must be so or you would not be risking yourself. Surely if there is a D'Karon or a similar threat, you will be capable of defending me and my guard until we are able to withdraw. And if there is no D'Karon, we shall finally have an opportunity to look into the workings of the machine of war you insist they have created without your will or desire. Or will I be sent home to my people with the sorry news that the Northern Alliance still has too much to hide to truly open their doors to the Tresson people?"

One of Ivy's eyelids twitched, then both of her eyes narrowed. "*Fine*," she said. The ear nearest to Celeste twisted toward him as he muttered instructions, but the malthrope ignored them. "I'll be taking Mr. Celeste, the carriage man, and three of our guards. Select an equal number of representatives, either on their own horses or to ride in this carriage, and we'll go. But we're going in just a few minutes, so act fast."

"Excellent," Krettis said.

Ivy thumped at the roof of the carriage. "Stop here, Lennis. We've got an emergency!"

The carriage lurched to a stop. As soon as it was stationary, Marraata, the attendant and record keeper, looked nervously to the ambassador. She braced herself for the stiff wind outside as Krettis opened her door and the pair stepped out. Ivy and Celeste slipped out the other side.

Their journey had taken them quite near the coast. They were riding along a carefully maintained road that traced along the spine of a strip of elevated land. It gave them a remarkable view of the local region. To one side, barely visible on the horizon and gleaming with the amber glow of the approaching sunset, was the Western Sea. To the other was a handful of sprawling icy fields, some frost-dusted clumps of gray-green trees, and the hint of mountains beginning to rise in the distance. Not far ahead and below was the huddled little nook of a town that would have hosted them for the evening.

"Okay, listen up!" Ivy bellowed, climbing up the wheel of the carriage until she was nearly level with the driver. "There has been a change of plans.

Most of the delegation will be continuing on to the next stop and staying there for a few days. I've never been there, but I'm told it is really a lovely place. I'm sure the Tressons will learn plenty. The rest of us need to take a side trip." She turned to the mounted soldiers who had been leading the carriage. "I'll be taking you three, along with this carriage and a small group of Ambassador Krettis's choosing. With any luck we'll all be back safe and sound in about two days."

She hopped down and came face to disapproving face with Celeste.

"This is *not* wise," he said.

"You saw what Myranda wrote. And you heard what Krettis said," Ivy said. "Besides, maybe if she sees what sort of monsters they were, she'll finally understand that we've been telling the truth."

"And if she is hurt or killed, we will have in the eyes of Tressor assaulted a diplomat sent in the pursuit of peace."

"Mr. Celeste, I won't let what the D'Karon did once happen again. We're pretty far from the front up here. Some of these towns are as peaceful as any place in Kenvard has ever been. I don't want one of those horrid things bringing violence here. What's the point of preserving peace with the Tressons if we let the real villains run free?"

"You aren't properly outfitted for battle, Ivy," he said. "Leave this to the army."

"I'm doing it, Mr. Celeste. I'm Chosen. This is why I exist. I wasn't ready for battle when this all started and I still did what I had to do, and I've learned a lot since then."

He stepped closer and lowered his voice. "And what if you lose control?"

"I won't," she said sternly.

"As I understand it, that isn't necessarily something you can guarantee. It is one thing for the D'Karon to potentially hurt or kill the visiting Tressons. It is another if you do it yourself."

"This needs to be done. Nothing else matters," she hissed. "Now are you coming, or should I leave you to conduct the rest of the delegation?"

"I was to be your adviser. I cannot do that if I am not by your side," he said.

Ivy looked at Krettis, who had assembled the best of her personal guards and was climbing back into the carriage. "Then we are going. It is my job to fight the D'Karon. Your job is to lead and help the other guards, and you are going to protect the Tressons. If anything endangers them, do what you need to do, keep them safe from danger." She took a breath and lowered her voice. "And I mean *any* danger." She put a hand on his shoulder and looked him in the eye. "Do you understand?"

"I do."

"Good." She opened her door to the carriage again. "Now let's go."

#

Ether's diplomatic journey had not begun under the best of circumstances, but she'd at least made a cursory effort to fulfill her role at first. She was quite poor at it, and though she asked the questions of Ambassador Maka that she'd been instructed were proper in such a circumstance, she made no effort or claim to be interested in his responses. Likewise she would answer any question he asked, but her near ignorance of the people of the north and the things that mattered most to them led to dry, flavorless answers. Since their discussion of family and purpose, her engagement with the diplomatic proceedings had steadily declined. She withdrew and introspected, sometimes allowing hours to pass without even glancing at her guest. Maka took the unusual behavior with almost saintly patience, taking the opportunity to fill the carriage with stories of his land.

She turned her eyes to him as the words of his latest observation and musing began to wash over her. It was truly astounding to the shapeshifter how a creature with less than a century of life could have gathered so many tales, and further astounding that he seemed so eager to share them with a person he knew to be disinterested.

"Ah! A sleigh. You know that my granddaughter Maandaa does not believe such things exist?" Maka said, pulling aside the curtain on the carriage window to admire the rough but sturdy vehicle in the fields beside the road. "She is the daughter of my youngest, Talla. They live quite near the edge of the desert, if you remember. The little girl has never seen snow. I tell you, if there was a way that I could bring her a handful as a gift, it would be truly something to see her eyes when she touched it. Ah! Perhaps someday she may come to this place and see it for herself." His wizened face creased with a wide smile. "Reason enough to do our best to preserve the peace, yes?"

"I suppose," Ether said distantly. "We have arrived. I understand the intention of this visit is to hear a performance of a lengthy musical piece composed by one of my fellow Chosen."

"Splendid! It will be wonderful to take in some of the art of your kingdom. And this piece was written by a friend of yours?"

"An ally."

"Ah," Maka said, nodding. "But one who would call you *friend*."

"The composer is a creature named Ivy, and I feel quite certain she would not openly refer to me as a friend. Our relationship is one of mutual animosity."

He laughed as Ether opened the door and stepped down. When it was clear he was having trouble, she offered her hand to help him.

"The friend who does not like us, and who we do not like," Maka said, still chuckling. "We have a word for such a friend in my tribe. *Duuwuldeya.* Friendly enemy. They say every circle of friends has one that no one likes, and if you don't know the name of that friend, then it is you."

Gregol hurried over to the pair with the desperation of a parent trying to take a sharp knife from a child. If Ether had any particular pride in the assignment she'd been given, she would have been quite displeased with the blatant distrust Gregol had in her ability to avoid creating some sort of incident. As it was she was grateful at times to have the older ambassador take Maka's attention. With each passing moment Ether found herself craving solitude all the more. The petty matters of state were proving a frustrating interruption to a line of thinking that she couldn't seem to reach the end of.

Around her, the small cluster of servants and helpers that poured from within each town to both serve the delegation and separate it from the rest of the populace went to work. Ether knew this town in the same way she knew most others. It was a somewhat unremarkable feature of the landscape, no more notable or interesting to her than the mountains rising up beside it or the forests scattered around it. The streets were wider here than in other northern cities, and though most of the homes were squat cottages with sloped roofs and crackling fires within, one was notably different. It was taller than the others, and much larger. It could comfortably fit every last resident of the town within its almost circular walls, and no less than four chimneys were sending out streamers of smoke into the afternoon breeze. The roof sloped sharply up toward each chimney, giving an almost crown-like appearance to the structure that seemed overly artful even by mortal standards.

"Have you been told of the festivities this evening?" Gregol asked, while a pair of Northern servants collected bags from the carriage.

"Ambassador Ether says it will be a musical performance of—" Maka began happily.

The crash of a bag striking the ground interrupted him.

All heads turned to the source of the sound, and a few hasty swords were drawn. It was a woman, not much more than fifty years old but with the beaten, worn features of someone with a life that had taken far more from her than it had any right to. She was one of the local servants, a worker at the inn that would play host to the delegation that evening. The soldiers didn't descend upon her, suspecting it was simply the work of twisted fingers growing too old for the job of a porter, but something in her expression kept them on guard. Her face was utterly transfixed with an agonized look of disbelief and joy. She covered her mouth, and tears began to flow down her face.

The rest of the surrounding crowd was just beginning to return to their prior activities, the other porters closing in to gather the bags she had dropped, when she cried out.

"Emilia!"

She had only been a few steps away from the group, so when she rushed forward there was no one who could stop her before she reached Ether. The woman threw her arms around Ether's waist, practically sobbing the name over and over again.

Ether stiffened, her face twisted in something between disgust and irritation. She might have reacted the same if a host's pet had jumped onto her lap without permission.

Around her the guards weren't certain what to do. Each of the servants had been vigorously cleared prior to the arrival of the envoy. There was no explanation for this.

"Remove yourself…" Ether fumed.

Guards assigned to the envoy backed Maka away, then began to bark orders to the woman, but she paid them no heed.

"Emilia, it has been so many years!" she wept, her face buried in Ether's shoulder. "Why didn't you write to me? Why didn't you tell me you were coming? Will you be staying in our inn?"

"Unhand the ambassador," demanded the guards.

"She can't hear you. She's deaf," explained the younger of the two porters frantically.

A guard took her by the shoulders and pulled her aside, placing her head squarely in the woman's vision. "You must release the ambassador and step away."

"Ambassador!" she said, confusion mixing with her joy. She turned to Ether, backing away as she did. "Of course! When you told me you were doing something important, I never imagined it was this! Oh, Emilia, I'm so *proud* of you." She reached out her hands. "My own *daughter*, an ambassador!"

"Daughter?" said Maka, gently stepping past his handlers and placing a hand on Ether's shoulder. "Is this true? Is this your mother?"

There was certainly a resemblance. The older woman had much the same shape to her face, similar eyes, and where it lingered among the gray, they even had the same hair color. One could easily call it a family resemblance.

Ether looked to him briefly. "I do not have time for interruptions. I am certain we are needed inside."

"Emilia, write to me when you are through! You must have so much to tell me after all of these years!"

The shapeshifter sent a silent glance in the old woman's direction, then paced coldly forward and through the doors of the inn. Her supposed mother smiled through her tears and clutched her hands, positively glowing with pride and joy.

"I apologize for that interruption, Ambassador Maka," Gregol began. "I would be pleased to tell you anything you might like to know about—"

"In a moment, Ambassador Gregol," Maka said.

The elderly Tresson strutted after Ether with a spryness that seemed out of place for someone of his age. His handlers, not expecting the burst of speed, scrambled to catch up. He passed through the doors of the inn and sought out Ether.

Unlike many of the other inns that had sheltered the delegation, this one was very simple. Thick plank walls patched with a muddy plaster held out the wind while a smoky fire chased away the cold. The main room was cramped even when empty. With the delegation, who had likely taken every available room, it would be shoulder to shoulder.

Ether had already had a terse exchange with the innkeeper and was heading down a narrow hall to her room.

"Ambassador Ether, a moment of your time," Maka said, touching her to catch her attention.

She turned. Her face showed no semblance of any emotions that might have been associated with a reunion with an estranged mother.

"What is it, Ambassador Maka?"

"If you do not mind, I would like very much to know why that woman seemed to believe you were her daughter."

"She was mistaken."

"Granted that must be the case, but she seemed certain. And no one will deny the resemblance."

Ether's expression soured ever so slightly. "I suppose she believes me to be the woman I appear to be."

Maka furrowed his brow. "I do not understand."

"I appear human to you, and so it is natural to assume that I inherited this appearance from a progenitor. Such is not the case. I assumed this form when it became clear that my would-be allies were unwilling or unable to interact with me in my natural form. The woman who stands before you was a foe. I believe she was a member of the Alliance Army, and at the time I am quite certain she had been subverted by a being known as Epidime."

"So somewhere there is another woman who appears as you do?"

"No. She was killed as a result of our clash."

Maka's face became serious.

"Did *you* kill that woman's daughter?"

"It doesn't matter."

"Ether, to that woman, it matters. She believes you are her daughter. She believes her daughter is still alive. What you have given her is false hope. You have drawn up something she had buried deep, made raw a wound that had begun to heal."

"That is not my concern."

"Ambassador, I submit that it *is* your concern. At this moment, you are representing your people."

"These are not my people. These are merely the residents of the land that I most directly defended in my opposition to the D'Karon."

"Regardless, at this moment, you represent them. And to represent them, you must care about them. That woman's spirit is soaring about something that is not so. If you leave her today without setting her straight, she will live what

126

remains of her life believing not that her daughter had died in the line of duty, but that her daughter was alive and well but choosing to ignore her mother. It will be a life of torture and uncertainty. I lost a son many years ago. If I were to see him one day and he behaved as you did, and then he moved on and I never saw him again… I do not know that I would ever think of anything else but what I could have done to lose his love for me."

"What would you have me do? Tell her of her daughter's death? From what I've seen of mortals, that would crush her. Despite its inevitability from birth, none of you seem willing to accept death when it comes."

"What you do is for you to decide. I cannot make your decisions for you. I can advise you that this is a matter that should be handled with care and delicacy. You must be mindful of her feelings."

Ether scowled. "Emotion… Few things have complicated and muddled matters more than emotion."

Maka nodded. "At times it can cloud the mind, make matters more difficult. But at other times it is the only thing that can give us the strength to go on."

"Ambassadors?" called Gregol, his voice showcasing the truly impressive anxiety that could be conjured in him by something as simple as a break to the intended routine.

"In a moment," Maka called over his shoulder. He lowered his voice. "You have said that you have no family. This is a woman who believes you are her family. You have suffered a loss, and though she does not know it, so has she. This is a pain shared by you. Perhaps this is a time to explore that."

"I have diplomatic duties to see to."

"Gregol and Zuzanna would embrace the opportunity to take your place for the duration of a meal," Maka said.

"I see no value in this."

He placed a hand on her shoulder. "Consider it a favor to me then. An act of compromise between our nations."

With that, Maka turned to the other Northern ambassadors, his arms held wide.

"Ambassador Ether has a small matter to attend to. I wonder if perhaps each of you would care to take her place. I am certain you will be able replacements for the evening," he said.

"Wha—yes! Yes of course!" Gregol practically sang, an insulting level of relief in his expression as he learned that he would finally have the ear of the senior ambassador.

Ether was left standing in the hall, her expression flavored with a simmering anger. This was not a task she would ever have chosen for herself, but something about being stepped over, pushed aside, infuriated her. She tried to quell these emotions as she did with all others. This did little good. Sweeping away the anger did little more than uncover lingering feelings that had been haunting her for too long already. Uncertainty, despair, and a dozen other shifting and confounding feelings that made it a bit harder to turn her mind to the things that truly mattered each day. Perhaps it would be useful after all if there was something else to occupy her mind.

She stepped out into the cold and glanced about. The gathered crowd of locals and servants had largely dissipated. The only individual with an apparent link to the inn and its staff was a young stable boy tasked with finding room for a dozen horses in a stable built for six.

"You. Were you present when the delegation arrived?" Ether asked.

Her voice startled the boy, who looked at her and froze.

"Er… yes, ma'am. Oh! I mean madam. Or… Guardian?"

Ether flipped her fingers dismissively.

"Did you witness an older woman accost me upon stepping from the carriage?"

"You mean Celia?"

"I do not know her name, but as I was only accosted by one woman, I must assume you are correct."

"I saw her. You… you're her girl, right?"

Ether's expression hardened. "Where is that woman now?"

"I think they've got her around back. Washing linens."

The shapeshifter nodded and marched stiffly in the direction he indicated. It never ceased to amaze her how poorly these creatures handled interactions with their betters. Stumbling over matters of title. They were children, fools, the lot of them. Though Maka seemed to have gained some insight into his fellow humans in his years, Ether could not imagine what the man hoped she might gain through this interaction.

A damp, musty smell led her to a small shack behind the inn. At the top of one wall was an ice-encrusted vent belching steam. She pushed open the door to find a room filled with a thick, hanging fog. It was quite warm, and where the hot, moist air met the cold, it was exceedingly unpleasant, but a single thought was all it took for Ether to whisk away her sensitivity to such things.

The older woman—Celia, if the stable boy could be believed—was stirring an enormous cauldron over a roaring fire. The water was cloudy, and billowing off-white mounds of cloth floated in it. Similar clothes, mostly underthings and bed linens, were piled on two tables on the opposite side of the room, and beside the cauldron a line had been stretched. Washed linens hung from it, drops of water falling onto an angled plank below them and running back into the cauldron.

The old woman looked up to the source of the frigid breeze.

"Emilia!" she said. "Oh, come inside, child. You mustn't stand there in the cold! This damp air will be the death of you!"

"It is of little concern. My business here is brief," Ether said.

"Bah, nonsense! You may be an ambassador, but you're still my daughter. And there are some things that a mother always knows best."

The D'Karon Apprentice

She stepped forward and grasped Ether's hand, pulling at the shapeshifter. "Goodness heavens, Emilia, you're already cold as death."

Ether stepped forward and allowed the woman to shut the door. The instant the breeze was cut off, the woman began to fuss with the contents of the tables, trying to neaten the piles and cover the most glaringly soiled articles.

"Heavens, it is all such a mess. I wish you'd written, dear. I wish I'd known you were coming. I would have made some time to meet with you someplace nicer than a musty place like this. To think, entertaining an ambassador…"

"Madam," Ether interjected.

"My own daughter an *ambassador*. Was there a ceremony? There *must* have been! Oh, if only I would have been able to see it!"

Ether turned Celia to her. "*Madam!*"

"You mustn't call me *madam*, dear. I'm your mother." Celia gazed at her face and smiled, tears beginning to roll down her cheeks again. "Oh… oh, there I go again. Come here, dear."

She rushed forward and once again threw her arms around Ether.

"Madam, please," Ether said, firmly pushing the woman back. "I am not your daughter."

Celia cocked her head aside. "But of *course* you are my daughter. It may have been a lifetime since I last saw you, but I'd know my darling daughter anywhere."

"I appear to be your daughter, but I am not."

The woman gave Ether a curious look. She then reached up and brushed some of Ether's hair aside, revealing a small dark patch of skin just below the hairline at the back of her neck.

"If you aren't my daughter, then why have you got her birthmark?" she said, her tone playful.

"I have assumed her form. My name is Ether."

"Assumed her form? You're not speaking sense, child."

Ether could feel her patience waning.

"I am a shapeshifter, and I assumed your daughter's form to better interact with humans, who are not comfortable with my true forms."

Celia shook her head dismissively and picked up the paddle to return to the cauldron. "Don't play games with your mother, dear. Now I know you've got very important matters inside, and it means so much to me that you took the time to see me, so let's not dillydally. Tell me, how have you *been*?"

"Do not dismiss me, human," Ether fumed.

"Now really, Emelia, that is no way to talk to your mother."

"You are *not* my mother."

As she spoke, Ether abandoned her human form, shifting effortlessly to a roughly human shape composed of crystal clear water.

Celia stood stone still. She raised one hand to her mouth, and her breath caught in her throat. A spectrum of emotions came across her face. Shock, fear, and confusion gripped her features, but slowly she reached out a hand and touched it to what had, moments before, been the skin of a woman she believed to be her daughter.

The older woman's fingers touched Ether's cheek, sending a ripple across her face. When she pulled them away, a drop of water clung to them, running down her fingers. She watched in disbelief, then looked at Ether one last time before her legs suddenly refused to support her any longer.

In a wave of bluish light that swept over Ether's whole form in the blink of an eye, she shifted from water to ice and reached out with her now solid fingers to catch the woman under the arms.

"Are you satisfied?" Ether asked, her face crackling as she spoke.

"B-bring her back. Bring Emelia back," Celia said, her voice bordering on terror now as she steadied herself against a table.

Ether released Celia and shifted with somewhat less speed and somewhat more care to her human form again, ice shifting to flesh, bone, and cloth.

The old woman's breathing slowed. "Ether... you said your name was Ether..."

"I am pleased you are finally comprehending."

"The... Guardian of the Realm?"

"Yes."

"I... I'm honored to meet you."

"Now that this has been settled, I will be on my way."

Ether turned to the door.

"Why my daughter?" Celia asked urgently.

The shapeshifter turned back.

"It was a matter of convenience. She was the nearest human when the need for form arose. It is simpler to duplicate a form than to manifest a unique one."

"Where is she? Why was she near?"

"Your daughter is dead."

Celia released a breath and stepped back. As intensely as she'd been tossed about by the revelations of the last few minutes, this blunt statement seemed to have the least impact of all. There were tears, but she did not sob or break down. She merely nodded, took another breath, and let the tears of sorrow mix with the tears of joy from moments before.

"Of course... she was an officer in the Alliance Army. It was... it was foolish to imagine she might have lived this long. So few do. Was it a good death? A worthy one?"

"She died in combat, serving the generals directly."

Again she nodded. "Good... good, she would have been happy to know it. A proud death. A noble one."

"I have reason to believe she was under the control of the general called Epidime. I assure you, it was neither proud nor noble."

"No," Celia said, wiping her tears away. "You may know how she looked, but it is clear you did not know Emelia. It was…" She paused, lest a tremor find her voice. "It was the death she would have wanted. Did she suffer?"

"She was killed by a sharp sword and a skilled hand. It was very swift. I don't imagine there was much pain."

"Good. Good. Thank you for taking the time to set me straight. I'm sorry to have bothered you. I won't take any more of your time."

Again Celia picked up her paddle and put it to work stirring the cauldron of laundry. Ether stood, studying the old woman. The shapeshifter's face was creased with confusion.

"Why?" Ether said.

Celia did not answer. Her eyes focused on her work and her ears unable to alert her. Ether touched the woman's shoulder and Celia turned to her.

"Why?" she asked again.

"I'm afraid I don't understand what you are asking," Celia said.

"When you believed your daughter was alive, you were overcome. There were tears and exclamations. You embraced me repeatedly. Now that I've given you what I understand is the worst news a mortal can receive of a loved one, you simply return to your task. Why? Why are you overcome with joy, but not overcome with grief?"

"This isn't the first time I've received this news, child. Oh, I mean… I'm afraid I don't know how to address you."

"I don't care what you call me. Answer my question," Ether said.

"I have lost a husband, a son, and… *two* daughters."

"It becomes easier with each loss?"

"No. Heavens no. Never easier. Just more familiar. It isn't a surprise any longer. You know the pain, how deep it will cut. And you know that you can go on."

"You had a husband. You loved him?"

"Of course I did."

"And he loved you?"

"Of course."

"You haven't replaced him."

"*Replaced* him? You can never replace someone you truly love. You might find someone new to love, but that isn't the same. Not by a long shot."

"Then how did you forget him?"

"Forget him! Perish the thought! There isn't a day that goes by that I don't think about him."

Ether stepped forward. "Then *how*? How do you cope with the void within you? How do you go on knowing someone you were destined to share eternity with is gone?"

Celia looked deeply into Ether's eyes. The shapeshifter blinked and felt a tear roll down her cheek. She turned away, feeling a hot flush of anger at her lack of control.

The older woman put a hand to Ether's cheek. "You lost someone, too."

Ether stepped away from the woman's touch and ignored the observation. "Others seem to throw themselves into their purpose, their calling. Others say things like family and career can fill one's mind and plug the holes within. But what of you? Have you any family?"

"I have a sister, but she lives near the Dagger Gales. I haven't seen her in fifteen years."

"Then you have no family, and your duty is to simple things like carrying bags and washing clothes. Why do you go on? What drives you? How do you continue to live your life when there is nothing else for you to do or to become?"

Celia smiled sadly. "We just go on. Sometimes the promise of another day is all we have. I may have lost my family, but they are still with me in my heart and my mind. I carry them with me, and as long as I carry on, so do they. That's enough."

"It takes great strength to do such a thing. I would not have imagined a mortal would be able to bear such a weight."

"I suppose it is the sort of weight mortals are best suited to bear."

Ether turned aside, the words filtering through her mind. She tightened her fists and felt the sudden, intense desire to be free of this place. "I will leave you to your work," she said before turning to the door.

"Wait," Celia said quickly.

"What is it?" Ether said, turning back.

"… Thank you for telling me what happened to my girl. And for letting me see her face again. This is the first time I've ever been able to say goodbye."

Ether lingered, eyes upon this frail woman. "Goodbye, Celia."

#

Turiel's eyes fluttered open. She was in total darkness, and she was lying on a cold stone floor. For a few moments, her addled mind disregarded the events of the last few months, and she believed that she was back in her cave, eagerly awaiting the return of Teht for further instructions.

Gradually her thoughts cleared, and she hauled herself unsteadily to her feet.

"Ugh… the portal spell requires a bit more nuance to cast than the keyhole," she said, shaking her head. "Still, if it only cost me a brief slide into and out of unconsciousness, I must have been close to proper execution. Not bad for a first casting."

She took a step forward and thumped into something heavy and wooden. Quietly cursing herself, she stirred the air with her staff and conjured a deep violet light. It spilled across her surroundings and revealed a small, cramped room. A heavy wooden desk sat near the center and shelves stood along two walls, but each seemed to have been largely stripped of its contents. The whole room had the overall feel of a place that was in the process of being moved.

Dust had caked most of the surfaces. She ran her fingers through it.

"This place hasn't been disturbed for weeks, or longer... Not a good sign. Teht insisted Bagu could almost always be found at this portal point."

Turiel peered at the wall. A map of the Northern Alliance was mounted there. It was stunningly comprehensive, with every city named and detailed in intricate writing.

"Troops... armories. There *has* been a war..." she observed. "And where are the borders? How... how could the whole of the north have allied? How long has it been..."

She shuffled in the dim light to the desk. A carefully written piece of parchment rested on it, its lettering large and highly visible.

"'The contents of this room are the work of dark magic. Any and all items found within are potentially tainted with D'Karon magic. Do not disturb anything without the blessing and guidance of palace mystics,'" Turiel read aloud. She snatched the parchment and crumpled it. "A matter best left to students of the D'Karon, that much is certain."

The front of the desk had six large cubbyholes, each stuffed with small boxes and tightly rolled scrolls. She pulled open the first of the scrolls. Her eyes darted across the words.

"Death toll... Production schedule... By the order of General Bagu..." She pulled out scroll after scroll. "Seasonal reports... Going back so many years... Gods, is it true? It *can't* be. This isn't possible... It isn't *possible*... The D'Karon wouldn't have bothered to take sides in a petty squabble... And if they did, the D'Karon have too much power, too many resources. It *wouldn't* have lasted this long unless they'd deemed it necessary. They would have had to *choose* to let the war last. There must be an explanation. There *must!*"

Turiel had not taken care to keep her voice down, and as her muttering turned to raving, voices began to filter through the thick door.

"Who is searching the general's chamber?" barked a voice angrily. "You know the chamber is off limits. I don't want to have to deliver another letter of condolence to the family of a foolhardy guard who didn't know a D'Karon trap when he found it."

"No one has been assigned to search Bagu's chambers, Commander. It has remained barred for weeks."

"Well then get this door open! There is someone in there, I can hear them."

Turiel muttered irritably at the bothersome din outside her door. "It seems my countrymen have become inconsiderate in my absence."

She pulled boxes from the desk and dumped out their contents, shuffling madly through them in search of some indication of why it seemed the D'Karon had both dirtied their hands with a war between the locals and held themselves back in order to allow it to continue.

Thumping footsteps and bellowing voices in the hallway went silent, then splintering creaks began to shake the door on its hinges. Turiel ignored them, abandoning the largely logistical matters she'd found in Bagu's desk and instead turning to the artifacts that had not yet been hauled away. At the base of one largely cleared shelf sat a sizeable chest. It was wrapped in heavy chains and secured with a stout lock. She drove her staff's tip into the lock and conjured a coil of black tendrils that tore it apart from within.

Turiel flipped the lid open. Behind her the door was beginning to succumb to the prying and pulling of the castle guards on the other side. She paid it no heed. What was before her was far too important.

Four things were nestled in the chest, ensconced in straw to keep them from damage. Three were brightly glowing crystals, each with the same violet color of the one mounted in her staff. The fourth was a large sand timer lying on its side. Her hand shook as she reached for it, as though it was a sacred artifact.

"The portal glass…" she breathed, clutching one of the brass struts that connected the mounting plates on the top and bottom.

She slid the device upright, then removed her other hand from her staff to more securely grasp the precious piece. Her weapon remained upright, drifting in the air beside her. A slight twitch of her head sent a wave of energy from her staff, blasting the pages and scrolls from the desk to clear it for the far more precious discovery.

Once she'd set it down, Turiel scrutinized it. All of the sand had gathered in the bottom bulb. She grasped the supports and inverted it. Rather than spilling through the pinch of the timer in a thin stream, the fine sand fell to the center but remained in the top bulb.

"No… no, the moment they arrived they began work on the full portal. The sand should flow." She shook the timer violently. Not a single grain fell through a pinch that was more than large enough to allow it. Her eyes darted about. "This can only mean that the portal is completed. The key is turned, the door is opened. But… but why can't I feel it?"

She shut her eyes and plucked her staff from the air. Her mind churned madly with doubt and confusion, but a moment of concentration began to tame it. For longer than she could recall, her every waking thought had been curled about the spells and incantations that would open the gateway to the D'Karon realm. Even half a world away, the unfinished spell she'd been working to open a second keyhole stood like a searing ember in her mind's eye. If there was a gateway anywhere in the world, she should see it like a full moon on a starless sky. And yet there was nothing. It didn't make sense. Nothing was making sense anymore.

Turiel scowled and shut her eyes tighter when the guards finally tore away the last brace and pulled the tattered door open.

"You there! How did you get here? You are trespassing in the royal—"

"I am trying to concentrate! Kindly be silent while I work at this riddle," she growled, irritably turning her back to the door.

"You will drop your staff and surrender yourself to the—"

"I said be *silent!*" she hissed, pivoting back to the door and opening her eyes.

The man before her was clearly a veteran guard, a few years older than one might expect to see in active military service. He still clutched a flat metal pry bar in one hand. Her mere gaze was enough to inspire the guard to take a few steps back, bumping into two of the men who had helped open the door. He dropped the bar and fumbled at his belt for his sword.

When the bar hit the floor, rattling noisily, Turiel slapped one hand over her ear and winced at the din. "What part of *silent* was too complex for you? There is important work to be done, and you are being terribly rude! How can I be expected to concentrate if you won't be *silent?*"

For emphasis she thrust her staff forward. A crackling bolt of black magic issued forth, striking the guard squarely in the chest. He wheezed in agony and launched backward, bowling his fellow guards aside. The whole group, five in total, went sprawling out onto the floor of the grand entryway of Castle Verril. By the time the first of them had scrambled to his feet, Turiel had stalked out of the room and squinted at the comparatively bright light of the vaulted hall.

"Ah, yes. Castle Verril," she said, taking a brief moment from her task to gaze about at the hall.

In her youth, she had briefly served under the king. She couldn't remember the man's name. Like most thoughts more than a few months old, it was a distant and blurred memory lost to time and madness. The entry hall, though. *This* she remembered. The plush carpet of regal blue. The pennants and banners hanging upon the walls and the brightly burning sconces on the walls and columns.

"Wh-what did you do to him?" cried one of the guards.

She turned, her expression souring. For the second time the inconsiderate palace staff had interrupted her thoughts. Did they not realize how *difficult* it was to gather her mind these days?

The man she had assaulted was shaking and pale. His breath had been reduced to wisps of curling black vapor, and his eyes were milky white.

"I illustrated to him the folly of interrupting my task. I would have thought it would have been sufficient to convince the rest of you as well, but clearly additional lessons are in order."

"Mystic! Call the palace mystic, and the healers!" cried one of the guards.

Two men hauled their stricken partner from the ground while the others raised their weapons and attempted to offer them some degree of protection.

Turiel shook her head irritably while the call for assistance rang through the halls.

"I am *quite* certain the palace staff was more mannerly in my day. At the *very* least they were more intelligent. Alas, I suppose things seldom *improve* with time. Now, the gateway. I can't detect it at all. Perhaps traveling here sapped my strength. I need to replenish." She looked briefly to the guards, who were now at the edge of the hall. "Bah, more trouble than they're worth."

She paced back into the darkness of Bagu's chambers. The open chest with its three gems offered the only light in the room now. She smiled as she approached them.

"Ah… thir crystals. And fully sated at that. To think, I didn't think I would ever have occasion to work with one any larger than the one Teht gifted to me."

The dark sorceress leaned down and clutched one of the gems. It was almost too large for her to properly grasp. When her flesh touched the smooth facets of the stone, her smiled widened. She could feel the gem tugging at her, drawing weakly at her spirit like an infant sucking its thumb. It was filled to capacity with stolen mana, but still it wanted more. Such delightful, artful constructions the D'Karon could make. A simple piece of crystal that fed like a living thing.

She lifted the stone from the chest and shut her eyes. A simple twist of magic, an unspoken command, was all it took to reverse the gem's thirst and send its power coiling up her arm and into her soul. It was invigorating, like a long night of sleep and a refreshing drink of water after a long journey. A few moments of glorious feeding left the gem dark and lifeless once more. Its hunger returned, and it tried to steal back the power it had given, but Teht had shared the technique for denying the hunger of the thir gems. She set it carefully into the chest again.

As it was designed to do, the gem had offered up all of the strength it had gathered. With strength came clarity, and with clarity Turiel was certain would come the long-awaited image of the open gateway in her mind's eye. She again tightened her mind in concentration and sought the portal.

Steadily the smile faded and turned to a snarl. There was no denying it now. If she could not find the portal with her mind and spirit in this state, it could only mean that there was no portal to be found. She turned to the door just in time to find a young woman step cautiously into view.

The woman was a mystic in only the broadest possible sense, that much was clear from a single glance. She was dressed in robes just a bit too pristine to have been worn by a seasoned spell caster, and the amulet she held shakily in one hand was still glossy from the jeweler's wheel. Her spirit had the pulse and vitality of one who had learned to focus, but it was fragile as an icicle, unforged and unpracticed. In her eyes Turiel saw the bone-deep fear of a novice who knew she was facing a master. To the woman's credit, she did not falter.

Power gathered within the woman as she pulled her freshly trained mind together about a spell. Her lips formed quiet, carefully phrased incantations. A golden haze filled the air between her and Turiel, and after a few more iterations of her chant the haze tightened into a glimmering shield.

Thus protected, she spoke. Her words had the slow deliberate cadence of someone with a tenuous grip on concentration.

"By the order of the crown of the Northern Alliance, I command you to—"

Turiel stalked forward and thrust her hand at the woman. The necromancer's fingers touched the shimmering veil of protective magic, and the golden shine parted like smoke. A gasp of fear was all the palace mystic could manage before Turiel's fingers were about her throat.

"You are a magician. *You* at least should understand the nature of the woman with whom you are dealing, correct?" Turiel said, her tone like that of a woman who had finally found an adult among children.

Her foe nodded stiffly, fighting for air.

"Excellent. Now, to the north there *should* be a portal. I am searching for it, but I cannot find it. Are you or any of the other palace staff hiding it somehow?"

The mystic shook her head. She had yet to get a single breath past Turiel's iron grip, and her face was beginning to redden.

"Have the D'Karon hidden it then?"

Again she shook her head. She'd released the amulet and clawed desperately at Turiel's fingers.

"Release her!" barked a guard at the end of the hall, the foremost of a dozen such reinforcements that had answered the call for aid.

Turiel made a sound of frustrated disgust and waved her staff in a small circle. Black threads poured from the cracks between the stones of the floor and formed a wall around her and her captive. The guards rushed forward and attempted to bash their way through the circle of black tendrils, but the spider-web-thin threads may as well have been inch-thick iron.

"But there *is* a portal, yes?" Turiel said.

Her captive shook her head weakly. The woman's eyes were beginning to flutter now.

"*Lies!*" Turiel spat. She hurled the woman against the conjured wall. "I know the portal exists. The timer has finished, so the portal has opened. Where *is* it?"

"It…" the woman gasped, "has been closed."

"Impossible! The opening of the portal is like the dawning of the sun on a brave new era for this world. You would have me believe that somehow the sun chose instead to retreat back beneath the horizon?"

"The Chosen closed the portal."

"What is this madness you speak? The chosen? The chosen *what?*"

"The Chosen warriors! The beings of prophecy who arose to defeat the D'Karon," the mystic said. Her eyes were wide with fear as the continued assault upon the conjured wall filled the air with chaos.

Turiel's confusion shifted first to realization, then to fury. "You speak of *the adversaries*. The foolish creatures that would stand in the way of my masters. That, *too*, is impossible. The adversaries could not band together unless the D'Karon attacked the people of this world unbidden, and they would never be so careless."

She leaned forward and grabbed the woman by the front of her tunic, dragging her effortlessly behind her as she stalked back toward the doorway to Bagu's chamber. The wall keeping the guards at bay shifted along with her, receding behind and emerging in front to keep her safe. When she stepped fully inside the chamber, the threads wove themselves into a solid black barrier across the doorway.

"What is your name, woman?"

"Y... you are a necromancer. I can feel it."

"That isn't an answer," Turiel said, throwing her prisoner to the ground beside the chest and leaning down to fetch a second thir gem.

"A proper wizard would never tell her name to a necromancer. It could give her power over us."

"You are hardly a proper wizard, that name nonsense is only for necromancers who haven't reached full mastery, and I've already got all of the power I need over you. So for the sake of civilized conversation, tell me your damned name."

"Kintalla."

"Kintalla, all that you've said to me is either fallacy or madness, but at the moment I don't have any evidence to contradict it. I *opened* the keyhole. And the portal would only be where the keyhole was centered. So I know precisely where it is."

"But it has been *closed*, I've *told* you," Kintalla said, taking the amulet in her fingers again.

Turiel frowned and slapped it from her hands. "Come now, I've let you live because I need to prove to you that all of your lies and foolishness can't keep me from the truth. Don't make me kill you before I do so. Then I'll have to find another witness, and this whole endeavor has been an untenable waste of time already." She paced to the map on the wall and held the glowing crystal to it. "When I created the first keyhole, naturally there was no portal point there, because the D'Karon had only just arrived. And Teht only gave me a small list of points, in the event I needed to contact them in a dire emergency. But I am quite certain they would have created a portal point for the keyhole as soon as they were able." She peered at the most northerly marked point on the map. "Ah, yes... they added *quite* a few more. But this one is the one I need."

She again stirred the air with her staff, summoning the swirling disk of black much more swiftly than she had the first time.

138

"Yes…" she said. "Yes, I see where my mistake was… This should be much smoother this time."

There was no apparent fatigue in her voice as she spoke, the spell being fueled directly from the thir gem in her other hand. When the black disk was through growing and the portal itself began to open, it filled the room with a vicious, biting cold wind. Turiel discarded the expended gem and grasped Kintalla's tunic again, hauling her up.

"What… what have you done?" the young mystic asked.

Turiel and Kintalla peered through the portal. The sun had set, and in the dim light of the moon filtering through the clouds it was difficult to see more than vague forms through the portal. There didn't seem to be any ground beneath it, and now and again something would slide past the portal with a ponderous, pivoting motion.

"Curious… I am not entirely certain this portal is properly aligned," Turiel said.

"You… you can simply open doors to other parts of the world?"

Turiel dropped the expended thir gem into the chest and retrieved the final one, smaller than the others, and tucked it into a pouch within her robes. "I wouldn't call it *simple*. Now, let me see." She leaned though the portal. "Ah. There seems to be something solid not far down. If you survive the fall, do let me know."

Before Kintalla could object, Turiel pushed her through the portal. The young woman screamed in terror for a few moments, then cried out in surprise and discomfort amid the rustle of leaves and the cracking of twigs.

"Ah, wonderful," Turiel said.

She stepped through and plummeted after Kintalla, landing not long after in the branches of what looked to have at one time been a tropical tree. The branches, now dead, were dense and thin, making for a relatively soft landing after the short fall. After a few moments to gather her wits and right herself, Turiel dropped down and felt the crunch of dry grass beneath her feet. Kintalla had fallen from the tree and was just now climbing to her feet, shivering violently in the howling breeze. Turiel, on the other hand, seemed completely unaware of the cold.

She brushed the twigs from her robe and shook free the crook of a branch that had become entwined with her staff. Above her, the portal snapped shut. Gradually her eyes adjusted to the light available, and what she saw was enough to give her pause.

They were atop a small clump of drifting soil that looked as though it had been swept up from another part of this world or some other. All around them additional fragments of earth, some as small as pebbles and some nearly the size of cities, drifted and circled in a bizarre galaxy of displaced land. No two of them were the same. A distant one glittered as if made of glass. Somewhat closer was a long, low stretch of prairie or meadow that seemed unbothered by the cold and looked to be home to some manner of beast that looked almost like a deer, but far smaller and with antlers infinitely more intricate.

Far, far in the distance, almost at the limit of their vision, the moonlight illuminated the snowy covering of the surrounding mountains. A nearly circular pit had been carved out, leaving perfectly sheer cliffs leading down into darkness below. The clump of earth they now rode atop was near the middle of this chasm.

"I am quite certain this is not how the portal was to look," Turiel said, her tone irritated. In the face of this impossible place the most emotion she could muster was that of a person who suspected a prank was being played.

"This…" Kintalla said shakily, "is where the portal *was*. Before the Chosen closed it. We call this place Lain's End now."

"Explain it. How did they close the portal? How did these blasted adversaries even manage to arise!?"

"I don't know. P-Please, we'll *freeze* out here."

"Do the adversaries still live?"

"F-Four of th-them do. L-Lain was the f-f-fifth."

"And *he* died here, I suppose. Hence the name? Very well, who are these creatures? I shall personally bring them to task for this travesty."

"If I t-tell you, w-will you help me leave this place?"

"I can't very well leave you here. That would be inexcusable. This place was meant for the D'Karon."

"V-Very well. Myranda Celeste, th-the wizard. She is Duchess of Kenvard now. Her pet dragon, Myn. An elemental named Ether, and a malthrope named Ivy. All but Ether can be found in New Kenvard."

"*New* Kenvard. Why would there be a new one?"

"K-Kenvard's capital was d-destroyed in the war! P-Please. We'll f-freeze! Y-you must get us out of here!" Kintalla begged.

Turiel muttered. "Oh, very well. But you must do me a simple favor in return."

"Anything!"

"I'm rather curious what is at the bottom. Do let me know if you find out."

"What? No! NO!"

The necromancer grasped Kintalla by the tunic one last time and heaved her toward the edge. Numbing legs and frazzled wits proved inadequate to let the poor wizard recover before pitching off the side. Turiel paced to the edge and peered over, watching the screaming form plummet swiftly into the darkness.

Kintalla's cries continued for quite a while, echoing up from the darkness long after she was out of sight. Indeed, there was no sudden stop to them, they just gradually faded into the howling wind as she fell into the chasm.

"I suppose it is entirely possible there *isn't* a bottom," Turiel commented.

She rubbed her chin and thought for a moment. As she did, she paced forward, black threads twisting out from the land and lacing together into a bridge to the next piece of land. It all seemed to happen effortlessly, or even without her notice. She paced along a meandering path, moving across temporary bridges to stationary clusters of stone. Her thoughtful pacing continued for some time before she spoke again, each twist and turn taking her closer to the nearest piece of solid ground, a narrow point due south.

"Let us see… there is no doubt that this is the site of the keyhole, and no doubt that the portal *must* have been finished." She casually crouched down a bit, avoiding the lower edge of a mountain-sized piece of stone as it rushed by. "If this place truly is the doing of somehow shutting the portal, then these adversaries are not to be taken lightly… If they can be killed for what they've done, they shall be. And regardless, the second keyhole *must* be opened. I will not deprive this world of the teachings and power of the D'Karon…"

She paused, eyes settling on the tiny clump of stone that remained between her and solid ground. It was barely three strides across and mostly circular. At its center stood a sword, but that didn't concern her. What seized her mind was the black stain across the surface of the stone, out of which the sword stood.

Turiel rushed across the bridge of threads and let it vanish behind her, kneeling at the edge of the silhouette burned into the stone. The shape was vaguely human in form, but just barely. It was twisted and unnatural, but Turiel held shaking hands out to it as though it was the still-warm corpse of a departed loved one.

"This is… this *was* Lord Bagu…" she said, her voice hushed with disbelief. "They… *killed* a D'Karon…"

Her hands tightened into fists, the right hand squeezing tight around her staff. With a vicious cry of anger, she thrust the staff forward, conjuring a blast of energy that struck the sword and dislodged it. The weapon went twirling into the shifting clusters of stone. Its blade sank deep into the underside of a passing boulder, embedding itself there.

"How dare they… How *dare* they!"

She crouched again and reverently touched the final resting place of one of her wisest and most powerful masters, then slowly climbed to her feet and conjured a bridge to the mainland.

"I'll… I'll…" she fumed, but after a moment she stopped, forcing herself to calm. "This is serious. There will be time for blind fury later. This is a time for cool heads and careful consideration."

She paced southward.

"I will find other D'Karon. The others *must* be here still, or at least other followers or creations. Yes… Yes. That is what I shall do. But first, I *must* see to my dear little Mott." She started to stir the air with her staff. "He must be beside himself with loneliness…"

#

Ivy's eyes were shut, her ears perked up and angled toward the door of the carriage. The tone of the journey had changed sharply once the group turned toward the D'Karon fort. Spirited, though admittedly adversarial, conversation had lapsed into complete silence. Their westward and northward journey had brought them toward the sea and its endless, damp, freezing winds. This had encouraged them to secure the windows and doors as tightly as possible, granting no hint of a view of the outside. Now the white-furred diplomat breathed in slow, controlled breaths. Her hands were folded and her toes were rocking on the ground in tense readiness. For all outward appearances, she seemed to be fully prepared to spring into a sprint at a moment's notice but using all of her willpower to avoid doing so.

"You seem to be… distracted, Ambassador," said Ambassador Krettis.

"I'm worried," Ivy said.

"Worried? About what?"

"I'm worried about what we'll find at the fort. It's one of Demont's forts."

"And what might we find in such a place that would worry you?"

Ivy shut her eyes a bit tighter. "Awful things… nasty things. Wrong things. Things no sane mind would imagine."

"Surely you can offer *something* by way of example. So that we might prepare ourselves."

The malthrope opened her eyes and looked at her Tresson counterpart. "Things like me."

Krettis arched an eyebrow.

"What you see here, what you were at first unwilling to talk to and what you still are unwilling to trust, was crafted in a place like the one we are about to visit. He takes things, innocent things, and he changes them. He twists them into weapons and monsters."

"He. General Demont? Fortunate for us all that you and your other chosen have killed him and his kind."

"Not him. We… *I* threw him away and slammed the door behind him, but I didn't kill him." She cast her eyes downward. "At the time it was a triumph that I'd managed to keep from killing him. He'd designed me to be a weapon. Sparing him showed that I wasn't willing to be one. But now I genuinely wish I'd pushed the blade through his throat when I had the chance. The thought that he or one of his kind might be back…" She visibly shuddered.

"Perhaps we shall be lucky then? Perhaps it is he who has returned. I shall have a chance to see for myself both that these D'Karon exist and that you are as dedicated to their destruction as you claim to be."

"You don't want that. You haven't seen what they can do, and you should be thankful for it. No one who has had to suffer through their reign would ever call their return *lucky*."

"You do not merely sound worried, Ambassador Ivy. You sound frightened."

"I'm terrified."

Krettis clucked her tongue.

Ivy shot her a hard glance, her lip twitching and her ear flicking. "What?" she said firmly.

"It is nothing. I was simply given to believe you were a warrior."

"You were wrong. I'm not a warrior. I never was. I'm an artist. It is what I am, it is what I always was, and it is all I ever really wanted to be. But I'm also Chosen, and that means it is my duty to face things like this. And though I'd much rather I was back in Kenvard practicing a new tune and visiting with the handful of people I can truly call friends, I would still rather clash with the D'Karon than leave the task to *anyone* else. I wouldn't wish that sort of thing on my worst enemy." She peeled her lips back in a brief snarl. "And what about being terrified suggests I am not a warrior?"

"A warrior would not be afraid."

Ivy shook her head slowly, a look of understanding slowly coloring her expression. "You've always been an ambassador, haven't you?"

"Yes."

"Never once seen a battlefield?"

"In Tressor we were never rendered so weak that our women were forced to take up arms. Our military is composed entirely of our strongest men."

Ivy cast a knowing glance at Celeste.

"I used to think of warriors the same way you do," she said. "I used to think I couldn't possibly be a proper warrior, because I felt the fear down to my core every time I looked out across the battlefield. But some of my friends, some of the fiercest creatures you could ever hope to meet, set me straight. There are plenty of people who could step out on a battlefield and not be afraid. A *child* could step into an arena against a tiger and not be afraid, because a child doesn't know better. A lunatic could face an army alone, because a lunatic wouldn't care. But a *warrior*? *A hero*? The thing that makes them what they are isn't that they don't feel the fear. It's that they don't let it stop them."

The rattling of the carriage began to slow. Ivy pushed the door open a crack, letting a stiff breeze in, and peered out.

"Stop in the middle of the next stretch there, please," she called to the driver. "That is as close as I want the rest of you to get. That's certainly the fort we are after. I'd recognize the sort of forts the D'Karon build anywhere."

As she pulled on her overcloak, she began to issue orders. Unaccustomed as she was to a position of authority, they came out as requests. "Mr. Celeste, please stay with the ambassador. I would prefer if *all* of the guards remained behind to keep you all safe. Is that acceptable?"

"You are a Guardian of the Realm and an ambassador. You have the highest authority here. If it is your wish, then it is acceptable," he said.

"Okay. Okay, good," she said, taking a slow breath. "I need a weapon."

Celeste began to unbuckle his sword.

"No!" she said, waving it off. "Not a sword. I don't... I don't like the way I act when I've got a sword in my hand. Come on. I'll find something."

She pushed open the door and stepped out. The others followed.

Their journey had taken them out along one of the unique features of the western shore of Kenvard. Many stretches of coast, this one included, were composed of uniform gray stone slabs that were so polished by the ice and wind that they seemed almost to have been cut by chisels and fitted together. The land fell sharply off into steep, sheer cliffs. Water splashed against the base of the cliffs just a few dozen feet below. It was not a dizzying drop by any means, but the thrashing water combined with the biting cold made death all but certain to anyone unfortunate enough to lose their footing. And losing one's footing was all too simple, as the constant sea-spray had formed itself into a thick crust of ice that crunched beneath their boots as the group stepped cautiously forward.

Ambassador Krettis squinted against the spray and gazed around. Their carriage had pulled to a stop near the center of a long, low slab that, to her evident dismay, was *not* a part of the mainland. The flat-topped island was the second of a string of three such plateaus that jutted out of the water. They were all at precisely the same height and perfectly level with the mainland. It almost looked as though some sort of calamity in the past had sliced away the ground itself, separating these remaining pieces from the shore. They formed something akin to stepping-stones leading toward the final island that was home to the fort itself.

To reach their current perch, the carriage and its escort had first crossed a fifty-foot-long bridge to reach a roundish stone island large enough to comfortably fit a cottage if someone were mad enough to build one there. From there they'd crossed another thirty-foot-long bridge to a much larger plateau. It was just a bit wider than the first island, but easily miles long, forming a strip of stone that led almost perfectly perpendicular to the shore. It was an elevated road of sorts, connected via a final bridge to the final island, which was home to the fort. They'd stopped a few dozen paces shy of this last bridge.

Ambassador Krettis eyed the bridges they had crossed to get this far.

"I must say... I am impressed by your construction skills. These bridges seem sturdy, and yet they are still but wood and rope. I would think this stiff wind and moisture would turn even the finest bridge to a rotten and splintered mess in no time."

"We build these bridges as we build ships, both rope and planks coated with pitch to ward off rot. I'm sure your own builders do the same," Ambassador Celeste said.

"Perhaps... I suppose I've never considered it. Most of the times I've crossed bridges I've not been so... *aware* of the consequences of their failure."

The gap that separated the long island from the fort was only a dozen feet, and the bridge that spanned it was as wide as the island itself. Beyond it lay a short strip of stone courtyard, then the low, rectangular structure of the fort itself. It was large. A small village could fit beneath its flat roof, and it occupied almost the entire island. What had not been covered by the simple stone building was home to an odd assortment of plants. There were a few sturdy northern pines and oaks, but joining them were shrubs and trees from all over the north. Some even had remnants of the broader leaves and smoother bark of Tresson plants. Most had withered and died long ago, the only evidence of their former lushness lingering as shriveled leaves encased in ice like a display piece in a museum. Now husks of trees stood dead throughout the courtyard. The remnants of gnarled vines clung to some stretches of the fort's windowless walls, and thorny skeletons of bushes stood beside the entrance like a grim warning. How such an assortment of flora had been assembled, and why it had been planted in a place that couldn't be expected to support much of it, was a curiosity.

"Such a strange place..." Krettis said.

Her earlier insistence that she be allowed to see the D'Karon facility had eroded somewhat, and for the moment she was content to observe from beside the carriage rather than following Ivy as she stalked toward the fortress itself.

"We call them the river stones," Celeste said, his eyes locked on Ivy as she stepped carefully onto the ice-crusted bridge. "For a day's travel in either direction one can find such islands stretching off into the sea. Some house sea forts to guard against invasion. Most are too scattered to be bridged as these have."

"Yes... I'm sure you are quite proud of your land's natural beauty," Krettis said. She'd managed to voice the final word with an almost surgically precise level of irony. "But I was speaking more of the structure. These plants did not find their way here on their own. I see a Taarsin cottonwood, or what is left of one. I can't imagine it chose to grow here."

"General Demont was a collector of such things. He was fascinated by plants and animals. I am told that early in his tenure, when he still had troops under his direct command, he would use them almost exclusively to gather samples of the wildlife and plantlife from across the kingdoms."

"An odd predilection for a military man."

"He was no more military than you, Ambassador Krettis. Like most of the D'Karon generals, the title was simply a means to an end, a way to exert authority in a time when the war was all that mattered."

"And yet you followed them."

"As I said, war was all that mattered. Your people were strong. If we were to survive, we needed their troops. Those troops came at a price. We paid dearly for the aid the D'Karon rendered."

He turned to the troops and the carriage. The soldiers were uneasy. A seasoned warrior knew a place of battle when he or she saw it, and this fort

Joseph R. Lallo

reeked of spilled blood. Even the ambassador had the cold, focused stare of someone expecting violence.

"Let us get this carriage turned around," Ambassador Celeste said. "Escorts, eyes on the fort and all be ready to move."

"Turning the carriage?" the ambassador said. "Surely you do not intend for us to leave without Ambassador Ivy."

"No," he said, ushering her aside so that the carriage driver could begin the complex maneuvers necessary to pivot on the relatively narrow island. "But if the time comes to move, I want to be able to move quickly."

"What manner of threat could this place offer if you have disabled and destroyed any remaining D'Karon troops and technology?"

"Such was our aim. And so we believed we had. But as I'm sure your troops can attest, the D'Karon are not so easily dispatched."

Krettis pulled her cloak a bit tighter and squinted against the sea spray. "The fort is a large one, but not so large that one could hide a regiment of soldiers for months. What surprises might be found?"

"Demont was the man responsible for crafting the creatures so often wielded by the D'Karon. Many such beasts are small enough to be missed but still large enough to be a threat. And the fort is larger than it seems. The D'Karon tended to dig deep for their forts. It may well fill the whole of this island, or even beyond."

"Wouldn't the lowest levels of such a fortress flood?"

Celeste turned back to the fort. "Perhaps. Perhaps by design."

#

Ivy shuddered and released a shaky breath as she approached the door of the fortress. She knew that the icy sensations rushing through her, growing with each step, had little to do with the wind and moisture. This was a D'Karon fort. *Demont's* fort. There were dark spells at work on such places. One could hope that such enchantments had withered and died without his oversight, but hope was a terrible defense against such horrid creatures as she knew the D'Karon to be.

The one heartening thing she'd observed as she approached was the state of the door. The massive wooden planks that made up the fortified entryway were splintered and shattered. Where they still hung weakly from their bulky hinges, they were blackened and charred. Ivy smiled. It was Ether's handiwork. The shapeshifter had scoured the Northern Alliance in the months following the war's end, and few things were more devastating than Ether's wrath when she found something she felt no longer deserved to exist. She was terrifying when she had reason to be and thorough to the point of excess in her devastation. If she had been here, then it was likely the inside would bear only rubble and ash.

Ivy flicked her ears and twisted them to the yawning doorway. Somewhere, deep inside, she'd heard something. It could have been the crackle of ice dislodged by the wind... or it might have been the skitter of feet. Ivy turned to a dead tree not far from the door and bounded up to it. With a firm grasp and a quick twist, she heaved at one of the lower branches and managed to tear an arm-length portion of it free. A club had served her well enough in the past. In the absence of the blades she'd come to embrace as her weapon of choice, it would do.

To her great relief, Ivy found that the inside of the fort was not entirely dark. Ether's typical level of fury had caused a long section of the roof to collapse, filling the center of the largely vacant floor with pale light. It also left the floor glittering with ice where the spray had settled. She took a deep breath, drawing in the scent of the place. It was musty and damp. Moldy cloth and rotten wood were the most prevalent scents. Beneath them a sharp, acrid smell asserted itself. It was strange, unnatural, but not unfamiliar. That smell was left behind at many a battlefield during her days fighting these creatures. It was the syrupy black muck that most D'Karon beasts used for blood. That it had been spilled was again a relief. Ether had found and destroyed some monster or another, but knowing that did little to quell the bone-deep anxiety and the terrible memories that the scent brought rushing out of her mind. Joining those scents was the smoky, charred sting of Ether's aftermath and... something else... something warm and alive, but unlike anything she'd smelled before.

Ivy tightened her grip on her makeshift weapon and cast her eyes around. Stone columns held up what remained of the roof. Here and there a pile of stony fragments or a scrap of leathery hide marked the remains of what had briefly been a D'Karon beast before Ether had snuffed it out. No hint of the source of the living scent. She licked her lips and swallowed hard. She was going to have to go deeper.

Her footsteps echoed in the vacated hall. Unlike the two other forts of Demont's that Ivy had the great misfortune of having visited, this one was not cluttered with bars and walls to hold various specimens. She approached the stairway at the far side of the floor and gazed down. Again she saw that it was not entirely dark, though this time it came as a source of concern rather than relief. Just barely detectable to her sensitive eyes was the gleam of violet light. She hesitated.

"Those gems... don't tell me there are still gems left here," Ivy said aloud.

When she moved again, it was with great caution. Her eyes widened to take in every scrap of the dim light, her ears darted madly at the source of every echo, and her nostrils flared to draw in the scent of her target, whatever it might be. Ivy rounded the turn of the massively wide staircase and moved to the next level. Now without a direct opening to the outside, the splashing waves and wailing wind could be heard only as a dull hiss filtered through thick stone. Her eyes adjusted to the indigo glow, which she could now see was coming not from full crystals but the shattered fragments of them. Again Ivy grinned. If there was anything Ether hated more than D'Karon beasts, it was D'Karon magic. Their gems burned the elemental terribly. Naturally she would have smashed them. Now all that remained of the horrid things, which had formerly been mounted on the walls, was a dusting of fine crystal slivers across the floor. They created just enough light to give the shadowy structures of the floor enough form for her to navigate. This level was marginally more crowded, a few broken walls marking where holding cells had been. The air was also thicker with spilled blood and charred flesh. Ether had been quite busy. But there was no doubt now that there was something alive. Without the wind pouring through the damaged door and roof, the trail was undisturbed, and the details of the scent were bright and clear in her mind. Clarity, however, did not dispel confusion in this case. She could detect canine elements, but also traces of goat and reptile and even human. It smelled like a small menagerie had been wandering through this place, but the scents were commingled and always present in the same mixture. Ivy didn't know what it meant, but she couldn't imagine the answer would be a pleasant one.

Ivy twisted her ears about and gazed across the floor. She was alone on this level, that much was certain. As her eyes became more and more adjusted to the low light, they were able to discern something chilling in the arched doorway of the stairs at the end of the floor. The light was brighter there… and the shadows were moving. She stepped lightly toward the stairs, careful not to make a sound. Each step allowed her to make out more details. A brighter light came in from the floor below, and as it shifted from side to side, it painted shadows across the rear wall of the stairwell. Steeling herself, Ivy began to descend, stopping when she reached the landing so she could peer around the bend.

Her eyes widened. Something was there, though seeing it did little to answer the question of what exactly it was. It was a jackal head perched at the end of a serpentine neck and body, skittering about on eight clawed spider legs and flapping black feathered wings. In its mouth was a fist-sized chunk of fairly intact D'Karon crystal, which it used as a makeshift torch to investigate the darker corners of a floor that had at least *some* relatively intact remains of D'Karon beasts.

In the brighter light, Ivy could see stony wolves and small, strangely smooth dragon-like beasts. The wolves at least were just as she'd remembered them, a rare but familiar part of the D'Karon arsenal. The other beasts looked like dragoyles, but they weren't much larger than the wolves, and their hides were much smoother than Ivy remembered from the dragoyles she'd fought. Their claws were also stretched with filmy fins.

The jackal-headed curiosity was clearly intrigued by the most complete example of these new dragoyles, as it was holding the gem close and sniffing at the beast. It sampled the scent with the excited, rapid sniffs of a puppy confronted with a new toy. Then, in a motion that was almost terrifying in its speed, the beast raised its head and twisted it aside, turning to the door and locking its eyes on Ivy.

She gritted her teeth and fought the urge to run, though a flutter of blue aura stirred around her as her fear began to leak through to the surface. The aura flickered again when the jackal beast skittered toward her. It moved in a darting zigzag, sweeping across the floor as a blur and coming to a stop a few paces away.

"Stop!" Ivy warned, her voice echoing through the fort.

The beast froze, then twisted its head aside. It took a single step forward with one of its entirely too numerous legs.

"Don't come any closer."

Now the thing twisted its head the other way. The curious puppy quality of the creature grew stronger with each movement. Aside from its nightmarish appearance, it hadn't made any motions that suggested it was dangerous. Indeed, as she watched, it set the crystal down and reached its head forward, sniffing at her feet. She held the club high enough to strike if she needed to, but something inside Ivy couldn't bring her to attack the creature.

"What are you?" she said.

It stepped forward again, more slowly now, as though it understood that her tone was no longer one of threat. When it was near enough to do so, it extended its neck enough to nearly touch its nose to her leg and sniffed her up and down, then twisted aside and rubbed its head affectionately across her thigh.

"Okay… okay, you're friendly…" Ivy said, though she was not entirely convinced of it yet. "I can't say I was expecting to find something friendly in Demont's fort."

The thing perked up at the mention of the general's name.

"Uh oh… I don't like that you know that name. Let's see how much you understand. Did he make you?" she asked, crouching down.

Her jackal-headed friend shook its head.

"And you understand Varden. That's certainly new," she said, brow furrowed in confusion as it rubbed its head against her neck.

She reluctantly patted the side of its long neck, mildly repulsed by the hairs that poked up between the serpent scales. As affectionate as the beast appeared, she was still coiled like a spring, ready for that to change at a moment's notice. After all, Demont had been more than capable of creating creatures that seemed quite friendly. She herself was evidence of that. Of course, she was also evidence that just because the touch of D'Karon magic had created something, that didn't mean it had to be evil.

Ivy cupped the beast's chin in one hand to keep its sweeping head still and leaned down to draw in a strong whiff of its aroma.

"No…" she said. "You aren't a D'Karon creature. There's too much nature in you. I don't know who made you, but it wasn't them. But what are you? And what are you doing here?"

The creature didn't respond. Ivy wasn't certain if that meant it was unwilling or unable to speak, but at this point there was little doubt it was at least somewhat intelligent and there was no reason not to suppose it might be smart enough to answer if it could. Instead, it skittered back to the dropped gem and picked it up in its teeth. It took a few steps toward the center of the floor, then turned back to her.

"What do you—*wah!*" Ivy yelped.

Her bizarre new friend had lashed out with its tail and coiled it around her free hand, tugging it lightly like a toddler who wanted to explore. Ivy forced away a flash of blue aura and gently pulled the coiled tail from her wrist.

"Easy, whatever you are. I'm nervous enough in this place without you moving about so suddenly." Ivy released an unsteady sigh and paced forward. "Have you found anything else alive in here? I came because there might be something dangerous here, and it doesn't seem like *you* are the sort of thing that I'd be sent to find."

It shook its head and hung it down briefly, its disappointment apparent. Ivy knelt down to inspect an almost intact example of the dragoyle-like creature. Up close, it had a number of features that at first struck her as more dragon-like than the rockier, simpler dragoyles she'd fought in the past.

"Maybe this was a new version? Demont *did* always like to improve his toys." She leaned forward a bit and grimaced as she picked up its limp claw. "Wait… no, this isn't like a normal dragon. This is more like a fish. I wonder if—"

Her thought was quickly cut short as the hairs on her neck stood on end. Something awful, something cold and supernatural, was happening deep inside the fort. Ivy had never learned much of magic, but she'd been its target often enough to recognize when it was at work. Even if such was not the case, every fragment of shattered crystal flared intensely bright for a few moments before fading again.

Whatever had happened, it thrilled the creature by her side. It sprang up and practically pranced about, zipping and darting around Ivy and nudging her to stand. She clutched her weapon tight and set her eyes on the next stairwell.

"That's what I'm after. I'm sure of it."

She set off for the stairs, the creature weaving ecstatic rings about her and lighting the way with its gem. Something about being certain that she would find something ahead took the edge from the fear. Ivy moved with purpose, running through the next two levels and turning a blind eye to the devastation Ether had left during her visit. After a third stairwell, the dampness in the air began to gather into pools on the floor. She splashed through a channel that could only have been designed to route the water toward a carefully placed drain, and through that drain she saw a brighter glow slipping through the corroded brass grating. Along with the light was a voice.

"No... no, no, no... Broken... All of it broken... How could this *happen?* Who would *do* this?" muttered a woman's voice, bordering on tears.

Ivy slowed when she reached the final staircase. Partially it was because these stairs were pouring with water and would be treacherous even at a walking pace. Mostly it was because if she was going to come face to face with this woman, she would do it with some degree of stealth. Her companion, however, saw no wisdom in either precaution. It streaked down the stairs ahead of her, clawed feet and spindly legs holding firm despite the slick surface. A moment after it disappeared around the bend of the stairs, its scrabbling footsteps were replaced with sloshing ones. The splashing steps drew the attention of the woman. She spoke, joy and relief mixing with the sorrow in her voice.

"Mott! My dear Motley, look what has happened! Thank heavens you are safe! I was afraid what had done this might have done something to you as well."

The malthrope crept carefully around the bend and took in the baffling sight. This floor of the fort was entirely flooded. The center was a walkway with only a few inches of water on it, but on either side the walkway descended in steps into the murky, sloshing water. From the scent, and the fact it was not frozen solid, Ivy could tell it was seawater. This portion of the facility must have been at sea level. What she could see of the submerged walls and walkways indicated that the room had been separated into a dozen or so pools. Each one held what was left of an aquatic or semiaquatic monstrosity. Like most of Demont's creations, there was some indication in each that it was at least based on a creature nature had intended, but in all cases he had taken horrid liberties with the forms. One monster looked like an armor-plated seal with undersized wings on its back. Another was some manner of nightmarish fish the size of a large dog and equipped with row after row of insectile legs.

At the center of the room, kneeling in the icy water with her arms wrapped tightly about the neck of the jackal-headed beast Ivy now knew was called Mott, was a woman. Based on her appearance she was not quite young enough to be Myranda's mother, but she might have been close, and tears were running freely down her face. A staff was submerged just below the water beside her, its gem glowing bright enough to paint dancing marbled patterns on the ceiling and walls.

Ivy faltered somewhat. This woman was a wizard, that much was clear, but she was no D'Karon. She was crying, and she showed genuine joy at seeing Mott. True, heartfelt sorrow and happiness were two things Ivy had never dreamed a D'Karon might show. Her mind mired in uncertainty, Ivy let her concentration lapse and mindlessly sloshed a foot down into the water. The splash echoed through the room and drew the eyes of both Mott and the grief-stricken newcomer.

The woman's lips peeled back in a snarl, and she snatched her staff from the water, brandishing it as the glow flared viciously. Ivy planted both feet and bared her own teeth, club held ready.

"Who are you, and what are you doing here!" Ivy barked.

"Who did this? And how dare you enter this place," the woman countered.

Her staff crackled with the beginnings of a dark spell, but Mott dashed out between Ivy and the woman and fluttered awkwardly up to block any possible attack.

"Mott, get down. What has gotten into you?" the woman growled.

It chittered excitedly at her.

"What are you…" she began, but she paused and looked up at Ivy again. Her face brightened with joy and relief and she dropped her staff once more, clutching her hands to her mouth. "Oh… oh thank *heavens*. They *weren't* all destroyed."

The woman began to rush toward Ivy, arms held wide, but the fox raised her club.

"Stay back!" Ivy growled.

"Oh! Oh, of course. Of course you are frightened. Why wouldn't you be? After what happened here, that is only right. My apologies. Greetings to you. I've come a long way to find you."

"Who are you? Why have you come?" Ivy demanded.

"I'll answer any questions you have, and I hope you'll answer some of mine, but would you perhaps do me the hospitality of continuing this discussion away from this horrid water? I'm afraid I'm a bit emotional. I'm having trouble shrugging off its icy sting."

Ivy glanced down. Now that the shock of the first meeting had passed, she was becoming aware of the biting pain in her feet from the sub-freezing seawater. The woman should have been in agony, as her feet were completely bare beneath the surface of the water. She backed up and climbed a stair or two. "Yes. I think that's a good idea. But move slowly."

"I don't think I could manage anything else. Mott, be a dear and carry my staff. I wouldn't want our host to feel uncomfortable."

The group tromped up to the next level, and at Ivy's behest, another level to the first marginally dry floor. All the while she kept an eye on the woman, but the only thing the stranger did was look over the remnants of the broken creations with the sort of heartbreaking expression one would imagine on the face of a recent widow.

"This is far enough," Ivy said.

Mott took this as its signal to trot up to a groove in the floor and twist its head aside, driving the staff upright. It then scrambled up to coil and perch precariously about the staff.

"Now what are you—" Ivy began.

"One moment... just one moment please," the woman interrupted. "Let me look at you."

She gazed upon Ivy with nothing short of wonder, reaching out with one hand as if to stroke the fox's face. Ivy pulled back. The woman continued to look over her face and hands.

"Beautiful," she uttered reverently. "Simply gorgeous. There is no other word for it."

Ivy looked at the woman askance. "Most people don't feel that way when they look at me."

"I'm not surprised... err... What is your name, dear?"

"Ivy," she said.

"Ivy? Ivy... Heavens, I just heard that name recently. Blast it, I suppose I haven't quite smoothed the wrinkles of the portal spell. No matter. You say most people don't see beauty in you. I say most people haven't got my eye for such matters, Ivy. Ah! And speaking of such. *Pink!* Pink eyes, Mott. *Unfinished*, and yet with such a magnificent hue. I'd never even considered it." She turned to the beast, which to all appearances was her pet, looking him over critically. "No... no I don't think pink would have suited you." She turned back to Ivy. "We had a terrible time finding the right eyes for him. The poor devil was getting impatient."

"What do you..." Ivy began to ask, thoroughly confused. Suddenly she shook herself, remembering the severity of the situation. "Tell me who you are and what you are doing here!"

"Yes, yes, my stars, yes. I'd forgotten my manners," she said. "My name is Turiel. And I came here looking for your father. I was a student of his, in a way."

"My... my father?" Ivy said quietly.

"Of course. Demont. His workmanship in you is unmistakable. A malthrope, too. Such a fine choice..."

Ivy's expression hardened, and she squeezed the grip of her club tightly. A flare of red washed over her, but she willed it away.

"Oh! That is an unexpected twist of magic. Is that some manner of connection with your emotions? Inspired! That is quite unusual for Demont, isn't it?"

She shut her eyes and fought to control her emotions. "You worked with Demont?"

Turiel rolled her eyes wistfully. "If only I had. I'm afraid I only met him briefly. Most of my interactions came by way of lessons from a young woman named Teht. Brilliant in her own way of course, but I don't believe she had the same insight and dedication as the others..."

Ivy's heart was pounding and her mind was aflame with fear and anger. It was all she could do to keep it beneath the surface. She wanted to put her weapon to work, to eliminate this woman who brazenly and gleefully embraced the horrid monsters who had held their world hostage. But there was something wrong, something different. The woman's eyes weren't the eyes of a D'Karon. They were wild, perhaps not sane, but they were sincere. She didn't smell of the D'Karon, didn't act as they did. She truly meant what she said. Her admiration of Ivy, or at least of her form, was honest and heartfelt, and she seemed to have a real affection for the creature beside her. There had to be more to this. If she could find the truth without bloodshed, then that is what she would do.

"How did you know the D'Karon? What did you do for them?" Ivy said, her voice almost cracking.

Turiel tipped her head to the side, concern creasing her expression. "Is there something wrong, dear?" she asked, reaching out to place a reassuring hand on Ivy's shoulder.

Ivy pulled back. "Please… just answer."

"What did I do for them? Some tasks, very minor from their point of view. I heeded their call, and I've been hard at work readying a contingency."

"Heeded their call?"

"I brought them here."

The grip of Ivy's club creaked in her hand, and her eyes plunged a few shades toward violet. "You… *brought* them…"

Turiel smiled. She'd admitted to setting loose a group of genocidal invaders, but from her expression she may as well have been speaking of donating to a needy orphanage. "How could I not? I needed their help. I needed to learn the things they could teach me. Your father, Demont—"

"He is *not* my father," Ivy hissed.

Now her expression became sterner. "Do not deny it. I know his touch. You should be honored. I can see that the soul and body are not matched. Surely you offered yourself to complete this masterpiece."

"I did not offer it. It was taken…"

Ivy's voice was cold, and growing colder. Her eyes were as deeply violet as the scattered gems around them. Blackness now stained the fur around her eyes as well.

"Taken? Ah. Still a matter of honor, to know that he found your soul valuable enough to be a piece of this glorious mosaic that he's made of you. And I'm curious, what is it that is happening now? The darkness, and the eyes. I'm fascinated."

"Darkness…" Ivy recoiled and shut her eyes. "Not that, not now!"

"These auras, they are emotion. That much is clear. I've seen some blue, which I imagine is fear, and I've seen red, which must be anger. Black? Something negative, certainly. Hate perhaps? All of this tinkering with state of mind, it seems more in line with Epidime's sensibilities…"

Turiel continued to muse, but for the moment, Ivy didn't have the mind to spare to listen to it. She'd kept her emotions under control ever since the final battle. It had been a point of pride for her that she'd not allowed herself to change. That part of her, that frail spirit at the mercy of her stormy mind, was supposed to be gone forever. But if ever she were to let the emotions take over again, it would *not* be hatred. Anger and fear, even joy and duty, were fleeting. But hate... she'd felt it only twice before, and it sank its teeth deep into her, threatening never to let go. That dark thing, that twisted, murderous monster was precisely what Demont would have wanted. She wouldn't, she *wouldn't* allow it.

For too long it was a losing battle. The hate was too strong. Images of all the evil that had been done by the D'Karon and on their behalf stung at her mind. Then something happened. She could feel a warmth about her, a connection that soothed her anxiety. It was precisely what she'd needed, and without it, she might have easily slipped away.

She opened her eyes, and for a long moment her mind seized. Turiel had wrapped her arms about Ivy, pulling her into a tight, nurturing embrace. She murmured under her breath, as if to a child who had fallen and scraped her knee. No magic was at work, it was merely an act of caring, of compassion.

"Dear, sweet thing," Turiel said. "I understand. It is too much. You weren't ready. Give it time, dear. You'll find the strength."

Ivy pushed Turiel away, more gently than she'd imagined she'd be able to do.

"Do you feel better, dear?" Turiel asked.

"Don't... don't touch me again."

"Of course not, Ivy. I apologize. But you needed something. You seemed so shaken. Can you tell me, what happened here?"

"What... what happened here?" Ivy said, already threatening to lose her recently regained composure. "Ether destroyed these things."

"Ether," Turiel said, stepping back, wringing her hands. "Ether... yes. Yes, she is one of the adversaries. I remember now. The adversaries..." Her eyes narrowed and she looked at the malthrope. "Ivy was one of the names that woman mentioned. A malthrope named Ivy. You are one of them. But how? He *made* you! How could you be corrupted in this way?" She seemed distraught, betrayed. "Why would you turn on your creators?"

"Do you *know* what the D'Karon did?"

"A war, yes... Yes I know that they were involved in a war. But to suggest they would do anything they didn't *need* to do is nonsense."

"Nonsense? *Nonsense?* Look around you!" Ivy said. She snatched up the sheared-away claw from a fallen creature. "Look at what Demont made! Look at *me!* These things were made to kill. And he used them. The worst of them were set loose into the world. His creatures have been killing the people for so long. We had to end them before they could do any more damage."

"If... if that is so, then it can only be because it was necessary. The D'Karon... the D'Karon are strong and wise. What did you and the others do to them?"

"Bagu is dead. And I killed Teht myself," Ivy said, her gaze steely and her grip on her weapon firm. "The rest were cast away, and we shut the portal."

"Teht... you killed... Ivy you... I *needed* them. They had so much to offer this world. So much to teach me..." Tears were in her eyes.

"They meant to control us, to take our world for their own."

"No... no, you don't understand. How can I ever hope to be what I need to be if... how can I ever learn to avenge my sister if..." Turiel stepped forward and clutched her staff, Mott skittering to the ground. "You need to go."

"Turiel, if you brought the D'Karon here, then you need to face justice for what happened."

"I brought them here. And if you forced them away, then they must be brought back."

"I won't let you do that," Ivy said, raising her weapon.

Turiel thrust her staff forward, its head burning and crackling violently. "I won't let you stop me." The very shadows began to shift and coil, creeping into the brilliant light as strings of inky blackness. "For turning on your creators you deserve so much worse... but you are the work of Demont. And in your eyes I can see that you are a child and you were not ready for the gift you were given."

The tendrils lashed out, coiling about Ivy's club and tearing it from her hand. The malthrope rushed forward, but threads netted together and ensnared her, hurling her back.

"Go, child. Your siblings are about to awaken, and they may not be as charitable as I have been."

Ivy looked desperately around her. The tendrils were piercing the remaining portions of the fallen creations, pulling them together. Jaws began to clack and snap even before the heads found their way to their bodies. More tendrils drove themselves between the cracks and wormed their way to the other floors. The shift and grind of motion rumbled all around her, stirring terrible memories of her other times spent in Demont's workshops. She threw herself against the web of tendrils twice more, clawing at it in a vicious attempt to get to Turiel.

"You can't do this! They'll kill people! You can't control them!"

Turiel turned and gazed at Ivy. "I don't mean to control them, Ivy. They aren't mine to control. I mean to understand them. Now please go, run. You are a fine piece of work, a masterpiece from the hands of the D'Karon who had the most to teach me. I don't think I could bear seeing you destroyed."

Mott chittered and whined, looking back and forth between Ivy and Turiel. The creature was clearly distraught, like a loyal dog that doesn't want to see a beloved master leave.

"There, there, Mott," Turiel said, running her fingers over the monster's head. "Perhaps in time she will find her way."

Ivy cried out and flared with red as she tried and failed to force her way through the tendrils, but it was no use. Every blow was caught and slowed by the ribbons of black. The care taken not to hurt her, and to keep her from hurting herself, was evident. For the first time she could remember, Ivy found herself wishing she could push herself past the breaking point and give in to the fury that had seen her through so many battles before, but her mind wouldn't allow it. The anger was tempered by fear. Fear of what would happen to her if she remained in this place, but more so fear of what would happen to the others if she wasn't there to help defend them. She had to get out. And she had to do it now.

She growled in frustration and turned for the stairs, quickening to a run. Behind her the tapping footsteps of Turiel slowly followed, conjuring more tendrils as she went, awakening more creatures. In four leaping strides, Ivy cleared the first stairwell and sprinted out onto the floor ahead. Mott had lit the way with his little gem on the way down. Without him the scattered slivers of crystal provided the only light, but Ivy's sharp eyes didn't need much. She could see black ribbons slipping out from between the stones of the floor, weaving themselves into the bodies of Demont's broken toys. The lashing filaments of darkness coiled and clutched about blindly, constantly threatening to trip the charging hero. When their thrashing finally brought them into contact with a fallen beast, they coiled about it and dragged it together. Other conjured ribbons abandoned their fruitless searches and continued upward into the ceiling and the floors beyond.

By the time she had reached the well-lit top floor, the shuffling and clawing of restored creatures was echoing all around her. Her boots slid and scraped across the icy crust of frozen sea spray as she ran, but she managed to stay on her feet. She squinted at the bright light of the outside when she finally reached the exit. Ahead, the carriage had been turned and the guards were standing with swords ready. The worrisome sounds had not gone unnoticed, even with the churning of the sea to dull them.

"Go! Move! There are things coming," Ivy called.

"You heard the ambassador!" Celeste said, snapping into action. "Ambassador Krettis, inside the carriage."

"What do you mean? What sort of things?" the ambassador asked as Ivy skidded to a stop before her and ushered her inside.

"You'll see them soon enough," Ivy said breathlessly, rather roughly helping her Tresson counterpart into the carriage. "And you'll wish you hadn't."

Once both Krettis and her aide were inside, Ivy stepped in but stood up and hung out the open door to face the fort behind them. Celeste did the same on the opposite side. They were barely rolling up to speed when the first monsters stepped into the light. It was a pair of stone wolves, stiff hair on their backs standing tall and sharp like porcupine quills. In three strides they had matched the ponderous pace of the carriage, and in two more they proved they could easily close the gap. Mounted guards turned their horses to face the foes, the three Alliance fighters then spread across the surface of the narrow island to block the way. They'd barely raised their swords when the wolves reached them.

"No!" Ivy called out.

She dove from the moving carriage and rolled once, landing on her feet and grinding to a stop before dashing for the soldiers. One wolf dove for a soldier and knocked him free of his horse, opening its jaws to snap at the man's throat. Ivy plowed into the hulking beast, hitting it harder than a creature her size should have been able to. She and the wolf tumbled back toward the fort, sliding near the edge of the island. The wolf slashed and swiped with its claws, teeth gnashing hard enough to send chips of stone flaking free, but Ivy somehow managed to keep the worst of the blows from her flesh. When the rolling slide stopped, they were only a few feet from the edge of the island, and the wolf had her pinned.

Acting on reflex more than anything else, Ivy coiled her legs and planted them on the belly of the monster. It was far heavier than a flesh beast would be, but desperation and fear are powerful things, particularly for Ivy. She cried out in effort and heaved with both legs, forcing the monster up onto its hind legs and back toward the edge. It roared and slashed at her, lacking the mind and instinct to preserve itself as her continued efforts pushed it farther up and farther back. The guard she had saved reached her and threw his weight behind a thrust of his sword. It struck the wolf square in the neck and drove it back just a few inches more. It was enough for the scrabbling hind claws of the beast to reach the edge. Icy stone crumbled away and the monster pitched off the side, clashing and clattering across the sheer stones and splashing into the frigid sea.

Ivy gave a stiff nod to the man who had helped her and turned her eyes to the fort. More creatures were pouring out. Most were ungainly beings meant for the sea, but some had the speed and size to threaten the retreating carriage. Then she turned her eyes to the carriage itself. The second wolf had one or two scores from the swords of guards running along its sides, but it had successfully pushed past them and was thundering toward the carriage. She gritted her teeth and sprang to her feet. The second group of three guards, these the personal guard of the ambassador, peeled off and turned to face the threat. Their bows were at the ready, and they let the arrows fly. Two missed their target, but one arrow drove itself deep into the chest of the charging wolf, splitting its rocky hide and eliciting a shriek of pain. Despite the successful attack, the mindless hunter did not slow or falter. It simply lowered its head and bashed through the cluster of men, upsetting two of them from their horses.

One man was lucky, dropping straight to the ground. The other was sent sliding toward the edge. Ivy streaked toward him, her long, bounding strides carrying her like a blur across the strip of an island. She slid to a stop and dug the claws of one hand into the icy stone while she reached out with the other to catch the wrist of the slipping guard. His momentum, and the weight of his armor, dragged the pair of them off the side, but Ivy just barely managed to keep a grip on the edge. They dangled against the blunt face of the sloughed-off wall of slate. She scrambled with her feet until she found firm footholds, then grunted with effort to lift the ailing man. The other two Tresson guards appeared at the edge. They dropped to their bellies, reaching for their countryman. They didn't so much as look at Ivy, far more concerned for their squadmate than her. That was just as well. She could take care of herself, that much she knew. It was the man who needed help. He might be hurt.

When they had hauled him to safety, she pulled herself up and assessed the situation. The carriage was a third of the way along the lengthy strip of land, with a great distance to cover before it even reached the next bridge. The wolf was clear of any of the guards, but the accumulated injuries had slowed it enough that it was struggling to keep pace with the carriage. Behind them, the next wave of the resurrected monstrosities was seconds away from reaching them.

"All of you, do *not* stand and fight! Get to the carriage and stay close, defend it!" she barked. "Just move! We'll worry about these things later!"

The soldiers mounted up, some with help, and rode out just as some spindly-legged creatures Demont must have based on elk began to clatter across toward them. Ivy ran. Her breath was heaving, her heart was pounding in her ears, and the blood was like fire in her veins. The intensity of the moment had set her mind alight, driving her forward faster than even the guards' horses. In just a few seconds she was closing in on the wolf. Despite its ailing gait, it had nearly closed the gap between it and the carriage. It took only a few moments to realize that this was due to the carriage itself beginning to slow. Ivy set her eyes on the wolf ahead and poured all of her strength into getting closer. When she'd matched its speed and was just a stride or two behind, she finally put what little mind she could spare to the puzzle of somehow striking it down. She had no weapon but her claws and teeth, neither if which would make so much as a scratch in the thing's hide.

A single idea, not wise by any means, asserted itself. For lack of other options, she put the plan into effect. She lengthened her stride, bounding from foot to foot, before finally extending it into a leap. Her intended target had been the monster's head, but she fell short, driving both heels square into the prickly nest of quills between the thing's shoulder blades. One or two of the needlelike barbs slashed through her boots, but the blow did its job. The wolf faltered, stumbling and slipping. Ivy tumbled forward, rolling a bit before recovering. Distantly her mind complained of stabbing pain in the soles of her feet, but she brushed the information aside, focusing instead on the carriage ahead of her. Her legs were beginning to give out, but she pushed herself and just barely managed to catch the flapping door of the carriage and pull herself inside.

Once within, she was met by the point of Celeste's sword. He held it just a whisper from her throat. Ivy kept still and looked about. Both Krettis and her aide were unhurt but recoiled in fear. It was not unjustified. Without the rush of battle to continue to seize her mind, realization began to dawn about how she must look. Her lips were peeled back, teeth gleaming. The quills of the wolves had met their mark more than once, tearing her clothes and staining cloth and fur with blood in more than one place. She was far closer to a change than she'd allowed herself to realize.

Ivy licked her lips and swallowed hard, gently pushing the blade aside. "I'm fine... I'm fine... Why are we slowing?" she said, collapsing into the seat beside Krettis.

The ambassador seemed as though she was on the verge of diving out the opposite door rather than share a space with the malthrope.

Celeste sheathed his sword. "Carriages and horses like this aren't meant for speed at the best of times, and we've pushed them hard to get here as quickly as we did. They haven't got the stamina to keep even this pace."

Ivy twisted aside and pushed the door open again to peer behind them. The half-dozen guards had caught up and were keeping pace, but easily a hundred twisted forms had belched out of the fort's demolished entrance, and if this fort was anything like Demont's others, then there would be hundreds more before the flow stopped.

"We've got to get to safety, and we've got to do something to slow or stop those things," Ivy said. She shut her eyes and took a steadying breath. "I... I might be able to help us pick up the pace. You've got to figure out something to do about the D'Karon creatures."

"What could you possibly do to help us maintain speed?" Krettis said, finally finding her tongue. "Do you intend to get out and push?"

"Where is my case?" Ivy asked, ignoring the ambassador. "Ah, here!"

She pulled open a sturdy wooden case and revealed an elegantly crafted violin. Her hands were still shaking as she applied rosin to the bow.

"A violin? What good will that do?"

"Plenty, if I do it right." She put the violin to her chin. "Can either of you keep a beat? That'll help. If you can sing, that'll help more."

"I... I can try," remarked Marraata.

"Good," Ivy said. She thumped her boot on the floor, tapping out a fast rhythm until the aid matched it. "Fine, that's fine. Mr. Celeste, make sure the guards stay close. It'll be easier if they're close. And if we need to go faster, tell her to speed up the rhythm. Let's begin."

Ivy put the bow to the strings, drawing out a fast and lively tune. At first it was shaky and sloppy, but as her mind soothed and the music gripped her, the tune became sharp, precise, and spirited. Her fingers danced across the strings, and the anxiety and fatigue drained from her expression. Then came the glow. A deep, golden aura that spread from her like the rising sun. Streamers of it looped and twisted in the air, weaving around the passengers and swirling out of the carriage. Ivy grinned as she felt the scrapes and gouges begin to ease away. Music never failed to stir a joy within her, and joy never failed to ease the pain and revitalize the bodies of the people around her.

#

Celeste watched the aura spread from Ivy and leaned aside to see thin wisps of it begin to coil toward the horses ahead and behind. Her song became louder, stronger, and the strength of the aura grew. There was no questioning the effect. The horses ran harder, both those ahead and those behind. Fatigue melted away and spirits lifted. They soon matched their earlier speed, and not long after began to move even more quickly. It was a mercy that the island was so straight, because at their present speed, navigating a turn with such a thick crust of ice would mean a sure skid into the sea.

He gazed back at the charge of beasts. Some of the smaller ones were keeping up, and if the carriage flagged again, the things would be upon them, but that didn't concern him. They could easily be dispatched with a few sharp swipes of a blade. What concerned him was a lumbering behemoth that had just pulled itself from the doorway. It was easily the size of the carriage itself. If he were to venture a description of the thing, he would have compared it to a crab crafted from the slag and debris from a blacksmith's forge. It was rust-brown and mottled, here and there gleaming in the light. Four stout legs, each armored with a thick jagged carapace, scuttled along at a width that might *just* fit the bridge ahead. Its motions were slow and lumbering, suggesting it was massively heavy, but the length of its legs and their sweep meant that it still covered a great deal of ground with each stride. The body, larger than that of a pair of horses, hung low to the ground. Getting past the armored legs to attack the thing would be difficult. Black orbs atop stalks must have been its eyes, but in place of a mouth it had only a group of slits that vented all-too-familiar black plumes of burning miasma. They had six guards, himself, and Ivy. They might be able to defeat the beast when it reached them, but not without losses… and if any of those losses were Tresson, that would be ruinous for the already ill-fated diplomatic tour. It would need to be stopped before that could happen.

"We need to go a bit faster," Celeste said.

Marraata nodded and thumped her boot a bit more quickly. Ivy grinned, lost in the music, and sped her tempo to match. The thrill of the challenge and the spirit of the music intensified, and with it grew the strength of the aura. Their speed increased. It wasn't much—the horses were probably running as

161

hard as they could—but it was enough to be sure they wouldn't be reached by the forward edge of the creeping mob before they hit the mainland. He looked ahead and saw the edge of the strip island and its narrow bridge rapidly approaching. An idea came to mind. One of the pointless luxuries that had been included in the carriage to make the journey more comfortable for the delegation was a pair of oil lanterns to light the interior. A small cask of lamp oil was strapped to the roof to store enough to refill them each morning. He hung himself out the door and grasped the edge of the roof. The oil cask was just beyond the edge of the roof, tied down with heavy twine. He tugged out the knot and pulled both the cask and the twine inside, thumping them down on the floor of the carriage.

"What do you intend to do?" Krettis asked.

"I intend to destroy the bridge," he said.

He pulled the nearest lamp from its mounting in the carriage and, using the twine, lashed it to the cask. Once the still burning lamp was securely fastened, Celeste leaned out the door to address the others.

"Driver. Ease up slightly and let the guards pass before the bridge! Guards, stay ahead and do not slow until the mainland!"

Their driver tugged hard on the reins. Invigorated as they were by Ivy's influence, it was no simple task to coax the horses into slowing. The open doors of the carriage flapped roughly, doing little to muffle the thundering din of the charging horses on either side. A peculiar look of manic exhilaration was painted across Marraata's face. There was the sense that she wanted badly to cover her ears, shut her eyes, and huddle in terror, but Ivy's contagious joy and her own task to keep its beat molded the fear into something akin to excitement. She faithfully pounded her boot, fueling the upbeat tune that in turn fueled their escape.

The last of the guards squeezed by the carriage with barely moments to spare. No sooner had the final horse slipped into the lead than the hollow thump of hooves on wood replaced the crackle of hooves on icy stone. Celeste held tight to the door frame of the carriage and lifted the cask of oil. The upright struts supporting one end of the bridge whipped by, one catching the door opposite Celeste and shattering it. He shoved his own door open and lobbed the oil cask into the air. It struck the bridge behind them, tumbling and spilling its contents. The lit lamp ignited the splashing oil, bathing the planks of the bridge in flame.

His job done, he ducked back inside and held his door shut, lest it be struck by the second set of struts. A horrid chorus of unnatural cries split the air behind them as the leading edge of the wave of D'Karon creatures attempted to cross the pools of flame.

"Will the fire be enough to stop them?" Krettis asked.

Her eyes were wide with panic and she'd dug her fingers into the seat for fear of falling. Most people found it very difficult to resist the uplifting effects of Ivy's aura, but as Ether and the D'Karon had frequently illustrated, if one was stubborn or unwilling they could shrug off both the positive and negative influence.

"I very much doubt it," he stated simply.

A few more seconds at their present speed were all it took for the carriage to cross the remaining island and bridge. Once firmly upon the mainland, Celeste again opened the door and leaned out.

"Here! Form up at the bridge and hold your ground!" he ordered. He then turned to Ivy and placed a hand on her shoulder. "That's enough, Ambassador."

She nodded and brought the tune to a stirring crescendo. When she was through, she beamed a broad smile at Marraata.

"You did *wonderful!*" Ivy said breathlessly, clutching Marraata's arm. "Ambassador, you didn't tell me your aide was so musical!"

"What possible difference would something like that make in a proper diplomatic exchange? And how can you think of such a thing at a time like this? There are *creatures* heading in this direction. We should retreat to a fortress or at least a city!"

Ivy brushed away some flecks of blood and pulled at her torn shawl. Though her joyful influence had all but healed her various scrapes and gouges, the stains remained.

"No. We've got to take care of this. I might be an ambassador now, but I was Chosen first, and this is my duty," Ivy said simply.

She stowed her violin with care and stepped through the splintered remains of the broken door. All six guards, the three Alliance on the left and the three Tresson on the right, stood at the mouth of the bridge, weapons ready. Just as Ivy's joy had allowed her to heal, so did it mend the worst of the injuries of those hurt prior to their retreat. The red-clad Tressons each had a bow drawn, but none had fired. Ivy quickly reasoned why.

"We need to work together, everyone," she said. "Those of you from Tressor, you have permission to fire on anything crossing this bridge that you believe would be a threat to your people or ours. Those things are D'Karon, *not* Northern Alliance. They are just as much our enemy as yours, so if you believe you have a shot, take it."

Her assurance prompted three sharp twangs of bowstrings. All three bolts hit their mark, shattering the singed but still dangerous beasts that had burst through the flames.

For a few tense moments, the rush of creatures across the bridge seemed not to be slowing at all. The alliance guards took forward positions and put their swords to work on the scattered beasts that made it past the arrows of the Tressons. With each moment though, more of the tar-soaked bridge took to flame, and the gauntlet of burning wood began to claim the smaller beasts and render the larger ones weak enough to be easily dispatched.

After a quarter of an hour the first wave of creatures had dwindled to nothing. The guards stood ready for what would come next, eyes peering through the smoke and flames of the bridge at the approaching second wave. Easily as numerous as the faster beasts, this group comprised larger, slower monsters, chief among them the lumbering monstrosity that had been Celeste's greatest concern.

The wave of twisted forms rolled forward. Though the bridge was now fully consumed in flames, it had been built of fine timber and stubbornly refused to collapse. This fact had not gone unnoticed by Ambassador Krettis.

"What do we do if the bridge holds?" she asked.

"We will have the carriage take you and your aide to the nearest town. Your guards too, if you prefer."

"And what of you?"

"We will stand and fight."

"You can't hope to defeat that thing."

"You'd be surprised," Ivy said.

"Even the crazed beast you became could not fell so massive a monster," Krettis said.

Ivy turned, cocking her head. "Crazed beast?"

"I saw in your eyes the blood fury. When I was told you would be my counterpart in this mission, I was warned that there were claims you could become some sort of rampaging monster. It was a harrowing sight."

The malthrope grinned. "Oh, you haven't seen that happen. Not yet."

"What do you mean? The madness in your eyes was unmistakable."

"I hope you never have to see me as the thing they warned you about. But if it happens, I assure you, you'll know it."

All eyes turned back to the charge of monsters. They were nearly upon the bridge now, and their pace had slowed as they fought and shoved to be the first to plunge into the flames. One beast, a thing that looked not unlike a bison with scales, thundered onto the planks. Three heedless steps brought its foot down on a plank too charred to support it, and the monster toppled down into the water to be swallowed by the churning waves. Half a dozen beasts made similarly ill-fated attempts to cross the bridge before the crab-thing finally thumped onto the blackened span.

By virtue of its size, the hulking creation had to plant its feet on the far sides of the bridge. It so perfectly fit the bridge one could almost imagine the structure having been built specifically to facilitate the monster's eventual escape. Walking as it was on the outer edge of the burning structure, it was supported by the thickest, most intact beams.

"Driver, eyes on the island. If that beast touches stone again, you will take the ambassador and her aide south. Do not stop until you are behind a fortified wall," Celeste ordered. "Tresson guard, you are not mine to command, but I would advise you to join them. Alliance guards, remain."

The D'Karon Apprentice

Step by creaking step, the monster rumbled forward, and the bridge refused to fail. Flames licked at its armored limbs, but it paid them no mind. Behind it the mob of waiting creations clambered onto the bridge. Many fell through widening holes in the burning surface. Ivy stood with feet set wide, balanced on her toes and ready to spring. The Tresson guards put fresh arrows to their strings and stood ready, each Alliance swordsman doing the same.

The final rocking shift of the beast's weight made ready to bring it to land when one of the main supports split, sending out a cloud of orange embers and causing the bridge to roll to the side. Nameless abominations pitched into the sea, and the behemoth that was leading the charge scrabbled and scraped at the land. In its thrashing, it demolished one of the surviving support struts and sent the remainder of the bridge plunging into the water. Without any rear footing, the crab creature's own weight dragged it backward until it dropped from sight, crashing along the rocks and splashing into the water.

The sense of relief as the final shreds of the bridge fell away was palpable. The soldiers eased, eyes still locked on the remaining threats but bodies no longer tensed. Ivy settled down again and looked to the surviving horde and the fort beyond. Without a route to the mainland, some of the leading edge hurled itself into the water rather than give up its forward charge. Others attempted to stop but failed, either due to their own momentum or the pressing bodies of the beasts behind. When the limited minds of the beasts finally came to terms with the blocked path, they simply stood, restless but without direction or ambition. They lacked the knowledge to cope with such an obstacle, and therefore could do nothing more than await instruction.

"What did you see in that place?" Celeste asked, turning to Ivy.

"Lots of stuff with fins and scales, so some of these things might survive a trip to the shore... though I don't suppose they'll be able to scale the cliffs very easily," Ivy said.

"You heard her. Eyes open, all of you," Celeste said, addressing the guards. "You, head south. I care not what route you take, but be sure to pass through two towns and warn them to have lookouts and armed men ready in the event some of these creatures reach them. Tell each of the towns to send runners of their own with similar warnings to their neighbors. You, head east, same orders. After that, return to your garrison. We will replace you from the local guards at our next stop. So ordered." The men rode off. "You, meet the rest of the delegation and warn them to be on high guard. Then remain with them until we meet you." The guard nodded and obeyed. Celeste turned back to Ivy. "What else did you see?"

"There was a woman, and a thing. Different from the D'Karon beasts. It was more... affectionate, I suppose. It certainly seemed more natural than the sort of things Demont dreamed up."

"Was this woman D'Karon?"

"No… no, she was human, I'm certain of that… at least, she *was* human. There was something off about her scent. She's… a mix of different scents. I think she's a little like the beast. Made of bits and pieces of other things. Whatever she was, she knew all about the D'Karon's works. I don't know much about magic, but it felt like she was doing the same things they were. I think she might have worshiped them. She recognized me as one of Demont's creations, and she seemed thrilled to have the chance to meet me because of that. It wasn't until she found out Ether had destroyed the creatures in the first place that she finally woke them and sent them on their way."

"And you are certain she isn't one of the D'Karon?"

"Positive. Not just because she was human but because she was… *kind*. She called her beast Mott, treated it like a pet. The D'Karon always seemed cold and distant. Demont used to treat his creations like tools. This woman, Turiel was her name, she spoke with passion, and when I nearly lost my composure, she comforted me. But… but she said she *brought* them here. She is the one who summoned the D'Karon in the first place. And she said if we truly cast them away, then she would find a way to bring them back."

"Then she must be stopped."

"Yes… yes, I know," Ivy said. There was a sadness, even an uncertainty, in her tone.

"You seem reluctant."

"Mr. Celeste, I don't know how to explain it, but… I really don't think she understands what she did was wrong. She didn't seem fully convinced there had been a war. When I told her we'd banished or defeated each of the generals, she said something about needing to learn things from them. She had a reason for bringing them here, but I really don't think she understands how bad the D'Karon were."

"Regardless, they can't be allowed to return. She *must* be *stopped*."

Ivy nodded. "But we'll need help. She's a wizard, and a powerful one. I couldn't so much as lay a finger on her before she threw up some sort of web to protect her. We need Myranda and Deacon up here, or at least Ether. Someone with magic."

"Myranda and Deacon are in Tressor. Even with the dragon I do not believe they could reach us quickly enough to be of aid. How would we summon Ether?"

"I don't know… She should have answered the same call we did. Where is that pad? I'll try again," Ivy said.

She and Celeste paced back toward the carriage. Seated on the floor of the carriage with her feet dangling toward the ground was Ambassador Krettis. The woman was trembling. The cold and damp may have been to blame, but judging by her face, that was the least of the causes. She was shaken to her core, looking for the life of her as if she'd done battle with those monstrosities herself, despite having been relatively safe in the carriage through the worst of it. Marraata was outside, pouring the ambassador a brandy to steady her nerves. The bottle was nearly empty, suggesting this was hardly the first drink she'd had since they'd reached the shore.

"Ambassador? Are you all right?" Ivy asked.

"I… I do not know what to say to you, Ambassador Ivy…" Krettis said. "What happened here… I do not know what to think…"

"I'd warned you it would be dangerous, Ambassador."

"If… if you were hoping to convince us that you were harmless, that you were no threat to us militarily, this was not the way. If you were hoping to illustrate that you were not in league with these D'Karon of yours… you make a strong display of their threat but… you could have been killed. *I* could have been killed."

"Again, Ambassador Krettis, I warned you it would be dangerous," Ivy repeated, irritation beginning to edge out sympathy in her voice.

"If I had been killed, war would have been certain. I cannot… I cannot imagine why someone would *arrange* something like this…"

Ivy clenched her teeth. "That's because I didn't arrange it, Ambassador. I didn't even want you to come. But now that you have, now that you've seen this, I hope you can at least appreciate the truth of what we've been saying. The D'Karon and their creations are a threat to us all. They are the enemy. And as much anger as your land and mine might feel for one another, if there is even a chance that the D'Karon might return, then we *must* be united against them, because if not, they will turn us against one another again and smile from the shadows as we do their work for them."

"I truly do not know what to believe," Krettis said, shaking her head. She downed her brandy and handed the glass back to her aide to be refilled. "I will tell you this, however, Ambassador. There are two things for certain." She took the now brimming glass. "The first is that your people are *quite* skilled at crafting a brandy." She drained the glass again and handed it back. "The second is that I have no desire to ever see anything of those beasts again. Let us move, quickly."

Ivy looked to the fort in the distance and the dregs of the unleashed creatures that stood aimless before the ruined bridge.

"You take the ambassador somewhere safe, Mr. Celeste. Continue the tour, if you think you can. I'll stay here."

"I can't allow you to remain here alone," he said.

"Someone's got to keep an eye on this place, and on that woman inside." He turned to the carriage.

"Ambassador Krettis, would you prefer the remainder of this diplomatic tour be postponed until the crisis at hand can be properly dealt with?" he asked.

"What I would prefer is to find a warm place to think, ideally one unmolested by abominations of 'D'Karon' design," she said.

"Would you feel at all slighted or disrespected if the ambassador were to briefly set her role aside?"

"Having seen the nature of those creatures and the lengths you would go to eliminate them, I believe it best for all involved if you remain in proximity to this threat."

"Very well. Driver, take Ambassador Krettis back to the delegation, see that she is made comfortable, and pending her further decision, either see to it that she is returned to the border or see that one of the lesser members of the delegation continue the tour. I shall remain here with Guardian Ivy."

"You don't have to do that," Ivy said.

"I have agreed to act as your adviser. This is a matter as worthy of my advice as any, should you need it," he said. He turned back to the carriage and its escort. All Alliance soldiers had been dispatched, so Celeste addressed the Tresson guards. "You are not mine to command, but if you are willing, two of you leave your horses and equipment for us and accompany the ambassador and her aide within the carriage as her personal guard."

"Do it," Krettis ordered her men.

"Many thanks. Driver, move out. Send three freshly rested men on horseback to this location as soon as they are available and Ambassador Krettis is safely in town."

All did as ordered, and Ivy transferred her things to the back of a loaned horse. In minutes, Ivy and Celeste were alone, eyes set on the fort. Ivy pulled up the hood of her overcloak, folding down her ears to pull it tight against the wind. She looked at Celeste.

"I'm surprised you didn't have some of the men stay behind," she said.

"Again, the remaining men were not mine to command, and I very much doubt a handful of soldiers will make for much more than fodder should that woman or her army reach the shore," he said.

"Aren't you worried what might happen to you?"

"You are a Guardian of the Realm. My daughter trusts you with her life, and our land trusts you with its defense. My concern is not what will become of me, but what value I can be to you in the meantime," he said.

Ivy smiled. "Myranda is lucky to have a father like you."

"Myranda hardly had me as a father at all. I left her to face an unforgiving world alone because I believed it was the best thing I could do for her."

"You did the right thing," Ivy said. "I think deep down you knew she'd be strong enough to find her own way." She reached out and gripped his hand. "But thank you for staying with me through this. I'm not as strong as Myranda sometimes."

"You're stronger than you think."

She looked back to the fort.

"I hope you're right. I really do."

#

The D'Karon Apprentice

Amid the crackling, nourishing flames of the fireplace in her room, Ether was thoroughly lost in thought. The recent encounter with that woman, Celia, had a greater effect on her than she would have anticipated, and certainly greater than she could explain. Her capacity to continue in the face of losses that must, at least to her, have seemed similar to Ether's own was a source of endless fascination. Naturally the reality of the situation was that Celia's loss paled in comparison to Ether's. The woman and those loved ones she had outlived were mortal, and therefore they'd lost no more than a handful of years together, whereas a timeless being such as she had lost *eternity*. Regardless, to the small and limited mind of the woman, a few years must have *seemed* like an eternity, and yet she pressed on in spite of it all. The woman had achieved peace and acceptance where Ether could find none. Mortals. A strength unique to mortals… it was absurd.

"Guardian Ether! Guardian Ether!" cried a voice amid urgent thumping.

The call of her name was iterated several times more before the shapeshifter reluctantly pulled herself from the flames and resumed her human form. She pulled open the door to find herself face to face with one of the younger and more skittish members of the diplomatic envoy, a page named Stefan.

"What is it?" she demanded.

"I'm sorry to disturb you," he said, though his tone and posture suggested a more accurate claim would have been that he was terrified to disturb her. "But one of—oh my!"

He averted his eyes.

"What is this nonsense?"

"You aren't decent," he said, stricken with shame and embarrassment.

Ether glanced down. Indeed she had resumed her human form without the pointless coverings they seemed so devoted to draping around themselves and stood before him completely bare. She quickly remedied the oversight. Her brief nudity was of little concern to her, but the fact she'd made such an error revealed a worrying degree of distraction.

"Deliver your message," she ordered.

He reluctantly looked back in her direction, his face beet red.

"One of the bags was moving and making a noise. It had been doing it for quite a while, and we thought it must have been a mouse! We aren't allowed to open the bags of those in the delegation, but one of the other ambassadors…"

"Is there an *end* to this, boy?" she asked.

"This was making a noise, and when we found it, it opened and started writing!" he said, offering up Deacon's pad.

Ether took it from him and wearily looked over the pages. Quite a few additional notes had been exchanged since Myranda's initial warning. Now there was an account of Ivy's encounter, and one from someone signing his correspondence "CL" that described a destructive event in the capital. The word "D'Karon" was scattered across the pages.

"This is not possible. If there had been D'Karon activity, I would have known," Ether said.

"Ah!" Stefan covered his ears.

"What are you doing now?" she growled.

"I am not to hear such matters, Guardian!" he said.

"I shall set this to rest right now," Ether said.

She focused her mind briefly on the task of sensing the unmistakable influence of the D'Karon and their magic. Within moments, her expression hardened. Though it was not the piercing, sour sensation she normally associated with their works, there was undeniably something similar. Scattered across the north and south, like drops of blood on a field of white snow, were the lingering traces of poorly cast D'Karon spells. Worse, she could feel them grow more refined with each casting. In time, these imitations would be as keen an affront to nature as the works of the D'Karon themselves.

There could be a disciple of the D'Karon, a wizard quickly learning their ways... and Ether had missed it. Worse, even alerted of the attack, she was having difficulty resolving where precisely the portals had come and gone.

"Why would they not have contacted me directly?" she seethed. "Why would Myranda and Deacon rely upon this *ridiculous toy* rather than seek me out with their own minds?"

"I'm sure someone else would be better suited to answer that question, Guardian. I'll fetch someone directly!"

"Is there some problem?" asked a voice from the end of the hall.

Ether turned to find Ambassador Maka standing at his door. Stefan turned and offered a deferential bow.

"Ambassador Maka. My apologies for disturbing you," he said, stricken with anxiety.

Maka raised his hands and lowered his head. "There is no cause for apology, my good man. I am an early riser of my own choice. I have been awake for some time. Is this a matter with which I may be of assistance?"

"I have received some news through a means I was not expecting, and I was musing over the exceedingly poor judgment that could have convinced my fellow Chosen from contacting me properly," Ether explained.

"Would this be Guardian Ivy, Guardian Myn, or Guardian Myranda, Ambassador Ether?"

"This matter would have been communicated by Myranda or her chosen mate."

"A matter of magic, then?"

"Yes."

"I believe they are in my homeland, and it is my understanding that our military would request they perform no far-reaching works of magic as a matter of courtesy and privacy."

"Yes," Ether said, impatience in her tone. "They *would* continue to obey so minor an agreement despite the consequences..." She turned to Maka. "Ambassador Maka, this matter is likely one beneath me, but it deals with a subject of such grave importance that its mere implication is enough to warrant my attention."

"I understand, of course. There are claims that you can, at your pleasure, duplicate yourself. Will you be doing so, to continue in your present capacity while addressing the second matter?"

"I prefer not to split my attentions unnecessarily. Recent revelations have made depth of focus a matter of careful consideration, it seems."

"Ah, a shame. I was intrigued by how such a thing might be achieved. No matter. Will the tour continue in your absence?"

"I am certain the others will make for more agreeable and conventional hosts."

"Perhaps more conventional, Ambassador, but I have found your hospitality most agreeable. Will you be returning?"

"I have committed to the whole of this tour. I intend to honor that commitment as soon as this matter is dealt with."

"Excellent. I have enjoyed our talks, and I look forward to continuing them."

"As do I. You are a man of considerable insight for one of so few years."

"Ha!" he said with a wide grin. "And *you* have a way of making an old man feel young again."

"You will inform the rest of the delegation of my departure?"

"Of course. Do not let us keep you from your task."

Ether did not waste another moment on the painful delays of protocol and pleasantries. She shifted sharply to a whirling mass of wind and whisked through the nearest loose shutter, leaving her pad in the hands of the startled and uneasy Stefan.

A feeling of unbridled liberation flooded her. Again the very air that enrobed the world mixed with consciousness, flowing through and around her. Thus freed of the burdensome form, her mind was free to pore over the tainted remnants of the horrid spells she'd been made aware of. Her first act would be to identify the proper destination. She could sense that Myranda and Deacon were headed quickly for one of the sources of such blight, and there was some talk about how her presence in the south might be problematic. That mattered little to her. If she had reason to do so, she would have few qualms about journeying to Tressor to investigate. But the workings in the north were far fresher and far closer to the proper casting of the spells. They were her greatest concern. Ivy, for all of her flaws, had investigated one of the most recent and abundant upwellings of magic. Though that fort and its well of dark workings would likely benefit most from her investigation, Ivy at least knew intimately of the D'Karon and their treachery. There was one point of concern that had been seen to only by mortals. It was the point farthest to the north, the capital. As she tried to focus on it, she felt as though this place had by far the greatest stain of magic. Portals to and from that place had opened more than once, and to different positions. It was the greatest incursion, and for that reason warranted the eye of the most skilled member of the Chosen.

She set her course for the Castle Verril and poured on as much speed as she could muster, whisking though the morning air and watching fields of white, silver, gray, and green rush by beneath her.

The first riddle solved for now, Ether could muse upon the more troubling matter of how she had failed to detect these spells.

I've spent too much time out of my native form. It has muddled my thinking. That must be the problem, she thought. As often as I've taken Emilia's form…

Ether paused. No. Not Emilia's form. My human form. There is no connection to that woman beyond the aesthetic. It is pointless to think of it as anything but an assumed appearance. And regardless, I've assumed the form so often it is simple, comfortable. It shouldn't limit my perception of such things. Yet there can be no doubt that having returned to a more appropriate form I can think more clearly, sense the world more directly. Yes… yes, I've simply numbed myself to the limitations of the form. In the future I shall forgo assuming human form, and such matters will no longer slip my notice.

For a few moments, and a few dozen miles, the answer had been obvious and satisfactory, but realization soon robbed her of the comfortable feeling of having solved this more troubling puzzle.

I'd been in the form of flame, replenishing myself all night. My mind should have been as clear then as it has ever been. And yet I had to be informed…

She considered the long night crackling in the hearth and the things that had occupied her mind during that time. As was too often the case, she'd been dwelling on the gnawing emptiness within her. The void left by the loss of Lain and the loss of her purpose. Cold realization poured over her as she finally grasped how deeply her mind and soul were stained by these petty mortal needs. A solution needed to be found before she slipped any deeper into the bleak state of mind that had driven her to this malaise. This void needed to be filled or else cut away. She needed to be rid of the longing and listlessness before she was rendered the same useless tangle of doubt and confusion that all mortals seemed to be.

This worrying preoccupation with her own preoccupation made the remainder of the journey seem to pass in no time at all, though traveling as the wind meant that such was not far from the truth. Dawn had only just finished breaking when her windy form pulled together into a roughly human shape in the courtyard of Castle Verril. Out of reflex and habit, she quickly resumed her human form, a fact that brought an irritated scowl to her already stern expression. It would be a difficult matter to train herself not to resort to humanity as a default form. She briefly considered whisking back to wind, or perhaps choosing stone or flame, but the palace was meant for creatures of roughly human form, and therefore it was simpler for now to remain as one, lest she risk igniting tapestries or crumbling stone underfoot.

"Oh! Guardian Ether!" said a uniformed guard, a young woman startled by Ether's sudden appearance. She gave an awkward bow. "We are honored by your presence."

"Are you the individual responsible for investigating the recent so-called D'Karon appearance?" Ether asked.

"No, Guardian, I—"

"Then summon the person responsible. I am neglecting other duties to see to this matter, and I do not wish to do so for any longer than necessary."

"Of course, Guardian Ether," the woman said, scurrying off.

Ether paced forward, crossing the courtyard of the palace and approaching the entry hall. It was unusually busy for so early in the morning, both servants and guards scurrying this way and that, each pausing to offer her a bow and an honorific-laden greeting. When she stepped from the icy, snow-dusted courtyard to an entry hall that was moderately less so, the severity of the situation was finally made clear.

A sizable portion of the entryway had collapsed. Centered on the left wall was a jagged hole, the stone around which was pulverized. Fractures were scattered about the opposite wall where fragments of debris had struck with great force, and a small section of the high ceiling had collapsed. The hall was normally draped with priceless banners and carpets, but they'd all been cleared away, no doubt to either repair the damage they'd received in the attack or to get them out of the elements lest they suffer greater damage. Though the lion's share of the mess had been cleared away and masons were already cutting stone to perform repairs, the rosy light of morning still shone through the narrow fault in the roof. A dusting of snow drifted lazily through the hole, floating to the floor, where it was quickly swept away by broom-bearing servants.

The shapeshifter stood in the center of the room and closed her eyes, opening her mind to a scene that was if anything *more* devastating. This place was stinking of D'Karon magic. Such had long been the case. The center of the apparent explosion had been the personal chamber of General Bagu, the most loathsome of the D'Karon generals, for decades. It would be years before his tainted influence could be cleaned from the astral fabric of this place. But now there was a new layer to the wretchedness. A fresh spell, flawed but enthusiastically cast by a mind well suited for such things.

Joseph R. Lallo

"Guardian Ether. It is my great shame to be meeting you under these circumstances," remarked a voice from the door leading to the throne room.

Ether turned to see the pristine, angular features of an elf. Even by human standards he would have been a young man. By elven standards he was practically a child. His hair was just less than shoulder length and looked like spun gold. The uniform he wore was an interesting one. It was finely tailored and dyed all three shades of Alliance blue, but was otherwise neither ostentatious nor ornate. Emblems on the shoulder and cuff identified him as a captain, but no medals, sashes, or ribbons were pinned or sewn in place, and it was layered for warmth. It was the garb of a respected soldier, but moreover a soldier who had work to do.

"Captain Croyden Lumineblade," he said, bowing before offering a hand and a crisp smile.

Ether glanced at the offered hand but ignored it.

"I believe we met briefly at the coronation reception," Croyden said, lowering his hand but maintaining the cordial demeanor.

"Yes," Ether said brusquely. "You were the queen's handler that day. And her plaything since, if I understand correctly."

His smile became brittle. "Ah. Well, I am pleased that the impression I had of you at that time remains an accurate one."

"I am eternal. My attitude does not change with time."

"Evidently."

"Tell me what happened here."

"What happened here was nothing short of an attack on the capital. A message was delivered via the enchanted booklet provided by Deacon that an invader may have infiltrated the capital. For many hours guards were on high alert, but no outsiders were identified until a voice was heard within Bagu's chamber. The seal had not been broken, and there is no other way into the chamber."

"Portal magic. It should have been plainly obvious that any portal would open directly into Bagu's chamber."

"A matter that we would have been mindful of if any but the D'Karon had insight into their spells."

"Clearly *I* have insight into their spells."

He almost imperceptibly gritted his teeth. "Perhaps the Guardian would be willing, in the future, to take the time to share this insight, such that we might better defend the capital. Shall I continue?"

"Yes."

"We opened the door and immediately a woman within assaulted the palace guards with magic. She did not appear to be of sound mind, and demanded silence. We summoned the palace mystic to defend us, but she was woefully outclassed. At that point the attacker subdued her and began to demand information of the mystic before retreating into the chamber. Moments

174

later there was an explosion, killing several guards and injuring many more. The attacker and the mystic are still missing."

"What information was she seeking?"

"The handful of guards who survived the blast was understandably shaken."

"Stop making excuses for their infirmities and answer the question," Ether said.

Any semblance of respect, or even patience, slipped from Croyden's face. "They feel certain that she was seeking some manner of portal, and there was some talk of the Chosen, for which she had another name. The adversaries."

"Mmm..."

"Regardless of claims to the contrary, I believe we are dealing with a surviving member of the D'Karon."

"That is because you are a weak-minded fool who does not understand the plainly obvious."

"Then explain the nature of this attack, and the fact it was so successful, if it was not performed by skilled sorcerers intimately familiar with our defenses?"

Ether waved her hand. "This is not an attack. And it is certainly not the work of a skilled sorceress. At least not as skilled as she might be. The D'Karon portal spells always spilled off energy when closed. This one was miscast. It was inefficient. And no D'Karon, certainly not a well-trained one, would ever sully such a spell in such a way. Take me to these survivors. I need to question them directly."

Croyden straightened. "No."

"I was not requesting permission."

"And that's just as well, because I am not granting it. Those men are still recovering. Some may not last the day. There is nothing you could ask them that I have not already asked, and I refuse to allow their last memories of this world be of you and your open contempt for them simply by virtue of their perceived inferiority. You are a Guardian of the Realm. Anywhere else your authority would surpass my own. But within this palace, and when the queen is away, my word is law and my decisions are final. I shall continue to treat you with the respect owed to your title. But that is the *only* respect you shall receive, and it is entirely undeserved."

"If your respect is to my title then you may as well abandon it," Ether said. "Titles are meaningless."

He raised an eyebrow. "Then am I to believe you would have me treat you as I would an equal?"

"Of course not. I am superior to you and you will treat me as such."

"Then why disparage the title?"

"Because my superiority is innate, not bestowed. Now take me to these survivors, or step aside and I shall find them myself."

Croyden widened his stance and folded his arms. "Ask your questions. If I do not have the answers you seek, then I will ask the men myself."

Ether narrowed her eyes. "You are stubborn and strong willed."

"Necessary qualities. I run the palace while the queen runs the kingdom. If not for a strong will, chaos such as this might well be an everyday occurrence."

"You do realize that I could easily cast you aside and question them regardless of your will."

"Not nearly as easily as you suppose. What are your questions?"

Ether took a breath. "Describe the appearance of the spells she cast."

"Her magic was bathed in violet light and often took the form of summoned strings of an impossibly strong black material."

"How old was this woman?"

"She was human and described as old for a mother or young for a grandmother. I would place her age at not more than forty years."

"Was she accompanied?"

"No, she was alone."

"What did her staff look like?"

"It was bone white with an indigo gem."

"Her clothing?"

"Tattered robes of black."

"Did she speak distinctively?"

"Native Varden. One man said she sounded more proper than most. There was agreement that her voice and words were not those of a sane person."

"… You *have* been thorough."

"Again, a necessary quality. What precisely do you hope to learn from these questions?"

"I am not certain, but as you say, thoroughness is a necessary quality. To that end, silence yourself for a moment. Half a kingdom away I was able to detect only that there was indeed some manner of D'Karon workings in this area, and now immersed in it I can detect its degree, but there may well be more treachery at work here than you have noticed or I have detected. We shall put that to rest now."

As before, she shut her eyes, but rather than simply taking in her surroundings she allowed her mind to spread, scrutinizing the mystic residues present. She could feel, in some measure, each spell both the woman and her captive had cast. The lingering echoes of the summoned tendrils still seemed to waver around her. But there was more. It was something distant, to the north. The sensation was much like this one. Associating a point in the astral realm with its counterpart in the physical realm was not always a simple task… but in this case it was a place known all too well to her.

"I must go," she said sharply.

The look of resolve and irritation on Croyden's face changed to one of reluctant concern. "Is something wrong?"

"That monster has sullied..." She stopped herself and eyed Croyden steadily. "I shall return."

Before he could ask another question, she shifted to flame and burst out the door. She looped over the castle and tore through the sky northward. In her mind's eye, mocking her like the splash of a vandal's paint across the face of a masterful portrait, was a glaring work of D'Karon magic in the center of the place known as Lain's End. That woman, that *thing* that clumsily wielded the weapon of her enemy, had used it to desecrate the site of the greatest tragedy in the history of this blighted world. Ether's fiery visage twisted in vicious anger as she stopped mere seconds later in the remnants of a mountain range.

For anyone else, Lain's End would seem the same inexplicable curiosity it had always been, save for a sizable gouge in the land not far from the tip of the pointed outcropping that reached out toward its center. The bottomless pit was still present, and the mysterious stones that hung and drifted over it continued their complex dance. Ether had spent too much time here, too many days staring unblinking at the aftermath of their final victory and greatest failure against the D'Karon. Black stains of dark magic hung like cobwebs from the edges of a sequence of stones. That anyone would sully this solemn place with more D'Karon workings stung Ether. The fact that this was the place formerly home to the portal that could have flooded the world with the D'Karon and their creations was worrying enough. Coming here meant the woman knew far more than she should about the D'Karon's plans, which in turn meant she might have some insight into how to once again render the otherworldly creatures a threat.

Then her eyes turned to the one patch of ground that had served as the focus of nearly every moment of her time here...

Her fists clenched, the flames of her body surging brilliantly bright, and her mind sizzled with hatred. The sword, *Lain's* sword, was missing. That monster had come to this place and *dared* to disturb the resting place and legacy of a creature so perfect, a creature who was her sole equal, a creature whom she *loved*...

She felt it stoke the flames of her anger, and as they seared her mind, she realized something else. Of all people, she heard the voice of Myranda in her mind. A memory of one of a dozen lectures the human had given her.

"I know you believe yourself above such things, Ether," Myranda had said. "But whether you embrace it or not, you are a part of this world, a part of its society. The things we think and feel, you think and feel as well. One day you'll understand how deeply emotions can drive us. And you'll see that it is the same thing that drives you..."

At the time she'd felt it was inane drivel, an attempt to drag her down to a level that a mortal mind could understand. But now...

Ether looked down. At her feet, the flames of her form had melted the ice into a pool of crystal clear water. Its surface churned and rippled in the biting wind of the mountains, but with a thought the shapeshifter turned to wind and willed it to stillness. The surface settled, and in it was her reflection. She dropped to the ground and reluctantly assumed her human form, gazing into the pool as it crystallized inward from the edges. There was something in her eyes. In them she saw the same pain she'd seen in the eyes of mortals more times than she cared to recall. Men and women gathered about the ruins of their homes. Soldiers standing at the edge of a bloody battlefield. And even in the eyes of the defiant Croyden Lumineblade when she'd left him in the castle.

"Damn them... This... this is their pain, not mine," she muttered. "This was never meant for me..."

She turned her eyes back to the stone that had formerly held Lain's sword. There were a thousand things she should be doing, but in that moment she knew that she could not leave without setting what had come to be a memorial to Lain's memory back to its proper place. The sword needed to be set back into the stone. His final act should be honored. Her eyes closed and she probed the place, but it was awash with the chaotic energies of the portals. Picking out the location of the sword was impossible. It would have to be found... if it still remained here at all.

Shifting to air would be the simplest, but the churning, rolling pieces of stone were adrift on a stormy sea of magic. As air, she was frail. In her present impaired state of mind, it was too dangerous. Fire would be better, intense enough to overcome the mystic currents, but it would require her to search this place inch by inch. That would take time and energy. But she would see it through. This place was her sanctuary, her cathedral. She would not allow this desecration to stand...

Chapter 6

Travel by dragon was normally an exhilarating experience, but in the day since they'd sensed the opening and closing of the portals, the journey had been a tense and silent one. The lush green fields of Tressor's farms now lay mostly behind them. Save for ribbons of green that traced along the banks of rivers, most of the land below had shifted to rolling dunes and windswept plains. It was a landscape every bit as forbidding as the icy wastes of the Northern Alliance, but with its own unique dangers. Cold nights were a concern, but the greatest danger came during the day, when a few hours of sun could easily bake an unprepared traveler to a crisp. The group had touched down to drink their fill at a stream and refill their canteens not an hour prior, but already the dry, constant wind buffeting them had begun to crack their lips and redden their eyes. It was uncomfortable for the riders, which made Myranda doubly worried for Myn.

"If you get thirsty or tired, don't push yourself, Myn," Myranda said.

The dragon didn't seem to notice.

"Myn?" Myranda repeated.

Now her friend shook her head slightly and glanced back, as if snatched out of deep thought. Myranda smiled.

"Just be sure to take it easy. It won't do us any good if you let yourself dry out," she said.

Myn rumbled a reply in the affirmative, then faced front again. It was nothing new for her to be distracted. The young dragon reveled in flight. Even with two passengers, she was more than willing to ride drafts and bob in breezes. She would even sneak in a twirl, loop, or roll from time to time. With so tight a schedule and so tense a climate, there was no room for such. That wouldn't typically matter, for even when flying in a more subdued manner, Myn always seemed endlessly interested in the lines of rivers and the points of towns as the ground crawled by below. But in the desert, such matters of interest were few and far between. That left just one thing to hold her attention, and it held it well.

Right on schedule, Myn's eyes flitted to their escort. Somehow, Myranda suspected even if they had permission to lilt like a leaf on the breeze or fly over a tapestry of different landscapes, Garr would still have been the thing that captured the dragon's attentions. The wizard felt a twinge of regret that the two dragons had met under such trying circumstances. Myn hadn't had many opportunities to meet her own kind, and her fascination with Garr was a sure sign that it was a piece of her life she'd been missing, even if she didn't know it. Rare was the minute that went by without Myn casting a curious look in his direction. She drew in a long, lingering whiff of the breeze to catch his scent, flicking her tongue briefly to taste it for good measure. The dragon may as well have been trying to memorize her counterpart's features for future reference.

Curiously, despite all of the obvious interest in her companion for the journey, Myn hadn't "spoken" with Garr. Beyond a rumbled warning when circumstances threatened to pit them against one another and the lecture about eating the meal Garr had offered, they were silent in one another's presence. Myranda almost giggled at the thought that Myn might actually be shy around her own kind.

This thought was still fresh in her mind when Grustim subtly waved his arm and then indicated a point on the ground below. Barely visible, a cluster of wood and sandstone structures blended well against the dunes. But it didn't take more than a second glance once it had been spotted to be certain that something had gone terribly wrong there. The wall surrounding the stronghold was intact, but it was perhaps the only part of the prison that was not damaged or recently repaired. With each second, they drifted nearer and were able to discern more details of the carnage. Large pieces of stone, in some cases whole blocks, were scattered about the courtyard between the largest of the buildings and the wall. What had at first looked like a pile of debris was in fact the remains of a squat tower that had entirely collapsed. By the time they were circling for a landing, they could see that even a short stretch of sandy earth and rough cobblestones had collapsed downward. Most concerning, just outside the eastern wall were five freshly mounded graves…

At the sight of a pair of dragons, a dozen guards moved out into the courtyard, first to assess any danger, then to frantically flag them down for aid when they were able to determine it was indeed a Dragon Rider. At an unheard order by Grustim, Garr swept his wings back and dropped from the air, landing hard in the center of the courtyard. Grustim continued the momentum of the landing into a leap from the dragon's back and a roll to his feet. When the green dragon shuffled aside enough to make room, Myn touched down as well. Myranda and Deacon climbed from her back, staff and gem in hand. The ground practically sizzled beneath their boots, and the whole of the courtyard felt like an oven. Wavy lines of heat distorted anything more than a few feet away, and the glare of sun against the tan stone was just short of blinding.

Now with a firsthand view of the damage, it was a wonder any of the buildings were still standing. Fractures wove up along the stone walls, branching up from the ground. Roofs had fallen inward. Walls had toppled aside. Even now some low-level soldiers were hard at work, having been pressed into repair detail. They troweled a loose slurry of mortar into what cracks they could reach in the handful of walls that might be salvageable, and scavenged bricks from those that were too badly damaged to save in order to rebuild those that had been utterly destroyed.

The prison fort was of a simple design. When it was whole, it had been composed of one large sandstone keep, five stories tall at its highest central spire and three stories tall elsewhere. Built large enough to house a large squad of troops, from the looks of the interior where the walls had given way, it dug at least as far into the ground as it stood above it. Five towers, built sparingly of wood, stood just tall enough to overlook the fifteen-foot wall that formed a pentagon around the courtyard, a tower at each point. One such tower had been reduced to splinters by flying debris. The others were intact but unmanned. The only other sizable structure was a large stable near the southern point of the five-sided wall. A few cases and crates, something akin to half-sized storage shacks, were nestled in out-of-the-way areas, and what was likely a well stood prominently to one side of the stronghold.

"What happened here? Is there still danger?" Grustim asked, speaking in his native language and thus sounding a good deal more precise and confident than in his exchanges with Myranda and Deacon.

"Does anyone need help?" Myranda added, dusting off her own knowledge of Tresson.

"We are both skilled healers," Deacon added, his mastery of the language easily a match for Grustim's.

The guards, lightly armored in off-white cloth padding, barked warnings and raised their weapons. The light skin of a Northerner was never a welcome sight in a Tresson military base, even accompanied as they were by one of the most revered units in all of Tressor. Myn planted her claws and spread her wings, curling her tail protectively around her humans and making her intentions remarkably clear regarding what would happen if anyone tried to lay a finger on them.

"Myn, that's enough for now. They are just on edge, and understandably so," Myranda said, offering a calming hand on the dragon's leg.

"Lower your weapons. These are representatives of a diplomatic delegation," Grustim instructed. "Tell me what happened here."

"Belay that order. Weapons high and prepare to take these aggressors prisoner!" growled a hoarse voice.

The command came from a form tottering out of the one side of the keep's main doors that was still able to swing on its hinges. He was a man, dressed as much in bandages as in clothes. Wrapped tightly in blood-stained linens, he had his right arm and leg both bound to splints. A crutch tucked under his left arm kept him upright, though just barely. Even his face was largely obscured by three loops of bandage across its right side.

Grustim stepped forward to greet the approaching man, who by sheer force of personality could only be the commanding officer.

"Commander," Grustim said, tapping his fist to his chest in a formal greeting.

"Brustuum," replied the commander, painfully mirroring the gesture. "Rider."

"Grustim."

"Welcome to what *remains* of my stronghold, Rider Grustim."

"It is my duty to offer any aid that is within my power to give, Commander Brustuum. Tell me, please, what happened here?"

"It was an attack, Rider. An agent of the north has broken the false peace that they dangled before us and assaulted a Tresson stronghold."

"A Northerner. You are certain?"

"Her flesh was lily white, and her accent was unmistakable. She even admitted to it. Shortly before unleashing her treacherous magic and taking the lives of fifteen prisoners and five of my best men. Two more are at death's door."

"If people are badly injured, you must let us tend to them," Myranda said, stepping forward.

"Stay back, Northerner. We've had enough of your *aid*. Now place your staff on the ground and prepare to be escorted to a cell. That goes for both of you."

The courtyard began to rattle with the ominous growl of a dragon testing the limits of her patience. Myn's jaws hung just slightly parted, a flicker of orange flame licking from between her teeth with each slow, hissing breath. Stalwart though the Tresson soldiers were, a furious dragon barely restraining itself from a rampage was the sort of sight that would give any creature pause. They held their ground, which was evidence enough of their bravery.

Commander Brustuum gazed up at the creature, who glared down at him in much the same way an eagle would glare at a rabbit.

"Is this creature not under your charge?" Brustuum said warily. Addressing Grustim.

"The beast is the personal mount of Duchess Myranda and Duke Deacon of Kenvard," Grustim explained.

"Nobility? Ah. So this is the 'diplomatic mission.' Curious how it found its way so readily to the site of the attack…"

Brustuum and Grustim continued their discussion, but Myranda couldn't keep her mind on it. Out of a hard-earned instinct to find and end suffering, on the battlefield or elsewhere, she'd begun to sweep around her, probing with her will. In the months since her final battle, Myranda hadn't needed to put her mystic abilities to use very much. Though they were unquestionably an asset, considering the circumstances that had made them necessary in the past, she would have been quite pleased never to use them again. As soon as the threat of another death at the hands of the D'Karon presented itself, however, her carefully trained will was ready and eager to leap into action. It took mere moments for the sharp sting of suffering to burn at her mind. She turned to her right and spied a hastily erected tent in the shadow of the wall. The injured men were certainly inside. She glanced at Deacon and found his attentions locked on the tent as well. When he turned back to her, it was with an expression that confirmed what Myranda feared. Without help, one of the men wouldn't see the next day. The other wouldn't see the next hour.

Without another thought for herself or the consequences her next action might have, Myranda paced steadily toward the tent. Her motions caused a ripple of activity around her. First, Deacon fell into step beside her, his fist gripping his gem tight and his will already weaving at least half a dozen spells of defense and recovery. A half-second later Myn followed, unfurling her wings and curling them low about either side of the wizards. Voices began to call out, soldiers demanding she hold still. Grustim called out to her, then grunted an order to Garr.

Two bounding steps from the green dragon brought it thundering in front of Myranda and the others, but Myn was ready, lowering her head and thrusting it forward, butting hard against Garr's own head as it lowered. The blow was a minor one, by dragon standards. It may have produced an ear-splitting clank of scale on helmet and horn on horn, but it caused little pain and no damage, more a test of strength than anything else. Myranda stepped aside, continuing around Garr as though he was little more than a simple obstacle. The male dragon tried to shuffle sideways and block Myranda, but Myn shoved harder, keeping her horns locked with his and just barely muscling him firmly enough to keep him in place.

Next the soldiers acted, heeding a bellowed order to subdue Myranda and Deacon. Without thinking, Myranda raised her hand to her side and sharply lowered it. The weapons in the soldiers' hands followed the motion, dropping suddenly to the ground as though they'd increased in weight tenfold. Some men attempted to raise their swords and pikes from the ground. Most peeled off and attempted to interpose themselves between the wizards and the tent, even if it meant defending unarmed. Deacon released his gem, leaving it to float beside him, and spread the fingers on his hand. The half-dozen soldiers stumbled and shuffled aside, pushed by a gentle but firm force. Try as they might, they couldn't push their way past the unseen wall that held them at bay. Finally there was no one left to stop them, and Myranda and Deacon stepped into the tent.

"I fear this was not the most diplomatic action we could have taken," Deacon said, casting an uncertain glance at the door before warding it with a simple but potent spell to prevent them from being bothered.

Joseph R. Lallo

"Perhaps not, but it was the most human one," Myranda said.

The inside of the tent smelled strongly of stale blood and long suffering. Seven cots had been arrayed along the floor of the long tent. Five were vacant. Upon the one farthest from the door, a man slept fitfully. Given the commotion still going on just outside the canvas of the tent, it was fairer to say that he was no longer strong enough to awaken. The cot nearest the door was occupied by a man who was coughing weakly. A sickening gurgle punctuated his breathing, and fresh blood seemed to be moistening a mound of bandages upon the man's chest. Two clerics tended the man, but it was clear from their expressions that they knew he was beyond their skills. They turned to the unannounced newcomers, eyes flashing with confusion and concern.

"Who are—" one cleric began to ask.

"I'm here to help. What happened to this man?" Myranda said.

For the moment, the promise of help from a woman who seemed confident she could provide it was enough to push aside any other concerns.

"There was an attack. He was pinned beneath a collapsed ceiling," the first cleric said.

"He seemed to be recovering, but an hour ago he started bleeding again," the second added.

Myranda crouched beside the injured man and shut her eyes, probing his body with her mind to learn the depths of the injury. She felt Deacon's will brush hers as he did the same.

"His ribs are broken. They've pierced his lung," Deacon said, confirming what Myranda had sensed. He turned to the first cleric. "Why didn't you have your healer mend his wound?"

"This *is* our healer," said the second cleric. "We had two, but the first was killed in the attack."

"And the other man?" Deacon asked. "How is he faring?"

"He is sleeping, but he is getting weaker each day," the second cleric said.

"I'll see to him," Deacon said, stepping quickly to the sleeping man's side.

Myranda looked at the clerics. "I need to set the bones. It will be painful for him, but it is better that it be done quickly. Then I will close the wounds and put him in a healing sleep."

"Whatever you must do, but please hurry," said the first cleric.

She shut her eyes again and focused, reaching out with her will and allowing it to curl about the damaged ribs. A less experienced healer would be tempted to move the bones slowly, gently. Myranda knew better. She'd mended her own cracked ribs too many times, and had learned after the first attempt that there was no way to do it that wasn't agonizing. Better to do it quickly than draw out the suffering. In total there were three ribs broken. Two on the left side, thankfully not driven into the lungs or heart, and one on the right, the one responsible for the most dire of the damage. When her mind was wrapped tightly about the bones, she drew in a deep breath.

184

"Hold him," she said.

When the clerics obliged, pinning the suffering soldier by the arms, Myranda snapped the ribs back into place. The man would have screamed if he'd been able. Instead he released a strangled, gurgling sound and descended into violent coughing. She reached deep beneath the pain and coaxed the fractures into knitting. If she devoted enough time and effort to it, she could heal the bones completely, but for now she just needed them strong enough to stay in place while the rest of the job was done.

The man was coughing harder, but Myranda pushed the sound from her mind. There was no use leaving the ribs to stand on their own. The way he was struggling he would very nearly break a healthy set of bones. She resolved to hold them with her mind while carefully weaving the next stage of the spell, pulling together the ragged ends of where his lung had been gashed. It took a terrific effort, but slowly she could feel the opening seal. Unlike the bones, this must be done in its entirety through magic alone. If his own healing was left to complete even the tail end of the job, one solid cough would undo all she'd done.

It took two minutes of intense concentration and a dozen quietly murmured incantations to bolster the effects, but finally the man's breathing eased and his coughing subsided. For the first time since she'd begun her work, Myranda opened her eyes. Though there was no doubt the man had vastly improved, his struggles and coughing had left him a horrid sight to look at. In clearing his lungs, he'd spattered the ceiling and walls of the tent with flecks of red. Myranda and the clerics had received their share as well.

With a touch to the injured man's face and a final twist of magic, Myranda nudged him into a badly needed slumber.

"He'll awaken in a day or two. He should recover fully," Myranda said, wavering slightly.

She wasn't truly fatigued by the exertion, but pulling into and out of the level of concentration necessary for such spells had a way of making one unsteady. At the slightest suggestion that she might need something to lean on, Deacon appeared by her side, steadying her.

"Fine work," he said. "As always."

Myranda turned to the second patient. "And how is he?"

"His wounds were healing badly, and there was a fever. Simple enough to ease."

"May you be blessed, good woman," said the first cleric.

"You have done the work of the divine today," said the second.

"No," Myranda said. "We did what anyone would have done. But you are very welcome." She sighed and turned to the door. "And now it is time to face the consequences."

"Shall we?" Deacon asked.

"Of course," she replied.

He set down his crystal. She did the same with her staff, and he lightly waved his hand across the simple cloth flap of the tent. The spell reinforcing it wafted away, allowing two soldiers to burst inside, swords drawn.

Myranda folded her hands in front of her, and Deacon did the same, stepping slowly toward the courtyard. The soldiers kept their distance, for the world appearing as though they were facing down a pair of tigers.

When Myranda and Deacon were fully into the courtyard, the level of chaos they'd left behind became abundantly clear. What had begun as a test of strength between Garr and Myn had clearly become something personal. Each was rumbling with a sound just barely short of a roar, and long furrows of the courtyard had been dug out by their claws as each was pushed back by the other in kind. The soldiers labored at their wits end, unwilling to venture near enough to put their weapons to use without fear of being lashed by a sweeping tail, and unable to fire arrows or throw pikes without fear of striking Garr, who was effectively a fellow soldier.

Grustim stalked up to the pair of wizards.

"Call off your beast and I will do the same," he commanded.

"Myn! Enough!" Myranda called out.

She stopped her shoving but held her ground, grinding slowly backward thanks to Garr's efforts until a similar order coaxed the green dragon to stillness as well. Each beast stood stone still, horns locked together, and gazing up into the eyes of the other. After a moment while the rest of the courtyard held its breath, Myn narrowed her eyes slightly and huffed a quick breath.

"Don't!" Myranda warned, but it was too late. The dragon had made her mind up.

Myn twisted her head sharply to the side and heaved all of her weight in that direction. It was just enough to throw Garr off balance, sending the male tumbling aside with an earth-shaking blow and knocking his helmet halfway across the courtyard. She then plopped her hindquarters down and craned her neck proudly.

Garr scrambled to his feet, a furious gleam in his eye, but before he could do anything, Grustim issued a throaty order. Garr turned to him with a sharp look of protest, but Grustim remained firm. Reluctantly the male trudged to Myn's side and sat heavily, glaring at her. Myn flicked her tongue once and lashed her tail, looking down at Myranda.

"We'll talk about this later," Myranda said with a shake of her head.

"You see!" cried Brustuum, stomping as angrily toward them as his battered body would allow. "You see the arrogance with which those of the north conduct themselves?"

"What did you think you were doing?" Grustim demanded, for a moment forgetting protocol and simply speaking to Myranda as he might to *anyone* who had taken her life and liberty into her own hands in a very tense situation.

"I refused to allow a man to die because of the distrust between our people." She offered up her wrists. "Throw me in irons if you must. I fully accept that I've acted without proper regard to the situation, but it had to be done."

She spoke without challenge or arrogance. This was not an act of defiance. Her words were sincere. What she'd done was an act of mercy for the men in the tent, but a tremendously dangerous one and certainly a breach of any number of well-designed protocols. A punishment was called for.

"I understand that something terrible happened here, and that it appears to have been done on behalf of my kingdom. I assure you this is not so, but I fully understand that you must err on the side of caution until it can be proved otherwise. None of us will resist."

"Men, secure the Northerners. Separate cells," Brustuum ordered. "And secure the dragon."

Myn looked down to the assembled soldiers. Unlike Myranda, her own gaze was dripping with challenge.

"Myn, go where they say, do what they say, and for heaven's sake, behave," Myranda instructed.

The dragon gave Myranda a pleading look.

"I mean it," Myranda said as a pair of heavy metal shackles was secured about her wrists. As she was taken by the shoulders and led toward the gate of the damaged keep, she turned to Grustim.

"I trust your capacity to handle this situation properly," Myranda said.

"Handle this situation?" he said, flustered for perhaps the first time in years. "I do not even understand what precisely this situation *is*."

"Then seeking understanding is an excellent place to start," Deacon suggested, receiving his own pair of restraints.

"I am *not* a diplomat!" Grustim objected.

Myranda glanced over her shoulder and gave a wry smile. "You can hardly do worse than I did…"

#

Grustim paced through the halls of the damaged stronghold, two steps behind Commander Brustuum. He had shed the heavy plates of armor, dressed now only in the padding and thin mail usually worn beneath it. In the earliest days of his training as a Dragon Rider the armor had been torturous to wear. Now, even when among fellow soldiers, he felt naked without it. Never had that been truer than at this moment. Something about this place, about the attitude of the commander who was his host, made him profoundly uneasy. He didn't feel as though he was among allies. Dragons, it is said, are fast and accurate judges of character. This was yet another trait that Dragon Riders seemed to absorb through proximity, because somehow Brustuum had rubbed Grustim wrong at first sight. With each word and every action, that feeling of distrust grew stronger.

He turned his gaze from the limping commander and surveyed his surroundings. The damage to the stronghold had been quite apparent on the outside, but it was even more so on the inside. Wooden support beams were splintered. The stone of some walls had been utterly pulverized. Grustim had good reason to doubt the roof would remain in place for much longer.

"You see… you see what comes of trusting monsters…" Brustuum fumed as he led to the end of a hallway that was, though not wholly intact, at least not in imminent threat of collapse.

A wooden door at the end, the only one that was still seated squarely in its frame, bore a recently applied brass nameplate etched with Brustuum's name and rank.

"You will accept my apologies for the disarray. My own quarters were badly damaged. I was forced to move my things rather hastily to this room. Please, come inside, sit down."

Brustuum opened the door and the pair entered. The room was somewhat more comfortably furnished than the rest of the keep, but in a very precise and austere way that seemed to transcend culture. These were an officer's quarters, appointed in a way that spelled luxury to a lifelong soldier and was barely tolerable to a civilian. Grustim had been in a dozen such rooms, and though they were no doubt furnished to the strict requirements of each individual officer, they may as well have been built from the same template. Comfort, in the mind of a fighter, came in a very simple form: a sturdy chair, a firm bed, and strong drink. The latter came in the form of a bolted liquor cabinet against the far wall, just at the head of the bed. It stank of recently spilled spirits, and when he lifted the bolt and pulled the door open, the wooden hinge ground with the sound of broken glass lodged within. The cabinet was largely bare, only three bottles occupying a space suitable for a dozen.

"Sit," Brustuum said, indicating a second chair set opposite a few planks of wood stretched between two sawhorses.

In the shadow of the recent disaster, Grustim supposed it was playing the role of a desk. He took a seat and watched as the commander set the bottle of liquor on the table, as well as a cracked ceramic pitcher of water and two glasses.

"May I offer you a drink?" Brustuum asked.

"Dragon Riders do not consume spirits," he replied.

"Such was my understanding. But from time to time I've known men to overlook the lesser aspects of duty and protocol."

"I am not such a man."

"Then you are a better man than I," Brustuum said with a stifled chuckle.

The commander eased himself painfully into his chair and poured a glass of water for Grustim, then poured his own tumbler two-thirds full of water before topping it with the contents of the bottle. As the clear liquor met the clear water, both took on a milky-white color and an almost pearlescent sheen.

Both glasses full, Brustuum and Grustim set their palms flat on the wooden plank and bowed their heads.

"May the nectar of your bounty sustain us," they recited quietly before lifting their glasses.

Brustuum sipped his drink with a sour look on his face. "You know, I genuinely hoped I'd been misinformed when I heard the delegation to Tressor would receive a Dragon Rider as an escort. Your presence unnecessarily elevates them. Of course, now I realize that with a dragon of their own, there are few who could hope to subdue them when they inevitably chose to break their treaty."

"So you were informed of the nature of the delegation," Grustim said.

"Indeed. I am one of only three commanders prepared for the arrival of the enemy. They had me searching for the agent. As you can see, I found her."

"Yes, I see that. I had some questions in that regard."

"As you would."

"What time of day did this occur?"

"Quite near midday yesterday."

Grustim leaned back slightly, gazing at Brustuum silently.

"And how many of your men were killed?"

"Five. Nearly seven."

"Yes. Nearly. But the seriously injured men will live, thanks to the efforts of the duchess."

"Small recompense for the lives already taken," Brustuum rumbled.

"How many men are under your command?"

"Fifty-six. Now fifty-one."

"And how many prisoners?"

"Fifteen. Sixteen including the escaped Northern agent. Two now, the duke and duchess."

"And their dragon."

"I suppose. Typically we wouldn't count livestock."

Grustim shifted in his chair. "So you lost *all* of your prisoners when the agent escaped?"

"We tend to cluster our prisoners together to simplify watch duty. The attack was centered on the agent's cell, so it killed them all. As well as the guards on duty and nearly myself."

"I see. I assume, remote as this stronghold is, you deliver and receive your messages via falcon?"

"Of course. And mounted messengers for shorter distances."

Another nod. "Describe this agent."

"Ah, finally we are past the formalities and foolishness and into the valuable questions. The woman was my height. Northern, of course. Dark hair falling well past her waist. Threaded with gray. Perhaps in her midforties.

Dressed in dark robes, armed with a bone staff with a purple gem. She kept a… creature. Nothing nature could have wrought."

"How did you capture her?"

"She came willingly, after we found that she'd ravaged a nomad tribe two days east of here."

"And that was how long ago?"

"Five days."

"And she was able to escape noon yesterday."

Brustuum sipped his drink with a grimace. "Yes, as I've said. Her escape was through some manner of mystically summoned window. Now, my recommendations for—"

"I'm not interested in tactics. Strategy is best left to strategists."

"Ah… Then you will deliver this information to your superiors?"

"When my mission is through."

"What, if not to aid in the capture and punishment of this aggressor within our land, is your mission?"

"My assignment was to accompany and aid the duke and duchess as they investigated the selfsame aggressor who you've let slip through your fingers. As you've seen fit to detain them and they are thus unable to investigate personally, that task is left entirely to me."

"You would serve the *Northerners*?"

"I would follow orders. Now am I correct in assuming the nearest liaison from the capital has been made aware of the woman's capture?"

"They have not yet been made aware."

"But you have a falcon, and you returned with her three days ago. Unless there have been changes since my last briefing, you would report any significant findings to Malaar, which is well within two-days' falcon flight."

Brustuum sipped his drink. "Our falcon was unavailable at the time of the capture."

"Then you will have sent a rider."

"Naturally.

"And a rider would take…"

"Four days, at best."

"I see. What route would this messenger take?"

Brustuum thumped his glass down roughly. "What possible difference would that make?"

"If you've sent him with news of the woman's capture, then his information is out of date or outright false. This is too sensitive a time to allow disinformation to circulate. Garr and I can easily intercept him and deliver a more complete and accurate assessment of the situation."

"Better to deliver the message yourself. Do not waste your time intercepting my runner."

"Assuming your runner took the most direct route, and I cannot imagine much value in straying far from it, then it would be no delay at all. I am curious why—"

His observation was interrupted by a cry from the hallway. "Esteemed Dragon Rider! Please, we require your assistance!"

After some thumping footsteps, the breathless voice made another plea. "Many apologies, but this… could become dangerous if it is not dealt with properly."

"What is it that cannot wait until the Rider and I are through?" asked the commander.

"We are having some difficulty with the Northerners' dragon. It and the Rider's mount appear to be getting agitated."

"Trained and untrained dragons can have violent interactions at times, Commander. If you are willing to postpone the rest of our discussion, I will tend to the situation."

Brustuum drained the second half of his glass and thumped it on the table. "See to it," he said.

Grustim stood and marched to the door as the commander refilled his glass. The Rider pulled the door open to find himself face to face with a man who had quite obviously been coping with a tinderbox of a situation and had no clue how to handle it.

"What is the issue?" Grustim asked, falling into quick pace behind the man, who spoke between brief, harried glances as he rushed back toward the exit.

"The, ah, the dragon. The red one. It… we… it seems to understand Northern, and Footman Quarnaam speaks a bit. It was listening. But once we ushered it into the stable, it… we… it won't let us close the doors."

"Won't let you?"

"Well, it will let us close the door, but it won't let us keep it closed, and I think it has something to do with *your* dragon."

"It isn't unlikely," Grustim said.

The pair made it outside in time to see the latest effort to secure Myn just finishing up. Five soldiers were hammering splintered and salvaged planks into place, securing a stable door that was a good deal more damaged than Grustim remembered from their arrival.

Garr was lying on the ground, his head held low and his eyes narrowed. The male's pointed snout was angled for the doors, eying it with the focus and expectation of a wolf waiting for a rabbit to poke its head out of its den.

The soldiers were working feverishly, despite the pounding sun, and looking incrementally more frenzied with each passing moment. By the time the final spike had been hammered true, most of the soldiers had run to a safe distance. The final worker dropped his tool and sprinted for the wall of the main keep, then turned and waited. For a few beats, there was silence save for the panting breaths of the workers and the howling desert wind. Then came the slow, deliberate creak from within.

After a few seconds, the new braces buckled, popping free. When they'd clattered to the ground, Myn gave a sharp nudge and the doors flew open, smashing into the walls of the stable hard enough to dislodge one door entirely. She then snaked her head forward slightly, matching Garr's same hard gaze. The two then commenced a grumbling exchange that was barely at the edge of hearing, yet loud enough to rattle pebbles across the ground.

"That thing is a vicious monster..." the footman leading Grustim said shakily.

"A vicious monster who waited until the workers were clear before forcing the door," he muttered under his breath. Grustim stepped forward, raising his voice: "Stand aside."

"You aren't going in there, are you?" called one of the soldiers in awe.

"I am."

He marched toward the door of the stable. Even with the horses moved to the shade of a tower for the time being, there was room for little else but Myn within its walls. As he drew nearer, her gaze flicked to Grustim and her muscles tensed. She pivoted her head to him and flared her nostrils, peeling back her lips to reveal a glint of teeth. The rumbling grew sharper, higher in pitch and more aggressive.

Grustim didn't falter. He simply ducked below her craned head to slip inside. Once there, Myn shifted herself, pulling her head inside and turning her body. The move achieved a number of things. First and foremost, it allowed the dragon, huddled as she was under the low roof, to look him in the eye again. It also blocked the door behind her and blotted out most of the light from the doorway.

Her growling was loud enough to shake dust from the rafters, but he simply stared at her evenly, arms crossed.

"Enough. You are being a child," Grustim said, adopting the Northern tongue again. "These men believe you to be mindless. I know better. So do not think that your posturing and grumbling can intimidate me. Myranda trusts you, and you trust her. This relationship the two of you have could not exist otherwise. It is because you trust her that I've given the woman what leeway I have. And it is because she trusts you that I believe her judgment is sound. But right now, this damage you are willfully causing is just foolish."

Myn's growling trailed off, but her expression remained hard.

"There are a number of things you must do, and you must do quickly if you are to have any hope of salvaging this mission for Myranda. First, you must stop this foolishness and allow yourself to be detained."

The dragon pulled her lips back again.

"You and I both know the stronghold could scarcely contain you, let alone this flimsy shack, but your very presence in this courtyard is pushing the soldiers to their wits end, so you must allow them at least the illusion of control. When humans do not feel in control of a situation, they begin to act rashly."

Myn shifted her head, glancing toward the wall in the direction of Garr and grunted again.

"Garr is the mount of a Dragon Rider. Most of the soldiers believe I have some supernatural control over him, and I have no reason to correct them," he said. "And on the subject of Garr, *stop taunting*."

She pulled her head back slightly and darted her eyes briefly aside.

"I can read your tone and posture as well as he can. You made a terrible mistake earlier. Garr has never been knocked down in fair sparring. To be grounded by a wild-caught, even a female, must burn at him terribly."

Myn drew in a breath and puffed her chest slightly.

"Don't be so cocky. You'd each been commanded to end the battle. He'd assumed you would fight with the same discipline as he. Instead you took advantage of him. He gave you more credit than you deserved. Don't expect so easy a time if the two of you come to blows again."

The dragon tilted her head doubtfully.

"Believe what you will, but Garr has been trained in combat and you have not. Challenge him at your peril. Or better, do not challenge him at all."

Grustim looked to the door behind Myn, then turned and paced toward the corner of the stable, mind deep in thought. Turned as he was, and with his eyes finally adjusted to the light, he found that in their haste to clear the stable for Myn the soldiers had forgotten two creatures. A pair of falcons, hooded and clearly flustered by the scent and sound of the massive predator sharing the stable, stood on perches in a large cage to one side.

The Dragon Rider stepped forward and looked between the bars. If they were still hooded, they'd been handled recently. He observed their legs. In Tressor, colored bands were used to indicate to and from what locations each falcon was meant to fly. There were roosts for only two falcons, and each bore a band indicating a destination of their sister stronghold in Malaar.

"Two falcons…" Grustim murmured. He turned to Myn. "I want you to answer some questions about Myranda."

Myn looked aside and huffed a breath.

"Now is no time to be stubborn, Myn. The man who holds power in this keep is not one for mercy. Hatred for the north drips from him, perhaps enough to blind him of his duty and his dedication to the truth. Honesty will help her. Anything less and I cannot promise there is anything that I can do."

She turned her gaze back to him.

"She treats you well? Listens to you, speaks to you?"

The expression this question earned carried the clear threat that any suggestion to the contrary would have swift and fiery results.

"And the madness your woman just willfully performed, risking her life and the ire of the entire stronghold for a pair of ailing soldiers. Was that genuine? It was not manipulation?"

Myn closed her eyes and nodded once.

"She would truly commit what in the eyes of the commanding officer is nothing less than an act of aggression to heal a pair of injured men, even if they were not her countrymen? Even if they were strangers who only weeks ago might have been clashing swords with her own people?"

Again, a simple nod was all Myn had to offer. Grustim cast his eyes down and wrung his hands.

"It pains me to suggest it… I do believe there has been treachery here… but in this instance the Alliance may be the least of the evils." He looked up. "Step aside."

She lightly scraped her claws into the floorboards of the stable, splintering one of them.

"What have I just said? The more you disobey, the more difficult it will be to convince anyone that Myranda and Deacon should be allowed to leave. You are only making things worse for them. Now would you *please* step aside?"

Myn tipped her head, smacked her tongue twice, as though these words were more acceptable to her, then carefully adjusted herself to clear the door. When she turned to face the exit again, she jerked her head back with a start.

Garr loomed in the doorway, eyes intently focused on hers. He lifted a foreclaw to allow Grustim to step from inside, then stepped down again when the Rider was clear, clawing at the ground as he did.

Grustim released a scolding command. Garr lingered for a moment longer before stepping back. The Dragon Rider looked at Myn again.

"I do *not* appreciate the bad influence you've been on Garr," he said to her. "He's never been this much trouble." He grumbled a new command, and Garr spread his wings, thrusting himself into the air.

"Where is it going?" asked one of the footmen, startled first by the suddenness of the departure, then by the realization that the one dragon remaining in the fort was the property of the enemy.

"I've sent Garr to hunt. I must speak to the dragon's keeper. Do not close the door to the stable," Grustim instructed.

"But we were ordered to secure the beast."

"And you have illustrated that you are not able. Leave the door open and there will be no further trouble." He turned to Myn and repeated the phrase in Varden. "*No* further trouble."

Myn grumbled something that likely would have been unrepeatable had it been in a human tongue, but folded her claws in front of her and laid her head on the ground to soak up some sun.

Grustim turned back to the soldiers. From their expressions, they were more than a little awed by his capacity to, from their point of view, coax dragons into following his commands through sheer force of will. Again, it was a useful misapprehension, and he wasn't eager to disabuse them of it.

"I need to speak to the dragon's owners," Grustim said.

The footman who had fetched him looked uncertain. "I believe the commander would prefer to deal with the prisoners personally."

"I respect the commander's wishes, but it is a matter that if left unattended, could make the dragon more difficult to control."

As he spoke the final words, he gave Myn a meaningful glance. The dragon, mischievously recognizing the need for a bit of emphasis, huffed a curling streamer of fiery breath from her nostrils. It was a gentle breath, doing little more than producing a flare of heat and light, but even a gentle flame bursting from a living creature was quite enough to make a firm impression upon those who had never seen it before.

"Right this way, Rider."

#

The damage to the stronghold was such that most of the hallways connecting the left and right sides were impassible. Only the entryway had been cleared, and only leading to the last two fully intact banks of cells. As the soldier led Grustim forward, then downward, he heard a voice speaking impeccable Tresson echoing through the row of cells.

"You are taking me to the duke?" Grustim asked.

"Of course. You said you needed to speak to the owner of the dragon," the soldier replied.

Grustim nodded. It was natural, he supposed, for the soldiers to assume that Deacon was the master. In Tressor a dragon, at least one owned by a human, was effectively a weapon of war. War in this kingdom was an exclusively male pursuit. In all of his interactions with the duke and duchess, however, it was abundantly clear that she was the one with whom matters of any real importance should be discussed. It was not until this moment that Grustim realized how natural and obvious that had become for him in their brief travels together.

As they drew closer, a few things became clear. The first was that Deacon either hadn't grasped the severity of the sentence he was facing, or else greatly misunderstood the nature of incarceration. He was chatting amicably with his jailer, or at least attempting to do so, with no indication that he was displeased or concerned about his imprisonment. Coincidentally, but not surprisingly, the subject was precisely the one Grustim had briefly been ruminating on.

"Really?" Deacon said, fascinated. "Not a single woman in your entire army?"

"There may be one or two female healers…" the jailer said. There was a weariness in his tone that suggested, despite the rather brief time he had been in charge of Deacon, the assignment had already begun to try his patience.

"But no one in battle? Why?" Deacon said.

"Because our army is made up of only the finest warriors."

"I apologize, but I fail to see how that answers my question."

"Men are clearly superior to women in matters of war. We are physically superior, more mentally capable, and overall better suited to matters of both combat and strategy."

Grustim was near enough now to see Deacon standing just inside the bars of his cell, head cocked to the side and listening intently.

"That has not been my observation. Certainly there are certain physical differences, which might broadly make men and women better suited to certain tasks, but in almost all cases I've found men and women quite capable of aspiring to a stunning level of competence in their chosen tasks, regardless of what those tasks may be. Have women routinely failed to satisfy the requirements of your army?"

"We do not recruit or conscript women, nor do we allow them to enlist."

"Then upon what do you base your—"

"Duke, I do not mean to interrupt, but there are a few matters that require your attention," Grustim said.

"Ah, Grustim!" Deacon said far more brightly than was suitable for a prisoner of war. "I was just discussing some very interesting topics with Footman Turill."

"No doubt. But I must ask some questions," Grustim said. He turned to the man who had escorted him. "You may return to the entryway and await me there. When I am through with the duke, I will need to speak to the duchess."

The escorting soldier nodded and departed. Grustim turned back to Deacon. When he continued, he was speaking Varden. "In your own language, I feel, it would be more appropriate."

"We can certainly do so if you wish, but the footman doesn't speak Varden, so he would not be able to contribute to the conversation," Deacon replied.

"That is ideal."

"Oh?"

"I have some questions. I appreciate you will be inclined to answer at length, but please be brief."

He nodded. "Not an uncommon request."

"First, you seemed certain we would find damage here. Why?"

"I was able to sense the casting of the spell, and the nature of this D'Karon spell is such that it unleashes a portion of its unconsumed energy upon completion."

"Is it a willful attack?"

"No. The burst of energy is a consequence of the D'Karon tendency to forgo counterspells or other means to complete a spell without expending the energy poured into it. If they had sought destruction, it would have been far more complete."

"So you would have me believe that what was done here was done by accident?"

"Perhaps not by accident, but the destruction was at best secondary to the purpose of the spell, which was to travel great distances quickly."

"Mmm… Is it safe to say if this agent of the D'Karon had wished to destroy the stronghold, she would have done so?"

"I cannot speak with certainty, as I do not know anything of the person responsible, but if the opening of portals is any indication of the knowledge and tactics available to her, then it is quite likely the destruction of an undermanned stronghold would be well within her capabilities."

"Then why would she not?"

"I cannot venture a guess."

Grustim nodded. "At the very least it would seem wholesale destruction is not the aim."

"I concur. May I ask, have you had much headway in your discussions with the commander? Does he seem a reasonable man?"

"We've not had much to say to one another, but I am not confident he will be inclined to offer you leniency, or even fairness, regardless of what we find to be the truth. You are, in his eyes, still the enemy, and having captured you he won't likely give you up unless forced. This far from a command, an official proclamation requiring it is unlikely to reach him anytime soon, and it would be quite simple for him to ignore it or deny he had received it."

"That is… most disheartening."

"I've been offered this opportunity to discuss matters with you because of the disobedience of your dragon."

"Myn hasn't done anything regrettable, has she?"

"She has been willful. In light of her age, the circumstances, and her lack of formal training, I would say she has been showing remarkable restraint."

Grustim glanced at the jailer. While he was not showing any sign of understanding, he was beginning to appear impatient, with the beginnings of suspicion showing in his gaze.

"I believe the time has come for me to move on to discuss matters with Myranda. You've been stripped of your equipment, correct?"

"I have."

"Am I correct in assuming that despite this, both you and the duchess are more than capable of escape?"

"We are quite skilled in unfocused casting, but we will not escape. We have surrendered. To escape after surrendering would jeopardize the lives of any Northerners who might surrender in the future. The precedent of Alliance members surrendering only to later escape would encourage Tresson soldiers to kill surrendering Alliance troops from that point forward. The circumstances would have to be truly dire for either of us to even entertain the possibility of escape."

"A wise view. Let us hope that we can all recognize dire enough circumstances should they present themselves. A final question. Your pad. The one through which you've communicated with the others to the north. Are there any tricks to its operation?"

"Simply open it and read it. If you wish to send a message, simply address it to the intended recipient with a double underline and write it with the stylus."

"And would you oppose my fetching it and reading its contents?"

"By all means, do so, if you feel the need or believe it will help. In fact, I'd been so distracted with the prospect of what we might find here and how to plan for it, I'd not thought to check if there were any new messages since after we took to the air again."

"Then perhaps the time has come to investigate once more."

Grustim nodded to the jailer and paced back toward the entryway. The soldiers who locked up Myranda and Deacon had wisely chosen to separate them as much as possible, thus putting them on either side of the impassible portion of the keep, roughly in the same cell on opposite sides. Unlike Deacon, who had taken the opportunity to indulge his rampant curiosity, Myranda was sitting quietly in her cell. Her jailer was similarly silent, though his eyes were locked on Myranda, mindful of what she'd managed in the courtyard and wary of what might happen if she chose to put such arcane powers to work again.

"Esteemed Rider," said the jailer, standing and thumping his fist to his chest.

"Footman. I need to speak to the duchess. Tell me, do you speak Varden?"

"I do, a bit."

"And do you read it?"

"I do."

"Do you know where the duke and duchess's things are being kept?"

"I do."

"If you would be good enough, go and fetch them for me. Their dragon has been misbehaving, and I believe there may be some indication of how best to properly deal with her disobedience among the duke's things. In his pack you will find a small booklet affixed with a bell. Bring it to me please. I will look after the duchess until you return."

"As you wish, Rider."

His escort and the jailer went on their way, leaving Grustim alone with Myranda.

"I'll make this brief, Duchess. I've spoken only briefly with Commander Brustuum, but I am not pleased with what I've heard. There is little doubt that a great deal of lies has been spoken about the woman responsible for this devastation and the circumstances surrounding her escape. Much as it pains me, I am quite certain the commander has told more than his share of them."

"Why would he lie about anything that's happened here?"

"I do not know. It is my intention to confront him with those things I know to be false."

"He doesn't strike me as the stable sort," Myranda said.

"Agreed. And regardless of the outcome, there *will* be consequences. If there is even a kernel of truth to what I've heard thus far, there can be no doubt that this attack, purposeful or not, was perpetrated by a woman native to your kingdom while our lands were observing a truce. That is an act of war, and more than enough reason for troops to march once more. If there is *no* kernel of truth, then a representative of my military took Alliance nobility prisoner without cause, which is more than enough justification for your people to resume the war again. I can foresee no circumstance in which what has happened here will not lead to more bloodshed."

Myranda took a slow breath. "What matters is the truth, Grustim. We were sent here to find it and to offer what help we could to the people who need it. I can assure you that Queen Caya, myself, and *all* who have a stake in the continued prosperity of the Northern Alliance have no interest in further combat. We will return to the front only to defend ourselves. But whatever happens will happen. What matters is that we find the person responsible for all of this and stop her before she can hurt anyone else or do any more damage."

The footsteps of the returning soldiers echoed down the hall.

"And if it is found that war is inevitable. How far does your dedication extend?"

"I will not leave that woman loose in your kingdom, and I will not allow her to escape justice if it is deserved."

Grustim stared at her evenly. "On this matter, we are of one mind."

The soldiers reached them, the jailer holding the thin booklet. He presented it to Grustim.

"Thank you. Well done," Grustim said. He flipped the pad open and reviewed the recent messages. As he did, he addressed Myranda one final time. "Your dragon has been… trying. Is there anything you might suggest that would make her somewhat more willing to behave?"

Myranda grinned. "I don't suppose you have any potatoes."

"They are not a crop cultivated this far south, and certainly not among the provisions of this stronghold," replied the jailer.

"I keep a few in my bag. If you offer one to her, she'll know it is from me. It might make her behave herself."

Grustim nodded again. "Something to keep in mind, should she become destructive again." He paused on one of the pages of the pad, a more serious expression flickering briefly across his face.

"If you are prepared, the commander has been anxiously awaiting your return, Rider," said his footman escort.

The Dragon Rider turned to the men. He held the pad in his hand, its pages facing Myranda. He subtly tapped the page, which described the attack on the capital. She read the words, though through a force of will he couldn't help but admire, Myranda managed to keep an even expression.

"I suppose I'd best not keep him waiting any longer," Grustim said, closing the pad and pocketing it.

#

When Grustim was led back into Brustuum's quarters, he found a meal had been set out. Like the quarters themselves, the meal was simple by most standards and extravagant by the standards of a soldier. It was stewed vulture, a delicacy in so much as any reasonably fresh meat was a rarity for those stationed in a desert stronghold, and vulture was among the only beasts that might venture near enough to the keep's walls to be hunted during the day. The smell of the dish was a unique one, as the greens were a combination of the tenacious and strong-scented herbs that could be gathered from the dunes, and various dried vegetables and fruits from the stronghold's stores. The combination of such bizarre and potent ingredients made for an aroma that was not only powerful, it was barely tolerable.

"Ah, well timed, Grustim. I thought it appropriate that we share a meal while we complete our discussions."

Grustim took a seat and looked firmly at Brustuum.

"I appreciate the hospitality, Commander. At present my curiosity exceeds my appetite, but I assure you I will partake when the mood strikes."

"Very well. You'll forgive me if I take my meal while we speak."

"Do as you will."

Brustuum dipped his spoon into the bowl. "Now where were we?"

"You were curiously intent on preventing me from tracking down your runner to save him the time and effort of delivering bad information."

"Ah yes. It should be no concern to you if my messenger does not carry the newest information. Instead, I would suggest you take careful note of my recommendations, then deliver the message of both the capture of the nobles and the nature of the attack directly to the capital, with information to disregard the runner's message. The messenger will not mind. My men are quite accustomed to desert exercises."

Grustim nodded. "So it would seem."

Brustuum paused in chewing. "… Your tone suggests there is more to that observation than the words imply."

"If I remember correctly, you say the prisoner escaped, and thus this disaster occurred, at noon."

"Indeed."

"And you lost only five men."

"That is correct."

"Out of over fifty."

"Yes. Is there a point to this reiteration?"

"Most of your keep is devastated. There are still piles of rubble blocking many passageways. How is it possible that only seven men were badly injured, and only five of them killed? At noon in a desert stronghold I would have expected the bulk of the soldiers to be indoors."

"My men are on field rotation. For five to ten days at a time."

"Where do these men go, and how far?"

"It varies. During our more recent maneuvers we were searching for, and eventually found, the woman who would go on to commit this heinous attack upon the base."

"And the current low complement of troops at this base is due to that?"

"It is."

"So you did not see value in recalling a squad of troops searching for a woman who you had already found. Despite the very real possibility that she would be armed with tactics that would make her difficult to contain."

Brustuum growled. "We had no way of knowing the woman's capacity."

"You described her as having decimated a nomadic settlement. One must assume there was *some* indication of her capacity there."

"I *do not* appreciate your tone, Rider."

"And I don't appreciate being lied to, Commander. Let me tell you what I believe. I believe you wish to dissuade me from finding your runner to the north because there *is* no runner to the north. At this moment, in your stable, there are *two* messenger falcons awaiting messages to deliver, and two roosts for them to do their waiting. If none were available when you first apprehended the woman, then certainly at least *one* of them had been available shortly after. And if not that, then surely in the day since the attack you would have dispatched one to request aid. Instead they both sit, unused."

"You assume too much..."

"It seems assumptions are all I have. I know for certain that some of your claims are lies, and until I am able to determine otherwise, I shall be forced to assume that any of what you've said could be untrue. The only evidence I have that you haven't simply fabricated the entire story is the fact that the duchess, through means of her own, has received word of a woman matching the description you gave. That woman attacked their capital, which I think you'll agree is a curious action for someone we are to believe is acting on their behalf."

"How has the duchess received a message? And how *dare* you believe her but disbelieve me."

"I do not take her word as gospel, Commander, but at least she hasn't told a lie to my face that could be easily disproved. Tell me. If I were to take to the sky and find the remainder of your men on their maneuvers before you can contact them, how much of what they say will corroborate what you've said?"

Brustuum clenched his fist around his spoon, brandishing it as if it were a knife. "You would enter *my* quarters and accuse *me* of such things? You would call me a liar to my *face!*"

"You are a liar at best, Commander. But that much I can abide. What stings me most is that you are inept even at that. You insult me by imagining I could not see through such hasty untruths. You claim to have lost over a dozen prisoners and yet I see no graves. Would you have me believe that those men are still within the ruins, baking in the desert heat without my knowledge? You are hiding things, Commander. You've been locked away in this stronghold too long, surrounded by people who are unwilling or unable to question your authority. It has given you the impression that you are infallible and beyond the reach of repercussion. I assure you, you are neither. Your inadequacy and poor decisions have certainly cost the lives of your men and may have cost the peace of our nation."

The commander slammed down his good fist, spilling the contents of his bowl across the table.

"This is an utter outrage, and if you believe that I will stand idle while you make baseless accusations, you are sadly mistaken."

"My accusations are hardly baseless, and standing idle is precisely what I expect you to do. I am at once a diplomatic escort, a military officer with a rank equivalent to yours, and above all, a Dragon Rider. No one with a head on his shoulders has ever willingly defied the will of a Dragon Rider."

"And now you threaten me?"

"I am merely informing you of what you seem to have forgotten. I would recommend you explain the irregularities of your story so that we might deal with them appropriately. My chief concern is why you failed to inform your commanders of the capture in the more than adequate time you had to do so."

"Men!" Brustuum bellowed.

Two armed soldiers entered, weapons ready.

"This man has confessed a greater loyalty to our enemies to the north than to his own kingdom," Brustuum stated, causing both men to brandish their weapons warily. Brustuum stood painfully and glared down at Grustim. "You have forgotten something as well, *Rider*. You may be a Dragon Rider, but you've sent your dragon away. And in siding with the duke and duchess, you have labeled yourself a traitor. Undeserving of mercy, worthy only of the swift execution that your crimes have earned you. Footmen, do your—"

"Commander, before you make the latest in a long line of tactical errors, I suggest you take a moment to consider what will occur *when* my dragon returns to find me killed. You have a fraction of your men, most of them injured, and a badly damaged keep. Garr is an impeccably trained dragon mount in prime condition. A dragon is not a horse, Commander. It will not remain docile and await a new Rider. He and I are brothers in arms, partnered for battle for years. He will be furious, and there is but one way for a dragon to deal with such matters. I wouldn't favor your odds even if your stronghold was at full strength."

Brustuum hesitated. "We have been *trained* to deal with dragons."

Having blades pointed at him seemed to have expended what little patience and restraint Grustim had left. "How *stupid* do you honestly believe I am, Commander? Your men thought they could lock the duchess's dragon away in a *stable!* They needed *my* help just to keep her inside! And even with the best training, which you most assuredly do not have, you aren't *equipped* to deal with dragons. The *only* way you and your men will survive this is if you stop this foolishness and tell the truth."

The commander stood as defiantly as he could with the injuries he'd suffered. Both of his men remained loyal and resolute, awaiting his next order.

"You are incorrect, Dragon Rider. You shall not be killed. You shall be captured. And when your dragon returns, you shall order him to destroy the Alliance dragon. You will do all that we say, or you will be killed. Is that understood?"

Grustim stood, unintimidated and unimpressed. "That the fate of nations could have fallen into the hands of a man such as you makes me wonder if the gods have grown weary of us." He crossed his hands behind his back. "Take me prisoner, if you believe it will do you some good. But while you await Garr's return, I urge you to take stock of the situation and reassess your decisions. I do not know all that you've done, but I know enough to be certain that you've committed a number of heinous deeds and that you are quite likely hiding things far worse. When the time comes, I'll do my best to keep you alive long enough to answer for what you've done."

"You are a boastful and arrogant fool, Grustim. If you are representative of the other Dragon Riders, it sickens me to think of the reverence that is wasted on you." Brustuum turned to his men. "Confiscate his armor and weapons, investigate everything you find, and throw him in a cell. Bind him and gag him as well. I do not know how the Riders command their dragons, but I do not want him issuing any orders unless under my command and supervision. You have your orders."

Grustim allowed himself to be removed from the room, leaving Brustuum to dig through his liquor cabinet in search of his bottle.

#

Myn lay in the stable, enjoying the warmth but increasingly displeased by the absence of Myranda and Deacon. She amused herself by locking a soldier in her gaze until he became visibly anxious at the stare. The people of Kenvard had become comfortable with her presence. Some of the children were even bold enough to scamper about her feet or try to climb on her back when she was padding through the streets. Though she would much rather be alone with Myranda, or grudgingly sharing her with Deacon, there was some measure of enjoyment at being a part of the lives of so many humans… at least until she grew weary of it. But these soldiers reminded her of the way the Kenvardians *had* behaved, when they had first met her. And the way most other people still did. A dash of fascination tempered with a torrent of fear. In the face of the

Joseph R. Lallo

people Myranda seemed to care about, such emotions were unwelcome to Myn. In the face of those who seemed to mean her only harm, it was quite rewarding to inspire such intimidation.

She'd been watching one man in particular squirm for the better part of an hour. Whenever her tongue flicked out, either to taste at the air or lazily lick her lips, the man practically leaped out of his skin. Thus, when the sun was briefly blotted out by a shadow despite the cloudless sky, her chosen target reacted with a startled cringe. A few moments later Garr shook the courtyard with a graceful but forceful landing, producing an audible yelp from the already tense soldiers. His stomach was subtly bloated, and his face had the contented ease of a carnivore after a heavy meal. Clutched in his teeth were the bodies of two creatures Myn had never seen before. He dropped them and sat on his haunches, eyes on Myn.

The female looked up at him reproachfully, then down at the prey he'd dropped. They looked to be birds, but far larger than anything Myn had seen in the north. Upright they might have stood as tall as a man, or taller. The heads and long necks had a sparsely feathered, almost half-plucked look to them, revealing coarse gray skin. Eyes larger than seemed necessary faced forward, and a cruelly hooked and serrated beak hung slightly open beneath them. Their bodies were plump and covered with sandy-yellow feathers ending in gray-brown ruffles at the tips of both the wings and the tail. Myn couldn't imagine such a beast ever soaring through the air, as the wings were pitiful in comparison to the body, but the legs more than made up for them by being absurdly muscular at the thigh and long and bony at the shin and talons.

Myn looked back to Garr, who licked a few stray feathers from his lips and stared down at her. He stood again and took two steps closer, straddling the dropped prey with his forelegs before plopping onto his haunches again. Now looking far more directly down at her, he released a throaty rumble that shook the ground with its intensity and put the soldiers even more on edge. She turned her head aside, ignoring Garr. He dropped his head low, swinging it between his legs and nipping one of the birds to drag it forward. He nudged it just under her chin, then raised his head up again. She looked up to him, sniffed at the bird, then looked away again. Her stomach betrayed its emptiness with a gurgle and growl, but she didn't so much as give the offered gift a nibble. He nudged the second bird forward to join the first, but she continued to snub it. Then she heard something strange, a smooth clack of stone on stone.

This, if only for its novelty, piqued her interest enough to look to the source of the sound. Lying beside the meal, glistening in the sun, was a perfectly smooth, rounded stone about the size of a large loaf of bread. Dust had stuck to it where it had bounced across the ground, suggesting it had been wet. Likely he'd been carrying it in his mouth, tucked under his tongue. A stone so smooth almost certainly hadn't been lying about among the dunes or in the dry plains surrounding the stronghold. It looked like a river stone. Garr must have traveled quite far in the hour or two he'd been gone to reach a river and return. She gazed intently at the stone, admiring it. The smooth gleam of its polished surface enhanced layers of different-colored stone. Fat lines of cream and yellow marbled the stone, interspersed with thinner ones of white, rose, and green. Just off center glinted a bright, shimmering stripe that caught the light with a metallic gleam. Though there was barely enough of it to notice via an instinct she'd seldom had use for, Myn could tell it was gold.

Garr interrupted her admiration of the stone with a soft, gentle rumble in his throat. She looked up to see him with an almost expectant look on his face, and behind it the tiniest glimmer of pride. She looked down again, taking in the beauty of the stone. And it was *that* which struck her most about the gift. Along the riverbed where he'd found the rock there were probably thousands of similar ones. Some would have been larger. Plenty would have had more gold, or been smoother, or been all one color or another. But Myn wondered if any other stone in the whole of the river would have been quite as pretty as the one he'd fetched and dropped before her. She looked again, feeling an odd flutter in her chest, but hardened her resolve and turned away.

Myn heard him stand again and release a quiet, breathy hiss. She noticed motion out of the corner of her eye and realized he was moving closer, reaching toward the stone. Without thinking, she thumped her paw over it and raked it into the shade of the stable before he could take it back. He backed away and dropped down comfortably to the ground. When she ventured a subtle glance in his direction again, his chest was puffed out in obvious pride and his lips were curved ever so slightly, giving him what on a more expressive creature would have been a wide smile.

She tipped her head, feeling a second flutter in her chest. It was a curious thing. A large part of her saw Garr and felt a flush of anger. The male was perpetually at odds with her, an obvious rival. In all of her life there had only *ever* been friends and rivals. Friends were rare, and when they were lost, they hurt terribly. She didn't want any more friends. All she wanted was to keep the ones she had, and for them to be safe. As for rivals, they were no problem. She knew how to deal with them, and dealt with them quickly and easily. But Garr seemed to want to be both. He wanted to show he was as strong as her, and he clashed with her each time his rider's will clashed with hers or Myranda's. And yet, he fed her. He worked with her to hunt, taught her better ways to stalk and fly. And he brought her this stone. Perhaps the rest he had done because it was Grustim's will that he do so, but the stone could only have been his own choice.

The young dragon huffed a breath in irritation and furrowed her brow. It was frustrating to have someone dance across what had been a simple line until now. She wished he would just make up his mind. Choose one or the other. Friend or foe. Then another thought flitted to the front of her mind, bringing with it another flutter in her chest so strong it almost burned. She shuffled backward into the shade of the stable and looked to where the stone had landed. As she scraped her claw across its smooth surface she supposed that, just maybe, he *had* made up his mind. And this was his way of showing it.

Her revelation was cut short when she heard sudden motion followed by a savage and unmistakable roar of anger erupt from Garr's throat. She snapped her head toward the courtyard and snaked it out to find Garr on his feet. His wings were unfurled and spread, his tail raised and sweeping. He faced away, his head angled at the entryway of the keep, but from the second thundering roar that issued forth, she didn't need to see his face to know his teeth were bared and his fiery breath was curling between them.

Another roar shook the courtyard. The intensity and fury behind it was almost contagious. Myn found her blood racing and her mind aflame. She looked to the entryway, finally spotting the source of his outrage. Grustim had been led out from within, hands tied. On either side was a soldier with a very sensible look of abject terror on his face. Behind them was Commander Brustuum. Unlike his men, he was wholly unconcerned. The commander began to bark orders in a language Myn hadn't yet learned to understand. Every syllable seemed to shake Garr with greater anger, and Myn found any doubt as to which side the male dragon was on fading. In this moment, Garr wanted nothing more than to roast every last soldier in the courtyard, and Myn had felt much the same since they took Myranda and Deacon away. At least for the moment, Garr and Myn were of one mind.

When Grustim spoke, evidently in response to something demanded by Brustuum, he spoke in the human language Myn *did* understand.

"Garr," he said. "The commander, who holds both the Alliance nobles and now myself as his prisoners, demands that you destroy the Alliance dragon and, from this point forward, obey only his commands."

Myn tensed her muscles and readied her claws in preparation for a clash she'd moments before convinced herself would never come. Garr did not move to attack. He didn't even shift his penetrating gaze away from Brustuum.

"We are both duty-bound to offer aid to the Alliance nobles. To do as he orders, you must abandon your duty and relinquish your loyalty."

The next words to come from Grustim were not words at all. At least, not in the way that humans knew them. Dragons had their own language, one that they seldom had notion to use thanks to the simple fact that most useful communication could come from a simple motion or gesture. But when the need arose, the draconic language could be spoken with all of the same clarity and specificity of any human language. Even then it was as much about motion and tone as it was about the sounds made. Grustim had delivered brief orders in a stunted form of this language throughout the journey, but this message he spoke like it was his native tongue.

He lowered his head, shifted his weight, and croaked an almost silent grinding in his throat. It was short, simple, and to the point. "In this choice, you are your own."

Myn did not understand why Grustim had spoken in such a way that she could understand, nor what the underlying meaning of his draconic phrasing might have been, but the very instant Garr heard the final command, he acted. Turning sharply to face Myn, and thus put his back to Grustim, he glared at her. She stood, not certain if he would obey the wishes of the commander, but not yet willing to trust that he wouldn't. There was scarcely room enough for her to crouch within the stable, so when she stood, she tore through its lightly built roof like paper. A pair of startled falcons burst from within, soaring off into the sky, and Myn stood ready to react to whatever came next.

Now it was Garr's turn to speak in the dragon tongue. Like Grustim's, it was a short, simple command.

"Down."

Both Myn and Grustim instantly obeyed. In Myn's case it took her back below the level of the wrecked walls of the stable. In Grustim's case it dropped him to the ground between his escorts. The male dragon belched a rush of flame at the stable. It easily ignited the desert-dried wood. The attack was far too high to strike Myn directly, certainly by design, and the heat of simple burning wood was of little concern to Myn as she remained crouched inside.

As he was incinerating the top half of the stable, Garr swept his tail at waist level. The scything motion struck both soldiers squarely in the chest, knocking them forcefully against the wall of the keep. The commander managed to stumble back far enough to avoid the strike, and bellowed an order to his men. Though Myn didn't understand the words, she knew he was ordering them to attack. A dozen soldiers, every last one available, readied their weapons. The boldest of them rushed at Garr, heaving pikes, firing arrows, and swinging swords. They may as well have been gnats. Swords struck his armored hide and bounced with barely a notch to show for it. Pikes splintered or fell harmlessly away after meeting their targets. Only the arrows did any good at all, all sticking tight into his scales and two piecing through.

Garr didn't pay any mind to the attackers. He turned and stalked forward, straddling the still-grounded Grustim and focusing on the entryway of the keep. The commander had dragged himself inside. The dragon thumped his head against the arch of the doorway, stout horns turning the stone to powder. Myn observed that the strike showed considerably more strength than he'd been displaying when they'd tested one another during Myranda's unauthorized healing. He swiped his tail blindly behind him, bashing a few of the swordsmen.

When the rest retreated and swapped melee weapons for ranged, Myn decided she'd waited long enough. She'd been told to remain inside the stable, but there was no longer any stable to remain in. She charged out and placed herself between the soldiers and Garr. The men must have assumed the blast of flame had been enough to end her, as her sudden appearance and earsplitting roar startled them even more than Garr's sudden turn. Desperate to put at least a moderately safe distance between themselves and Myn, the men scattered and retreated. Once they were on the move and slipping quickly toward panic, Myn found it simple enough to keep them from becoming a threat again. It would have been easy to trample them, roast them, or otherwise dispatch the humans, but Myn knew that Myranda would never forgive her for taking the life of a human she didn't have to, and senseless death didn't appeal to her. Keeping them on the run was more than enough, and stoking their terror into a frenzy was deeply satisfying in light of their behavior.

#

"Listen, you will stop talking or I will personally gag you," growled the Tresson soldier guarding Deacon's cell.

The flickering light from a dim oil lamp caused the shadows of the bars to dance across Deacon's face as he listened to the impatient order of his keeper. A floor removed from the surface, the air was a good deal cooler here, but that did little to improve the mood of the guard.

"Naturally I apologize if I've overstepped my bounds, but a brief incarceration while our respective representatives come to an agreement is no reason to curtail the diplomatic exchange that was to be a very valuable result of this mission."

"You are a *prisoner* in *enemy territory.* You ceased to be a diplomat the very moment your people attacked ours!"

"But we need not be enemies. The woman who attacked you is a mutual adversary. Surely your king and his advisers have policies in place for dealing with external threats common to both the north and—"

"*Close your mouth!*" fumed the guard.

A worrying rumble punctuated his demand, causing walls to crackle and release cascades of broken powder.

"What is that!?" spat the guard.

Deacon having completely eroded his patience to nothing, his exclamation had an angry and accusing tone that suggested he suspected Deacon was somehow at fault for this as well.

"I do not know, but it had a worryingly structural sound to it. I am not certain how much longer this stronghold will remain standing. I would suggest you evacuate."

"I do not take suggestions from *prisoners*," the guard said.

He'd reached the end of his wits now and was oscillating madly between anger and confusion. A voice echoed through the hall and swiftly gathered his full attention.

"All soldiers to the courtyard! Kill these things, *now!*"

The D'Karon Apprentice

It was the commander, his voice a potent mix of agony and fury. Without a moment's hesitation, the guard abandoned his post and heeded the call to action. Deacon stood and stepped to the bars, watching him go, then cast a concerned glance at a fresh fault that had opened in the wall across from him. Even between rumbles, powdery stone was falling in a more or less continuous cascade. It was now safe to say that the building wasn't so much standing as collapsing very slowly. He shut his eyes and reached out with his mind. It took but a moment for him to sense the familiar warmth and clarity of Myranda's thoughts. It was no coincidence that she too was reaching out. When their wills entwined, each appeared as a presence in the mind of the other, suddenly together despite the quaking walls that separated them.

Myranda, I believe the time has come to abandon the stronghold, he thought.

Agreed. I don't know what is happening, but I'm certain that sound is a dragon's roar, and I don't imagine Garr would do so lightly.

You see about whatever is happening on the surface. I shall gather our things and ensure that no one else is in the stronghold.

Be careful, Myranda said.

You as well, Deacon replied.

They broke their connection, each with a job to do. Deacon touched the bars and flexed his mind. The lock was simple by any standard. An industrious prisoner could likely have picked it with a thick splinter of wood. For a wizard with even the most cursory knowledge of gray magic, manipulating its workings to open the door was as simple as lifting a latch. As he stepped out, he brushed his fingers against the walls. Ribbons of blue-white began to mingle with the crumbling masonry, shoring it up enough to stop it from quaking, at least for a moment. Without his crystal he didn't have the strength of will to support more than a small section of the place at a time, but he'd learned much from the Earth masters of Entwell. The whole of the stronghold was either wood or stone. He attuned his spirit to each, and in his mind's eye those sections of wall and ceiling most in danger of collapse lit up clear as day. He lent what strength he could spare and quickened his pace, dedicating the remains of his attention to finding if anyone else needed their help.

The packs containing their equipment were simple enough to find. A wizard's casting gem may as well be a beacon in the night. He could feel it like a warmth against his skin, one floor below. As for other people who might need help, the only living things that felt strong enough to be humans were already outside or on the move toward the exit. They were in less danger than he was. On the same level as their things he felt a flicker of life, but it was insignificant, more likely a rat or a cluster of insects than anything that might need his aid.

He reached the stairs before the next rumble shook the facility, and the keep was striped with new faults that needed to be strengthened. He split his

209

mind further and quickened his pace. The stairs down had partially collapsed, but from the looks of it, most of the damage was from the initial disaster and simply had not yet been cleared. He sidled past it and took the rest of the staircase two at a time, bursting out of the stairwell at a full run. None of the lamps on this level had been lit, but he'd conjured so many strips and patches to hold the place together, the ambient glow was more than enough to light his way. Deacon held out his hand and gently called for his gem. It answered with a brilliant glow that poured from his pack, marking the storage cell to be at the far end of the current hall. Distant roars preceded the roughest impact yet. A section of ceiling shattered to his right, sending a torrent of fractured stone and splintered wood toward him, but he raised his hand and conjured a shimmering shield. Time was clearly running out.

Deacon covered the last few paces of the hallway, manipulated the lock, and pulled at the cell door only to find it buckling against the floor. This close to his gem, the merest thought was all it took to call it to his hand. It touched his flesh, and the strength and clarity of his mind compounded. He funneled much of the added strength into reinforcing the sagging roof, and a portion of the rest into ripping the cell door from its hinges. Rather than attempt to haul everything he, Myranda, and Myn had been carrying onto his back, Deacon simply willed the packs into the air.

After two steps toward the stairs, though, the added light of his glowing gem illuminated something that caught his attention even amid chaos. Through a hole in the floor he could see that one of the cells below was occupied. At first glance his heart nearly stopped at the thought that he might have missed such a thing. The cell, in fact, seemed to be *crowded* with people, all standing. He could see at least eight, which in a single cell left barely room to move. Another shake and rumble caused more of the floor to collapse, revealing a handful more in an adjoining cell. When he'd had a moment to process what he was seeing, he realized, though they were on their feet, they were not humans. At least, not anymore. There was only the faintest flicker of life to them, and entirely no will. Each of them had the dark skin of a native Tresson, some darker than others, but the color was flushed and subdued. They were husks. Bodies drained of life but not yet allowed to take their rest.

A thunder-crack of splitting wood signaled the failure of one of the few remaining support columns. There was no more time for investigation. He would simply have to hope that when the stronghold finished collapsing, somewhere beneath the rubble would remain some evidence of what had happened here.

#

Myranda rushed up the steps. She could feel that Deacon's influence was, for much of the keep, the *only* thing holding the walls together. The hallway was littered with fallen bricks. Ahead, where it turned toward the entryway, stood a press of people with their weapons drawn. They were crying out in

210

anger and fear. Two rows of three men hunkered down into the hallway to protect Brustuum, who was behind them and still attempting to climb to his feet. An earsplitting roar caused the men to tense further, then a vicious blow to the entryway from the outside dislodged a section of wall. A falling brick struck Brustuum and threw his head back, thumping it into the solid stone of the floor and threatening to bury him in the rubble.

The commander dragged himself free of the toppling bricks, then looked up to Myranda, eyes widening in surprise and anger.

"You! This is *your* doing! It *must* be! Men! Subdue the duchess!" he slurred, the recent blow to the head robbing him of some clarity.

The order fell on deaf ears, the threat of a rampaging dragon requiring the full attention of every able soldier. Myranda stepped to Brustuum and hauled him to his feet, throwing his arm around her shoulder.

"You unhand me! You unhand me, woman!" he cried, head sagging and eyes unfocused.

"Commander, your men have their hands full and your keep is crumbling. For the moment I suggest we put our differences aside in the interest of survival." She peered through the entryway, just barely able to see the wild eyes of the dragon over the heads of the defending soldiers. "What is happening?"

"Is it not obvious?" Brustuum raved, fighting to maintain his focus. "Your influence has poisoned the mind of a Rider and his dragon. They have turned their backs on their kingdom, and now the dragon wishes to kill us all."

"If he wished to kill us all, he would fill this hallway with flame and be done with it," Myranda said.

Garr withdrew from the doorway and took a few paces back. The soldiers braced themselves as he heaved a shoulder against the stone wall, shaking the building and causing the left side of the entryway to buckle. She thrust out her hand and pulled her mind to the task of keeping the roof from coming down on top of them, willing blocks back into place and holding them there.

"Myn!" Myranda called.

The response was immediate, a distant grinding slide, then a thundering gallop. The red dragon burst into view of the doorway, wedging Garr out of the way and lowering her head to peer inside.

"Kill it! Kill them both! Kill them all!" Brustuum barked, his voice at the cusp of delirium.

Some combination of anger and pain had stripped away any semblance of logic and reason from the commander, reducing him to little more than a ranting lunatic. Soon even the words were lost in a sea of loudly muttered drivel, as though he lacked the energy and patience to form words any longer. Myranda raised her voice, speaking with calmness and clarity. In the midst of madness, a voice of reason was a difficult thing to ignore. The Tresson soldiers forgot for a moment that Myranda should have been considered as great a threat as the dragons and simply let her speak.

"Myn, the keep is on the verge of collapse. We have to come out. I don't know what's happened to Garr and Grustim, but I don't think anyone wants to see any more blood spilled today," she said.

"You'll have no argument from me, though you may have difficulty keeping the commander safe from Garr," called Grustim, unseen beyond the doorway.

"I'll see to him," Myranda said. She addressed the Tresson soldiers between her and the outside, who were still stretched tight as bowstrings. "Either move forward or move aside, please."

Rather than risk being the first to venture out to a courtyard currently home to two dragons, both of whom had been out of control until recently, the men flattened themselves to the walls and allowed Myranda to pass. She stepped into the baking hot sun of the courtyard but found herself instantly in the shade as Myn stood over her and practically trembled with joy at seeing her again. The dragon reached her head down, eager for a scratch, but Myranda gently pushed her back.

"In a moment, Myn," she said, taking a few steps more, the injured commander by her side.

To her left, between Myranda and the tent that served as the ailing keep's temporary infirmary, stood Garr. He had his feet set wide, his claws dug deep, and his eyes fixed with burning intensity on the commander. Farther away, near the flaming remnants of the stable, stood Grustim, arms crossed and face serious.

"What exactly happened? What is wrong with Garr?" she called to him.

"The commander began making unreasonable and unwise demands of me. Opposing him would mean abandoning my loyalties to my kingdom; following his orders would mean abandoning the mission assigned to me. Rather than bring shame upon myself and my mount, I saw fit to relieve Garr of his duty. He is no longer my mount, no more mine to control than Myn or any other wild dragon. It would appear he was as displeased with the commander as I, and without the concern of breaking oaths, he was and is free to act on it."

The green dragon lowered his head, his snout drawing near enough to the commander to brush his injured arm. The commander looked defiantly back, painfully clawing at his side with his bad arm, searching for a sword that wasn't there. Broiling breath, heated by barely contained flame, spilled around Myranda and Brustuum.

"Garr, the commander is keeping things from us," Myranda said. "We need to know them. That alone is reason enough to keep him alive."

He seemed unmoved by the appeal to reason, his grating growl thumping in Myranda's chest as he peeled back his lips. Finally Myn had enough. She shuffled aside and gave Garr a firm butt to the side of his head, forcing his head up and away. He snapped toward her and rumbled something, curling his tail and fluttering his wings. Myn huffed something in return and looked him hard in the eye. The pair stared at each other for what seemed like a minute, then Garr shut his eyes and lowered his chin in a slow nod. The dragons parted, clearing the way to the infirmary. Myranda led the commander toward it. His raving was quieter still, barely a murmur, his mind a broken wheel spinning loosely on its axle. He merely shuffled, leaning heavily upon Myranda.

The dozen or so soldiers who had been trying and failing to control the dragons cautiously emerged from the scattered hiding places they'd taken refuge in before the sudden influx of sanity brought by Myranda's arrival. Some attempted to raise their weapons, but seeming to sense the motion rather than see it, Myn's eyes flitted in their direction and the soldiers quickly thought better of it.

"Myranda?" called Deacon as he stumbled out the door, his mind firmly turned to the task of keeping the stronghold standing.

"I'm here, Deacon," she replied.

"Is everything safe?" he asked.

"Safe as it is likely to be until we can sort this situation out," Myranda said.

He guided the bags that were drifting behind him out into the center of the courtyard and let them drop. His hands were shaking, and the hand clenched about the crystal was white-knuckled with his grip.

"There are six men in the entryway. Are there any others within the keep I might have missed?" he asked no one in particular. When he spoke again, his voice was labored. "An answer, ideally a swift one, would be much appreciated."

"We're the only ones inside," said a voice from within.

"Then I would vigorously encourage you to leave, because I do not believe I have the strength to prevent the collapse of the keep for much longer."

A few seconds passed before the first of the men ventured out. When he was not snapped in half by a dragon, the others followed.

"Thank you," Deacon said, lowering his arm and sagging to the ground.

As soon as the glow in his gem faded to nothing, a deafening roar of clattering stone and splintering wood filled the courtyard. A cloud of dust and debris rushed up from every door, window, and gap in the lower walls as the tallest portions crumbled into themselves. The whole structure slumped into the ground, with the exterior wall falling last.

The final rumble and clatter of stone and wood settled into silence, with all eyes looking to the pile of rubble that less than a minute prior had been a tall and proud stronghold. The eyes then turned to the one person who seemed to have her wits about her; Myranda.

Joseph R. Lallo

"If anyone is hurt, bring them to the infirmary. Deacon and I can tend to your wounds. When we are certain that no one is in danger any longer, we will address what has happened and what is to be done about it."

Chapter 7

By the time the assorted injuries had been tended to, the punishing sun had begun to slide from the sky, leaving the now-homeless soldiers to shelter in the long shadows cast by the defensive walls. Wisely, much of the food for the keep had been stored against the wall in a sequence of long, low storage crates, no doubt in order to ease the difficulty of loading and unloading. The water came from an exceedingly deep well, so there would be plenty to drink. The firewood and lamp oil was also stored separately in the courtyard, so the most immediate consequence for the collapse was a lack of shelter. Though it would make for an uncomfortably cold night, it would only really be a concern during the worst heat of the day to follow, and for that there was time to prepare.

Myranda wiped her hands and stepped out into the light. The worst of the injuries had been the commander's own, and though he certainly would have preferred to suffer through them rather than even ask to receive treatment at the hands of either Myranda or Deacon, the duchess had taken it upon herself to mend the worst of his injuries and gently pushed him into a deep healing sleep that should take care of the rest before morning.

"Was anyone else hurt?" Myranda asked, looking about at the Tresson troops.

"The two men struck by Garr's tail were in rough shape," Deacon said. "But I've seen to them. How are the soldiers we treated upon our arrival?"

"Sleeping comfortably. In a day or two they should be fully recovered as well."

For the first time since the walls of the keep had begun to shake, Myranda took a moment to appreciate all that had happened, and the significant results thereof. Though not told to do so, the soldiers had all dropped their weapons before taking to the shelter of the outer wall. Their expressions covered the range from barely masked fury to utter terror. Garr had settled onto his haunches, eyes locked on the infirmary tent that held the commander. The tenseness of combat had yet to leave his muscles. At a glance one could imagine the beast snapping back into a rampage at the slightest provocation. Myn, on the other hand, was quite at ease. She hopped to her feet and snatched up the remains of two enormous birds, trotting happily to Myranda and dropping them at the wizard's feet.

"Yes, Myn. They're lovely. But where did you get them? We *did* tell you to stay inside, didn't we?" Myranda said, scratching vigorously at Myn's offered brow.

The dragon gave a quick glance to her Tresson counterpart by way of an answer and rumbled with a purr of contentment at the attention she was receiving.

Myranda turned to Garr. "You have our thanks."

Garr ignored the comment, far too intent on glaring at the tent. His gaze was locked precisely where the commander was resting inside, despite the fact he couldn't possibly know where the man had been placed. Myranda wondered what mix of senses allowed it. When Myn's stomach gurgled loudly, she set the thought aside.

"Myn, have you eaten at all?" she asked. "For heaven's sake, as much as I appreciate you bringing me a meal, don't forget to take your own share first. You've been doing far hungrier work than I."

The dragon pulled her head reluctantly away and snatched one of the birds, gulping it down with zeal before padding off toward the collapsed stable to drag over a burning timber.

While Myn assembled what soon became clear was a fair approximation of a cooking fire, Grustim stepped up to Myranda.

"I must say, I would have expected the two of you to be more shaken by the collapse. I was concerned you'd be killed."

Myranda looked briefly at the pile of rubble. "It's nothing we haven't had to deal with before. It is embarrassing how often, in fact."

"Indeed," said Deacon brightly as he stepped to Myranda's side. "Our friend Ivy has pointed out we've seen almost every building that's ever held us crumble to the ground. It's something of a tradition at this point."

"Not the best habit to get into," Myranda said.

"Nevertheless, I must offer my profound apologies for the danger I placed you in. Without orders, he can be single-minded. It is a great relief that his thirst for vengeance didn't claim your lives."

"Myn can be the same way," Myranda said. "The two are quite alike."

"What happens to Garr now?" Deacon asked. "If I understand correctly, he is no longer your mount. And thus, I suppose, you are no longer a Dragon Rider."

"That is up to him. He is free now, and as such he may choose his own way. I've once before had to relieve him of his duty, and he saw fit to renew his oath to me. It is my hope he shall do so again. If not… a Dragon Rider's life is a difficult one. It would be a lie to say I do not dream from time to time of being rid of it. But not until I'm through with this mission."

"Yes," Myranda said, stepping to the packs that Deacon had gathered. "The mission."

She opened one of the packs and revealed a knife and some pots and pans.

Deacon looked to the rubble once more. "As diplomatic ventures go, this hasn't been a marked success thus far."

"Did you find anything that you can share? Are we any closer to understanding who is responsible and how to stop them?" Myranda asked.

"Mostly what I learned was that Brustuum was lying. How much of what he said was a lie remains to be seen. But I have my suspicions," Grustim said.

Myranda began to prepare the desert bird to be cooked while Deacon found his book and stylus and made ready to record.

"Please, share them," Deacon said.

Grustim closed his eyes to gather his thoughts. "Brustuum… he claimed to have had the woman for only a few days. I suspect it was far longer. Even if it was just a few days, he'd violated protocol by not sending word of her discovery. He was holding her here in secret. I don't know what he had planned for her, but rather than keeping his men on hand, he sent them out… they'll be returning before long. It will be telling when they do. Either they were off performing desert drills, in which case they will be carrying light or training weapons, or they were sent searching for the woman he had already found, in which case they will be heavily armed."

"We shall have many questions for him when he awakes," Myranda said.

"Did he say anything of any magic she worked while she was here?" Deacon asked.

"Just that she escaped with two windows she opened through magic," Grustim said.

"That much fits… but I saw some… *things*. They were human. At least, they *had* been human. In the lower level cells."

"What do you mean?"

"Husks of men. Drained of life. They were the work of a necromancer, I'm sure of that," Deacon said.

"How many?"

Deacon shut his eyes to remember the scene. "Eight in one cell, seven in another. I'm not certain if there were more. I was in a rather significant rush at the time."

"Fifteen total. Those would be the prisoners," Grustim said. "What would be the result of rendering men into such a state?"

"Those men would be her thralls, servants to her will. And a necromancer can gather a significant amount of mystic energy by draining life in such a way," Deacon said.

"Enough to mount an escape as she had?"

"That would depend upon her level of training and discipline. But it should certainly get her close, in any case," Deacon explained.

Myranda set a portion of the meat over the flames to cook and joined the discussion. "How quickly could someone be drained in that way, Deacon? Is it possible she quickly sapped enough strength to escape while the guards were unaware?"

"It is possible, I suppose, but surely it would have done her more good to sap the guards themselves. Unless those still outside the walls are better equipped, I don't detect any enchantment that could have protected them. Though… is it possible she *did* attack some guards and we didn't find them?"

"He lost five guards. We know that much. If he'd lost more, he would have eagerly expressed his outrage at their loss as well."

"Well perhaps those five who were killed were drained."

"No. There are five fresh graves beyond the east wall. A Tresson, even a deceitful and traitorous one like Brustuum, would never commit a body tainted by magic into the earth. Our dead are offerings to the Great Ones. It would be an insult to knowingly offer a work of dark magic to them. That is why the prisoners were not buried, I'm quite certain. The unclean are to be burned, and there is no evidence of a pyre." His face hardened. "He's had plenty of time to burn them… And there are no other graves… He was *hiding* them… Just as he was hiding so much else."

"I don't understand it… We will simply have to ask when he awakes and hope he is reasonable enough to answer," Deacon said.

"I'm through appealing to reason," Grustim said, suddenly stepping toward the infirmary. "Can you wake him?"

"He needs at least half a day to heal," Myranda said.

"If his mind is sound, or at least he can understand my questions and I can understand his answers, then the more broken the rest of him, the better it suits my purposes."

Myranda stepped in front of him. "What are you planning?" she asked firmly.

"If Brustuum was hiding those prisoners, then either he could not protect them and was seeking to hide his failure, or he had plans for them. At best he is a fool undeserving of his rank, and at worst he allowed or encouraged a hostile mystic to commit abominations of gods and men upon them. In either case it is now clear that it is my duty, and also my pleasure, to do whatever it takes to find the root of his treachery."

"It looks and sounds to me that what you have in mind is torture."

"I will have my answers through whatever means he renders necessary."

"I cannot abide such cruelty," Myranda said.

"Then I suggest you turn away," he said, stepping past her.

She reached out to catch his arm. "There has to be a better way."

Garr, for the first time since Myranda had stepped out, let his gaze slide from the infirmary. His potent stare now locked on Myranda. More specifically, it locked on her hand, where it touched Grustim's arm. The creature did not look on with anger or threat. He simply made it clear that he was now watching.

Grustim pulled his arm roughly from her grasp and turned to her. "Listen to me, Duchess. You have a firm hand but a soft heart. That is a fine mix for a woman charged with mending a broken world, but in times of war sometimes a heart of stone is the only one that will do. You say that you and others like you defeated the D'Karon within your own borders, and from what I've seen, you certainly have the ability. But if you were able to see your way through to the many unpleasant things that needed to be done, I must believe that there was at least one among your number who would do those things that a soft heart could not abide."

"… There was."

"And would you have found your way to this peace you seek to protect if not for those distasteful acts?"

"Perhaps not."

"Then turn away and let the deed be done."

"But he is your countryman. You relinquished your mount rather than raise a weapon to him before," Deacon said.

"What I've seen and what I believe are enough to convince me he is undeserving of further consideration." The Dragon Rider turned toward the men huddled against the wall and addressed them in their native tongue. "I have reason to believe your commander allowed your prisoner—a Northerner by birth, if the account is to be believed—to work dark magics upon prisoners of Tresson blood. Can any of you confirm or deny this?"

The soldiers stirred and murmured a bit but gave no indication that there was any certainty.

"Seven soldiers were injured, five of them killed. With the commander, that makes for an eight-man guard. Am I correct to assume that all of the men injured or killed were a personal guard of the commander's own selection?"

Now the murmur was clearly to the affirmative.

"And if he were to commit acts unbecoming of a Tresson commander, is it proper to assume that these acts would be done exclusively by his most trusted men?"

They gave another affirmative response.

"And if through his choices or failings a Tresson commander should allow his fellow Tressons to come to harm, should he face judgment?"

"Yes!" came the reply, this time in one voice.

"And if through his actions he should choose to hide those choices or failings, what shall be done to uncover them?"

"Anything necessary to find the truth!" they proclaimed in unison. More and more it seemed this was a practiced refrain.

"And if the truth is certain and the actions are unworthy of a Tresson subject, what is the price for such deeds?"

219

"Death by exile!" they answered.

"I, as a Tresson soldier of equal or greater rank, mean to have the truth. If I seek it, will any of you stop me?"

"No, Dragon Rider!"

Grustim turned to Myranda again. "You have your ways, Duchess, and we have our own. I do not ask you to embrace them, but I ask you to respect them."

Myranda looked him in the eye. She saw much there. Intensity, hate, righteous fury, but more than anything, she saw resolve. He would see this through, not out of cruelty, but out of duty.

"Do what you must," Myranda said quietly, lowering her head.

As Grustim continued to the infirmary, Myranda sat beside the fire and tried to steel herself for what would come next. Deacon sat beside her and tended to the flames and food.

"You placed Brustuum in a healing sleep, did you not?" he said.

"I did."

"It will take considerable... force to awaken someone in such a state."

"I believe Grustim is prepared to apply whatever force is required to get the job done," she said.

Myranda tried not to think of what Grustim would do, or how he planned to do it. But the more she tried to push those thoughts away, the more she felt worse thoughts drift in to replace them. He'd spoken of a heart of stone, those willing to do the unthinkable in pursuit of a cause. In a way, the description fit Ether well, but the shapeshifter was not the person she'd thought of when he made such a suggestion. He may as well have been speaking specifically of Lain. Myranda held the fallen hero close to her heart, and held him in the highest regard, but he of all people would never have wanted her to forget what he was. By his own choice, Lain had been a killer. So much of their quest would never have been possible without the dark deeds he was willing to perform. Somehow she'd been able to set that aside.

A yelp of pain, followed by a muffled howl as it was forcibly silenced, heralded Grustim's swift defeat of her nurturing sleep. The sound instantly forced to mind what sort of similar things might have been done in the name of peace in the past.

Perhaps sensing the dark directions her mind was headed, Deacon spoke up. "Myranda, the pad from my pack seems to be missing," he said.

She turned to him, taking a moment to shake herself from her thoughts. Doing so instead reminded her of something equally unpleasant.

"Grustim had it... Deacon, the portal to the north? It *was* in Castle Verril. And there must have been a second one out of there. Damage was done to the castle. People are missing. People may have been killed."

He took a breath and placed a hand on her arm. "We knew it was a possibility. Do you have the pad now? Was there anything more?"

"No. He took it with him. I have to assume it was taken when they stripped him of his weapons and armor. It may even have been destroyed."

"They would have to work fairly hard to destroy one of *my* books, and if they'd done so, I would have known. I'll have it in a moment."

Deacon stood and paced to the rubble, gem in hand. He stood at the edge of where the door had once been and gazed over the shattered stone of the mighty stronghold. After working out roughly where he wished to focus his efforts, he raised the gem. The powerful light of the sun made the polished egg of crystal seem to glow brilliantly even when at rest, but as he focused his strength through it, it came alive with its own cooler glow.

"There… I see it." he said quietly.

He spread his fingers, and the smallest of the stones began to shuffle obligingly aside. It took more effort, but not long after, the larger of the stones followed. Brick by broken brick he excavated a sloping path down into the rubble, ending in a mound of lacquered green armor battered on the floor of a former cell. Deacon let his focus lapse. A few of the smaller stones tumbled back down into his cleared passage, but it remained otherwise intact, allowing him to step down into the ruin and gingerly push aside the topmost plate of armor to find his pad. It was badly creased and partially torn, but otherwise quite whole.

Deacon fetched the bundle of pages. Another pulse of light within his gem suggested he'd worked an enchantment, and slowly the torn pages began to mend, the creases eased away, and the ground-in dust drifted off in the breeze. In seconds the book was perfectly repaired with no evidence of so much as having been dropped to the ground, let alone suffering through a building collapse.

He flicked through the pages, as usual quite unaware of how astounding it must have looked to the soldiers who witnessed the event.

"This is… very distressing," Deacon commented, his eyes darting over the contents of the final page. "Have you read this?"

"I only saw a glimpse," she said.

"Here. The woman has found her way to another of the D'Karon forts. There was a clash with Ivy. We know more about her now, but most worrying are her plans," Deacon said.

Myranda squinted as the light of the setting sun glared off the page. Though her fair skin was ill-suited to it, she'd not taken refuge in the shelter of the wall. The soldiers sheltering there were enough on edge without having to share space with Myranda and Deacon. This was particularly true when considering Myn's unwillingness to leave their sides for more than a few moments at a time. The thought of her faithful friend lumbering up and frightening off the troops she deemed to have settled too close to Myranda was enough to persuade her to endure the sun for a bit longer, even if it was already baking her.

Myn soon noticed the difficulty and settled down between Myranda and the sun, casting her friend in a cool shadow and setting her paws protectively on either side. She glanced at Deacon, who was still standing in the brunt of the sunlight but was too distracted scribbling down his recent findings in a larger book to notice. Reaching out with a paw, she nudged him closer until he was beside Myranda, sharing the shade. Then she set her paw down again and craned her head in contentment, huffing a breath of satisfaction. Myranda placed a hand atop her paw in thanks.

"She wants to bring the D'Karon back? Is that even possible?" Myranda asked.

"They were brought here once... And if it is indeed the case that she was the one who brought them here the first time, then it isn't a matter of possibility, it's a matter of time. I admit, I've not studied the portal spells as closely as I might. They are precisely the spells those of Entwell resolved never to study. Even looking upon their workings makes me uncomfortable. But the spell is not a complicated one, merely a potent one. It would take monumental amounts of mystic strength. The combined might of the Entwell masters during a blue moon ceremony might *just* be enough. But given enough time and the proper focus, even a novice wizard could work the spell."

"How much time?"

"For an individual gathering power on a scale subtle enough to have gone unnoticed until now? Not less than a century. Likely much more. Three hundred years wouldn't be outside the realm of reason."

"One hundred fifty years of war, plus however long it took the D'Karon to start the war... if she set her mind to the task immediately after the last one..."

"She could be quite nearly ready," Deacon said. "As with the D'Karon, any new and potent supply of power could speed the process enormously."

"And what would happen then? Would it be another portal, like the one we closed at Lain's End?"

"No. This would be small," he said. He held his hand out toward his pack and called a book to it, flipping through and revealing page after page of otherworldly writing. "It would allow spirits through, not even flesh. But that would be enough to allow beings like the D'Karon generals to pass back into our world and take form."

"That looks like D'Karon writing..." Myranda said, eying the pages as he scanned through them.

"It is. I've transcribed the D'Karon spell books we've found into my personal grimoire. We can't hope to combat their workings if we don't understand them." He continued looking over the page, muttering to himself. "It was foolish of me to avoid studying their portal spells. They are forbidden *precisely* because they are the greatest threat. If they already exist, then there is no wisdom in avoiding the knowledge any longer..."

"We need to be certain of how much time we have, if any. We need to know the urgency of the situation," Myranda said. "Is there any way we can detect that?"

"With the full portal, perhaps, but not with this initial one. It seems to have been *designed* to be virtually undetectable. It would certainly stand to reason, as it is doubtless the most fragile spell they have."

"So if we find it, we could undo it?"

"Well, again, the D'Karon do not work their craft with the expectation of ever undoing it, but the keyhole, at least until it is finally cast, is in most ways just a very well hidden reservoir of energy. It can be sapped, drained, dissipated. Ideally the power would be relinquished slowly, or else we'd have a situation much as we faced in the Dagger Gale Mountains a few months ago."

"That *must* be avoided. We lost a large portion of a mountain range. If that were to happen within Tresson borders as a result of something we or another Alliance subject has done, it could only be considered an attack on an unprecedented scale. We may already have passed the point that peace might be salvageable. If a swath of their land were to be consumed in a wave of chaotic energies, I doubt the resulting war would ever end."

"We could condense the energy, I suppose. Gather it into some manner of artifact until it could safely be dealt with."

"Wouldn't that do little more than postpone the problem?"

"Sometimes postponing the problem is the best we can do at a given time. It will certainly be the swiftest and safest way to reclaim the stolen energy. With the energy gathered, the keyhole spell would collapse harmlessly and the solution of how best to return the energy that went into its creation could be addressed at our leisure."

"Let us suppose we chose to do such a thing. Can it be done at a distance? If we were to learn the location of the keyhole, could we gather the energy from here?"

"No. The nature of the spell makes interaction from afar at best unstable, and at worst impossible. We would need to be able to physically touch the point in space that is being prepared to open. If the wording here is any indication… finding the keyhole might be *very* difficult. It cannot be seen with the eyes, steps have been taken to make it nearly undetectable through magic… It is a fairly simple spell, but much of what little complexity there is in casting it is tailored to make its presence known only to its creator."

"What if Turiel is no longer able to fuel it? Does it matter if we leave the spell half-cast?"

"I would strongly advise against it. Like most D'Karon spells, it will drink up energies around it even without the hand of a wizard guiding it. That's one way we might find it, but without knowing how it has been tended to thus far, we don't know how strong or weak that draw might be. If it is very strong, it will be simple enough to find, as it will present itself as the same withering lifelessness that characterizes their gems. If the draw is weak, it might lay hidden, quietly sipping at the ambient magic for... perhaps *thousands* of years. But it *will* eventually drink its fill, and then the keyhole will open."

"So if we do not deal with this now, there is the very real possibility that we will have guaranteed that at some point in the future a door will open again, and perhaps at a time when we won't be there to defend against the D'Karon."

"I'm afraid so."

"Our goal is crystal clear, then. As important as it is to find the woman who has been tending to it, it is *more* important that we find the keyhole," Myranda said.

"Yes..." Deacon said distantly.

He continued to flip through the pages of his books while Myranda silently watched the meat cook and considered the path ahead. Every few moments another muffled howl of agony echoed out from the infirmary. Myranda began to wonder just how much this peace would ultimately cost. Rather than let the sounds of Grustim's work bore into her mind, she plucked up the pad and stylus and began to compose a message to the others.

#

"How much longer before we have the materials to seal the hole?" Croyden asked, gazing up through the fault in the roof as a pair of workmen stood beside him.

"Three more days to have the stone cut," said the first.

"Another day to bring it here," said the other.

"Will there be sufficient time for the ceiling to be mended before the queen's return? I do not want... Oh, lovely."

He looked in annoyance at the familiar swirl of wind approaching.

Ether whisked in through the hole in the roof and touched down in front of Croyden, bringing with her a stream of stinging ice crystals that pelted those in attendance and sprinkled the floor. When her windy form was near enough to do so gracefully, she shifted to her human form again.

She began speaking to Croyden without regard for the conversation that had been going on. She didn't even acknowledge the presence of the workers.

"All of this that happened here," she said, with an encompassing wave of her arm, "does it stab at your soul? Does it feel as though something sacred has been desecrated, something precious taken from you?"

Croyden looked at her curiously. There was an edge, a fire to her words that had been absent before, and that same fire was reflected in her eyes.

"It spits in the face of all I've come to stand for. It is an affront to my kingdom and a personal insult that cuts me to the bone."

"Then you and I have much to discuss..." she said. "Follow. I wish to speak to you in a place where others will not hear."

She paced toward the throne room. Her crisp turn and quick pace made it clear she had no doubt whatsoever that he would follow. Croyden had never encountered someone so effortlessly presumptuous.

"I have duties to attend to, Guardian Ether. I cannot abandon them simply to humor you."

She spoke without turning. "Your duty is to protect your kingdom and enact some measure of justice upon those responsible for sullying it. I mean to aid you in that. Now follow."

Croyden tried to quell the surge of irritation that her curt attitude conjured so efficiently.

"See to it that all materials are prepared as soon as possible, and when the schedule is solidified, inform me. I want the castle whole again for the queen's return," he said.

The men moved quickly to their tasks, and Croyden set off after the infuriating shapeshifter. She pulled at the heavy door to the currently unoccupied throne room. The door was utterly massive, reaching from the floor nearly to the vaulted ceiling, and made from the thickest wood anywhere in the castle save the gates. The doors were meant to be large enough when opened to allow the throne room to serve as a continuation of the entry hall, yet sturdy enough to be barricaded and protect the king and queen from anything short of a siege weapon. The handles for the door were brass rings the size of serving trays, spaced regularly from bottom to top and meant to be attached to ropes to help a team of men open and close them quickly. Ether grasped the lowest ring and hauled the door open with little apparent effort and no concern for the colossal breach in protocol that such a thing represented. Once inside she looked about the room with disinterest, then turned to await him.

"Quickly," she snapped, pointing her finger at the floor beside her.

His expression hardened further. The woman may as well have been addressing a disobedient dog. Nonetheless, he'd heard stories of Ether's feats and seen firsthand the devastation she could produce and the ferocity with which she fought when she deemed such a thing necessary. The strength necessary to open the door was the least of her attributes. She had been and continued to be a strong ally and, in any case, was not the sort of person one should willfully irritate. He stepped beside her, and she pulled the door shut with a thunderous rumble.

"The woman responsible for this is dangerous for many reasons. First and foremost is her mastery and apparent fascination with D'Karon magic."

"That much is clear."

"Silence yourself until I am through," Ether said. "The D'Karon seek power above all else. Not something so petty and impermanent as the sort of power bestowed by politics and wealth, but raw mana. They have devised means to harvest it that are grimly efficient, and if she hopes to work their spells with any regularity she will need them. To prevent things like this from happening again, you must do what I would have hoped had already been quite nearly completed. You must destroy any D'Karon influence left. Do you know what a thir gem is?"

"I imagine they are—"

"Do not imagine. Be certain. They are the stones so often found in the facilities the D'Karon had claimed or constructed. They drink away one's strength and take on a brilliant violet light. They must be destroyed, turned to powder. Any fragment larger than a walnut may have some value to her."

"We are quite aware of that and have been actively seeking and sequestering all such gems."

Ether's lips pulled into a grimace. "Do not sequester, *destroy*. There were gems in that chamber. She found them, she used them, and that hole in your palace was the result. Anything and everything that the D'Karon touched should be treated with distrust, and all that they created should be destroyed. Not collected, not studied. Destroyed. D'Karon works are an abomination and should be treated as such."

"Understood."

"Your second point of concern is the woman herself. She is what you would call a necromancer, and as such has the tremendous capacity to harvest strength on her own, quite likely enough to fuel some of the lesser D'Karon spells in the short term, and in the very long term she might match their greatest feats."

"And you are certain she is a necromancer?"

"I only speak with certainty."

"And *how* are you certain? How can you determine such a thing?"

Ether released a mildly exasperated breath. "The same way you can determine if something is red rather than blue. When one is familiar with the finer details and able to perceive them, it is plainly apparent. May I continue, or do you wish to continue to interrupt me with your inane prattle?"

Croyden crossed his arms and held his tongue.

"As a necromancer, she regards any living thing as a source of energy and any dead thing as a source of raw materials. She can commune with the dead to learn what they knew, she can resurrect the fallen to serve her whims, and she may even have the ability to return herself from death if not properly dealt with. She should not be faced directly. Anyone near enough to make contact risks only making her stronger."

"Noted. Ranged tactics and mystics only. Would you be willing at this point to endure some of my inane prattle?"

"If I must."

"Where did you go just now, what did you find there that inspired you to be helpful so suddenly, and why did you feel it necessary to enter the throne room to dispense this information?"

Ether looked at Croyden evenly. "I am a creature of the world as a whole. Not a single kingdom. Not a single race. I serve as a protector for the world as a collective, and therefore I call no one part of it my home, despite what your military and government would choose to believe. But to the north of this palace... *Lain's End*... that is the one place I would lay claim to. As near a home as any place in this world. It is my sanctuary, a place to be alone with my thoughts and to ponder what the past has brought and what the future may bring. She *soiled* it. Brought D'Karon magic to that place once more. And she soiled the memory of Lain himself. I *cannot* let that stand. And I realized that the same burning that I felt, I saw in you when I arrived."

She looked away, her words as much intended for herself as for him.

"I have not been myself of late. I am troubled by things that should not concern me. With little choice, I've reluctantly sought wisdom from those who have been at the whims of such nonsense all of their lives. Mortals. They have made claims of understanding my difficulties, and they have offered solutions that are as useless as they are foolish. They speak of family, and duty. You, though. You are different. You are an elf, and thus more than mortal. And you do not have a proper family and never have."

"Do not have a proper family?" he said. "I had a mother and a father... though I admit I was never introduced to the latter."

"He was and is a traitorous scoundrel. Your life could only have been enhanced by his absence. And your mother was worse, a traitor to not only her world but to her destiny. She got what she deserved, though far too long after the damage was done."

Croyden narrowed his eyes. "My mother was ceaselessly devoted to her kingdom. I shall brook no claims to the contrary."

"Your mother was Trigorah Teloran. She was Chosen, or at least was meant to be. But her devotion to the meaningless borders men draw between one another led her to turn her back upon her true duty and instead serve the very beings she was selected by the gods to defeat. At best she was a shortsighted woman with poor judgment. At worst she willfully embraced her world's would-be usurpers."

"I've heard enough," Croyden said. "Your advice regarding the proper tactics when defending against the necromancer shall be taken into account in our future encounters. Now please open this door."

"I am not through."

"You may not be through with me, but I am quite through with you, Guardian. I have tolerated your venomous tone for a good deal longer than I would have preferred, but when you insult the memory of my mother, you cross the line."

"You *must* lend me your aid," Ether commanded. "I require your insight."

Joseph R. Lallo

"Regardless of whether or not you require it, you most assuredly do not deserve it. And if your opinion of me is so low, one wonders why you would seek my counsel at all."

"Because you are brash, willful, proud, and blunt. You have no real family, you are in a position of comparatively great responsibility, and you have recently lost someone who could well be your only genuine connection to another individual. I see much of myself in you. And at this moment you and I feel similarly regarding the actions of the necromancer, but while you are apparently composed, I am very nearly at my wits end. You *must* share your insight into how to cope with such emotion."

"You see much of yourself in me… In an exchange positively fraught with disrespect and derision, to compare me to you is, by a wide margin, the worst claim you've made thus far. If your mind is causing you troubles, then I will happily leave you to them. Now open the door."

"*My mind is all I have!*" Ether growled. "You do not understand that, nor could you. I am not a creature such as yourself, a husk of bone and sinew playing host to a brief and ephemeral consciousness. I am little more than a mass of pure elemental energy bound together through sheer force of will. My will is everything. And I am losing my focus. This woman who plagues the both of us, the necromancer who threatens your peace and toys with the tools of the enemy… I should feel her presence. In the months gone by I have swept from one side of this land to the other, seeking out and crushing even the slightest remnant of their influence. Now there is a woman cutting a clumsy swath across the land with their teachings and *I cannot detect her*. In the past it would have taken a peerless will to evade me. Now this woman is but a vague sensation at the edge of my mind. I cannot focus my attentions sufficiently to find her, and if this lack of focus is allowed to spread, what then? Will I soon lack the will to maintain form? Will I once again be spread to the far reaches of this world, unable to gather myself together again? All because of this *blasted* plague of emotions that your kind has somehow foisted upon me? *You must help me!*"

He looked her evenly in the eye, noting the flash of desperation mixed with the wall of arrogance that seemed to compose the bulk of her personality. If there was one thing he'd learned about her, it was that she seldom saw fit to misrepresent herself. She had far too high an opinion of herself for that. So her concern was genuine. It was odd to see even a flicker of vulnerability in a being so thoroughly certain of her own superiority.

"And what would you have me do, Guardian? I have no secret to ease your mind. I cannot even begin to understand the source of your unease."

"Then at least explain why so many mortals offer up the same pointless advice. How can so many of you claim family as a source of strength and a solution for inner strife when the one being who might have been near enough to be considered family is the *source* of my troubles."

228

"How so?"

"Lain. First he denied me his love, and then he was taken from me before he could see the error in his ways."

"Mmm… And this is the only source of your troubled mind?"

"No. My primary purpose, the literal reason for my creation, has come and gone. In very real terms, I have outlived my usefulness. These two feelings are the seeds from which all others sprouted."

"And how have you attempted to solve this problem thus far?"

"As I have solved all others. I have set my mind upon it. Reflected and meditated upon it. I have sought the solution from within."

"I think perhaps the nature of your difficulties is reflected in the words you've chosen. You are upset not because he did not find love but that he kept it from you, and not that he died but that he was taken from you. And when these feelings began to burn at you, you sought the answer in yourself. Have you ever, in all of your years, thought about anyone but yourself?"

"I have until now devoted myself to my duty as a Chosen One above all."

"And that duty, as you have said, is the reason for your creation. In effect, the duty and the Chosen are one and the same. This, I think, is why family is so important. Family is something that you care about above even yourself. It is perhaps the one thing in your life you would do anything for. And the one thing that can be relied upon to do anything for you. It takes you out of yourself. Opens the door to your heart and mind. Lets you see that there is more to the world than the darkness that may linger inside."

"Foolishness…" Ether said, though in her tone there was the slightest dash of uncertainty. "And even if this were so, how does one develop such feelings for others? Surely one cannot will oneself into caring for others."

"No, I suppose most of us are lucky enough to have blood ties and to be surrounded through our lives by those who care about us, and who earn our affection in kind."

"Blood ties… Yes… yes, if there is something of yourself, literally a part of you in someone else… then the connection would be inherent."

"One would hope such a connection would come in time to any who—"

"I require a child."

Croyden blinked. "What?"

"If what you say is so, then the connection I require can most simply be had in a blood relation, and as I have none existing, the only solution is to create one."

"I think perhaps you misunderstand my meaning."

"Give me a child," she said firmly.

He coughed and took a step back. "I'm sorry?"

"If you require, I would be willing to assume a form to better suit your tastes."

"Guardian Ether, flattered though I may be at the suggestion, the decision to have a child is not one to be made lightly. And as you say, I am 'the queen's plaything.'"

"A matter easily rectified," Ether said, her features subtly shifting until she was visually indistinguishable from Queen Caya.

"It is not a simple matter of appearance, Guardian. And I'll thank you not to impersonate our queen. It is a crime with a very stiff penalty."

"I was led to believe that the act of procreation is one endlessly sought by the males of each race. It is curious that you would resist this opportunity."

"There are any number of reasons I could offer with regard to why I would actively avoid this opportunity, the least of which is that no amount of shape-changing could ever render you suitable for my tastes."

"Absurd... though with the task at hand, the months necessary to produce an offspring would likely represent an unacceptable delay. Still, it is a matter to revisit when the present crisis has passed."

"For our own sake and that of any potential child, let us hope that a better solution presents itself in the interim," Croyden said. "Now if you would kindly open the door so that we may each continue with our tasks?"

"Of course. With this matter investigated I shall return to the site of the clash with Ivy. It is doubtful the necromancer has lingered, but there may remain some indication of her further ambitions. I thank you for your insight. It at least colors that of others with potential value. I may seek your counsel again."

She pushed the door open, shifted to wind, and departed. Croyden stepped forward and watched the swirling form vanish through the damaged roof.

"'I may seek your counsel again,'" he repeated. "A more ominous phrase I've never heard..."

#

Ivy and Celeste stood beside a fire as the cloudy sky over the fort turned from golden to rosy. It would be some time yet before the soldiers would return, but between the provisions left in the soldiers' things and some swift foraging by Ivy, they were able to erect a tent to keep the worst of the wind and moisture from them. Much of the time since then had been spent in silent vigil. The stirring forms of Demont's many creations gradually became still, until they had one by one collapsed. With little to occupy him any longer, Celeste became restless. Spending years in a dank, frigid cell has a way of making one anxious to fill every moment of freedom with something. Anything was better than stillness.

He first gathered and organized the provisions available, then sifted through the equipment that may prove useful. Among them was a pair of short swords, as well as a Tresson longbow and a supply of arrows.

"My fingers aren't what they should be anymore," he said, testing the tension of the bowstring. "Of the two of us, I believe you should be the one to handle the bow."

"I really don't think so," Ivy said, shaking her head. "I don't think I know how to use one."

"You don't think you know?" he said. "One would imagine such is a matter one would be certain of."

"When the D'Karon were still... *making* me," she said with a shudder, "they would force things into my mind. Some of it stayed in place. Some of it didn't. And the things that stayed... I don't like using them. I feel... wrong when I do. Like I'm not the one deciding what I should do. It's hard to control myself."

Celeste beckoned. "Here. You shall see then."

"I really don't want—"

"Ivy, precision with a bow is a valuable skill. Uncertainty or discomfort with any weapon, particularly for one so often tasked with combat, is simply not something that should be allowed to remain," he said firmly. "Take the bow."

She reluctantly did so, holding it gingerly and regarding it as though she'd just been handed a venomous snake.

"Do you favor your left or right hand?" he asked.

"Left."

"Then this bow will not be ideal for you, but one cannot always depend upon one's preferred bow. Give me your right hand. The bow goes here. Seat it here, against your thumb."

He guided her hands swiftly but surely, giving Ivy little time to object or fixate on her anxiety.

"These three fingers here, to grip the string. These two will hold the arrow, so you want the gap between them centered."

His orders were simple and precise and came in rapid bursts. Ivy couldn't suppress a grin at how easily he slipped into the role of instructor. It made her imagine him as he must have been in his youth, training soldiers, or raising Myranda.

She followed his instructions as precisely as she could. When his words weren't clear, or when she misunderstood them, he would gently shape her grip or guide her stance with a quick tap here or there. Before long she was fitting her first arrow. He offered up a scraggly, ice-coated bush in the middle distance as the target. She did her best to follow his instructions, drawing the bow, sighting as he described, tipping the bow what she judged to be the sufficient amount, and letting an arrow fly.

It fell woefully short, striking the ground and flipping through the air.

"It would appear you escaped having *this* knowledge forced upon you," he said.

"Yeah, I guess so."

"Ready another arrow. Your claws may be a bit of a problem. I want you to try this grip instead, if you can manage it…"

Again he coached her through a few minor changes. As much as she'd wanted to avoid using the bow, for fear of feeling a dash of the lingering control that Demont and Epidime had so carefully woven into her during her time in their clutches, now that she knew it was her skill to learn, she felt a flush of pride with each improvement. Such improvements came quickly as well. Celeste had many strengths, but two of his greatest seemed to be his patience and his eye for detail. Each time she drew the string, he knew immediately if she'd done it right or, if not, how to fix what she'd done wrong.

"You're a wonderful teacher," Ivy said.

"You've not hit your target yet. You should ready a fourth arrow. Remember, there is a stiff wind. You'll need to aim into it."

She reached back toward the quiver he'd helped her position on her back, groping blindly for the fletched end of an arrow.

"Is this how you taught Myranda to shoot?" she asked, finally snagging one.

"No… I taught her a bit, and my brother taught her a bit more… but there was never much time for that. Her mother wouldn't have any of it regardless. Myranda was destined for better things than to follow her father to war. … No, pinch here, and hook your thumb."

Ivy adjusted. "I hope… I hope you don't mind me asking, but… is there something wrong between you and Myranda?"

"Of course not."

"It's just that Myranda spoke all the time about how she always kept the hope that you might be alive. You were always on her mind."

"And she was always on mine while I was locked in the Verril dungeon."

"I imagine you must have been thinking of her. So if the two of you felt so strongly, I would have thought once you found one another again you would be inseparable. It seems like you're always handling something within the city and she's always handling something else."

"Myranda has many responsibilities. I do what I can to help her."

"I know, and I know she appreciates it, but there are times when I know you could leave something to someone else. Sometimes you must be choosing to work apart from her rather than with her."

He paused, and there was the sense that the silence was not to search for words, but to summon the strength to speak them. "She grew into the woman she is today without me, Ivy. I had a place in her mind through all of this, but not a place in her life. She doesn't need me any longer; it would be selfish and pointless of me to impose myself."

Ivy loosened her grip and turned to him. "You don't really mean that."

"She's a grown woman. What use does she have for me any longer, beyond those ways I can help in repairing our homeland?"

She shook her head, glancing briefly to the fort to assure there was still nothing new to be concerned about. When she was satisfied, she set down the bow and slipped the quiver from her back.

"I think you could benefit from a bit more instruction," he said.

"Mr. Celeste, right now I think you're the one who could use some instruction. Tell me, what was Myranda like when she was a girl?" Ivy asked.

"She took after Lucia… her mother," he said.

He took the brief interruption in his teachings to pluck a tin mug from beside the fire. Inside was some warm broth he'd prepared. He sipped a bit to take the edge from the chill and his hunger.

"In what way?"

"Very studious. I was certain she would grow to be a teacher as Lucia was."

"She sort of did," Ivy said. "She taught me a lot. And she still does." She stared for a moment. "When she was young, when you'd come home after a long mission, how did she act?"

Celeste gripped the mug tightly in his fingers to warm them. "She was always so happy. The look on her face could light up a room. Once, when she saw me through the window, she ran out into the snow in her bare feet to greet me. She was such a sweet little girl."

Ivy placed a hand on his shoulder. "That feeling doesn't go away, Mr. Celeste. Did you remember many of the other children back in Kenvard? The ones your wife taught."

"Some. I was not home as often as I would like."

"There was a little girl about Myranda's age. A gifted artist and musician. Her name was Aneriana. That was me… or at least who I was."

"I do believe I've heard stories of a child who was something of a painter and a musician. She played the flute."

Ivy nodded. "They say the flute was my instrument." She grinned and gave a hollow laugh. "I've tried. I have a flute back in New Kenvard. It feels right when I try to play, but it isn't. These lips aren't really made for the flute. It is funny. When you're a natural at something, it's hard to learn a new way to do it. I imagine I'll get it eventually. But that's not the point. The point is, I have barely anything left from that time. When the D'Karon took me during the massacre, they didn't want Aneriana. They didn't have any use for her. The body was worthless to them, and the mind even more so. They tried for years to wipe it all out, worked as hard as they could to blank the slate and leave me a clean canvas to craft their own weapon. They came very close. Most of my memories are from my time in their clutches, and even then just the last few months of it. But sometimes at night, if I shut the world out and close my eyes, I can feel the shape of the memories I lost. I get a flash of something. The smell of my mother's bread. A glimpse of my father's face… they are the most precious moments I have. Sometimes, I know I shouldn't, but I feel so envious of Myranda. That she has you. So don't you dare think that she doesn't have a place for you anymore."

The malthrope released a shaky breath and wiped her glistening eyes. For a moment she and Celeste simply turned to the fort to resume their vigil. The light was dimming quickly. Within the hour it would be night again. By now Celeste's eyes likely couldn't pick out the dark forms of the monsters on the island. Before much longer, even Ivy's sharp vision wouldn't be sufficient.

"Are we certain the sorceress is still there?" Celeste asked. Ivy wondered if his question was born of genuine concern or simply a desire to shift the subject away from the sensitive direction it had taken. "There was little indication of her arrival. She may have departed just as silently."

"No… I can feel that she's still there. I can't describe it exactly. But I'm certain she's still there." Ivy's ear twitched, and she glanced to her pack. "Oh! I think that's Deacon's pad!"

She pulled open the flap and quickly found the fold of leather and parchment. When it was free, the shuddering stylus jumped to life and began to scrawl out a message on the page.

"It's Myranda's writing," she said, releasing a sigh of relief. "I was getting worried about her."

"What does it say?" he asked. "My eyes aren't what they once were."

"She says, 'We have reached a small stronghold. The woman, Turiel, was here. Possibly for some time. A commander here may have kept her in secret. We hope to have that answer soon. Lives have been lost by Turiel's hand. The stronghold was damaged and now is destroyed. We were briefly taken prisoner, now free. If Turiel hopes to restore the D'Karon, she will have started to open a keyhole. Her work must be reversed, and with great care. Therefore it must be found. We will search, but the surest way is to get the information from Turiel herself. If at all possible, Turiel must be kept alive until we can find and eliminate the keyhole. If she dies and we have not found it, we can never be sure if we'll be able to keep it from opening and allowing the D'Karon to return.'"

With that, the stylus fell still again, the message complete.

"Goodness…" Ivy said, staring at the dire message on the page. She looked back to the fort. "We need to do something."

"What can be done?" Celeste asked. "You've said yourself that you cannot face her alone. And there is no way to know what she has been doing in the fort. She may be even more formidable now."

"Maybe… maybe if I let myself change. I've beaten magical things before when I was changed. I know I could defeat her if I was angry."

He shook his head. "Even if you could depend upon yourself to change, which as I understand it you cannot be certain of, do you think you could hold yourself back? Could you keep yourself from killing her?"

"I… I'm not sure I could…"

"Then better not to risk your life and hers."

"But we're the only ones near her. Something has to be done, and we're the ones to do it."

"Sometimes the wisest thing is to keep vigil until reinforcements arrive."

"You said it yourself, a few soldiers won't make a difference against her. And what if she leaves before someone who can help us arrives? We'd have to find her again, and who knows what sort of damage she could do before then? There's got to be a way…" She clutched her fingers and looked nervously to the fort. "You're smarter than me, Mr. Celeste. You must have *some* idea. If you can think of anything, anything at all, tell me."

Celeste gazed into the fire briefly. When he spoke, it was not with the tone of one who had a moment of inspiration, but as one who simply had taken the next step down a line of reasoning. "Perhaps it is wise to remember that you are not only a Guardian, but an ambassador."

"What do you… oh… you mean I should try to talk to her again?"

"I don't think you should try it at all. But if something must be done, and quickly, it may be a solution. You said she was kind. That she comforted you."

"We had a little bit of a falling out at the end of it," she said with a weak grin. "But… maybe… maybe it is worth a try. I got away from her once. If something goes wrong, I'm sure I could get away again."

"Then we shall need to find a way for you to reach her."

Ivy looked to the charred remnants of the bridge. In the fading light she could see that some of the supports and dangling ropes still smoldered. She paced carefully to the near bridge, the one that was still intact, and peered down. The waves were choppy and rough below. Despite the salty seawater, the cold had left a sort of slush across the surface.

"If you are considering climbing down and swimming, forget such foolishness," Celeste said. "The water will numb you in moments. Even if you could survive the swim, numb fingers attempting to cling to an icy cliff side are a recipe for death."

She looked to the fort again. After a moment of thought, she pulled her cloak a bit tighter and began to march toward it.

"What are you doing?" Celeste asked, walking briskly after her.

"I don't know. But sometimes when I'm neck deep in a problem, that's when I figure a way out of it. I'm hoping that happens now. Go back to the fire. Watch the equipment and keep an eye on me."

"Ivy, I can barely see in this light. In a few minutes I won't be able to see at all."

"I promise you, if something happens between me and Turiel, you'll be able to see it."

"You shouldn't go alone," he said.

Joseph R. Lallo

"We need someone to stay back and spread the word of what happened, *if* something happens." She glanced ahead again, a flicker of doubt in her gaze. "You and I both know if something happens to me, you're better suited to figure out how to handle it than the other way around. Don't worry about me. I've faced worse than this before." She shrugged and smiled. "Hey. Probably I won't get any farther than the bridge, right?" She looked about briefly. "I suppose I should bring a weapon…"

"No," he said. "If you are going as an ambassador, then it would send the wrong message to do so armed."

"Right… Right, that makes sense. See? The two of us are a great team." She gave her cloak one final tug and huffed a breath. "I'll be careful. It'll be fine."

With a stiff nod, she set off toward the burnt bridge, hoping it wasn't terribly obvious how much her final statement was intended to bolster her own confidence rather than his. Once she was on her way, she did her best not to look back to Mr. Celeste. As worried as she was about what could happen, she was more worried about what he must think of her for going out with such a malformed and, frankly, *foolish* idea. In very short order Mr. Celeste had become an important person in her life. She couldn't decide if she was venturing off to do this in an attempt to impress him or hesitant about doing it out of fear of disappointing him.

Each step toward the ruined bridge gave her a clearer look at the remaining creatures. Most lay in unnatural, limp positions. They looked for all the world like puppets with strings that had been cut. Others, like the bridge itself, still smoldered with a weak glow, mostly between joints and in the hollows of their eye-less sockets. None of them offered so much as a twitch of motion at her approach. This, at least, set her mind a bit more at ease. In Ivy and Celeste's vigil, they'd not seen anything scale the cliff and venture off toward any potentially undefended innocents, but they weren't certain they hadn't missed anything. If these monsters, so near their creator, had fallen still after only hours, there was little concern that any others might have survived the waves, the cliffs, and the journey to even the nearest town.

Ivy stopped just short of the charred wooden planks of the bridge they'd destroyed. With little else to do, she took a deep breath and called out.

"Turiel!" she cried. "I need to speak with you!"

The fort was still quite a distance away, and Ivy's voice had the wailing wind and chopping waves to compete with, so she had little hope that she'd actually been heard. She placed two fingers into her mouth and curled her tongue, conjuring a piercing whistle that she'd only a few weeks prior learned to do from one of the hunters in Kenvard. Doing it wasn't quite as simple for her as it had been for him thanks to their anatomical differences, but with a little adaptation she'd been able to get the hang of it.

She gave three more powerful trills with no apparent response from the distant fortress and was about to turn and return to the shore when a dark form flitted out from the doorway and flapped awkwardly through the air. As it got closer, the thing lilting through the air like an old rag caught in a gale turned out to be the mixed-up concoction of a creature that faithfully served Turiel.

It dropped heavily to the ground, knocking one of the smaller unmoving creatures aside, and glared at Ivy across the gap. Despite its primarily canine head, it did a remarkably good job of communicating a look of disappointment.

"Um… Hello… Mott, was it?" Ivy said.

Mott threw his head up in a decidedly theatrical manner, looking away from her and uttering a disdainful chitter.

"I, uh… I'm sorry about before," Ivy offered.

The creature skittered its many legs and turned its back to her, flapping its undersized wings. It was as near a physical interpretation of the word "harrumph" as the beast was able to deliver.

"Listen. I know you only want to make Turiel happy and to do what she says. Just… just tell her Ivy wants to talk. No fighting, I just want to talk."

It curled its serpentine neck back, glancing at her with one eye.

"Look," Ivy said, turning slowly and holding her hands out. "I didn't bring any weapons. I don't want anyone to get hurt. I just want to talk. Just ask her. Please?"

Mott skittered back around again and crouched low, waggling its body and fluttering its wings. For a nonverbal creature, it did a remarkably good job of making its intentions clear.

"No! Don't try to jump! You won't—" Ivy called out.

Predictably the creature didn't pay any attention to her, springing out over the water and working its poorly suited wings with the wind. The flailing and flapping did extend its leap quite a bit, but not nearly enough. It dropped like a stone as soon as it was below the top of the cliff and the wind was no longer aiding its trip. With a meaty thud it struck the icy cliff just below and to the side of the ruined bridge on Ivy's side.

Acting more out of instinct than logic, Ivy raced to the edge and held tight to the sturdiest remaining bridge support. As soon as she looked over the edge, she could feel the world begin to spin. Though she'd been working hard to overcome her many weaknesses, one flaw she'd not been able to correct was the fear of heights. Nevertheless, and out of a concern far more genuine that she would have expected for the familiar of a woman who might be actively seeking the slow demise of her own world, Ivy felt the need to help Mott. His spiderlike legs scrabbled and scraped at the cliff face, but he was so far managing only to barely keep from sliding farther down, and then only *just*.

She looked around quickly and found a short length of support rope on the second strut that had been largely spared the worst of the flames. She hauled it up and pulled it over, dumping its slack down to Mott. He clamped on to it with his jaws, but the buffeting of the swirling breeze combined with the ice-encrusted stone caused the dangling beast to bash painfully against the cliff. Ivy pulled slowly and steadily at the rope to avoid dislodging Mott, and before long he was scrabbling his way up onto relatively solid ground.

Mott swung quickly around behind Ivy and then chomped his jaws on to the hem of her cloak, urgently pulling her back as well. When they were both safely away from the edge, the creature wrapped himself around her legs. From tail to head, he was able to manage several full coils, embracing her tightly with his head resting on her chest. He churred affectionately and licked at her chin once before uncoiling himself.

"Okay… friends then?" Ivy said, reaching down to pat the scraggly and scaly head.

He chittered and wrapped his tail around her leg again, flipping his head entirely upside down so that her fingers instead were patting his chin. Ivy took the hint and started scratching it.

When the beast decided he'd had enough, a decision that came rather suddenly, he flipped his head around and chomped lightly on to her hand. He didn't bite hard enough to cause any pain, just in the sort of playful way that a not overly well-behaved dog might. Then he pulled back.

"So what are we going to do now? You're definitely not going to be able to make the jump back," Ivy said.

Mott "sat," which was a far more complex and curvy motion for a creature with eight legs and a serpentine spine, and raised his head high. The sound that croaked forth couldn't have possibly cut through the wind and waves to reach the fort, but even to Ivy's untrained senses there was something more to it than what she was hearing. As quickly as it had begun, the croaking ended. Mott then wrapped a few more coils around one of Ivy's legs. From the chill of his body as it touched her, even through her clothes, Ivy reasoned he was after some warmth. She managed to kneel beside him, shuddering a bit as his coiled tail squirmed before sliding free, and then threw her cloak around him. Clearly appreciative, he released another low, contented churr that made Ivy feel oddly pleased with herself.

The pair waited and watched for a time, but within a few minutes, Mott's head perked up and his alert green eyes locked on to a slow moving form approaching along the rocky island between them and the fort. As the form drew nearer, Mott became incrementally more excited.

The form, moving a bit unsteadily, revealed itself to be Turiel, though despite the mere hours that had passed since their clash, the sorceress looked *years* older. Her single streak of gray hair had thickened to pepper most of her head. Lines cut deep into her face, and her movements were stiff and uncomfortable. As she passed the lifeless creatures, they stirred briefly, mechanically shuffling out of her way before dropping down again.

Turiel stopped at the opposite side of the bridge and gazed across at Ivy. She looked weary, both physically and emotionally. Rather than the anger or distrust Ivy would have expected, her eyes were twisted with distant, helpless sorrow.

"So you've returned," she said.

Though the woman made no attempt to raise her voice, it reached Ivy effortlessly. The sound of the waves and the gusts seemed to part around it, allowing it to reach her ears with crystal clarity.

"Listen. I think… I think the two of us need to discuss some things. We may have had a misunderstanding before. I need to know for certain what you've done and why. Would you be willing to answer some questions?"

"You're curious. Of course you would be. Seeing what I've seen of these creatures, it stands to reason you would be. Come…"

She tipped her staff forward. Swirling ribbons of black poured forth, as if dumped from a bowl that had been balanced upon the staff's end. The ribbons arched and coiled through the air, driving themselves into the ground at Ivy's feet. They split and splintered, expanding out into a dense ebony net that eventually rose at the edges to form a handrail.

Mott scampered out onto the new bridge, barely a quarter the width of the old one, then turned and ran back to Ivy to again chomp on to her cloak and tug her forward. A thousand thoughts rushed through her mind, including her doubts about the strength of the conjured bridge, her even greater doubts about the trustworthiness of the woman who'd conjured it, and her doubts about how much success this mission could possibly have. None of them mattered, because Mott turned out to be a good deal stronger than he looked, and a few well-timed yanks were all it took to get her to stumble onto the bridge.

She shut her eyes tight and allowed Mott to lead her forward, because though the bridge appeared to be strong, it was by no means steady. Each gust caused it to sway, and it dipped worryingly beneath her step. Still, it supported her as she stepped gingerly across, and when she finally felt stone beneath her feet again, she felt a hand take hers and guide her a few steps farther.

"There. Safe and sound," Turiel said, patting Ivy on the back. "You should have told me you had problems with heights. I believe I could have made the bridge a bit wider."

"You…" Ivy said, more of a flutter in her voice than she would have liked, "you could have built a bridge the whole time?"

"If I'd had a mind to, dear," Turiel said, leaning heavily on her staff as she continued back toward the fort. Again, each creature scattered across the island that lay in her path rose to its feet just long enough to clear the way, then clattered lifeless again to the ground.

"Then why didn't you? Why did you let these… *things* fall, or leave them to wait?" Ivy asked.

"I have no interest in spreading chaos or misery, Ivy. I simply wanted the creatures to live again. It was silly of me though. I was hasty. Both in my zeal to awaken these sleeping masterpieces and in my reaction to you. I hope you'll accept my apology."

"Mistakes were made," Ivy said steadily.

"These... these creatures. The more I study them, the more I understand that he'd not taken the time to finish them. Each was a test, a sample. I could work for months to craft such things from whole cloth. It would have taken me ages to create the things within this fort. But as fine as they were, they were incomplete. Limited. They were not *ready* to live on their own, and it would take more strength than I have to keep them living. I squandered too much just to wake them. But in my studies, I realized that just as I had expected too much of *them*, I had expected too much of *you*. You were unfinished, dear. Far more so than I'd realized. You were abandoned for this reason or that before you were complete. That is why you behave as you do. That is why you don't understand what I've done and why. That is how the adversaries were able to claim you, to turn you to their cause. I should have been more patient with you. I hope you can forgive me."

"It depends on what sort of answers you can give me," Ivy said.

"Of course. Ask. I am an open book. Nothing would give me greater pleasure than to know that I helped you to become the work of art that you were *meant* to be, so I will naturally do my best to aid your development."

Ivy breathed slowly and wracked her brain for the best way to proceed. This woman was... off-putting. Now she'd slipped back to her matronly demeanor, but there was no telling when she'd become a murderous lunatic again. Could Ivy risk asking immediately? Should she play the part and ask her simple questions first?

As Ivy's mind raced, Turiel faltered, stumbling as her leg buckled. Mott darted forward, offering his head to catch her. In spite of herself, Ivy approached to help as well. She didn't care if it was an act or not, something about Turiel suddenly seemed so frail now, so broken.

"What happened to you?" Ivy asked. "You look... so much *older* now than you did..."

"The spirits take their toll, dear. The spirits take their toll."

"I don't understand."

"Magic is a mix of one's own spirit and those sympathetic to one's aims. If you embrace those spirits as I have, it adds great potency to one's spells."

"But my friends cast spells like yours all the time, and they don't age so."

"Magic such as mine... it attracts the sort of spirit who drinks quite greedily in exchange for its aid. But the aid is often worth it. Don't worry about me, dear. My best years are behind me at the moment. But it's a simple trick to get them back when I need to. I overreached a bit, that is all."

"But how? How can you turn back the years?"

"Magic, my dear. Always magic. The same current that drains the land may feed it if properly directed. My focus has always been the passage of life to death and death to life. What can be done to another can be done to oneself. I gave rather deeply of my strength, but a bit of time to focus myself or, failing that, a willing donor of a few years will give me youth enough to continue comfortably."

"A donor."

"Oh, yes. The young squander their years. Better to let someone with the wisdom to put them to good use take them instead."

"That's... awful," Ivy said.

"It really isn't so unpleasant," Turiel said. "Oh... heavens. You mean for the *donor*. Yes, I imagine it can be a bit jarring. But it is all for a good cause."

"And that cause is... bringing back the D'Karon."

"One can hardly imagine a higher purpose."

"But I've told you, the D'Karon are *evil*," Ivy said.

Turiel turned to Ivy and shook her head sadly. "I know you believe that. The adversaries had their way with your mind. We'll untie those knots... Though I must say, from what I've seen... the D'Karon haven't left the legacy I would have anticipated."

"They coaxed the world into centuries of war!" Ivy said.

"Centuries is a *bit* of an overstatement, dear, but much as I was hesitant to believe it, the proof seems quite irrefutable."

"Knowing that, why would you ever bring them here again?"

"They *must* have had their reasons. Perhaps they were attempting to teach us a lesson about the futility of war?" Turiel said.

"... By forcing us to kill each other without ever allowing it to end?"

"The most difficult lessons require the firmest hand," Turiel said.

"You don't really believe that's true, do you? You can't possibly believe this war was for our own good!"

"Calm yourself, dear. We wouldn't want you losing yourself," she said, patting Ivy gently on the back. "But no. I'll allow that the war is a rather... disconcerting development. However, all the better reason to bring them back to us. No surer way to find the truth than to ask!"

"But why is it worth that risk!?"

"Why? Oh, Ivy. Look at *you!* Yes, they've done some terrible things, and I hope to one day understand why such things were necessary, but look at what they can do when they turn their minds to it." Turiel stopped and took Ivy's hand, holding it up and spreading her fingers. "Look at the beauty, the precision. They *made* you, and yet you are every bit as right and proper in this world as a being born of nature. They do the work of the *gods*, Ivy." She released Ivy's hand and brushed back the malthrope's hood to stroke her hair. "And they weren't even through. You are approaching *perfection* and were just the beginning of their skills. They could work wonders for us. Teach us to do such incredible things. I submit that unlocking power like that is worth any price."

"But why do you need it? Why does *anyone* need power like that?"

Turiel's expression became distant. "We all have our reasons…"

"Tell me. Tell me *your* reasons. Tell me what you believe made all of the death they brought worthwhile?"

"Bah!" Turiel said, almost playfully. "Death? Death is nothing to fear. Nothing to mourn. Death is a door we all must pass through. Death, my dear, is the proper way of things. We shall all spend much more of our existence in the gentle embrace of death than in the madness of life. War is a terrible thing, but not for the death it brings. It is awful for the damage it causes, and for the time it wastes. Life *is* precious, and it is precious because it is so brief and scarce. There are far better ways to spend it than to hasten the death of others for no reasons other than politics and principle. Better we should use our years to discover great things, to *do* great things. And when greatness, *true* wonder and greatness, is cut short, *that* is the tragedy of death."

Turiel's foot struck a patch of ice and she stumbled again. Ivy kept her on her feet.

"I'm sorry, dear. And thank you. I just can't seem to keep my feet under me. Let us get inside, if you don't mind. Better to finish our chat there, away from the wind."

They continued to walk the daunting length of the island that Ivy and the others had raced across in their escape. Along the way, she tried her very best to ignore the assorted ghastly footprints left behind by the horde of *things* that Turiel had awakened. In time they finally reached the fort.

"Oh," Turiel said, shaking the frost and ice from her robes. "So good to get out of the damp."

Ivy peered around the interior of the fort's first floor. It had changed greatly since her first visit. Once emptied of the twisted, shattered creatures that it had been built to contain, one could almost forget the dark origins of this place. In construction it was little more than a sturdy stone warehouse, a bit scarred from battle and discolored here or there, but otherwise indistinguishable from any innocent room in a well-built stronghold. In decoration, it was much, *much* different. Turiel must have gathered every last flake of thir gem and arrayed them along the ceiling and walls in artful, swirling patterns that were striking in their beauty. The fragments of stone bathed the floor in violet light, making the atmosphere feel almost cozy and welcoming. Then there was the matter of the… furniture.

Some beasts, it seemed, were too broken to be repaired. Or perhaps their design was so bizarre and otherworldly Turiel couldn't determine how to put the pieces together. Rather than waste them, though, she'd put them to good use. Large, smooth plates and bits of carapace had been fused together into an unnervingly… *living* chair. No part of it really resembled a creature anymore, but the oily black sheen and curving shapes made it look as though it might have been part of a great beetle or other insect. And as she stiffly turned to take a seat, the spindly legs uncoiled slightly, lifting the seat to meet her and easing her down again.

She set her staff aside, a claw flicking out from beneath the seat to grasp it, then eased luxuriously back. Mott clattered across the floor and crunched his jaws around the leg of a similar, though smaller, chair and tugged it forward. It shuffled along on its remaining three legs until it was positioned behind Ivy. Mott then gave Ivy a playful nudge to the abdomen, causing her to stumble back onto the seat, which tipped her back into itself before becoming still again.

"Now, where were we?" Turiel asked, sighing contentedly and twiddling her fingers beside the head of her staff.

Mott took the hint and spiraled up the staff, thrusting his head out beside it to receive affection from her long, slightly split nails.

"You were telling me about your reasons for bringing them here."

She shook her head. "You don't really want to hear that story. It is a sad tale. A matter of my own concern. Nothing that should trouble you."

Ivy took a breath. Now was the time. "Then tell me how. How did you bring them here?"

"Ah! A very *valuable* lesson. One that every D'Karon, each of their followers, and wisest of their creations ought to know," she said, leaning forward as if she were about to tell a beloved nursery rhyme to an eager child. "The workings of the spell are intricate, but nothing that even a novice wizard couldn't manage. Now, repeat after me—"

"No, no!" Ivy said. "That, uh… that part can wait. I'm more interested in how *you* brought them here. The story of when you cast the spell."

"Ah… I suppose an example or two makes the lesson easier to learn. It was many years ago, after my sister died… Again, that is a matter of my own concern. But I was seeking answers, hoping to reach out to her, to learn what happened to her, and how I might right the wrongs surrounding her death, or at least to finish those things she had started. As far into the beyond I reached, though, I could not sense her. So I pressed on, pierced deeper. I probed the veil, stretched it and explored it. There were so many voices. Each night there were more. The ranting of a thousand new spirits joined the chorus whenever I learned a new technique or tightened my mind about the task with renewed strength. But never was there a voice that was familiar. Never was there a voice that was *hers*.

"In time, though, I reached a place in my searching, in my listening, that was quiet. I had thought I'd reached beyond the beyond, past where even the most far-flung of spirits might wander… but then I heard it. A whispering voice, a yearning will. It was seeking someone, anyone, to listen. I did not understand the words, but night after night I sought it again. And somehow without understanding, there came knowledge. I learned the spell, the keyhole. It was so simple, so elegant, and yet so profound in its power and brilliance. And with it came the promise of more if only I could cast this first spell. I knew that *this* knowledge came from those who might help me finally tend to the matter of my sister properly.

"The instructions were simple. First find a place safe from those who might seek to break the spell. Someplace no one would ever go on their own, yet a place strong with magic. The Ancients were the natural choice, in the Dagger Gale Mountains. It took me... oh... I imagine it was over a century to gather the strength to finally open the keyhole. And the best place I could find in Tressor was not nearly so potent, so it is taking ages longer, but someone with your power, and your connection to the D'Karon, could surely open it far more swiftly..."

Turiel trailed off, her eyes suddenly wide with realization.

"You... you could *help* me." The necromancer was inspired, almost giddy with the prospect of joining forces with Ivy.

"Perhaps... perhaps if you told me where the keyhole was..."

"Tell you! If I had the strength to spare at the moment I would just *take* you. Even *with* you, it could take years, but I *know* together we could do it."

"But if you could just tell me, perhaps we could go together and... is something wrong?"

The joyful expression was slowly fading and her eyes were drifting aside. She looked as though she'd heard a curious sound and was trying to determine its source.

"That's intense... a pinpoint of magic..." she said vaguely. "And coming quite swiftly and quite directly."

Ivy began to feel something as well. The air had a tingle and a vitality to it. She realized that the sensation was familiar, and at this moment she wasn't certain if she was relieved or panicked.

"Ether..." Ivy said.

"Ether... Ether. Mott, from where do we know that name?"

Mott chittered and spiraled down the staff to dart to the doorway.

"Yes," Turiel said. "Yes, the *shapeshifter* we were told about." She turned to Ivy and narrowed her eyes. "Another one of the adversaries... Did you *lead* her here?"

"No. I assure you, I didn't lead them here, but when you use your magic to move from place to place, we can detect it. That's how I found you, and I promise, that's how she found you."

"And what will she do when she gets here?"

"She's the one who destroyed this place to begin with."

Turiel's chair thrust upward, and Ivy's did the same, standing them up and leaving them face to face. She grasped her staff and glared at Ivy.

"And what will *you* do when she gets here?" Turiel asked.

"I'll help you. I'll hold her at bay. I'll reason with her. I'll do whatever you need me to do, but *only* if you tell me where the second keyhole is."

The necromancer glared at her, stricken with indecision. "I want desperately to believe you, but I do not know how much of their treachery clings to your mind. … And I'm concerned for the strength it may take to defend myself against a foe strong enough to banish the D'Karon."

Ivy clenched her fists and gritted her teeth. Her heart was fluttering in her chest, and flares of blue were beginning to mix with the violet light of the room.

"Then let me help you," Ivy said.

The wind outside seemed to have reversed itself, shifting from blowing behind the fort to rushing in through its door. Turiel's gray and black hair streamed and her tattered robes billowed, but she gazed, unblinking.

"I need to know what you know. And you need to know what I know. You've offered me the benefit of your strength. I believe, if you are sincere, I have a solution for each of us… But it will require trust."

Ivy looked to the door. She could hear the unnatural whistle of Ether's windy form approaching. There was no telling what Ether would do, but she very much doubted the elemental would control herself, even if she knew that crucial information could only be found in Turiel's mind.

"If you feel you can trust me, then I can trust you. But please, for both of our sakes, *hurry!*" Ivy said.

"Then you have both my thanks and my apologies. But rest assured that you *will* recover. I would never damage so perfect a creature as you."

Ivy held her breath, unsure of what to expect. Mott galloped over to her and curled his tail around her, chittering sweetly and rubbing his head on her in what felt curiously like an emotional goodbye. Turiel gently placed her hand on Ivy's head…

In the same moment, there was everything and there was nothing. She saw her life, what she could remember of it and brief instants of the pieces she'd had stripped from her, fill her mind. Mingled among the memories and visions were alien thoughts and feelings, moments of another life. Moments of *Turiel's* life.

The torrent of feelings, memories, and emotions was almost enough to overcome her on its own, but as two lives flashed before her eyes, a third sensation asserted itself. She could feel her strength wicking away. Her eyes locked on those of the necromancer, the room for once brilliantly lit by Ivy's icy-blue aura. Years were melting away from the woman. Black once again whisked away the gray in her hair. Lines faded to smooth, flawless skin. Fueled by the rush of energy spilling from Ivy, the woman was restored from someone beginning to bend under the weight of the years to someone in the prime of life.

Turiel's hand lifted away, and Ivy felt the room spin around her. She felt drained and drawn; her mind was swimming. The assault had pushed her to the very brink of unconsciousness, but as she stumbled back, Mott scuttled behind and helped keep her on her feet while the renewed and invigorated Turiel stepped toward her.

"I wish you a swift recovery, and know that your strength will not go to waste," Turiel said.

The necromancer tenderly kissed Ivy on the forehead and lowered her gently to the floor. As the darkness finally claimed her, she heard a few final words.

"Come, Mott. Quickly. Let us prepare you to defend Mommy..."

\#

Ether's howling form roared down from above and hung before the yawning door of the fort. The already potent fury broiling her mind burned brighter as she saw a small army of D'Karon design marching on clattering claws and scrabbling feet back into the fortress. She drew her form together and sparked it to flame, darting to the ground and charring the slowest of the creatures into cinders. Through the door, barely visible in the violet glow and the light spilling off from her own burning form, twisted black and purple shapes clattered and crawled into an ever larger mass. She streaked inside and set her brilliantly glowing eyes on the sight before her.

Turiel stood in one corner of the room. She held her staff high, its gem pouring indigo light and waves of black. Like a conductor leading an orchestra through a spirited symphony, she wove intricate patterns through the air. In the center of the floor, the creatures that had until moments earlier lain lifeless and awaiting orders at the end of the stone island fed themselves into a chaotic swirl of lashing black tendrils. The threads plucked away plates of shell and whole chitinous limbs, joining them again into a form that was becoming familiar. It had a long, serpentine body, spindly spider legs, and a sleek canine head. The form was that of Mott, but crafted from scale, bone, and armor plate. It was massive, barely small enough to coil in the available space, and each detail was stouter and more vicious than before.

"Ah... the elemental. They call you Ether, I am told," Turiel said, venom in her tone. "But to me you will only ever be an adversary. Your name is meaningless."

Ether ignored the woman's words, narrowing her eyes and gazing up at the patterns in the ceiling. The D'Karon crystals were scattered there, and few things were more painful and detrimental to her than those gems. The flakes were small, and their hunger largely sated, so they did not feast on the shapeshifter's energies as larger stones might. Nevertheless, even as they were, she could feel their presence like a thousand needles.

"You'll forgive me, Ether. I am only *just* peeling back the layers of what I've learned about you. Since I've awoken I've been trying to pull together the edges of my sanity into something resembling a whole. I've not had much success." She rubbed her temple. "It is beginning to become bothersome. But mental infirmity is no excuse to abandon one's purpose."

The flames of Ether's form continued to sizzle as her eyes shifted now to the motionless form huddled in the corner behind Turiel. It was Ivy. She was sleeping, at least; perhaps worse.

A renewed anger rushed through Ether. Something inside her recoiled at the thought of something happening to Ivy. It came almost as a surprise to her. The malthrope was a liability, practically an abomination, and yet she felt nothing less than raw fury at the thought of someone doing the beast any harm. As much as she had despised Ivy in the past, they had been through many battles together. The creature was *Chosen*, and they were united in a cause. That, Ether told herself, was the reason for these feelings.

"What have you done here?" Ether fumed.

"What have *I* done? If I have been informed correctly, *you* are the one who desecrated this place. *You* were the one to shatter the works of Demont the Crafter. I've merely done what I could do to heal the damage you caused."

"… You are a creature of this world. Is it true? Is it true that *you* brought the D'Karon here?"

"It is by leaps and bounds my greatest achievement. And is it true that *you* are responsible for banishing them again?"

"It is the whole of my purpose."

Turiel clacked the point of her staff down to the floor angrily. "Then it seems we each are destined to be at the throat of the other. Because if you would chase away beings of such wisdom and power, then you are nothing less than a demon."

"You will release Ivy from your clutches. I will not see her harmed while I mete out your punishment."

The sorceress stepped closer to the sleeping form of the malthrope like a protective mother staring down a charging bear. "I *will not!* You've done enough, twisting this poor defenseless child to your ways. Her mind is a tangle with your lies. Leave her to me and *perhaps* she may be salvaged."

"If you know anything of what has happened in this world, you know that you brought a terrible evil upon your people and a blight upon your land. And you know that I and those like me made short work of your beloved D'Karon."

"Short work is a boastful claim. But yes. I've learned much of what you've done. And I've learned much of what was done to you. None of you are invincible, Ether. And I now know your weaknesses."

Turiel raised her staff and knocked its head to the ceiling. The fragments of crystal she'd embedded there drifted down like fireflies disturbed from the branches of a tree. In rapid succession the points of light drove themselves into the hide of Mott's latest form. Curving, precise patterns of crystal studs traced themselves out on Mott's tail, the clawed pincers of his many legs, the horny ridge of his forehead, and along his black daggers of teeth. What remained of the gems drew stripes along the rest of his tail and armor. In essence, Turiel had armed her creation with the one weapon that might truly sting Ether.

"This does not need to occur, *adversary*. I will permit you to leave this place. I *urge* you to leave. It is never too late for a creature to learn the error of its ways, and enough damage has been—" Turiel began, her voice steady, reasonable, almost *pleading*.

She did not reach the end of her thought before Ether burst toward her, columns of flame billowing behind her.

Mott was swift, swiping his tail with great force and greater precision. It swept through the air, demolishing the support beams in its way, and clipped Ether a split second before she could lay a searing finger upon Turiel. A purely physical attack would have been of little use against Ether's flaming form, but the gem studs raked at her like thorns, driving her back.

Ether cried out in pain and flitted back to safety, but the sheer size of Mott's new form left no place within the now-cramped interior that the monster couldn't reach her. He released what would have been a gleeful chitter at his natural size. Scaled to his new form, it was a rumbling roar that seemed to come from the very bowels of the underworld.

Though the giant thing moved with greater speed and precision than one would have thought possible, it was still no match for Ether. She drove her body forward, dropping low and facing upward as she skimmed across the ground. Her upraised hands burned deep, smoldering furrows across Mott's armored underside. It was almost wholly without the protection of gems, and the deep gashes prompted an otherworldly howl of anger and pain.

Mott scuttled aside, smashing apart two more support columns and causing the heavy stones of the roof to begin to rain down. The already damaged roof was now well and truly collapsing, albeit gradually. By the time Mott had shrugged off the falling stones and spotted Ether again to snap at her, she was upon Turiel. The sorceress was ready, conjuring a thicket of black threads. Ether flitted aside but several of the threads slashed through her being, sending an entirely new surge of pain through her.

Rather than retreat again, Ether pressed on, stoking her flames hotter. The mystic fire burned through the black tendrils, but Turiel conjured more to replace them, hurling some of them forward at Ether and weaving the others into a protective mesh to deflect the falling stones and the slashing fingers of the elemental.

The pain was intense, but it was nothing Ether hadn't learned to deal with in her dozens of encounters with the D'Karon. And though she could feel the gems chip away at her strength with each glancing blow from Mott's teeth and tail once the creature was in a position to strike, it was doing little to threaten the vast reserves of magic she'd accumulated in the period of relative peace since the end of the war. It wasn't until most of the roof had fallen away, ending the rocky cascade that had been pummeling Mott, that the hulking creature could once again direct his full attention to Ether. His jaws yawned wide and snapped shut around her, driving gem-studded, arm-length teeth through Ether's insubstantial form.

His attack didn't last long before Ether's intensity incinerated the teeth, but it was enough to convince her she would have to abandon her flaming form lest she make the mistake of overexerting herself as she had so many times before. When Mott recoiled, howling in pain again and clawing at his ashen and smoldering teeth with two of his legs, Ether shifted to wind and slipped around and between the weave of black magic that had held her at bay.

When she coalesced again, her form a tangible mass of tightly whirling wind, she took up nearly all of the available space within Turiel's protective net. The sorceress spun to face her, but Ether struck first, drawing the air from the woman's lungs and conjuring a wind that forced her back against the net that was to have protected her.

"Listen to me," Ether said, her voice issuing from the core of her windy shape. "You may have heard the legends of this world, the stories you humans tell of great heroes. Many such figures of your history are renowned for their mercy. *I am not*. I have no use for mercy, and you have done nothing to deserve it. You should use what little time you have left to give thanks that I do not have the time to make you suffer properly for the evils you have wrought."

Turiel, still struggling to draw a breath, dispelled her own protection. The threads vanished like wisps of smoke, leaving the wind that had pinned her to them to send her hurtling backward. She was dashed twice against the mounds of fallen stone before Mott's coiled tail snatched her from the air and lowered her carefully to the ground. He then struck with the tip of his tail, driving it like a scorpion's stinger into the whirling form of the shapeshifter. Ether effortlessly scattered to avoid the attack, which instead pulverized the stone of the wall that had been spared the collapse thus far thanks to Turiel's efforts. It began to tumble down, threatening to crush Ivy's prone form, but Ether drew together again and tightened her focus around the stones. Bringing them to a halt through wind alone took enough of her dedicated strength that Turiel finally managed to wrestle a breath into her lungs.

"Mott!" she croaked. "You'll injure Ivy!"

The creature released a yelp of concern and dismay, then skittered back to avoid causing any greater collapse and further endanger the sleeping malthrope. As the walls all around them shuddered and collapsed to expose them to the roaring winds and churning sea, Ether drifted between the monster and Ivy. She pulled herself together into her stone form and dropped heavily to the ground.

Rather than waste her time on further threats or conversation, Ether simply thundered toward monster and master alike, crushing stone to powder beneath her rocky feet. Mott snapped at her with his already damaged mouth, but just as he was faster than seemed possible for his size, so too was Ether far more nimble than a stone construction ought to be. She sidestepped, allowing the monster's head to punch through the weakened floor, then delivered a punishing blow to the back of its head.

Reeling, he pulled himself from the damaged floor and tried to snap at where she had been, but Ether had clawed her way onto his neck and was hammering and slashing relentlessly at the tough shell. The wounds she opened offered little more than a faint glow, not a drop of blood.

Turiel filled the air with more of her black tendrils. Where they struck Ether, they bored into her surface like roots splitting stone over the seasons. Where they struck Mott, they mended his wounds and strengthened his armor. Mott managed to whip his tail upward and coil it around Ether, tearing her from his neck and constricting her form. The lines of gemstone studs ground into her rocky skin, but unlike against her other forms, the gems did little good against this one. The constriction, however, was beginning to wear on her, causing cracks to feather through her limbs. Thus immobilized, the sorceress had little difficulty perforating and cocooning her with filaments of dark magic.

A low, indulgent churr of fiendish glee rumbled through Mott, and for a moment Turiel allowed a grin to flash across her face as she felt the colossal power of her foe begin to flicker and wane. Between the monstrous tail and layers of filament, no part of Ether was visible anymore. A subtle, grating crumble rang out, and both tail and cocoon began to collapse inward. Then came a hiss and a brilliant flash as Ether shifted back to flame with a fierce cry.

The heat was phenomenal, even compared to what she'd displayed earlier in the battle. Her formerly pinned arms sliced effortlessly through the tail's tough hide, causing the huge limb to fall away in writhing loops. The threads binding her crackled to nothingness, and before Turiel could conjure more, Ether was upon her. The blazing elemental swiped her brilliant flaming hand down upon the wrist of the sorceress's staff-bearing hand. Like the armor, the flesh and bone offered little resistance.

So fast was the attack, and so thoroughly did it sear Turiel's arm, that the sorceress didn't make a sound. She merely stumbled backward and fell, cradling the wound while her staff clattered to the ground.

The result was immediate. With the staff no longer actually in her grasp, its amplifying effect on her focus vanished. This left her without the level of control required to keep Mott's massive form intact. Plates of armor began to peel away as he roared and writhed, falling to pieces. In the space of a few seconds, the behemoth was reduced to a motionless husk, no longer recognizable as what it once was.

Ether let her fiery form fade, though the anger within her was not diminished in the slightest. Steadily she allowed her flaming substance to be replaced with flesh and blood. For reasons she could not fully explain, she felt the need to see this horrid creature with human eyes, and to face her as something she would perceive as one of her own. Thoughts and concerns, things left undone, teased and prodded at her mind. She ignored them. The need to see this woman, and to see her suffer, was far too important now.

Once she was fully human, dressed in a billowing white robe and with her disgust and anger clear upon her face, Ether stalked over to where Turiel had fallen.

"You," Turiel began, breathlessly, "are precisely the monster I imagined you to be."

"I cannot say the same of you." She kicked the staff aside, the sorceress's severed hand still gripping it. "No creature, living or dead, has committed so heinous a crime as you. Yet somehow you seem to be nothing more than a human seduced by D'Karon teachings. It brings me no pleasure to kill you. It is merely a task that must be done."

"Tell me… what will happen to the child? To Ivy? She is of the D'Karon as well."

"It is true that she is touched by their evil, but at least she has turned herself from them. She has fought for this world, abandoned her masters. She is redeemed."

"So she will be spared?"

"She will."

Turiel's expression became less pained. She seemed almost serene, ready to accept what was to come.

"All is well then. She has much promise…"

"Ether…" called Ivy weakly, her mind finally beginning to recover.

"Rest, Ivy. I will see to you when this blight is wiped away."

"You… you can't…" Ivy said, trying to stand. "She… she knows something…"

"There is *nothing* this *thing* could know that would make her worthy of being spared."

"You have to… if you don't…"

Ether's fingers began to take on the brilliant glow of flame again, and she leaned down to the sorceress. Turiel seemed ready for her punishment. Behind her, something seemed wrong, however. The crackle of settling shell and armor had become sharper for a moment. Now a tapping sound was just barely audible over the howling wind and crashing waves.

She turned to find that Mott, his flesh raw and bruised and three of his eight legs badly broken, had dragged himself out of the wreckage of his former self. The massive form must have been little more than a suit built over him. He had made his way to Ivy and was nuzzling her. His face was forlorn, his movements sluggish. Ivy was lying back against what remained of one wall. She rested a hand on Mott's head.

"You get away from her…" Ether hissed, turning and stepping quickly toward Ivy, mindful of what Mott might do. Even in his reduced form, he was still more than capable of tearing out a throat, and Ether would not allow these things to take her ally from her. The world had lost too many Chosen already.

"Ether... I don't know if... I don't think that..." Ivy muttered, nearly delirious.

"Be still," Ether said.

She reached down and grasped Mott by the wings with her still-flesh hand. He did nothing to resist, only slacking his neck to try to keep it near Ivy for as long as he could. When that was no longer possible, he turned his head weakly to Ether and gazed at her pathetically.

Ether moved her hand closer, ready to run her blazing fingers through his head and end his misery. A moment before she could do so, however, his gaze sharpened and he pulled his head away. Then, amid a crackle and peel, the wings Ether held came free and Mott fell to the ground, scuttling with purpose toward where Turiel had fallen.

The shapeshifter slashed with her fiery hand, sending a lance of flame outward that splashed against the mismatched creature, but Mott merely squealed in pain and continued his escape. Ether glanced up and instantly understood. Turiel had dragged herself to the staff. Once it was in her hand again, she was able to invigorate Mott.

Furious both at the job left undone and her foolish oversight of the staff, Ether burst fully to flame and streaked through the air, but Turiel and Mott had slipped through a wide fault in a wall and reached the edge of the steep cliff that made up the walls of the island. With a final shove, Turiel slid off the face of the cliff. Ether had already inexcusably underestimated the woman once. She would not leave the fall and the churning sea to finish the job she'd failed to finish herself. She swept over the edge and down toward the plummeting woman. Ahead, directly below her, a ring of roiling black energy encircled a window depicting some piles of rubble and a floor of damaged stone. Turiel and Mott plummeted through. Before Ether could follow, the necromancer willed the portal shut.

Ether braced herself as an explosion of energy splashed against her, forcing her fiery form back and taking a massive bite out of the cliff side. It was painful, but she was able to endure the blast without any lingering ill effect. Nevertheless, the damage was done. Her own blindness and oversight had allowed that *thing* to slip from her fingers once more. It burned her, shamed her. More than anything, it worried her. This affliction of her mind had caused her focus to suffer, that much she was certain of. Such had robbed her of the clarity of thought that would have made tracking this sorceress to the ends of the earth as effortless as it would have been in the past. But this was not a matter of focus, or at least not a matter of *mystic* focus. This was a matter of judgment. If her feelings were clouding her *thinking* as well as her concentration, then what could be trusted? How could she fulfill her task?

She whisked back to the surface and touched down, shifting to humanity once more and moving quickly to Ivy's side.

"Did you... is she..." Ivy muttered. Her voice was less slurred, but she still clearly had to work at even forming the words. Her mind was not as it should be.

"She and her pet escaped."

"I think... I think that's best," Ivy said. "I don't know if... I don't know if I know what I need to know."

Ether leaned low and took Ivy's hands, hauling her to her feet and supporting her. "You are not well. Your mind is weaker than usual. And I cannot remember a time when your spirit has been so drained."

"She did something," Ivy said, her eyes beginning to clear and her words becoming steadier. "I told her I needed to know where the keyhole was, and I promised to help her if she would tell me. She touched my head. It felt like..." she shuddered, "like what *Epidime* would do when they were trying to teach me. I think she was trying to show me where the keyhole was, but I don't... it's all a jumble in my mind. Can you track her? Follow her?"

"Not at this time," Ether said.

"Why not?"

"I am not myself right now."

"You're *never* yourself. Why should that—"

"Now is not the time to try my patience with your words," Ether fumed.

"Okay... okay..." Ivy said. She shook her head. "We've got to get word to Myranda and Deacon then. Mr. Celeste is on the main road. Or he should be..." She gazed out across the land. "Yes, I think I see him. If you can take me there, we'll write what happened in the pad. They'll see it. They'll know what to do..."

"Very well," Ether said.

She shut her eyes, and a moment later her human form vanished in a burst of swirling wind. She rose into the air and directed the flow of wind to coil about Ivy, lifting her as well. In moments she whisked over the stretch of sea and stone between the fort and the mainland.

Ether set Ivy down by the road, a short distance from where Celeste anxiously waited. From the looks of Ivy's frazzled expression, the short trip from the fort's island had not been a pleasant one.

"Ether," she said, stumbling dizzily toward Celeste until he caught and steadied her, "I'm afraid of heights, and I can barely think right now. Don't you think you could come up with a better way to carry me than with just *wind*? That was *terrifying!*"

"I have little interest in your comfort. You are Chosen. You are strong enough to endure such things."

"Guardian Ether," Celeste said with a respectful bow of his head, "it is as always an honor to have you among us."

"Yes, it is," Ether said simply.

"What happened in the fort?" he asked, addressing Ivy.

"She was reasonable again, at first. But when Ether was on her way, she started to panic. I think she tried to share some knowledge with me, but she did it the D'Karon way. She forced me to know it. It's still lost in my head at the moment, and I don't know if what we need is among the memories she inserted. Even if it is, I don't know where to find it."

"The sorceress used a D'Karon portal to escape," Ether explained. "She may be anywhere the D'Karon have prepared an exit. Any of their forts, and any of a dozen other places. My own focus is ailing. I do not know that I can detect where she has gone reliably. Myranda or Deacon may be able to do so. And they will have to do so quickly. I badly injured the woman, but she is quite skilled, and quite powerful. She will recover quickly."

Celeste pulled the pad from the pack and readied the stylus. "Tell me what Myranda needs to know."

#

Myranda sat with her eyes on the infirmary. The sun had finally slipped below the horizon and the heat had begun to wane, relieving Myn of her shelter duties. The dragon had gradually inched farther away from her and Deacon, rummaging through the remnants of the smoldering stable. Garr had taken to rummaging as well, poking his snout and dragging his claws through the rubble of the keep. Every few minutes he pulled something from the stone and set it aside, huddling close over the growing mound of recovered items.

Despite the curious actions of the dragons, Myranda couldn't tear her attention away from the tent. The sounds of pain… the sounds of *torture*… had long ago ceased. Now she was stricken with the thoughts of what exactly Grustim had done, and what had become of Commander Brustuum…

Myn finally seemed to find what she was after, tugging a stone from the burnt structure and trotting back to the others. She dropped the stone on the ground and settled beside Myranda again. As the dragon lapped her tongue lightly over the smooth stone, Myranda finally pulled her mind away from the tent and looked to her friend's new toy.

"Where did you get that, Myn?" she asked. "That doesn't look like the sort of stone one would find in the desert."

The dragon glanced at her, then quickly at Garr. Her glance probably wasn't intended as an answer, though it left little doubt. Instead she seemed to be glancing to ensure that the male hadn't heard the question, or at least not seen to what Myranda was referring. Satisfied that he'd not noticed, Myn quietly plucked the stone and crept around to between Myranda and Garr, such that when she placed it down again, her body blocked his view of it.

Myranda grinned, momentarily forgetting the weight upon her mind.

"Myn… did *Garr* give that to you?" she whispered.

The dragon gave another sly glance toward him before licking away the last of the char that had collected on the stone. Myranda smiled warmly.

"It's so nice to see you getting along with one of your own. Perhaps, when all of this is through and the peace is more secure, we can bring Garr and Grustim up to visit us. New Kenvard isn't so very far from the border," she said, scratching Myn on the brow. "Deacon and I invite friends and family. There's no reason you shouldn't invite some of your own."

Myn tipped her head into the scratching and shook the ground with her rumbling contentment, much to the concern of the soldiers. Despite the decline of the sun, they had opted to remain near the wall, starting small fires and preparing their shares of the provisions.

"Myranda," Deacon said, suddenly fumbling with his bag.

It was the pad, the tiny bell rattling with a muted sound while trapped within his pack. He pulled it free. The cover quickly flipped open, and the stylus scrawled out words in a large, careful hand.

"'Turiel escaped. May have shared knowledge with Ivy. May have taken knowledge from Ivy. Used a portal. Must find,'" Deacon read aloud. "Your father is extremely efficient with his writing."

"If she used a portal, why didn't we sense it?" Myranda asked.

"She used *two* portals here. This fortress is drenched with the residual aftereffects of D'Karon magic. Passively detecting the distant use of a new spell of the same kind would be like happening to spot a candle we didn't know to look for a half a field away while staring through a bonfire," Deacon said. "In hindsight, it would have been wise for at least one of us to remain remote to this place... though I suppose Grustim *did* make it clear that we were not to leave his supervision..."

While Deacon reasoned his way back through the course of events that had led them to miss this crucial piece of information, Myranda snatched up her staff and set its head in her lap. For a man who, when he had a mind to, had crystalline mental clarity and impenetrable focus, Deacon's propensity to allow his mind to wander was astounding.

He was, however, entirely correct about the stain that the D'Karon magic had left. In her mind's eye, it hung all around them, like a thick fog choking out the healthy, vibrant glow that existed in those places untouched by their influence. To see past it, she had to deepen her concentration and expand her view beyond the stain. It was precisely the sort of magic she'd promised not to deploy within Tresson borders, but in light of recent disastrous events she very much doubted there was any merit in restraining herself any longer. At this point the only thing that mattered to her was preventing *further* disaster. And this woman, this Turiel, brought disaster with her everywhere she went, and her stated goal was to return to this world the *greatest* disaster that had ever befallen it.

The key difficulty of tracking movement through such means was that the spell left massive, unmistakable scars wherever the caster *departed*. The marring where they *arrived* was barely a ghost of an echo by comparison. The mind's eye, no matter how rigidly one trained it, was drawn to the most substantial disruptions, making glimpses of the lesser ones fleeting and imprecise. It was to the north, certainly. And it was closer to the west coast than the east.

Then, all at once, it snapped into clarity. Deacon, having reached the end of his line of reasoning had taken his own gem in one hand and *her* hand in the other. Given time to steady the storm in her mind, Myranda would certainly have reached this same state. Deacon, perhaps even more quickly, could have done the same. But together it seemed effortless. For a precious moment Myranda allowed herself to bask in the strength and serenity that came not from her, and not from him, but from the pair united. It was something that this purpose or that always seemed to push aside, but there was no doubting that the two were perfectly attuned, matched together on a metaphysical level, and in a way that she had too often taken for granted. She resolved, as soon as the task was done and they and their world were permitted a moment of peace, to make it clear to Deacon how much it meant both to have him by her side and for him to have the patience to remain there when so much else required their attentions.

The moment passed, however, and the gentle feeling of completion was chased away by the cold truth that their focus had revealed. Only a single fleck of black was different from the others, an exit that was not also an entrance. This was the place that Turiel had arrived but not yet departed, at least by the same mystic means. It sat at the northern edge of a dim but strengthening mass of souls. The souls were instantly, chillingly familiar. It was a place she knew.

As quickly as it had come, the focus was gone, broken by a voice.

"Duchess Celeste."

Myranda opened her eyes. Grustim stood before her. Still affected by the sharpened focus, in the space of a single moment she saw a thousand telltale signs of the deeds done within the infirmary. Flecks of blood, not his own, smeared his hands. The depressions left by cords wrapped tight around them still lingered across his palms. Most of all, there was the look in his eyes... Torture left a stain on the soul just as black and just as deep as the one D'Karon magic left on the world.

"I am afraid Commander Brustuum cannot tell us precisely where Turiel first arose. He does not know. She was *certainly* fostering this keyhole you've spoken of, but it is also certain that she first arose some weeks ago, and that she came from a place far deeper in the Southern Wastes than we first believed. She'd traveled from there to a nomadic tribe near the west coast, and Brustuum's men captured her there and sequestered her here over a month ago."

"Deacon, you stay here and work with him," Myranda said, climbing to her feet. "If you can get close to the keyhole, do it. We'll all work on finding its precise location. The nearer you are, the more quickly you can tend to it."

"Certainly," Deacon said. He began to dig through his bags to find a certain book. "Grustim, can you show me on a recent map—"

"Wait. Duchess, why assign this task to him?"

"I have to leave."

"Why?"

"Because Turiel is in New Kenvard," she said, agony hardening her voice.

"You know this? That she is there, and that she is still there?" Grustim asked.

"She opened a portal to New Kenvard not more than a few minutes ago," Deacon explained.

"Then deliver a message to the local defenses," Grustim advised.

"I shall begin the message immediately," Deacon agreed.

"Regardless, I will be there to help them," Myranda said.

"You do not have *permission* to leave. There is work to be done here," Grustim said.

Myranda was beside Myn, readying to climb onto her back. She turned to Grustim. "Grustim, when I was six years old, I watched my city be overrun and my people destroyed. For years I thought it was your people who were responsible. I later learned it was the D'Karon. It remained in their grip until the end of the war, and since then I have been doing all I can to restore it. And at *this moment* the woman who brought the D'Karon to our world has set foot there. It is my home. I will *not* allow harm to come to New Kenvard. Not again."

"Even with Myn to carry you, you are *days* away," Grustim reminded her. "There is no telling where she will be by the time you arrive. And even if you were *hours* away, you are suggesting that I allow a member of the Northern Alliance to ride a dragon through the skies of my land unguided and unwatched? You have proved yourself to be honorable and trustworthy, Duchess, but what you are asking must not be allowed."

"Grustim, I apologize deeply, but I am not suggesting and I am not asking. If I can keep my home safe, I will. If I can be there to heal the damage that is done, I will. This is something I must do." She climbed onto Myn's back. "You will not stop me."

Grustim turned to his former mount. Garr was standing among the rubble, watching intently as the exchange grew more heated. He stepped forward. Myn turned. The two dragons locked their gazes. Not a growl or roar was exchanged. Not a wing or tail twitched. There was only the stare, the silent measurement of the other.

When the decision came, it was clear to even a novice in the ways of dragons precisely what decision was made. Garr's tense stance eased, he shifted his gaze to Grustim in what might have been shame and might have been defiance, and then he finally sat. There was no fear, no intimidation. He wasn't backing down from a challenge or bowing to a superior opponent. He simply chose that in this moment, in this instance, this dragon and her rider should be left to their task.

Myranda didn't linger, nor did she gloat. She looked first to Grustim. "If, when we are through, you feel justice is deserved, then justice will be served. You have my word." Her eyes turned to Deacon. "Be safe. I'll return as soon as I can."

"Until then, may we each find what we are searching for," Deacon said.

With that, Myn curled her neck and plucked her stone from the ground, flashing a quick glance at Grustim before dropping it beneath her tongue, and the pair took to the sky with a few powerful thrusts of her wings.

Myranda, in times of great need, had learned the techniques to funnel her own considerable mystic strength into that of her mount to speed their motions and to ease away fatigue. She'd used it to great effect in more than one chase that would have exhausted a normal horse, and the same tactics had helped Myn match even Ether's speeds for short periods of time. As the seemingly endless desert opened up beneath her, Myranda knew that Grustim was right. Under the best of circumstances it was likely a longer journey than could reasonably be made in a short enough time to make a difference, but that didn't change a thing. She would reach them. She was the duchess now. It was more than her home, it was her responsibility. She would *not* see it fall again.

#

Deacon stood beside Grustim, watching Myranda and Myn soar off to the north. He understood precisely what she was doing and why, but there was the concern that Grustim and, moreover, the whole of the Tresson people might not. He turned to the Dragon Rider, expecting to have to calm him down and make it clear that Myranda meant no disrespect, but at the moment, it seemed the ire was not between Grustim and Myranda, but Grustim and Garr.

The Rider stared at his former mount with a look of disappointment and irritation. He was "speaking" with the beast in the grunting, growling imitation of the natural dragon language that Deacon had become increasingly fascinated with during their time together. It wasn't precisely the language he had learned when under the tutelage of Solomon back in Entwell, but that much was to be expected. Languages had regional variations, and soldiers had their own jargons. Adding in the varied anatomy of the two speakers made for a linguistically remarkable demonstration. By the end of the exchange, Deacon was fairly certain he'd worked out the nuances of the speech.

"… She is not of our land," Grustim rumbled.

"She is of our kind," Garr replied.

"It is not our way."

"To protect our own is our way. To serve our own is our way. The Rider is wise and just. The mount is strong and loyal. They are of our kind, and they are of our way."

"… I saw the stone."

Garr craned his neck, pride on his face. "She kept the stone."

"She is a child, though she does not look it."

"Children grow. I am patient."

"It was not the way of a mount."

"I am not a mount."

Grustim crossed his arms. "It is well that you are not."

Deacon cleared his throat. "If I might interject?"

Grustim kept his gaze on Garr, but when he spoke, it was in Varden. "This is why it is unwise to mix females with males in times of war," he muttered. "Females and males do foolish things when they are mixed." He turned. "You and the duchess. You are married?"

"We are."

"How is it that someone such as you could catch the eye of a woman such as her?" he asked.

"I'm afraid I don't understand your confusion, and I'm not certain this is the proper forum for such a discussion."

Grustim looked to the soldiers at the wall, addressing them as a whole. "Prepare yourselves for the sentencing of your commander, and fetch for me any region maps or field maps that have survived."

The men snapped to action. Grustim turned back to Deacon.

"It will take a few moments for the commander to be readied by the healers in the infirmary, and in that time the soldiers will fetch the maps we need to put the information I received from him to good use. But at this moment I am a Dragon Rider stripped of his mount, forced to pass judgment on a man of my own nation, and forced to stand idle while a trusted ally chose to side instead with your woman and her mount. Forgive me, Duke, but your woman has seized my thoughts, and I would appreciate an answer. How is it that so forceful a woman could allow herself to be joined to so forceless a man? *She* is clearly the figure of authority between you. She is the one with the vision, with the intensity, with the passion. You… what *are* you? You are a shadow. You make no impression. There is nothing to you but to serve her. It is baffling to a Tresson to see a man defer so completely to a woman, but more so it is baffling to imagine that a woman of such quality could ever tolerate a man lacking such substance. The two of you may as well be brother and sister for all of the passion I see between you."

Deacon furrowed his brow. "I am sorry that you have so low an opinion of me, sir, but to garner a high opinion was never my aim, so you will pardon me if I am not offended. As for Myranda and I, our feelings for one another are a private matter, and what I've done to earn her is simply to be the best that I can and make it clear to her how much I value her."

"No… I refuse to believe that a headstrong woman such as her would ever turn her heart to you without *some* manner of grand gesture, *some* showing of your worthiness of her."

"I permanently altered the mystic makeup of my left hand when I pierced a hole in the very fabric of reality in order to journey from my home to her side and offer aid in a time of profound travail, utilizing a spell the very existence of which has sullied my name and barred my return to the place of my birth," Deacon explained. "Is this a sufficiently grand gesture to satisfy your curiosity?"

He raised his eyebrows. "That would explain much."

A soldier marched up to Grustim and revealed a stitched cloth map, tersely informing the Dragon Rider that it was the most accurate map to be found in the ruined keep. From the looks of it, the map was quite new, and it was made with care and precision.

Grustim spread it on the ground, weighing down the corners with stones. "According to the commander's claims, Turiel came from somewhere in this region," he said, running his finger across the southern coast. "It is a wide area. Even if we knew what we were looking for, it would take weeks to do a thorough search."

Deacon tipped his head to the side, eying the map.

"Is something wrong?" Grustim asked.

"This line here," he said, running his finger across a thin gray embroidered thread. "What does this represent?"

"That is the leading edge of the Southern Wastes."

"But here, this city. On my map, I'm certain the Wastes fell far south of it. On this map there is so little space between them. Could my map have been *that* inaccurate?"

"Your map was likely based on one from before the war. It is over one hundred years old."

"And that would alter the edge of the Southern Wastes?"

"Indeed, the forward edge has crept northward with time."

"… The Wastes are growing… Of course…"

"Is that relevant?"

Deacon waved his hand over the map, and the lines took on a brilliant glow. For the second time he conjured a map in the air. As he maneuvered it in front of him, he explained his thoughts.

"The D'Karon spells invariably feed upon the mana of a region. The *life* of a region. If this woman is a necromancer, she would be particularly skilled at consuming the vibrancy from the area. Over the duration of the war, or longer, she could *certainly* have had an effect on the landscape that has spread over the years. If the Wastes, or at least the degree to which they have spread, is a result of her harvesting of power to feed the keyhole, then the effect would be *centered* in the Wastes."

"No. We already know from the commander that woman had been much farther south."

"You need to think as a whole."

He traced his hand carefully along the ragged edge of the Wastes, then continued the curve out into the surrounding sea and circled back into the original curve. The center of the resulting circle seemed to fall just barely on the edge of the land.

"Here. Somewhere in this region is the center of the influence on the Wastes. We begin our search there."

Grustim looked to the cloth map, then wet his finger and touched it to the soil to leave a smudge of mud in the indicated location. "It certainly falls within the stretch the commander indicated. If you are correct, it would cut the search from weeks to days…"

A subtle commotion drew his attention to the infirmary. The commander was on his feet and walking toward them. Myranda's attempts to cure his ills had largely taken hold. He was limping and still wrapped in bandages, but otherwise seemed not much worse for wear. The bandages, tellingly, had considerably more fresh blood on them than when Myranda had treated him.

"A moment, Duke. I must see to this," Grustim said.

He stepped toward the commander and each came to a stop near the bonfire upon which Myranda had cooked the food. When Grustim spoke, it was in Tresson, and it was with the attention of every last one of the troops on hand.

"Commander Brustuum, your orders were to secure the source of the disturbance to the south and to turn her over to your superiors."

"It was," Brustuum answered.

"You stand accused of abandoning those orders and acting according to your own agenda."

"I have done so, but what I have done was with the strength and honor of my nation in mind."

"And tell your men what you did with the strength and honor of your nation in mind."

He hesitated only briefly. "I kept the woman here, questioned her. I resolved first to prove that her actions were indeed a purposeful act of war. When I learned of the power she held, the knowledge she had, I knew it belonged under the control of our great army."

"And how did you intend to secure this knowledge?" Grustim prodded.

"I had her demonstrate her abilities."

"You know what you did, Brustuum. Tell your men."

"… I allowed her to draw power from our prisoners and had her instruct our mystics in the methods."

The soldiers in attendance murmured in horror and disgust.

"Draw power... You let her drain Tressons of life. You *fed* your countrymen to someone you believed to be a Northern Aggressor. And with the power you gave her, she did all of this," Grustim said, sweeping his arm around the stronghold. "Your arrogance and dereliction of duty brought this upon you and cost the lives of your men."

"My intention was—"

"This is not a matter of intention!" Grustim spat. "This is a matter of duty and honor, and in your actions you have abandoned both. Do you deny this?"

"I do not."

"Then your punishment is clear. Your dagger of command, Brustuum."

The commander drew a short, simple dagger, clearly more ceremonial than functional, and handed it to Grustim. The Dragon Rider set its grip into the flames of the fire.

"Soldiers, open the gates."

Those nearest the heavy gates marched solemnly to the task of pulling them open. As they worked, Grustim laid out the punishment.

"It is fortunate for us that you chose to commit your crime here within the great desert. It saves us the effort of bringing you to this forsaken place. You will now be left to the mercy of the land. You shall be sent into the sands. Because you have abandoned your obligations to your military, you shall not have the benefit if its resources. No water, no food, no shelter, and no equipment. This place is quite far from any cities, far from prying eyes. It is a fact that has helped you to keep your treachery from the eyes of your superiors. It also means there is little hope you will reach anyone who might offer you aid. But this is, after all, a death sentence. You shall be refused any aid you may request. And to ensure this..."

He held out his hand, and as though it had been previously arranged, a soldier walked up and presented him with a heavy leather glove. He slipped it on and plucked the dagger from the flames by the blade.

"Hold him," Grustim ordered.

The same soldier stepped behind his former commander and gripped his head, holding it firm while Grustim approached. In two quick, efficient motions he pressed first one side of the pommel, then the other to Brustuum's cheek. The crossed lines on one side interlocked with the scythe on the other, forming a single branded symbol. Brustuum, to his credit, did not cry out or flinch as his flesh was seared. He simply maintained a steady look in Grustim's eyes.

"Take him," Grustim said. "See that this last measure of his duty is faced with honor."

Two more soldiers stepped forward and took Brustuum by the shoulders, but he pulled himself free, determined to walk on his own.

"I can face the consequences of my actions. But I hope you can face the consequences of yours," he said.

Grustim didn't do him the courtesy of a response. He merely watched as the disgraced commander was marched toward the fading light of dusk. As he passed Deacon, he gave the Northerner a look of disdain, then glanced at the cloth map before continuing to his punishment.

Deacon stepped to the Dragon Rider's side. "I of course defer to your customs, but are we certain it is wise to leave his fate to chance?"

"In Tressor, only our holy men and magistrates have the authority to take a life. For the rest of us, we must leave the deed in the hands of the gods and the land. I would prefer to deal with him more permanently, but without rules and without duty there is chaos. We've set the task at hand aside for too long, however."

"Yes... yes, I agree, of course. Do you agree with my assessment, regarding where to begin our search?"

"Your reasoning is sound."

"Then I do not think we can afford to delay. I think you, Garr, and I need to set off for the Southern Wastes immediately."

"I agree. But that choice is no longer mine. Garr has been freed of his oath to me. I am at this point no more a Dragon Rider than you. That he has remained behind is more than I would have expected of him."

"But you said you've released him of his oath before."

"I have. The first time he took to the mountains and returned three months later. True freedom from their duty is something most dragons never have, and never seek. More than any other beast, a dragon understands loyalty and honor. Garr is a fine soldier, but in those moments that are his own he is... perhaps driven by *different* instincts than most."

Deacon turned to the dragon. Garr stood among the rubble. He'd been watching as the sentencing and discussions had progressed.

"Garr..." Deacon began. He cleared his throat. "You'll forgive me if my diction is not as precise as Grustim's." When he spoke again, it was the guttural rattles of a human approximation of a dragon's tongue. "Thank you for your aid. You have your freedom now. It is deserved. You should enjoy it. But much—"

"Stop," grumbled Garr. He lowered his head. "I do not like you. I do not dislike you. What you say does not matter to me. The woman I like. The dragon I like. The woman likes you. The dragon likes you. What you ask was my duty. What you ask is his duty. I have reasons to do it. The dragon. If the dragon would like this, it would be another reason to do this. A very good reason to do this."

Deacon grinned, abandoning Garr's language. "It seems I always must work hardest to earn the respect of dragons. I can assure you that Myn will appreciate anything you can do to help us keep this terrible thing from occurring."

Garr raised his head and flicked his tongue across his snout. He then turned and lowered his head, snatching something up from among the rubble. With it clutched within his jaws, he padded to Grustim. He lowered his head once more and dropped the pieces of Grustim's armor at his feet, then stepped back and bowed to the ground. Setting his head and neck on the earth, he rattled out a vow.

"I pledge my tooth and claw, my scale and flame, to you and to your blood until such time as our oath is broken," Garr rumbled.

"And to you I pledge my mind and hand, my armor and blade, to you and to your blood until such time as our oath is broken," Grustim said.

Garr huffed a breath and rose to his full height again. Grustim began to put on his armor. It was an incredible testament to the quality of the armor that it was barely marred despite enduring a building collapse.

"It is not lost on me that you had already gathered the armor," Grustim muttered. "I wonder if you were waiting to be asked."

"Regardless, I must ask, how quickly can we reach the possible location of the keyhole?" Deacon asked.

"Garr has not rested. None of us have. But he is well fed and well trained. We may be able to reach it in a day and a half, but we will be exhausted. And there is the matter of carrying you."

"Is that a problem?"

"I am a Dragon Rider, and he is my mount. *No one* but I may ride on his back."

Deacon released a breath that was just shy of exasperated. "And I'd believed *Entwell* was a rigidly codified culture. I suppose I shall need to be carried then?"

"Indeed. It is not the most pleasant way to travel."

"I've had worse. Let us not delay any longer. There is work to be done."

"Indeed. Garr, find your helmet. We shall at least face the challenge ahead properly equipped."

Chapter 8

Ivy was still reeling beside the fire when Deacon's writing began to scratch itself out on the pad. Ether had gathered additional wood and stoked the flames quite high before stepping into the flames herself to replenish what she had squandered in her battle with Turiel. This left Celeste to squint at the precise lettering.

"I believe… my daughter and her husband have found Turiel's destination. It says… she has appeared in New Kenvard."

"No… no, no, no," Ivy murmured. "She can't go there."

"I shall require some time to recover my strength if I am to make so vast a journey quickly enough to be of any use to combat her," Ether said, her voice crackling from the flames.

"This information will be long stale by then. She moves far too quickly. If we are going to effectively combat this woman, we need to know more about her. It isn't enough to know where she is. We must know where she is *going*," Celeste said.

"She… she left… she gave… she *forced* a lot of her mind into mine," Ivy said. "Why must they always toy with my mind…"

"What have you learned of her? What did she tell you?"

"It isn't like that. She didn't tell me anything. There aren't facts… Well, there *are*, but they're wrapped in experiences. And she…" Ivy held her head, "she can't think straight. Her thoughts are swimming in my head. She's not *sane*. It is like a hive of bees…"

"There are two things we need to learn. Where the keyhole is located, and how she intends to open it. Do you believe those things are within the memories she's given you?"

"I don't *know*. I asked her to tell me where to find the keyhole, so it must be there, but she gave me so much more than that. And they aren't *my* memories. It isn't as though I can simply think back to the moment in time that I experienced these things. I *didn't* experience them, and I don't know when I might find the moments when she did. Her thoughts and mine are jumbled up."

"Start at the beginning then. Why is she doing what she's doing?"

"Sister," Ivy said instantly. "That much is certain. Her sister is constantly on her mind. She never thinks of her name. Barely thinks of what she looks

265

like. It isn't… it isn't even as though she is a person anymore. She's this all-powerful figure, this presence that fills her mind. Sister."

"What do we know about this sister?"

"She's… I have to think back so hard just to see her face… Yes… Yes she was tall. Thin. She was older, but just by a few years. Both knew magic, but her sister knew more… or at least knew it better. Turiel spoke to the dead, she could give and take life. Her sister could *change* things. She worked enchantments. There was this one instance, long ago, when she made a pendant or brooch. It was supposed to bring luck and protect from misfortune."

"What happened to her?"

Ivy shut her eyes tighter and seemed almost pained by the remembrance, as though the intensity of the memory harkened back to a tragedy in her own life.

"She believed she was the finest wizard in the world and sought to prove it. She entered a place… a cave. She was determined to do it alone. It was… it was the trial of the cave. She was facing the *beast* of the cave. And she failed, vanished. It was devastating to Turiel. That beast… that beast is just as big a figure in her mind. A towering darkness, casting its shadow across all that she does. They are like… the two sides of a coin. The ultimate good and the ultimate evil. White and black. In the face of the perfection of her sister and the evil of the beast, nothing she does is ever truly good or evil in her mind. It is like nothing she can do will ever matter until the beast is defeated. And to kill the beast, she believes she must become even more powerful than her sister was. That's what all of this is about."

"The beast of the cave? But as I understand it, there *is* no beast of the cave."

"Lain was through the cave many times. Myranda was through it once. Deacon lived with the people of Entwell his whole life. None had seen or heard the beast. It *doesn't* exist. Her sister must have been killed by the cave."

"Unless she survived."

"I don't know. She's… *hundreds* of years old. She lost her sister… I think Deacon said Entwell is… maybe four hundred years old? I think her sister went through before that… I don't know. The years back then were different. The fifth year of this queen or the seventh year of that king. None of them make sense. I really don't know how long ago any of these things are. There are long periods of just sitting in the mountains in the north, or sitting in a cave in the south…"

"The cave. That is what we're after. Do you remember anything about it?"

"It was dark. It was filled with animal bones. She almost never left it. She…"

Suddenly Ivy gasped and her eyes shot open.

"What is it?"

"Teht… I saw her." She was almost shivering at seeing the face of one of her keepers. "Teht visited her so often. Turiel adored her. Took her instruction to heart and was so hungry for more. In my... in *her* memory there is such affection for her." She squeezed her fists tight, subtle flares of red and whispers of black sparking around her. "I can't *stand* it. To have those feelings inside of me. That *face* in my head..."

Celeste gripped her hand. "They aren't your thoughts. Set them aside. You need to focus. *Where* is the cave?"

Ivy squeezed his hand tightly. "She... I can't... every time she steps out of the cave, it's just... dry and cold. The horizon is flat. There aren't even any plants. And I... wait..." Her hands loosened and she reached out. "The pad, give me the pad!"

He quickly handed her Deacon's pad and the stylus, and instantly she began sketching, never once opening her eyes.

"I can see it. She looked back upon it once, when she left to begin this. I can see the cave, and the cliffs."

The tip of the stylus sketched madly at the page, tracing out with remarkable fidelity a cave-riddled cliff side. When she was through, though it was no doubt a perfect representation of what the true cliff looked like, there was nothing terribly distinctive about it, and she knew it. She opened her eyes and looked over the drawing critically. The page was very small, but she realized there was one feature that stood out. She circled it and flipped to a new page.

"This, back here. It's a pointy mountain, or a spire. Very tall and narrow, and beside it there is a tree. Even taller than the spire, and with very few branches." She sketched the spire in greater detail as she described it. "You can probably see it from a long way away."

When she was through, Celeste took it and looked it over.

"Short of a point on a map, I believe this is as accurate as we can hope to have. Is there anything else you can tell us?"

"She won't hold anything back. Anything that she can do to bring her closer to her goal of vanquishing the beast is justifiable in her eyes."

"A beast that does not exist. Do you believe she might stop her quest if she were to learn the truth?"

"I don't think so. She'd never believe it. It would be like telling a monk that his gods did not exist. Her belief goes down to the core."

"Anything else?"

"She's... gleeful in what she does. Eager. And she is resourceful. If she has the *remains* of a creature, or if she senses that someone has *died* in a place, she can turn that to her advantage. She can... *recruit* the dead in the same way that you might recruit the living. The more violent and tragic their deaths, the more easily she can use them. And she..."

"She has greater power where someone has died violently?" Celeste interrupted.

"Yes."

"… She is in New Kenvard. She has the whole of the Kenvard Massacre to feed upon. And she is a stone's throw away from the front, where generations of lives were lost."

Ivy's eyes widened as the depth of the realization struck her. "Gods… You're right…"

The fire flickered and then dimmed, swirling and wicking together as Ether shifted back to humanity.

"Then there is no more time to waste restoring my energies. Prepare yourselves. Comfort will not be a consideration. We must move with speed. And we must move now."

#

Turiel rolled herself painfully onto her back. Her arrival in the palace of Kenvard had been far rougher than she'd intended. Part of it was the speed at which she'd had to enter the portal. The plummeting entry had been turned into a swift sideways tumble as she passed through the conjured gateway. But if she'd understood the placement of the exit point properly, she should have arrived in a hallway. It would not have been comfortable, but she should have struck smooth ground and slid to a stop. Instead, she'd found only mounds of jagged, broken masonry. It had taken almost an hour of careful working of her magic to repair herself sufficiently to sit up, which meant she was only now seeing the nature of the devastation in what should have been a glorious palace.

The sun had set, sending a deeper chill over the land and casting her in near-complete darkness, but that was little concern to her. Years within the cave had trained her to make do with barely the flicker of a candle. Even the rising moon filtered through the thick clouds of the north was light enough to reveal that there was little left of this place. Work had been done to at least prepare it to be rebuilt though. Here and there the most intact of the stones had been piled neatly, narrow paths of jagged brick had been cleared to allow workers to access the most unreachable or worst-damaged parts of the fallen structure, but save for scattered remnants of a spire and the crenellations atop some of the rubble, this once grand palace looked more like a quarry than the glorious symbol of a kingdom's wealth and power.

"No. How could this happen?" she gasped, genuine horror in her voice. "I remember Kenvard. Mother was a servant to the king here. I… I learned my first incantations in these very halls."

She stood and paced unsteadily to where her staff had landed, or at least to where the head of it had landed. The long fall and sudden stop had a similar effect on her staff as it had on her. Its white body was broken and splintered, revealing its hollow, red-stained interior that suggested her staff did not merely *appear* to be bone, it truly was. The gem was feathered with fractures, held together only by the staff's clawed tip. With it in hand, she began to conjure tendrils, but they withered and faded. She sighed lightly and focused instead on conjuring just one thread. It wove down and pierced a fragment of the broken staff, drawing it near and stitching it back in place before a new thread replaced it and sought out the next piece.

Her eyes still sweeping over the castle and the city around it, she set the staff beside her to continue its task on its own, then turned to the twitching heap that had been Mott. He had been in poor shape even before diving off the side, and now he was hardly recognizable. It was a grotesque sight, and but for his lack of blood, it would have been gory and hideous. Instead it looked like a demented taxidermist had grown weary of his latest project and thrown the scraps in the trash.

Turiel reached out for him with her right hand, but instead held forth only the cloth-draped remnant of Ether's attack. Again she sighed, more disappointed than in pain, and instead reached with her left. Mott's form shook and twitched, then began to crackle back into shape. As soon as enough legs were whole enough to carry him, he dragged himself over to Turiel and heaved his head into her lap.

"This place was glorious. Its walls were impenetrable, Mott. Look at them. Even now they stand. The one part of the city that doesn't seem to have been patched at all. ... I know there was a war, and they say it was because of the D'Karon. It certainly seems they were at least involved. But even if there was a war, this could not have happened. Not Kenvard. Not this glorious capital. I need an answer, Mott."

Her familiar looked up to her and chittered.

"I know they will be coming for me, but this... this *requires* an explanation. Let us see what we were able to pluck from that dear misguided child's mind. Perhaps she knows more of what happened."

Turiel shut her eyes, her remaining hand idly stroking Mott's head while she sifted through recollections that were not her own. Like the staff, and for that matter like the city of Kenvard, she could feel that Ivy's memories were badly broken. Winding backward through them, she could see the battles the creature had fought, her many clashes with the D'Karon, and the way the other adversaries had treated her. Turiel's face became pained. She saw only kindness and dedication in the actions of these monsters she'd been told were the hated adversaries... True, the shapeshifter was brash, foolish, and arrogant, but there was no doubting that at every opportunity, the D'Karon had done harm while the adversaries had healed or prevented it to the best of their power.

These could not be lies... They were memories, pulled directly from Ivy's mind. These were the things she remembered, *as* she remembered them. It could only be false if the memories had been inserted or twisted by another. She dug deeper into the memories. Some of her training had come from the skills mastered by the one called Epidime. He was a master of such manipulation, and having learned the beginnings of his tactics, she at least knew how to recognize when such things were at work.

"Ha! Here! Her mind *has* been manipulated," she said, triumphant in the belief that she'd found evidence of the adversaries' treachery.

Quickly she realized she was mistaken. The hallmarks of manipulation did not come in the form of pleasant memories inserted, but in other things. Raw, blunt training and understanding, forced unwillingly into her mind. And this was done *not* by the adversaries, but by the D'Karon themselves.

"She… she *was* an adversary first… It *was* the D'Karon who changed her…" She gritted her teeth. "This was *not* what I was after. That is a concern for another time. This is Kenvard, once great and now ruined. *That* is the riddle at hand."

Turiel brushed these discoveries aside and delved deeper. She saw flashes of a terrible battle Ivy had been a part of, and a brief imprisonment within the very castle that now stood in ruins. It was whole then… but not as she remembered. Perhaps the greatest damage to the place had happened after, but there was something before it. The sorceress plunged deeper, pushing beyond the manipulations and erasures at the hands of the D'Karon. She found her way into the haziest, most distant memories Ivy had. And there she saw it. The city she remembered. In fact, if anything, it was larger, more glorious, more thriving and vibrant… and then she saw the gates fall, and the people scream. She saw the red uniforms, Tresson soldiers… but no. This memory was vibrant in the way that only great tragedies can ever be. Every detail was burned deep and true into her mind. Turiel knew the living, and she knew the dead. She knew how a proper thing moved, how a proper thing looked, and she knew such things in a way far more intimate and detailed than most ever would. These soldiers moved wrong. They were flooding the city, razing homes and slaughtering locals, but they were not Tresson soldiers. They were not even humans. Not proper humans anyway, or elves or dwarves. These things were created. Concocted. They were made expertly and efficiently, controlled by unseen hands. And there was only one group who could have made so many, and so well.

"The D'Karon… the D'Karon *did* do this. No… no, I refuse to believe it. This must be the manipulation of the adversaries. If they were strong enough to banish the D'Karon, then it stands to reason they may have ways to twist minds just as Epidime could, but in ways that I cannot detect. I need someone beyond their influence. … I need the *true* eyes that witnessed this massacre. And in that, at least, I'm spoiled for choice…"

The sorceress stood, her bones finally mended and both her staff and her pet whole again. The strength was flowing quickly into her. She blinked her eyes a few times and let the forms felt on the edge of her mind flicker into being. There were spirits, hundreds of them. They wandered what had been the halls of this fallen castle. They traced the lines of the streets and drifted like dry leaves through the air. As one so deeply connected with the dead, Turiel could have called upon each of them to tell the story of his or her final moments... but there was no use in doing so. She knew how to read the souls of the departed, and it took the merest glance to know that most of these lingering spirits were those taken quickly. Their lives ended in sudden sparks of fear and confusion. They would have little to add. She needed someone else. Someone with a steadier mind, a sharper recollection. And so she continued on her way.

Turiel could feel the influence of the D'Karon deep in this place. It had been their stronghold for some time, but like Castle Verril and unlike Demont's coastal fortress, attempts were being made to reclaim it. She could feel that the gems and enchantments that her D'Karon masters always set down were being gathered up and scrubbed away, but such things could not be disposed of without care, and it took time to do so properly. As such those most dangerous things, the most mystical and mysterious, had been gathered up and locked away. So much power concentrated in so small a space made it easy to find, despite attempts to the contrary by whoever had placed them. She paced along the narrow, excavated pathways through the ruin until she came upon what appeared to be the largest mound of intact stone in the whole of the wreckage of the castle. It was clearly placed there purposefully, and yet it seemed to have been piled atop a portion of the floor that was quite intact.

She angled her damaged staff toward the mound and, with great effort, began to shuffle the stones. Blocks from the center of the mound slid forward. Blocks to the side slid farther out. Piece by piece she constructed a crude arch to hold up the rest of the stone such that the core of the stack could be cleared away. When the final few bricks dragged themselves free, they revealed a well-secured trapdoor. Not only was there a stout lock of complex design, but there were at least three warding spells, each quite potent. Though lifting one of the stones with her will and dropping it upon the lock a few times rendered it useless, the spells were another matter. She would not be opening the door while they were in place.

Her knees and hips crackled uncomfortably as she lowered herself to the ground and set her staff down to spread her hand against the cold wood of the trapdoor.

"... Yes... I can feel you inside, both of you... This magic may keep me from opening the door from the outside, but the fool who cast it must have been fearful that a poor innocent might be trapped, because from within it is undone quite simply... Rise for me... Open the door so that I might ask you a few questions and set my mind at ease."

She focused all of her will into conjuring a single thread and wormed it down through the cracks of the wood. Piercing the protective spells, even in this tiny and precise way, took every ounce of mystic focus she could muster, but finally it was done. She probed about with her tendril in search of flesh. It took time and required that she slip her influence past what felt like a closed

271

crypt, but finally the seed of her spell found purchase, and from within, there was motion.

Turiel stepped back. Below the trapdoor heavy, plodding steps approached, followed by the long, slow ring of steel. The door shuddered once, then slowly opened. Whatever figure opened the door chose not to reveal itself, so Turiel instead marched down the steps. Mott trudged after her, still not fully recovered or, at least, not fully empowered by the necromancer's magic. He fetched her staff and descended into the darkness.

As she stepped into the blackness, familiar violet light began to flicker and flare. At the same time she found herself weakening. Rather than fear or horror, this sensation brought a grin to her face.

"Ah… thir gems… Remarkable that whoever locked them here managed to keep them from drinking their fill."

She closed off her strength to them to spare herself further drain, then looked upon what their light revealed. The trapdoor led to a sort of storeroom. Crates were packed with assorted broken artifacts from the time of the D'Karon reign in this place. Quite a few shattered gems shone from within their crates, but one or two whole ones flickered there as well. She selected one and fitted it in place of the fractured one in her staff. Then she turned to some of the other artifacts. Carefully sealed, ornate metal boxes were stacked against one wall. Mounds of partially shredded spell books joined them, as well as bundles of scrolls and bolts of cloth. Most chilling, however, was the pair of caskets set upright against the far wall. One was still firmly shut. The other lay open.

"Ah, of course. My apologies. Where are my manners?" Turiel said, turning back to the staircase. "I thank you for your aid."

Standing beside the door was a figure who seemed to be more armor than man. The equipment might once have been gleaming and pristine, but no longer. Now it had deep, shining scars from where stone had scraped across it, and many plates were dented or bent almost beyond recognition. A helmet with a mangled faceplate hid the face, but two eyes shone from within with an unnatural light. At his hip hung a sword, its grip dripping with jewels and its blade and pommel bearing a familiar insignia formed from a curve and a point.

"My name is Turiel. I do not mean to interrupt your slumber, but there have been some matters of great importance. If you will stand ready, I believe your crypt-mate may be of equal or greater aid."

She turned to the remaining casket and pointed the head of her staff. The lid slid aside, revealing a frail young woman with pale skin. Every inch of her was crisscrossed with faint scars, and here and there her skin glittered with embedded crystal. There was something unnatural, eerie about the wounds though. The scars were pure white, save the gem-bearing ones, which were pure black. None were faded, each fresh and new, as though they'd all only *just* healed. Her clothes were relatively fresh. She wore dark funereal garb.

Under the influence of Turiel's will, she stepped out, far more steady and whole than the armored man, and took her place by his side.

Mott, now lively once more since Turiel had replaced the staff's gem, skittered over to a crate and shoved it forward with his head so that Turiel could take a seat.

"Now, time is potentially limited, but I see no reason not to treat this situation with the proper decorum. My name is Turiel. Who are you?"

"Rasa, the swordsman," murmured a hoarse voice from within the armor.

"Aneriana," said the woman. Her voice was clear, pristine.

Both of them spoke lifelessly, mechanically. The information they gave lingered in their minds and flowed from the spirits and those drifting in the ether around them. They were puppets, soulless and unthinking.

"Ah," Turiel said, nodding slowly to the woman. "You, my dear, are the one I seek. I understand that you were at the center of this castle when it crumbled to the ground."

"I was," she said.

"As was I," said Rasa.

"Really? I must say, to have experienced the same force that leveled a castle, you both appear quite whole. And as this occurred months ago, I would not have expected to find bodies so free from rot." She looked to Aneriana. "You, my dear, are practically alive. How is it that you have been spared the ravages of death? And how is it, though your soul is bound to another, you answer the call of my spells as though you still had one of your own?"

"We are Chosen," said both of them simultaneously.

"Elaborate."

"To defend their world from the creations of other gods, the divine powers of this world created or selected five warriors," Rasa said.

"We were to be two of those Chosen, but we lost our lives, or our souls, before the five could be joined in the Great Convergence," Aneriana said.

"Our bodies remain, touched by the divine, and thus spared true death while there remains a task to be done," Rasa said. "When you speak to us, you speak, in part, to the divine, and are privy to some things known only to them."

Turiel's expression hardened. "Touched by the divine... speaking for the divine... Yes... there is a power about you, even in death. Pray tell, these 'creations of other gods,' have you a name for them?"

"In my time held by them as a tool to be used against my fellow Chosen, I came to know them as the D'Karon," said Aneriana.

Turiel released a breath and shut her eyes. "Tell me, these... creations of other gods, must we assume they mean us harm? Are we so fearful of the knowledge from beyond our world that we must defend ourselves even from those who might bring us wisdom?"

"No," Aneriana said. "The Chosen were forbidden to unite until the D'Karon made clear their intentions. Only when the D'Karon had willfully taken the life of a native of this world, purposefully and intentionally without heeding the orders of another, could the final Chosen arise and the Convergence occur."

"As the D'Karon said would be necessary for the adversaries to arrive. And a D'Karon did this?"

Rasa answered, "In the months prior to the Convergence, the D'Karon known as Epidime assumed control of a beast now known as a dragoyle. He took my life."

Turiel narrowed her eyes. "Epidime... he allowed this to occur?"

"He caused it to occur," Rasa said.

"Why would he do such a thing?"

"I do not know. I cannot know," Rasa said.

"Aneriana. When Kenvard fell, you were there."

"I was. I was the target of the Kenvard Massacre."

She raised an eyebrow. "The target?"

"The D'Karon knew of the coming of the Chosen. They knew of the prophecy, and knew if they could secure the Chosen, the world would be without its strongest defense against them. They found me within Kenvard and knew that the fates of many Chosen would bring them together in this place. So they laid waste to it to secure me."

Turiel was silent for a long time. When she spoke, it was with grim realization—and stabbing regret.

"The D'Karon... they slashed across this world. Twisted two nations into war. They brought ruin to great cities to claim single individuals. They manipulated the rules of a game played at a cosmic level. They stand in direct competition with the powers of creation. And I brought them here..."

"The D'Karon prey upon fear and anger. They find those with needs that seem impossible. They called to you. You were the first manipulation in the game," Rasa said.

"Yes... This was all about my sister... I committed... *all* of this... to bring justice and closure to my sister." She raised her eyes, determination beginning to show through. The corner of her mouth rose into what could almost be called a smile. "The lambs have been slaughtered. The butcher's work is done. All that remains is to make the stew. It would *truly* be a crime to bring about all of that for nothing... I've come this far for a cause. The only proper thing to be done is to take the final steps."

"What you did centuries ago, you did not knowing the pain and damage you would cause. What you do now, you do with full knowledge of the consequences," Aneriana said. "If your love for your sister has driven you to these lengths, perhaps the thing you should ask yourself is if she would have wanted it."

"No," she said. "I think that is the thing I should ask *her.* Regardless of what they've done, there is no arguing with the ability of the D'Karon to reach beyond the veil. I may have done things that did not serve this world, but *everything* I've done has served *my* purposes. I will bring the D'Karon here, and I will seek their council to finish the task that set me on this path."

"Perhaps…" Aneriana said.

"No more 'perhaps.' No more judgments from an empty shell. Rasa, you are dismissed."

With those words, the reanimated swordsman clattered to the ground in a heap of lifeless armor.

"And as for you, Aneriana. Something was taken from me shortly before I came to you, and I have an uphill struggle to victory. Mott," she said, beckoning her familiar.

He trotted up and wrapped his tail around Aneriana's arm, pulling it out to her side. Turiel pulled her knife from her robe and raised it high.

"I believe if anyone could benefit from a touch of the divine, it is me…"

#

A desert is a harsh place regardless of the hour. The pounding rays of the sun claim many lives, but the cold of night is no less dangerous. Brustuum had marched through the frigid night, blasted by a dry wind that had left his lips cracked to the point of bleeding. The layers of bandages had spared him the worst of the cold, and he'd since torn a few away to wear as a mask, but now he was staring at a horizon reddening with the sun that would offer the mercy of dawn's warmth followed by the ordeal of the day's heat.

The former commander had marched without rest with a very specific destination in mind. Grustim had followed each step of the banishment ceremony, leaving him with the scar on his cheek. No city and certainly no encampment of soldiers would take him… but there was a chance. Things had been set in motion before they had fallen apart. He knew things Grustim did not know. In the distance, between two tall dunes to the east, dust and sand were rising.

He quickened his pace as much as he could manage and walked along the peaks of dunes to increase the likelihood he would be seen. Ahead, the cloud of dust resolved itself into a covered carriage with a pair of armed escorts. The soldiers were swathed in light cloth, first to protect them from the cold of night, and soon to protect them from the pounding sun. Sharp eyes trained for desert combat took no time at all to spot him, and calls went out for the carriage to stop.

They guided their horses to the foot of the dune, then climbed down from their mounts and began to scale it. He moved down to them quickly, ensuring his mask was still in place. He would only have a few moments of their mercy before the finer points of their training could seep to the surface. They would check his cheek; they would seek his dagger of command. Finding both no blade and the mark of banishment, they would turn him away. He had to reach the carriage before then.

"Water," he croaked, stumbling quickly down the slope. "I need water and I need shelter."

"Commander Brustuum?" asked one of the soldiers, his voice familiar.

Brustuum nodded, in part as an answer but primarily in satisfaction that his navigation and timing had been sound. These were precisely the people who might help him, not out of honor, but out of dishonor.

"What has happened?" asked the second soldier.

"Northern treachery. The keep has been attacked... destroyed..."

He lurched forward, exaggerating the toll the desert had taken upon him, though only slightly. He needed them to believe that he was at death's door. The charade was enough; they maneuvered him to the door of the carriage and pulled it open.

Inside, alone, was a man in military garb far too pristine to have ever been put to use. He held in one hand a pipe, and in the other a silver goblet filled with a spiced wine.

"Esteemed Patron Sallim, Commander Brustuum needs water and shelter from the winds. The keep has been attacked, and he has been cast out."

"Brustuum? Of course, of course," Sallim said, shifting aside to offer more space on the seat opposite him.

The disgraced commander pulled himself into the carriage with more energy than he'd shown in his journey down the dune, and for a brief moment both soldiers disappeared from the doorway to fetch food and water.

"Commander what could have—"

Brustuum leaned forward and tugged his bandage down, revealing the crusted-over scar on his face. At the sight of it, Sallim's eyes widened and his voice dropped away.

"We need a word, alone," he said.

"You are—"

"Bearing the same mark that *you* will wear when the truth comes to light, so unless you wish to receive it now, I advise you to listen carefully."

A soldier appeared at the door, a skin of water and a wrapped bundle of dried fruit in hand.

"Leave it on the floor and close the door. Brustuum and I have matters of great sensitivity to discuss," Sallim said. "We do not continue forward until I say so."

The soldier obeyed, sliding the provisions to the ground and shutting the door behind them.

"What *happened*, Brustuum?"

"A Dragon Rider and some representatives from the north. They came in search of the woman we captured, but she had escaped."

"Escaped! Brustuum, you assured me—"

"Enough! It could not be helped. She was a sorceress of a far higher order than either of us could have imagined. The Dragon Rider determined that we had kept her in secret, and he knows… he knows much."

"You did not tell him of my involvement, did you?"

"I did not, but he is thorough. If he is allowed to continue his investigation, he *will* learn that you were aware of our capture of the sorceress. There will be no hiding that you allowed this to happen just as surely as I."

Sallim's eyes darted about like a cornered rabbit.

"This… this cannot be… This cannot happen. I… this is *my* army. These are *my* soldiers marching this sand. The horses they ride, the food they eat, it is paid for by the gold of *my* family. Damn you, Brustuum, I will not have my cheek branded by a dagger I paid to forge!"

"Keep your *voice* down, you fool!"

"What is to be done?" Sallim asked in a panicked hush.

"They learned from me where we believed the sorceress had been hiding in our land, and I believe they refined that information further. There was a marked map, quite near Lost Shepherd's Point. I am certain that one or all of them will travel there, likely to see to the spell that the sorceress had been casting. We must go there. We must catch them there. If we find the Dragon Rider, he must be killed. That, at least, will spare you from further investigation and retain your rank and your life. If we find only the Northerners, they must be captured. That will prove that they had the darkest of aims for our land, as we always knew they did. It will prove that what we did was the wisest and best decision. It might well save us *both* from the punishment I have earned, but more importantly it might spare our land the touch of further Northern treachery and allow us to make a final push to extinguish the Alliance threat once and for all."

"Yes… yes, of course."

"To achieve this, we will need the full force of your reserves. Every soldier near enough to Lost Shepherd's point to reach it within a few days will need to be deployed immediately. At best you will be facing a dragon. A worst you will be facing a dragon and two potent mystics. Can you get word to the proper individuals to ensure deployment?"

Sallim pulled open a case beneath his seat and began to scrawl a message in a shaky hand. "I'll send the falcon to my quarters with orders to send the messages via mystics. I can have cavalry in place, thirty to fifty men, in less than three days, if the falcon flies fast and true and the mystics do their jobs."

"Then send them there, and we should head there as well. If this is a moment of triumph, we should be on hand to make it clear that *ours* were the minds wise enough to see the danger where others dismissed it."

"But from here it will take more than a week for us to reach Lost Shepherd's Point."

"It is just as well. Even if we miss the moment of glory, very shortly it will serve us both if no one knows where to find us."

"Yes… yes of course." Sallim thumped the roof. "I want us heading to Lost Shepherd's Point, immediately!"

\#

Myranda lay low to Myn's body, trying to hug tight to her back just as Grustim did atop Garr. Her mind was tightly focused on the task of keeping the dragon's energy up. Her eyes were shut, her breathing shallow. Myn could be trusted to find her way, and every last scrap of concentration would be needed to prevent the faithful creature from exhausting herself.

Only once before had Myn flown so quickly, and it was after Myranda had been drenched with excess power while attempting to destroy the open portal. Now she was casting her spell not only without an overabundance of power, but without sleep. Already the worst of the desert was beginning to give way to the more vibrant farmlands of Tressor's heart.

Doubt crept into her mind. What good would she be if she exhausted herself to reach her home? Would *any* amount of speed be sufficient to be of any use? Turiel had faced and at least *survived* both Ether and Ivy, two fellow Chosen who were *more* than formidable…

She shut it all away. There wasn't any room for doubt. New Kenvard was her home, and it needed her. For too long she had walked the north, and now the south, as her people suffered. Now she had the power to do something, to change something. Though she was forced to do battle when necessary, in her heart she was a healer. Her purpose for the last few months had been to mend the wounds of her world and to bring her homeland back to its former glory. To her there was no higher calling, and if it meant she had to give the last full measure of herself, then so be it.

Chapter 9

Myranda was roused from near unconsciousness by the sudden shift forward and downward. Myn, her motions labored and sluggish, was landing. It was impossible to know how much time had passed. The depths of her concentration made the journey seem like an eternity, and yet she was not cognizant of the passage of time. It was at once an odyssey and an instant.

There was no doubt she'd reached the north, however. Traveling by air was a brisk, chilling endeavor, but the air of the Northern Alliance had a painful bite that reminded Myranda just how quickly she'd become accustomed to the warmth of the south. Worse, in her haste to leave, she'd not taken the time to don the layers of warm clothing that would keep the frigid air at bay. It was thus a task for her ailing mind to ward off the bulk of the iciness.

"Myn…" she slurred, blinking away the tears in her eyes and gazing down at the slush and snow coating the fields below. "Are you well? Do you need to rest?"

The dragon's pace suddenly quickened, as though she were a student caught dozing off during a lesson. Myranda knew the poor creature must be at the breaking point. As hard as she'd worked to keep the dragon strong, Myranda knew that the body could only go so long without real nourishment, and there was no substitute for proper sleep.

Night had come while they were traveling, though Myranda didn't know if it was the first night, the second, or even the third since she'd departed. She had the vague memory of stopping briefly and only once, somewhere in Tressor she had hoped would be far enough from prying eyes. At the moment, though, that didn't matter, because two far more pressing things were on her mind. Below and ahead, the city of New Kenvard drew nearer, and it couldn't be clearer that something had happened there, and likely still was.

Its streets were dark, the first sign that something was wrong. There was an enormous amount of work to be done to restore the broken city to its former strength, and the people of Kenvard—*her* people—were more than eager to put their hands to the task. The portions of the city that had been repaired were lively and bustling deep into the night and woke before the sun. There should at least be warm lights glowing in the windows of the homes and businesses nearest to the gate. All was dark and silent.

Beyond the obvious, there was something in the air that only a wizard could truly appreciate. Compared to how still and silent the streets were, the air hummed with an unnatural energy. The city itself seemed to be restless, anxious. She could feel raw emotion weaving through the very wind: anger, fear, confusion. Some of the feelings poured from the residents, huddled within their homes and certain that the dark history of the city was about to repeat itself. Most came from elsewhere, hundreds of minds and souls that seemed to know nothing else but fear and hate. It was something she'd felt at the edge of her mind on nights when the moon was full and the city was still; her carefully attuned spirit was sympathetic to the lost souls drifting in this place, but never had it been so sharp, so intense. Myranda felt as though a thousand indistinct voices were screaming in her mind.

Myn touched down with a heavy gracelessness that underscored the depths of her fatigue. Myranda tumbled from her back, her thin summer boots crunching down into the crust of fresh snow. With no evident explanation, an assortment of carriages and wagons were abandoned near the gate of the city. As she and Myn trudged closer, a pair of familiar faces from the town guard rushed out to meet her.

"Duchess! There is—" the first began.

"Has anyone been hurt?" Myranda asked quickly.

"No, Duchess. The woman arrived two days ago, but few have even seen her. She… she hasn't let anyone leave the city. Everyone who approaches is able to enter, but the horses refuse to leave, and even those who try to leave on foot can't summon the will to step more than a few paces from the walls. The only damage that has been done is a farmer's wagon that was destroyed. He was not inside at the time."

"Have you seen the woman responsible? Is she still here?"

"No one has been able to get close, but we know that she is in the palace. There's… something there. Duchess, she had a… a *thing* with her. It just left the city. It was enormous. I can't begin to describe it. It moved through the north quarter and over the wall."

"Thank you. I want you, *everyone* to get indoors, but everyone should be ready to flee the city. I'll do my best to deal with the woman quickly and calmly, but if the worst comes, I promise you, I will find a way to free the city from her grip so that the rest of you can escape."

"Duchess, are you certain you are strong enough to do this? Are you certain you don't want the guard at your back?"

"She's a sorceress. I don't want anyone without a focused mind and the proper training to go near her. Keep your weapons ready and defend the people, but do not attack and do not worry about me and Myn."

Before the guards had a chance to object further, Myranda and Myn marched along New Kenvard's main street. In the old days the primary road curved around the edge of town and wove back and forth, rendering the wide and open path as indirect as possible in its route to the castle's main gate. Myranda had decided that in rebuilding the city, as a way of showing trust and openness in the aftermath of the war, the street would lead directly from the main gate to the palace gates. Her father, mindful of the city's defense, had not been fond of the idea, but Myranda felt strongly that the best way to defend the city and its people would be to do all that could be done to prevent another war, and this would be yet another layer of motivation to do so.

Myranda tried to gather her strength as she paced along the short stretch of street that had been completed thus far. It was a failed endeavor. She had barely any will left, and from the way Myn's tail dragged and her head hung, without the strength Myranda had been sharing she was on the cusp of collapse.

Only a few dozen paces farther and the road gave way to churned-up, icy earth and scattered rubble. Myranda worked hard to keep her footing, stumbling once and finding Myn quick to lower her head to nudge her back to her feet. The exhaustion was swiftly becoming a distant concern in the face of the growing influence of swirling spirits. The air was thick with unseen wills and minds. For Myranda it felt as though she were trying to push her way through syrup. Even Myn, with her untrained mind, seemed increasingly uneasy. It would take the merest flex of her mind to render the torrent of spirits visible to her, but she dared not. These souls, tormented and angry, were the men and women of her childhood. But for the grace of fate and the hand of a fallen ally, she would be among them. The task ahead was great enough without seeing faces she'd last seen on the most horrific day of her life.

As she climbed the mound of stones that were once part of the palace's outer wall, the press of spirits began to assert itself in a way that Myranda could no longer ignore. Voices whispered in her ears, half-understood cries of anger or pain. Emotions that were not her own caused her heart to race and her hands to shake.

Then, as she crested a second mound of stone that ringed a mostly cleared courtyard that had at one time been the palace entry hall, the force and emotion slipped away. It felt as though she had slipped into the eye of a storm. Ahead of her, Turiel was sitting in a chair assembled from rubble, joined by several hundred tiny black strands.

The sorceress looked as young and vibrant as she ever had. Myranda's epic expenditure of magic and utter physical exhaustion made it appear as though the black-clad necromancer might be a year or two younger. Her thin black lips were curved into an easy smile, and she was carrying on a merry conversation with the empty space beside her chair. Her left hand stirred the air, accenting words with broad gestures, while in her right she clutched the black and white shaft of her repaired staff. The fingers of this hand seemed paler and more delicate than those of her left.

"No, no, I understand that, but you must see things *my* way. They *were* right to do what they did. It was an extreme measure, but as current circumstances indicate, Aneriana *was* a threat to them. You would have done the same. And I…"

She turned to Myranda and Myn, seeming to be pleasantly surprised by the sudden appearance of the wizard and the dragon. "Oh!" She turned aside again. "I *am* sorry. I think you'll see when the task is done." She turned to Myranda again, throwing her arms wide. "Myranda, Myn! It is so *lovely* to finally meet you!"

Myranda gripped her staff tightly and focused her mind as best she could. Myn set her feet and spread her wings, smoke and flame curling from her nostrils.

"Please, please. There is no need for that. Myn, my dear. Mott dug up a gift for you."

She tapped the staff on the ground. A coil of black unwound from it and speared a large burlap sack sitting amid the rubble behind Turiel's makeshift throne. She guided the bag in front of Myn and upended it, spilling some fresh potatoes onto the ground before her.

"Naturally he would have liked to give them to you personally, but I sent him on a bit of an errand. I really think the two of you would make fine playmates for one another."

The dragon peeled her lips back in a snarl and raked the offering aside.

"Turiel, tell me—" Myranda began.

"Myranda, please, sit down. You look fit to collapse," Turiel said.

She sent out two fresh filaments, but Myranda slashed her own staff through the air, striking them down.

"As you wish," Turiel said with a shrug.

"You speak to us as though you know us," Myranda said.

"I do know you. I know you precisely as well as your dear friend Ivy knows you. I thank you for your kindness to her, by the way. Many in your position could never have found it in themselves to open their heart to someone so clearly molded and colored by the enemy, but you took her in, guided her. I speak as one with an unshakable appreciation of all the things the D'Karon have crafted, but I truly believe the best of what Ivy is comes from her soul and what you have helped her to make of it."

"I am told you intend to bring the D'Karon back to this world," Myranda said.

"I mean to do so, yes, and it is quite likely they will return to their agenda, whatever that might be," Turiel said. "This, I imagine, is not acceptable to you. I certainly wouldn't blame you. Unfortunately, this puts us at odds with one another. It's a shame. You seem such a sweet girl."

"I can't let you do this."

"I don't expect you to let me do it, and normally I would be genuinely concerned. But the rather unpleasant history of your homeland and my own particular skills have placed me in a *very* advantageous position. I would ask you to stand aside and let me pass, I really don't want to hurt you, but I think we both know it would be a waste of breath."

"We defeated the D'Karon. We will defeat you," Myranda said.

"Myranda, you are no stranger to the ways of magic. You must have felt the *presence* here. The people of your home, the victims of the massacre, they are *angry*. They are *fearful*. They thirst for *revenge*. You and I know that the D'Karon are the real culprits, but these people went to their grave truly believing that it was the Tressons. *Rare* is the spirit who can learn and grow after they release their grip on the mortal coil. These are the imprints of a whole city that wants nothing more than to see the blood spilled on that day paid back in kind. And that is what I am offering. You've no doubt noticed you've been spared their relentless chaos during our conversation. Do you know why? Because I've *asked* them to. And dark emotions are *dense* with power. It is glorious. I've nearly drunk my fill of it, and there is ever so much more to be had. Perhaps not enough to finish the keyhole, but we both know where I can find the rest. When we're through with our little chat, whether you see the error in your ways or not, I'll be on my way. This is the endgame, Myranda. I'm so sorry. But I want you to know that I don't have any rancor or spite toward you."

"Then *don't do* this."

"Most of it is already done, dear. The storm of souls is roiling. The mystic power is all but fully harvested. Nearly every victim of the massacre is unified in their desire to see me march across the border and harvest what remains to be collected from the spirits I'll find there and the soldiers who shall fall trying to defend it. Only one spirit seems opposed. You're shutting her out right now. In light of the other spirits about, that's a wise decision, but I've convinced the worst of them to keep their distance. For your sake, dear, I think you should have a word with the most stubborn of the spirits."

"You are trying to get me to lower my guard."

"I am, but if you saw what I see, you wouldn't be arguing. I'm doing this *for* you, not *to* you. It is a peace offering. And she seems quite interested in speaking to you... though she keeps calling *you* Myn, rather than your dragon, so I suppose she may be confused."

"She... she called me Myn..." Myranda uttered, her voice distant.

Almost against her will, Myranda let her tightly focused mind shift from blocking out the circling spirits to letting them show themselves in her mind's eye. Instantly a brilliant column of shifting, vaguely human forms flickered into being around her. She could hear them screaming and see their eyes wide and wild. It was a terrifying sight, but one that faded from Myranda's mind almost instantly. Something infinitely more important had taken form before her.

It was the ghostly form of a woman perhaps an inch shorter than Myranda. She looked to be a few years Myranda's senior, and the resemblance between them was pronounced. She was dressed in thick layers, some warm woolen leggings topped with a winter skirt, a jacket, and a gray cloak. Her outfit was neat and professional, the traditional garb of a Kenvardian educator. Though her insubstantial body was muted in its colors, the vivid red shade of her hair was unmistakable.

Myranda covered her mouth, and her vision blurred. "Mother…" she said, tears as present in her voice as her eyes.

"My dear, sweet Myn," said the spirit before her in a voice straight from Myranda's memories.

It was more than she could bear. The tears flowed freely down her face and the breath caught in her chest. Any doubt or suspicion fell away. There could be no deception in this. This was Lucia Celeste, looking precisely as she had the last time Myranda had seen her… the morning of the massacre.

Lucia stepped forward, her hand reaching out in an attempt to brush away the tears. Myranda felt the touch as a distant chill against her skin.

"Mother, I didn't… I didn't know… If I'd known I could have contacted you…"

"Don't… don't, child. Look at you. Look at the woman you've become. I'm so proud of you."

"Why are you still here? Why haven't you moved on?"

"I don't have the answers. I wish I did. Perhaps I knew that someday you would return, that we would have this moment. Perhaps I knew that our fallen city would see life and freedom again at your hands."

"Mother, I… Turiel…"

"I understand. She needs to be stopped," Lucia said.

"Please! Have your moment. I am in no hurry. Mott still hasn't returned, and I would very much like to introduce the two of you before things are forced to become unpleasant," Turiel assured her. There was nothing mocking in her tone. She seemed genuinely pleased to have facilitated this reunion.

"I don't know how much longer we have," Myranda said.

"You look so tired, Myn," Lucia said, again trying to cradle Myranda's cheek.

Myranda smiled through the tears. "No one has called me that in years. No one since you. That's her name now." She glanced to her companion.

The dragon was looking down at her, vague confusion in her expression. The sharp shift in tone seemed to have thrown her. Without any mystic training, she was only weakly aware of Lucia's presence.

"I know," she said. "I've been watching. It has been a joy to see you and your father working together. Myranda… I want you to tell him that I don't blame him for what happened. And tell him to remember that he is still your father, and you are still his daughter. Never forget that you will always need each other."

"I'll remember. I'll always remember," Myranda said.

"Oh…" Turiel cooed. "Don't hold back! Hug her."

Myranda and Lucia looked at the sorceress, each with distrust in their eyes.

"Please!" She clicked the tip of her staff to the ground. "It is my gift to you."

A considerable dose of mystic power flowed into the air, swirling free. The magic was dark, almost black in color, but as it wafted through the air, it lightened, slipping entirely from Turiel's influence and taking on the same faded cold-blue glow of Lucia's form. It gathered around her, feeding her strength until there was the semblance of substance.

Myranda could feel that the power was no longer the necromancer's, that she'd legitimately offered it freely to strengthen Lucia's spirit. She did not pause to consider the riddle of this woman's behavior. She stepped forward and threw her arms around her mother, and felt her mother's arms in return.

She was not greeted by the warmth of a true embrace. What she found instead was something less, and yet something more. It was distant, but real, like a memory of a hug from her childhood somehow drawn into the present.

"I miss you so much…" Myranda whispered.

"I'll never be far away," Lucia murmured in return.

"It is a true mystery to me why so many view necromancers to be evil," Turiel mused, sincere tears in her eyes as she watched the reunion. "Who but we could bring an opportunity such as this to life?"

The tenderness of the moment was finally brought to an end by the clatter of falling stone. A form pushed itself through the churning column of swirling spirits. It was Mott, or more accurately what Mott had become once Turiel had begun to gorge upon the strength of the spirits she had summoned. He looked much as he had before, a jackal head fading into a coiling serpent body with spidery legs and massive wings. The scale, however, was entirely different. Mott was a match for Myn's height now, his muscular serpentine neck as thick and heavily armored as hers. The wings seemed to have been crafted, dragon-like in structure and scale, but inky black and glossy like nothing from nature. As a whole, he almost looked to have been coaxed to this new size specifically to be a match for Myn.

"Ah! Mott. As you see, we have guests," Turiel said. "Myranda, Myn, Lucia, I present to you my dear Motley. I made him myself. Though I tried to build him into something fearsome using the knowledge and materials I was able to glean and salvage from the D'Karon, I simply lacked the depth of knowledge to remake him properly. Fortunately I still remember a bit of what I learned from my dear sister. With the proper power and a bit of knowledge, one can sculpt flesh into the shapes one needs. Mott, tell me, did you do as I asked?"

A baritone chitter rolled from his eager jaw.

"Good, good. Always good to plant a few extra seeds, just in case this season's harvest falls flat. And… oh… I believe the pleasantries are about to end. One of your allies with whom I've had the misfortune of clashing in the past seems to be drawing near."

The wind was indeed kicking up, and doing so in a way that was far more directed and willful than a simple gust or storm. Ether was coming, in one form or another.

"Turiel, please," Myranda said. "You don't need to do this. I assure you, anything you need, anything you wish to do, if it is within my power I will help you. Release the city and end this quest to bring back the D'Karon."

"But it is *not* within your power. It was not within the power of the finest mystic our world has ever known, and for that reason the only recourse is to reach out to minds greater than ours, and those are the D'Karon. My sister fell to the beast of the cave, and with the knowledge and training of the D'Karon, the beast of the cave will fall to me!"

"Turiel, there *is* no beast of the cave."

She narrowed her eyes. "You'll get nowhere with lies, Myranda."

"It is the truth. I've crossed through the cave twice. Those who enter are killed by the cave itself or make their way to a place called Entwell."

"You would have me believe that you could do something my sister could not?"

"It isn't always a matter of skill. Unless you know the dangers and can prepare, luck is even more important. Just tell me your sister's name. She may have made it through, and if you are still alive, she may still be alive in Entwell."

The wind was growing more powerful. Turiel had to raise her voice to be heard.

"If my sister was still alive, I would have felt her presence."

"The mountains around Entwell prevent all but the simplest spells from passing through them. It is what has kept the place so well hidden."

Turiel remained silent for a moment. "That is all terribly convenient, Myranda."

"What have you got to lose by letting me help you? What have you got to lose by seeing if there is any truth to what I say?" Myranda called, the wind howling.

"I could lose it all, Myranda. And too much has been done in the name of this cause to squander it on the word of someone who would do anything to stop me."

"Will you at least tell me how long ago it happened? When did your sister die?"

"It was in the twentieth year of Queen Marrow the fierce. Her triumph over the beast was to be her gift to the queen on the anniversary of her coronation. That much I can never forget. Bid your mother farewell, Myranda. I shall be taking back the strength I have lent her."

Lucia turned, the ghostly glow of her body beginning to grow sharper.

"Myn, my dear child," Lucia said, reaching out and touching Myranda's cheeks. "Take it, and use it well… I'll be with you always."

She stood on her tiptoes and gave Myranda a gentle kiss on her forehead. From the point where her lips pressed to Myranda's skin, the young wizard felt an intense warmth that seemed to wash through her, revitalizing her. By the time she realized that somehow her mother was making a gift of the borrowed power, it was too late to say or do anything but accept the strength she'd been given.

The image of her mother faded before her until it was simply one of a thousand points of light thrown about by the mystic torrent swirling around them. A few final tears ran down Myranda's cheeks and she held out her hand, but the brief respite was over. Her purpose was calling once again.

"Now really, giving up my generously offered power to your daughter? That is genuinely rude," Turiel remarked.

With the fresh magic pulsing through her, Myranda felt almost like herself again. A few days of rest or even a few hours of meditation would have done far more good, but as a gift, it was a godsend. Even after dosing out enough of it to restore Myn to some semblance of fighting shape, Myranda had enough focus and energy in reserve to defend herself and her home… though knowing that the merest fraction of Turiel's power was enough to restore her to this degree was concerning. The woman must be *swimming* in power…

#

The source of the wind, which had now been joined by the first stinging flakes of a fresh snowfall, finally arrived. Myranda had been expecting Ether's windy form, but instead the shapeshifter had assumed a form they'd seen her take only a handful of times. She was a griffin, her front half with the features of an eagle and her rear half with the features of a lion. Her feathers and fur were both slate gray, and two figures were tightly clutching her back. From the looks of it, the form she'd selected was barely large enough to support their combined weight. Perhaps it was for that reason that the wind had been raging along with her, to aide her in lifting them and speed their journey.

She circled around and came down above Myranda, bringing herself to a swift and graceful landing. Ivy and Greydon Celeste shakily tumbled down from her back. The very instant she was no longer supporting them, Ether shifted to flame and launched herself at Turiel.

The dark sorceress raised her staff and stood, sending what at first seemed to be a black cloud from the head of her staff to swirl about Ether's fiery form. As it grew closer to her blazing glow, slivers of the light slipped through, and it became clear that the attack was simply the densest, most agile cluster of black filaments Turiel had yet summoned.

Ether moved like lightning, flitting this way and that in her attempts to reach Turiel, but every tongue of flame was scattered and broken by the thrashing of the threads, and every momentary pause was punished by a dozen of them lancing through her.

"Mott, dear, if the dragon does anything unpleasant, you see to her. I'll handle the elemental," Turiel said, the merest flutter of effort in her tone.

"Myn, stand guard and be ready to protect the city," Myranda crisply ordered. "Don't fight unless you have to. I don't want this clash to threaten any of the people. Kenvard has seen enough bloodshed for a hundred lifetimes."

"Myranda!" Ivy said, running up to her and throwing her arms around her. "I'm so glad to see you. Please! Give me something to do! Every decision I make on my own seems to go terribly wrong."

"How are you? Are you strong? Rested?" Myranda asked.

"I'm not hurt, but I can barely think straight," Ivy said, stepping aside and looking upon the manic clash going on. "How did Mott get so *big*?"

"We've been traveling for two straight days. Barely a nibble of food and only what rest can be had while clinging to the back of a griffin," Greydon explained. "I don't imagine any of us are as strong as we might be."

"When fate sees fit to challenge us, it seldom waits until we are ready," Myranda said.

"Have you been crying?" Greydon asked, wiping away a tear.

She took his hand from her face and clutched it tight for a moment. "I have so much to say to you, but there is no time now. Please, get to the town, make sure no one panics, make sure the town guard is prepared to keep the people safe, and find out the status of the troops. We've all been out of communication for two full days at a time when war could come at any hour. If we cannot contain Turiel, she will seek the front, and she *cannot* be allowed to reach it."

Greydon gave a stiff nod and moved as quickly over the rubble as his limbs would allow.

The air filled with an inhuman shriek of anger and all eyes but Greydon's turned to Ether. She was at the center of a thicket of threads, searing her way through them as quickly as Turiel could conjure them and inching steadily closer. She was blindingly brilliant, illuminating Turiel's features as she began to show the stress of battle.

Myranda stalked forward, her own staff raised, and began to pull her mind to the task of dispelling the dark workings of Turiel's own magic. Each wave of blue-white light that pulsed from her staff's gem caused the lashing swirl of black threads to wither just that much more and allowed Ether to advance just that much closer.

"I'm begging you, Turiel, before anyone else gets hurt, let us discuss this reasonably. Let us—"

"I am truly sorry, Myranda, but I'm years past the point of reason," she interrupted. "And what I do now, I do only because you've forced me to."

She dropped to one knee and clutched her staff tight with both hands. The threads slashing at Ether instead wove themselves into a dense shield to protect her. Answering some unheard call, the swirling torrent of spirits curled around behind her and descended upon the heroes like locusts upon a field.

Icy phantom fingers clutched Ether's form and hauled her back. Spirits fell upon Myn, each ghastly blow seeming to cut into not the flesh but the soul, jolting the dragon with pain that went beyond the limits of mere injury.

Myranda burst forward and thrust her staff down, driving it into the cobbles and wrapping her mind tightly around it. The rush of spirits parted around her like the flow of a river around a bridge's supports.

Myn ducked down into the void in the storm of souls that Myranda created, and Ivy huddled close. For a few heroic moments it seemed that Ether would still get her hands about the throat of the necromancer, but floating as she was in the focal point of the spectral flood, it was only a matter of time before she was thrown back. She shifted to stone midair and thumped to the ground. The rush of angry spirits forced her back across the ground, but she dug her toes into the bricks beneath her and stomped forward.

Myranda squinted through the brilliant flow of spirits, their unearthly chill cutting her to the very soul. Ether's determination was remarkable. Even as the constant assault of the massacre's victims caused cracks to feather her stony surface, she didn't falter.

Turiel watched as Ether drew nearer, but the sorceress appeared unconcerned in the face of the furious shapeshifter. She'd let her shield fall away and now wore an expression that was almost bemused.

"I would suggest that you are pushing me to make a very unpleasant decision, but I believe it has been established that you don't care about such things, do you, Ether?" Turiel asked calmly. "Very well. Mott, defend Mommy."

The screeching rush of spirits suddenly scattered, becoming less focused on Ether in particular and more of an indistinct hailstorm of unguided rage. Ether thundered two steps closer before Mott's massive jaws snapped around her, grinding angrily at her body before he whipped his head aside, hurling her in a high arc over the city walls.

Myn took the act as an invitation to finally charge into battle, leaping over Myranda and enduring the stray attack of an angry spirit as she kept her eyes set on the monstrosity ahead. She drew in a deep breath and released it as a shaft of flame toward Mott. He yelped in surprise and coiled his long body barely around the attack, essentially dodging in all directions at once. It spared him the burn, but left him in no position to dodge the dragon's charge. A titanic, fleshy thud and a yowl of pain signaled the impact as Myn drove her lowered head into the armored scales of Mott's underbelly. Scratching, spindly legs wrapped around her, driving their claws into her scales. His long body constricted around hers, immobilizing her legs and wings. It took every ounce of his strength and all of his attention, but Mott was just barely able to keep Myn occupied, tangling with her and rolling about the ruins of the castle.

"Now do you see what you've done?" Turiel called to Myranda. "I've lost the attention of the spirits. What they do to the city and its people is entirely on *your* head."

Myranda turned to the reconstructed southern side of the city. Indeed, though they were not doing so in a concentrated or dedicated way, the points of light representing the angered shades of people she'd once called her countrymen were diving and sweeping among those places where the living residents of New Kenvard had taken shelter.

The young wizard did not take the time to waste words. Almost without thought she found herself rushing over the piles of rubble, raising her staff and steadying her mind. Spirits were things of magic and emotion. Some, like that of her mother, were thinking things, capable of compassion and reason. Those who tore at the town were not. The aspects of the heart and mind that defined a human or other sapient creature had been burned away in the heat of the tragedy that had ended their lives. These were *not* the people she had known in life. These were the stains in the living fabric of her world that were left by the massacre. They were shadows, twisted and grotesque mockeries of what they had been. Until whatever held them here could release them, Myranda knew that they felt only the torturous need to spread their dark feelings to others.

She had to forget who they were and treat them as the force of nature they had become. And unlike a normal storm, which could be held at bay by a sturdy roof and stout walls, these spirits passed effortlessly through the wood and stone. Their grim attacks could only damage the living. The people were defenseless. Myranda had to do something to give her people a chance.

By the time she skidded to a stop in the center of the restored portion of the city, she had her answer. Now the only concern was if she had the skill and strength to work the appropriate spells, and if Turiel would allow her to do so…

#

Ivy stood her ground among the rubble of the castle. A blue aura flashed and swirled about her, but she managed to keep her terror in check. The only weapon she had, besides the teeth and claws she knew would do her little good against someone like Turiel, was the bow and arrow. She set her feet and reached back for the quiver, her shaking fingers finding the fletching of one of the shafts. As she nocked the arrow and began to draw the string, the malthrope saw Turiel turn her eyes to Ivy, seemingly disappointed by what she saw.

"Ivy. You know what I know now," Turiel said, her posture relaxed and her voice reasonable. "And I know what you know. Life has been difficult for us both, but you *must* see that even if these people have always meant the best for the world, I must honor my task. I mustn't let my crimes be without reason!"

"Turiel, there is a better way," Ivy said.

"No! There is *not!* The D'Karon are the only way!" Turiel growled. She stirred the air with her staff. "And they have left enough of themselves behind in this city to *prove that!* Do you recall what the D'Karon made of this place once it was theirs? I know that you do. I saw it in your mind. It was a place for the *manufacture* of their foot soldiers. This is the place where so many of their nearmen were created. And though you and the others have worked to clear them away, there were still *plenty* of pieces to be put to good use. And I've been quite busy with them."

Threads began to spiral down the staff and slip between the cracks of the stone at her feet.

"Don't! I won't let you!" Ivy cried.

She took aim and fired. Alas, a few hours of training even at the hands of someone as skilled and patient as Celeste were not sufficient to keep her hands steady and her aim true in such trying circumstances. The arrow hissed through the air, missing Turiel by more than a foot.

Ivy cried out in frustration and reached for another arrow.

"There, there. No one is perfect," Turiel said encouragingly. "I'm sure in time you'll—"

The necromancer stopped suddenly and looked up, raised her staff above her head, and braced it with both hands. A fraction of a heartbeat later, a form from above came slamming down atop her. It was Ether. She must have shifted to wind and climbed high above the battleground, then shifted to stone again above her target. Unlike Ivy's arrow, the shapeshifter's aim was true. She struck with such force that both she and Turiel punched through the stone floor, crashing down into the lower level of this section of the fallen castle.

Ivy raced up to the hole and peered down just as a flare of fire cast light all around. Ether was in her fiery form now, swiping and darting around Turiel as she frantically raised any defense she could to deflect the willful flames. The malthrope's eyes widened as she saw what *else* the light fell upon.

All around the fierce battle was devastation. Not a single support column was fully intact. Many sections of floor had fallen away to still deeper layers of the castle's catacombs. Walls were mostly rubble and fractured stone. She wondered how the heaps of collapsed palace walls that were mounded above had remained where they were rather than collapsing further into the hollows and voids below. From the worrying way the ground shuddered and quaked with each blow from Ether or Myn, she very much doubted the castle would remain as intact as it was for much longer.

Worse even than the likely collapse was the fact that Ether and Turiel were not alone in the bowels of the castle. Motion drew her eyes to the shifting shadows cast by the mounds of stone. Several hundred forms, most dressed in twisted but functional armor, were pulling themselves from the rubble. Nearmen... Ivy had been foolish enough to believe that she'd been done with them, that she'd seen the last of the blasted playthings of the D'Karon. Seeing them again, knowing what they had done, and that so many of them had been lurking even in their inert form within the place she called a home was enough to tip the emotional balance firmly in the direction of anger.

Her fist tightened around the grip of the longbow and long wisps of red aura flicked and rolled around her. She dropped the bow and slowly slipped the quiver from her back, teeth bared and eyes darkened. As much as she'd tried to suppress the emotions that would claim her mind and body, those things that would turn her into the weapon the D'Karon had meant her to be, in this moment the strength that flooded through her and the pure, righteous fury that welled in her chest were welcome. Right now a weapon was what she needed to be. But tooth and claw would only get her so far. She needed to be properly armed if she was to be any good to her friends.

Realization dawned a moment later. This was New Kenvard. This was her home.

"Keep her busy, Ether," Ivy called, her lips curving into a fierce grin. "I'll be right back…"

#

Myn struggled against Mott, but the stitched-together concoction of a beast was far stronger than he had any right to be. His powerful tail was clutched so tight around the dragon she could scarcely breathe, and his long neck was cinched tight around her head and snout, leaving her flame to spray uselessly from her nostrils. The one saving grace was that it was taking every ounce of his considerable strength to keep his grip on her, and as eager to please as he was, he lacked anything resembling skill and tactics. His combat was centered on raw strength and frenzied attacks.

She rolled to the side and shook her body, managing to dislodge the coils trapping her wings. Instantly she put them to work, catching the rushing wind and flexing hard. Three mighty flaps got Mott and Myn airborne. The familiar tried to work his own wings to bring their flight under control, but the tug-of-war in the air was impossible for him to win. Instead, every flap of his wings drew more and more of his long body away from hers until finally her claws were free.

The dragon slashed viciously at Mott, carving deep gashes into his armored hide. If the monster had any blood to spill, there was little doubt it would be running freely. When her jaws slipped free of his coils, she belched a potent blast of flame that seared and blackened the scraggly fur of Mott's face, inspiring the monster to release her entirely.

For several seconds the two creatures hung in the air measuring the other and planning their next attack. As Myn tensed herself to swoop in and attempt to end the battle, she realized that the gashes on his belly were visibly closing. Even the blackness of his fur was fading quickly. He was healing. In seconds the worst of the damage was gone.

Mott grinned, his eyes flashing with defiance as he finished recovering. The creature seemed to be utterly reveling in the thrill of combat, madness driving his motions as he caught a fresh gust of wind with his wings and was pulled higher before tucking them back and plummeting toward her.

She pulled aside, but his body lashed wildly from side to side and his spearing legs spread like a net. The sheer size of the attack made it impossible to dodge cleanly. The very tip of his tail caught the base of her wings, and he coiled three quick loops about them, robbing her of her mobility and sending the pair plummeting down like stones.

They struck the ground with punishing force in a still-ruined section of the northern portion of the city. Mott, though he took his share of the impact, never stopped tearing and scrabbling at Myn. The tips of his spidery legs worked like the picks of a mining team, chattering and chipping at the same concentrated section of Myn's side until finally they broke through her scales.

The dragon howled in pain, throwing her mouth wide. A small shiny stone, one that had been pinned carefully beneath her tongue until now, flew free and clattered to the deserted street.

Myn tore herself away from Mott and rolled to her feet, collecting herself while Mott retreated again to let the latest damage mend itself. As he did, he clacked to the dislodged stone and sniffed at it. It wasn't until she saw Mott nudge it with his nose that Myn realized she'd lost Garr's gift. Seeing him touching the prized possession caused her to grow rigid with anger.

Mott glanced up and saw the look of challenge in Myn's eyes. He grinned mischievously, scuttling over the stone and raising his two foremost spider legs over it. Myn released a warning rumble, but this only seemed to encourage the creature. With a fiendish chitter of glee, he stomped and smashed at the stone, driving it into the street.

The sound that came next was enough to give even the manic familiar pause.

Myn's claws cut deep into the stone of the street and she drew in a breath, releasing it in a roar of utter burning fury. Eyes gleaming with white-hot rage, she broke into a charge. Mott's ears flattened to his head, his eyes widened, and he pulled his neck back. The canine features and posture gave him the uncanny look of a mutt who had just discovered he wasn't the biggest dog in the pack.

#

Myranda finally unleashed the spell she'd been crafting. Though she'd had great success producing off-the-cuff effects by carefully weaving her will into the elements around her, something that would remain strong and focused to its task even after she'd moved on was another matter entirely. Deacon made it look like child's play, but it was akin to building a castle without any planning and expecting it to stand against a storm.

She poured the last dose of her will into place. The effect was, to her great relief, immediate. The rampaging spirits had left her with more than a few ghostly scrapes along her arms and across her face as she tried to focus, but it was worth it. Where once they had passed through the restored walls of the repaired section of the city, now they clashed and rebounded from them. Myranda had imbued the physical structures with a measure of substance even in the spectral realm, allowing them to offer the same protection from spirits as they did from creatures of flesh and blood.

A few of the spirits had been trapped inside, but her subjects were no fools, and a spirit is no fonder of being a prisoner than a living being. The instant a door or window was opened, the insubstantial form swept clear. Slowly the spirits began to withdraw from the inhabited part of the city. One of the enchantments she'd layered upon the stone was a twist of magic that had roughly the same effect as a bright light cast into a cluster of insects. It filled the spirits with unease, repelling them.

Myranda stumbled as the focus of her mind finally released. The borrowed strength was all but gone now, and judging from the almost searing glow in her mind's eye that was surging from the remains of the castle, Turiel was anything but defeated. She tried to head for the palace again, but her limbs were slow to obey, numbed as they were by the cold and the attacks she'd weathered.

"Myranda," her father called, rushing to her side.

"Is everyone all right?" Myranda asked.

"People are frightened, and some people have felt the touch of these... things in the air. But the cries have died down and no one has called out for the healers," he said. "Myranda, you cannot push yourself this way. If you are too weak, you must leave it to others."

"The others are doing all they can. I must do the same," she said. "What have you heard of the troops?"

"It isn't good. Things have grown tense. Troops are streaming to the front. The region is a powder keg. Spotters say just across the border, Crestview has called up a whole regiment of soldiers. We've been forced to do the same. If there is any sign of hostility at the former front, there will be a full-scale battle."

Myranda put her fingers to her face, trying to clear her thoughts. "Father... if I were to go to the front, do you believe I could command the troops? Could I maintain discipline, even in the face of orders that may be against all they believe?"

"Myranda, these are Alliance soldiers. They will follow your orders."

"Good... then stand ready... Turiel's focus is shifting, I can feel it. She will move to the front, and I truly do not believe we will be able to stop her. If she makes it there, I must follow, and I must make it clear, crystal clear, that our troops are dedicated to stopping her and her creations. The Tressons are *not* the enemy. Turiel is. This is not an attack by the north upon the south, this is an attack by a madwoman against our whole world. We are *allies*. Do you believe you can make the soldiers understand?"

"They won't need to understand. They will do as they are told because you have earned their trust and respect and they have pledged their loyalty to you."

Myranda nodded, then raised her eyes to the churning spirits above. Now repelled by the shelters keeping the people of the city safe, they seemed drawn instead to the ruins of the castle. The ground shook and rattled with unseen impacts. Some came from the north, where Myn's savage roars and Mott's startled yelps told the story of at least one battle that was going well for the heroes. The rest seemed to originate from below the ground itself. One by one the spirits slipped down through the debris of the castle, joining the source of the battle.

She turned to her father. "If you're satisfied the people here will be safe, take some men and wait by the southern gate. Turiel… she's terrifyingly powerful. I can feel her will from here, the instructions and commands she is giving. If we can't stop them, something will be coming this way, and it will be moving fast."

"We will be ready," Greydon said. He touched her arm. "Be careful, Myranda."

"I'll try," Myranda said, rushing toward the castle. "But the time for care is a rare luxury these days."

She'd only just quickened to a sprint when Ivy skidded out of a side alley and nearly crashed into her. The malthrope was carrying a bundle of cloth and tugging at the twine that secured it.

"Myranda!" Ivy said, startled by her near collision.

"Ivy, what's going on in the castle?"

She answered while keeping pace with Myranda, still distracted by the cloth bundle. "Ether and Turiel are fighting, and Turiel is starting to wake up the bits and pieces of nearmen that were in the catacombs. Or put them together. Or make new ones. I'm not entirely sure, but there are a lot of them. A hundred at least. … Come on! Stupid knot!" She finally gave up on finesse and dragged her claws through the twine, sheering it easily into pieces and revealing the contents of the bundle.

Two stunning and ornate blades had been carefully wrapped in the cloth, each with a horizontal grip, a wide blade, and a faintly glowing gem set in the center. They were curious weapons crafted specifically for Ivy, something their designer called Soul Blades.

Grinning like a child given permission to play with one of her favorite toys, Ivy clutched the grips and brandished the weapons. The gems took on an increasingly intense glow, the color yellow with pulses taking it closer to orange at times. Matching blades that were nearly long enough to drag the ground continued the line of her arm, and elegant carvings and etchings made them as much the appearance of museum pieces as weapons of war. Such was the hallmark of their maker, a man called Desmeres Lumineblade.

She had only just properly armed herself, and hence had a moment to spare a glance toward the castle again, when Myranda held out a hand and stopped her from running.

The wizard and her ally stared at the ring of rubble that separated the courtyard battleground from the rest of the city. Something was cresting over it… No… *many* things were cresting over it. They weren't the intangible spirits that had caused so much damage thus far. In fact, with each new dim form crawling over the rubble, there seemed to be one fewer of the floating spirits. These were human forms.

"The nearmen…" Myranda said, her voice hushed. "She's… Turiel is allowing the spirits to take the nearmen as hosts. She's given flesh to the lingering remnants of this city, echoes of lost lives. Things that know only hatred and fear…"

"Why would she do it?" Ivy said, taking a steadying breath and brandishing her blades. A telling dose of blue briefly swirled within the gems.

"To free her mind of the burden of controlling the nearmen? To draw our attentions away from her? What does it matter? If they truly are fueled by the desire for revenge, then they now have all they need to take that revenge. A hundred men in Alliance armor rushing in a blood rage for the border, and with troops already tense for war… we can't let them by, Ivy. Not *one*."

Ivy nodded, her eyes gleaming almost as much as her blades, clearly pleased to have a simple task with a simple solution.

"Okay then…"

#

Ether was rationing her power, trying to rely as much as possible on physical strength rather than magic. She spent most of her time as stone, absorbing attacks and answering them in kind. Only when it would reap tremendous rewards did she squander the power to flash to flame, and even then only briefly. In any other battle the tactic would have brought the clash to an end minutes ago. At this time, and in this place, Turiel was inexhaustible. Even so, she was only mortal. A physical form such as hers could only channel so much power at a time, and it could only endure so much damage. Every blow, even a glancing one, took its toll on the necromancer.

"The gods chose wisely when they chose you as their protectors," Turiel said, her voice strained as she barely deflected a blow that could well have ended her.

The shapeshifter didn't dignify her with banter or threats in response, choosing instead to keep up the intensity of her attacks. At the edge of her mind she became aware that things were not progressing as she'd expected. As the necromancer grew more desperate and closer to her limit, her attacks should have become more frenzied and frequent, or so Ether anticipated. She expected the spirits to be sicced upon her like attack dogs, or for the nearmen being drawn from the wreckage to hurl themselves upon her. Instead, the nearmen were ignoring her, and the spirits seemed to have vanished entirely.

Turiel tipped her staff forward and blasted Ether with an incredibly potent burst of energy. The shapeshifter scattered into her wind form, dodging the blast. Until now she'd avoided the form of wind because this disciple of the D'Karon was clearly no stranger to their penchant for absorbing power, and her windy form was a veritable banquet of energy without much at all in the way of defense. Even in the brief moment she'd spent in the form, she could feel Turiel eagerly pulling at her reserves. Ether did not give her a chance to capitalize, instead whisking above her foe and drawing swiftly to stone again.

Her heavy form dropped down atop Turiel, too near to dodge and too massive to deflect. The blow forced her to the ground. Ether reached out with her stony hands, closing them about Turiel's throat. The necromancer's eyes were wide, her expression glazed with insane exhilaration. Black bands, stouter by far than anything she'd conjured to this point, burst from the ground and coiled around Ether, splitting until they'd encircled her very fingers.

For the moment, the strength of each was a match for the other as she lay pinned. Her voice a whisper slipping through her half-strangled throat, Turiel spoke again.

"I would have dearly loved to finish the lot of you before reopening the path for the D'Karon. I suppose it should be no surprise to find those warriors who could overcome the wise and powerful D'Karon would be more than a match for myself, even diminished by one as you are."

Ether felt a surge of anger at these final words. Seeing it flicker through the glassy stone eyes brought an even broader grin to the face of the foe.

"There… that is something, isn't it? I dealt little with Epidime, but he had always insisted the greatest weakness was always the mind…" Her eyes darted indistinctly for a moment, remembering. "Ah. Ah! Ivy is *certain* you had love for the fallen one, Lain…"

"I will *not* hear you speak his name!" Ether hissed, squeezing tighter. "You defiled his resting place! His name is too good for your traitorous lips!"

The shapeshifter could feel the strands of magic burning at her, trying like leaches to drink away her power. If she was anything but stone it would be unbearable, but even so, they were like living iron, peeling her grip open and inch by inch lifting her away from the pinned necromancer.

"And there we see the wisdom of his words," Turiel said. "Look how it scatters your mind so, robs focus from the task at hand. You really have *no* idea how to cope with such things… Your beloved Lain… he's passed on, hasn't he? Dead, and without a trace? Pity… I'm sure his body would have been a fine thing to breathe life into. In death he would no doubt have made a fine ally for me. Perhaps his soul is still lingering in that place? Would it please you if I plucked him from his rest to tell you what you already know? That he didn't love you in return? That he could *never* love you?"

Ether fought viciously against her bonds, but they were just strong enough to keep her in place. Her mind burned with hate and pain at Turiel's words, stealing away precious focus from her efforts. Smaller threads snaked around Turiel herself, sliding her from beneath Ether and dragging her upright, like the strings of a puppeteer. The bands holding Ether did the same, leaving the pair eye to eye. Turiel's lips were tight together, her brow knitted with conflict.

"Apologies are in order. That was uncalled for. Effective though it was, I'm afraid such attacks are not to my taste. I'd never sought Epidime specifically as a mentor for that precise reason. There's no reason to be *cruel*. I only want you dead. I don't want to torture you." The conflict left her face, replaced with certainty. "But I *will* finish you if you give me the chance. Another time, elemental, and this battle would be yours. But not here, and not now. In this place of death and fear, *I* am the one who will be standing when the battle ends. Your power will wane. Mine will continue to flow. Remain as stone and I shall grind you to powder. Turn to flesh and I shall rip you to shreds. Turn to anything else and I will drink away your power. Leave this place and I will go about my task. I think the choice is clear."

Ether's fury was bold upon her face, her eyes locked upon Turiel's. As wise as it might be to retreat, to regroup, and to face this foe again with her allies to help her, Ether knew that she could never allow such a thing. As she ran through the ways she might regain the upper hand, and tried to push away the sting of emotion that was even now sapping her focus further, she realized that while many forms were in motion around them, nearmen rising under the control of vengeful spirits, one of them was unlike the others. It was a pale figure, moving slowly but with purpose…

Turiel noticed the look in Ether's eye and turned to the approaching form, stepping aside to give the shapeshifter a clearer view.

"Oh good gracious, Aneriana. I believe I was clear when I said I was through with you. Back to your slumber with you," Turiel said.

Though the final words seemed a simple statement, Ether felt a pulse of power behind them. Turiel was trying to dispel the unnatural life that animated the much abused being. Nevertheless, still she stalked. She had only one hand remaining, the other having been taken to replace Turiel's own. But in her one hand was a gleaming sword.

Turiel placed her hand on her side and tipped her head. "Well then… you aren't acting alone, are you? Is that… so it is. Really now, Lucia. I'm genuinely regretting giving you a moment with your daughter. Evidence that no good deed goes unpunished. And did Rassa give you *permission* to use his sword?"

"You want to hurt my world. You want to hurt my city," said Aneriana, her voice entwined with that of Lucia Celeste, who had for the moment taken refuge within her form just as so many other spirits had slipped into the nearmen. "You want to hurt my *daughter*."

"All of those things are merely the unavoidable consequence of my *true* aim. There's nothing personal in any of it. Now please. Be *gone!*"

This final command was accompanied by a swipe of her staff, but Lucia responded in kind, whipping her arm with unnatural speed and sending the sword hurtling in Turiel's direction. Turiel's attack did its work, striking Aneriana's body and Lucia's spirit as one. The body tumbled to the ground, and the spirit was banished from within, but not before the blade met its mark as well. It sank a third of its length into the shoulder of her staff arm.

The sorceress stumbled backward, crying out in agony. When she clutched the blade to pull it free, her cries only increased as flickers and flares of golden light curled out from the weapon wherever it touched her. She lurched in pain before finally wrenching it free. The wound gaped for a moment, light shining through but no blood flowing. Then the same threads that accompanied all of her spells bridged the opening and began to pull its ends shut, but the injury seemed reluctant to close.

"Quite the..." she gasped, stumbling back against a pile of rubble, "remarkable sword..." She coughed, flecks of black spattering her lips and chin. "It shouldn't even have reached me."

Ether redoubled her efforts as she felt the bands holding her weaken in response to the attack.

Turiel turned to her, gritting her teeth and trying to maintain her hold, but it was clear that Ether would soon break free.

"I suppose you think this is the tipping point? That you've won now?" Turiel said. "The first lesson I learned from the D'Karon, the very *reason* I was sent to open the second keyhole, was that one should *never* have only one plan in place. As we speak, my dear Mott is ending that dragon of yours."

The ceiling of the chamber shook, dust pouring down and whole stones dislodging and clattering to the ground.

"There? You see? That is probably the sweet little darling coming home now to—"

A second rumble shook the chamber, and a section of roof slumped inward under the weight from above. When the dust cleared, the slightly brighter light of the now-visible night sky revealed both Mott and Myn. The familiar looked badly battered and was barely moving. Straddling the beast was Myn, scored with slashes and dripping blood from a few wounds, but with triumph in her eyes.

"Ah..." Turiel said. "Well then... I can only imagine how well the rest of my precautions are faring."

Ether tore one arm entirely free from its bonds while Myn stalked toward Turiel.

"I… believe Kenvard has given me all the strength it can spare," she said. "Best to leave this place."

She clacked her staff down, and six black voids appeared, growing swiftly into portals arrayed around her. With a flick of her wrist she sent the prone form of Aneriana flying through one of them. The sword was sent through another, and those bands still binding Ether began to drag her through a third. She fought against them, unwilling to lose the time it would take to return to this place from wherever she might be sent.

Myn stalked closer, attempting to reach Turiel, but the portals were close around her. Though each was far too small to allow her through, Myn was cautious not to venture too near. She'd seen what could happen to anything that only passed partway through such a thing before it closed.

"You seem a reasonable beast," Turiel said, slipping through one of them. "It would behoove you to leave this place before any of these gateways close… beginning with *that* one."

In response, one of the six portals began to swiftly contract. Ether was almost free, her eyes set upon Turiel as the dragon looked to her.

"Go, beast! I will see to her," Ether demanded.

Myn swiftly obeyed, leaping into the air and whisking toward the rebuilt portion of the capital with the speed of a creature that knew all too well how potent the forthcoming eruption of magic might be. Ether finally fought free of the final bond just a moment before she would have been dragged through one of the portals and instead bounded through the one Turiel had used to escape. It led to the windswept and icy stone surface of Demont's fort that had played host to their prior battle, but Turiel did not seem to be present. Ether looked all around, the portal behind her beginning to close, then finally took the gamble of shifting to wind. It would leave her open to attack, certainly, but it would also allow her to search the area in moments.

The instant she shifted to air, her awareness became unfocused. Encompassing every breeze and current of air, she became painfully aware of two things. The first was that Turiel was not here, or at least, was not here any longer. The other was that there existed a second portal…

She streaked toward it, hooking over the edge of the seaside cliff and discovering that this escape portal was located halfway down the cliff side. The bite taken out of the cliff beside it suggested it was precisely where the first portal had been, the one that brought Turiel to Kenvard. It too was closing. She quickened her pace, rushing toward it, and managed to slip through an instant before it closed entirely.

Ether realized as she whisked into the portal what Turiel had done, and cursed the cleverness of it. Of the six portals she had opened, not one but two of them had been to Demont's fort. She'd slipped through one and back into the other. Ether caught only a brief glimpse of her, riding atop a badly ailing but still very much alive Mott. After that, the first of the portals closed, unleashing its torrent of energy with Ether directly beside it.

#

Myranda and Ivy had their hands full with the rush of possessed nearmen charging from the castle. Both of the heroes had the misfortune of having been a part of many battles before, but in nearly all of them their foes had been trying to kill them. The armored, mindless things rushing through the ruined streets of New Kenvard were barely aware of Myranda or Ivy, their eerie eyes set to the south and their movements tireless and unnaturally fast. Myranda attempted to dispel the spirits driving them, but either Turiel had worked a spell to protect them, or the years of torment had hardened their will. Only focusing on one at a time could tear the souls from their hosts, and more often than not they found their way back inside. The only way was to defeat the nearmen and deprive the spirits of new vessels.

This, at least, was a task Ivy was grateful to do. Chasing down and slicing up creatures that weren't technically alive and didn't even fight back was a delightfully uncomplicated way to indulge the predatory instincts she'd been forced to suppress for so long. For once, she was putting weapons to work not out of fear or anger, but out of duty and defense. She sprinted through the streets, bounding over mounds of rubble and flicking her blades through the air. Their spectacularly sharp edges slipped effortlessly through armor and artificial flesh alike, causing the sprinting soldiers to collapse into dust. Thrill and exhilaration flowed through Ivy as she chased down those nearest the walls, then slid to a stop to angle her ears toward the pounding boots of her next target.

The wizard took to the task a bit more grimly. She couldn't move as quickly as her ally, and as crucial as it was to strike down these soldiers, it burned at her to have brought battle to her streets again. Nevertheless, there was a job to do. She summoned flashes of flame to sear away some nearmen. Others were buffeted with intense winds to gather them into clusters before striking them with bolts of destructive magic. She worked precisely, surgically. There must be *no* damage to the rest of the city. Too much time and effort had been invested rebuilding her home for it to be broken again.

For all their efforts, Myranda and Ivy couldn't stop every soldier. Some made it as far as the wall. Celeste had gathered the guard and spread them among the choke points, the streets and alleys between the buildings. Bows were pulled taut; volleys of arrows launched at the fast-moving forms as they emerged from the shadows. Some fell, others didn't, passing instead to the next line of defense. City guards with swords struck and slashed, men with great shields formed mobile walls, pushing the nearmen back and jabbing them with pikes. The scattering of foes that made it through and survived to scale the wall or whisk through the gates were targeted by a final row of archers stationed on the wall itself. With the open field south of the city sprawling out before them with no cover, the nearmen were easy targets.

Joseph R. Lallo

The flood of haunted constructs had slowed to a near stop when the thunderous bursts erupted from the ruined castle. One by one the portals shut, releasing their miscast overabundance of energy as raw destruction. Massive plumes of dust and stone rose into the air. There was little structure still standing in that part of the city. Most of the castle was little more than gravel at this point. But even if it had still been the grand symbol of her land that it had been in her youth, Myranda's concern for its destruction would have paled in comparison to the other things threatened by the blasts. Ivy skidded into the main street and locked Myranda in her gaze, the two heroes of one mind.

"Did they all get out!? Is Myn okay? Is Ether?" Ivy cried.

The malthrope turned and looked with agonizing concern over the center of the city. Myranda swept instead with her mind, but the burst of D'Karon magic hung like a thick, toxic fog over the city. It blotted out everything else.

"There! There, I see Myn!" Ivy said, jumping up and down and waving her blades in the air.

Myranda looked to the sky and could just barely make out the silhouette of her friend wheeling down from the cloud of dust and circling toward them.

Ivy hung her blades at her belt and ran to the dragon as she touched down wearily. The malthrope dove at Myn, wrapping her arms around the base of her neck and hugging tight.

"Myn, did Ether get clear? Did she follow Turiel?" Myranda asked.

The dragon turned and looked to the castle, her expression anything but certain.

"No…" Ivy said, looking again to the castle.

Through the concern, Myranda forced herself to remain focused on the task.

"They were portals, weren't they? Turiel opened portals?"

Myn nodded. This much was certain.

"What about Mott? Was he still alive?"

Myn nodded again. Myranda brushed her fingers across the dragon's hide, looking anxiously at the assortment of injuries great and small.

"You're hurt…" Myranda said. "Let me—"

The dragon pulled away as Myranda readied her staff to heal her and gave the wizard a defiant look. She was evidently mindful of how near her limit Myranda was and how much of their task remained.

"Don't be stubborn, Myn, you need your health. Just hold still so I can—"

Myn huffed her breath and stomped a foot, her expression quite firm.

"Fine, I don't have time to argue. If you feel strong enough, go and find Mott. There's no sense trying to track Turiel by the portals, she could have used any of them. But with her beast, we'll at least have more to go by."

Myn nodded and galloped off toward the castle. Ivy dashed after her, and when Myranda was confident the town guard could handle last of the flood of nearmen, she followed. She'd not made it halfway there when Myn came bounding back, fury in her eyes. From the way she was whipping her head about, gazing at the sky and sniffing at the air, Mott had not been where she'd left him, and there was no trace.

"No," Myranda said, her fingers tightening around her staff and her eyes shutting tight. "I won't lose her after getting so close. This woman, as mad as she may be, is frighteningly clever. Her goal is to get to the front. If the massacre was able to provide her with this much power, then I hesitate to imagine what the front will provide. Kenvard is by far the closest D'Karon portal point to the front. She wouldn't have left this place."

She gazed up at the sky, following the tower of choking dust up to the clouds.

"She covered her tracks, mystically and visually. Brilliant… Myn, can you fly?"

Myn responded by unfurling her wings and looking to the sky. Myranda climbed onto her back.

"Ivy, I know you don't want to hear this but—"

"I'll stay here and see if I can figure out where Ether went," Ivy said, predicting her assignment.

"Tell father to head south as soon as he's certain the city is secure. If Turiel reaches it, I suspect she won't be difficult to find…"

"I will, and when I've got Ether sorted out I promise I'll be by your side as soon as possible."

Myranda nodded. "One way or another, Ivy. This ends today."

#

The journey south had not been a pleasant one for Deacon. He and Myn had gotten off to a bad start, but when the time came to fly with her, she'd at least always allowed him on her back. As such was against a very ancient and sacred tradition among the Dragon Riders, Deacon had been forced to endure the multiday journey clutched in one of Garr's forepaws.

"Dragon Rider Grustim!" he called out as best as his constricted chest would allow.

His host offered no response. Deacon knew from experience that was not an indication he'd not been heard, simply that Grustim didn't feel as though a response was worth his time or effort.

"I think perhaps Garr's grip is a bit too tight."

As a dragon mount, Garr's training was extensive, Deacon had no doubt. Likely the beast had been taught precisely how to carry a human in this way without injuring him or her. If that was the case, however, Deacon suspected Garr was following the letter of the training rather than the spirit, because the clutch of the dragon's claws around him seemed to have been very precisely calibrated to fall just short of crushing his bones.

"Better that than the opposite," Grustim observed.

303

Joseph R. Lallo

One positive outcome of the uncomfortable journey was the peerless view of the ground it afforded Deacon. Fear of heights was not a problem for him, so the view was not only fascinating but crucial, as it had revealed to him something quite curious.

Dark forms had been moving across the Wastes, small clusters of troops on direct courses from at least three small cities and settlements. All were heading in the same direction as they were. Even as Garr shifted his angle of flight and began to drop down to the surface, another group of soldiers came into view.

"Grustim, are the Wastes commonly used for training and readiness drills?" Deacon called.

"Not this far south, not this many, not at this time of year, and not during a time of military uncertainty."

"Then why are so many troops headed south?"

"I do not know, but I strongly suspect it is not a coincidence, pleasant or otherwise. And certainly not in our favor."

"I suspect you are correct."

A few minutes later they set down, and Deacon was rather forcefully dropped to the ground. He stood and dusted himself off, resolving to take some time when the current crisis had ended to determine why dragons seemed to more often than not take an instant dislike to him.

The Southern Wastes were a dry, arid, and cold place. Not as frigid as the Alliance, but cool enough that Deacon found himself longing for the traditional Northern garb. The air had a very slight salty sting to it, hinting at the sea that lay unseen beyond a line of low mountains to the south.

Deacon held up the page of his pad covered with the thin, precise lines of Ivy's sketch and compared it to the landscape to the south. It was clear why Grustim had been concerned about the amount of time it would take. Never before had Deacon seen a mountainside so littered with caverns and crevices. Considering their destination only needed to be deep enough to shelter a single woman, even narrowed as their search was they would have to visit hundreds of them.

"Are you certain you can trust the sketch to be accurate enough to identify the place?"

"Ivy has a great many gifts. Though music may be her calling, her skill with the pen and with the brush is no less remarkable. If this is how she rendered it, then it is at least as accurate as Turiel remembered it."

Grustim paced along, his armor jingling. "And how is this ally of yours privy to the memories of a foe?"

"As I understand it, there was some manner of exchange that occurred between them," Deacon explained without looking away from his task. There was no indication in his tone that he felt anything he'd said thus far was out of the ordinary.

"I'd known the Alliance methods of war were different from the Tresson methods. I'd not realized how great the difference was."

"I can assure you, Turiel's methods are not typical of the Northern Alliance." He tapped the pad. "This, the feature she indicated and detailed... there are only a handful of stretches of the coast visible that are high enough to host it. It is simply a matter of finding the proper angle. This upright here will become visible if we head to the east, I feel," Deacon said. "Not more than a few hours and we'll have it."

"And you cannot speed matters with your magic?"

"I've been seeking it since we took to the air. All I can say with any certainty is that it is quite near."

Garr stopped and raised his snout, shutting his eyes and drawing in a long, slow breath. Without any other indication of danger, Grustim reflexively tightened his grip on his lance and began to scan the horizon.

"What is it?" Deacon said, turning to his escorts.

Rider and dragon turned simultaneously to the north. Garr craned his neck, and Grustim climbed first to his back, then to his head, balancing effortlessly atop it and taking stock of the horizon.

"The troops. In the distance I can see at least three squads heading toward us."

"Is it possible they saw a Dragon Rider and felt there may be a crisis that could benefit from their aid?"

"Why they are coming this way is of little concern. When they reach us, they will find you with me and there may be questions, at best. Depending on who dispatched them and why, there may be *no* questions. Do your work quickly. If they find us and seek to stop us, we will be left with very few options."

"Understood... I believe we need to go that way, east. A fair distance."

Grustim dropped to the base of Garr's neck, and the dragon snatched Deacon up. A few strides and a snap of his wings took them into a glide that practically skimmed the ground. Deacon kept his eyes trained south, watching the shape of the landscape shift. Miles whisked by and his wind-burned eyes focused on a single point. It was a steep spire, similar to the one Ivy had drawn, and with each moment it seemed to match the image more closely. Then, as they neared a section of cliffs that was taller and more intricate than the rest, he saw his first glimpse of the tree she had drawn.

"We are close! A bit farther southeast!" he called. "Farther... Farther..." His eyes flicked up to the land and down to the page.

Grustim grunted an order to Garr at the precise moment that Deacon's hand shot out to a feature on the land.

"Footprints!" Deacon called.

Garr's flight shifted seamlessly into a trot. He eased into a three-legged run with the remaining claw clenched about Deacon. When he had slowed enough, he dug his claws into the frigid earth and ground to a stop. He dropped Deacon, who stumbled briefly but managed to stay on his feet rushing toward the mountains.

There was no doubt anymore. The footprints were few and far between, swept clean by the constant wind in all but a few sheltered dips and gullies. Finally there was the cave. It was an unassuming one. Not the sort of shelter one would willingly choose. The mouth was tall and narrow, and a quirk of the mountain face seemed to funnel gusts of wind inside despite the constant breeze coming from behind the mountain.

Deacon stepped inside, Grustim close behind.

"Someone lived here?" the Dragon Rider said, eying the surroundings.

There was evidence of habitation. A few empty bottles and casks, and a stunning variety of animal remains, but nothing as basic as a washbasin or even a bed could be seen.

"I wouldn't call what she was doing here 'living,'" Deacon said. "She must have spent most of the time in deep meditation. It is deeper than sleep. Quite near death. I cannot fathom the focus she must have developed. The power she must hold. Do you realize the strength of mind, the singularity of attention and desire it would require?"

"If there is work to be done, do it. I would prefer to be gone before the soldiers arrive. And there is no doubt they *will* arrive."

"Yes… yes of course."

Deacon pulled his gem free and buried himself in the task. In his mind, the physical world dropped away, the veil pulling aside to the plane of spirits and magic. Most anywhere in the world had a vitality and life to it. The most innocuous stone was in some way pulsing with the power of the eons of its existence. But this place was cold, lifeless. It was as though his mind, Grustim's, and Garr's were the only points of light in an otherwise empty and darkened pit.

"It is… it is truly remarkable… the power that has been gathered here… but to the mind, in the astral plane… it is entirely absent. So well hidden… The *skill* it must take to achieve such a deception, such a grand illusion. *Using* magic to *hide* magic," he uttered, in genuine awe.

"These D'Karon took your nation to war. Held you by the throat and sent your people to die for their ends, correct?"

"Not my birth nation, but my adopted one, yes."

"And yet you admire their works?"

"Ah… I apologize. It has been repeatedly observed such a behavior is… nonstandard. … Wait… yes… yes I feel the threads… the seams of it… *Here*…"

He held out his hand and touched a point in the air just a few inches from the ground. The gem in his fist, already glowing with a warm light, suddenly began to pulse brighter, its color shifting from white-blue to amber-gold, and from amber-gold to deep violet.

The D'Karon Apprentice

He could feel it, a point in space at once gorged and ravenous. Wrapped about it was a simple, elegant spell. That it could hide something so powerful was like concealing a battle-ax beneath a silk kerchief. And then, with a flex of his mind, he pulled the sheet away.

The reveal of the unfinished spell was not a grand and showy thing. There was no burst of light or crackle of energy. It was simply as though it had never been there, and then a moment later it had always been there. Twisting in the air was a knot of shimmering light. Compound curves, like reflections of reflections, continued inward into a depth and complexity that seemed to be without end. The longer he stared at it, the deeper it seemed to become, as if the fist-sized churning mass of energy was miles deep.

More chilling than the impossible complexity of it was the sensation. There was a will to the thing. It was mindful of its purpose, like a chained dog watching an intruder, patiently waiting until the trespasser came near enough to be bitten. In the back of his mind, he could feel the D'Karon on the other side. Watching and waiting, banging on the door and demanding to be let through.

"You've revealed it. Now destroy it," Grustim said, shattering the awed silence.

"Grustim… it is not an overstatement to say that I am among the dozen most knowledgeable wizards alive today. I have seen acts of power that could lay waste to whole kingdoms at a single stroke. And I say this not out of ego but so that you will understand that it comes from a place of considerable experience when I say that this cave contains the sort of concentrated mystic energy that I've witnessed only a handful of times. I cannot destroy it. It cannot be destroyed. It can only be changed. Turiel's work was very nearly done. If she is allowed to return here after having harvested any appreciable power, the keyhole will be opened. Undoing it must be done delicately. If I make a false move… neither of us will ever know."

"That may be difficult," Grustim said, turning to the fields to the north. "The soldiers will be here soon, and I am quite certain they will not be pleased to find you working potentially disastrous spells."

#

"I'll stay and find Ether," Ivy muttered to herself, both frustration and genuine concern flavoring her voice.

She climbed over the thrice broken remains of the castle, pawing through the mounds of stone with one hand while holding a torch in the other. Her steps were unsteady, due in large part to the heavy bundle of firewood strapped to her back. She held the torch high and scoured every dancing shadow, looking for some hint of a clue as to where her ally might have gone.

"What was I thinking? I don't know magic. It isn't like she has a scent for me to follow! She might not even be here! She could be anywhere in the north!"

She crawled down into the pit that had been excavated by the latest set of portal blasts. "Ether! Ether, if you can hear me at all, answer me!"

Her sharp ears twitched and pivoted, scouring her surroundings every bit as much as her eyes did. The wind wailed, the fire crackled, and her own heart pounded in her ears. Stones clattered under her feet... and also elsewhere, farther into the damaged halls.

Ivy couldn't explain it, but she knew instantly there was a will behind it. She scampered down to the source of the sound and held the torch low. It wasn't a needle in a haystack. It was infinitely worse. If Ether was here, she could be anything. Any animal, a flicker of smoldering flame, a pool of water, even the air itself.

"Where are you, Ether?" Ivy said, squinting at the stone.

Finally she saw it, a curve of stone that had certainly been a finger. And here was a hollow that might have been the back of a knee. Ether had been stone, and what remained of her was here.

Ivy turned and dropped the bundle of firewood onto the stone and pulled a cask of lamp oil from her belt, dumping it over the wood. When the cask was empty she touched the torch to the wood.

"Come on... Come on, Ether..." Ivy said, watching anxiously as the wood took to light.

Several minutes passed with agonizing slowness, then finally stones began to smolder and spark, both those below the wood and beside it. One by one they peeled away and swirled into the flames. Each one caused the flames to swell and intensify. Then, almost imperceptibly, a voice crackled from the flames.

"Back away..."

Ivy obeyed, and not a moment too soon. The flames grew orders of magnitude more intense, the wood reducing to ashes in moments. The fire gathered, flicking together into Ether's form and then shifting to flesh, blood, and cloth. She stumbled forward, Ivy catching her.

"Turiel... she..."

"Myranda went after her. She's probably at the front right now, or will be soon."

"We need to join her," Ether said, trying to stand. "She needs our help."

"You're not in any position to help anyone, Ether," Ivy said.

The malthrope held her tight and helped her stand up straight. Ether shook her head and clenched her teeth, furious at her own weakness.

"Thank you, Ivy," she said, stepping unsteadily from her support but gripping her arm tight for balance.

Ivy looked Ether in the eye, genuine confusion in her expression.

"Wow... you *really* aren't yourself right now."

"I've not been myself for some time. My mind... I don't think my former self exists anymore. These feelings..." Ether returned Ivy's gaze. "You...

you've played your music and helped others before. You've put bow to string in order to heal and energize Myranda and the others. It has never been of any use to me."

"Uh-huh," Ivy said, uncertain of what Ether was working at.

"I've always affirmed that I have no emotions, no need for them. You've constantly affirmed the opposite, claiming I have emotions, but that I know only anger and hate. ... My mind... my mind is awash with this *poison* you call emotion... But... but perhaps in that I can find some of the strength you've found. Perhaps..."

Ivy's eyes opened and she clutched her hands together, practically vibrating with excitement. "You want me to play for you!?"

"It *may* have some value," Ether said.

"Come on! Come on, come on!" Ivy said, clutching her hand and tugging her forward. "It works better when there're other people to join in the fun, and I think the people of Kenvard need a pick-me-up! I know I've got a spare fiddle I can use."

#

"Here... oh, my dear Mott. Right here... can't you *feel* it?" Turiel said, stroking her fingers through the tufts of hair running like a mane down the massive creature's back.

The pair had been flying through the clouds for a few hours. The time had given Turiel a chance to heal herself and her pet, though at the cost of a small share of the power she'd gathered in Kenvard. Flying through the freezing clouds, they'd been pelted with ice and covered with frost. Turiel seemed, as with all matters of the body, to shrug it off as, at worst, a mild annoyance. They had been navigating based wholly on the lure of restless spirits and generations of death that traced a line from west to east.

Now, just as the clouds were thinning, that line was beneath them. Mott circled down toward the rust-brown line of churned-up earth that marked the bloodiest nearby stretch of the front. Mott, as a creature crafted from mad whims and in defiance of nature, was fairly ungainly in the air. At no point was this more apparent than when he tried to land. His long tail dangled down behind him, dragging along the ground until his upper body came slapping down onto his coiled legs and his head flopped to the ground. The impact produced an unpleasant, fleshy sound, suggesting it had done a fair amount of damage, but through great effort Mott had spared Turiel any serious distress.

The necromancer climbed down and drove her staff into the earth, dropping to her knees to scoop up soil. Her eyes were wide and her grin wider, like she was looking over a banquet table heaped with delicacies after a long, hungry day. The reddish-brown soil ran between her fingers.

"I can feel it. I can feel the blood that has been spilled here, Mott," Turiel said, her voice hushed. "Wonderful... Glorious... The war... do you see? Do you see the brilliance of the D'Karon? This battlefront was like an altar, and every man and woman killed during the war was like a sacrifice to their greatness. And that power. That glorious power is here. Don't doubt it represents a piddling amount for them... but for me it is so much. Enough to bring them back, and with enough to spare to show them how effective, how powerful I can truly be."

Mott stood, curling his tail around to adjust his jaw, which had been somewhat dislocated by the rough landing. He chattered something, eyes peering to the west.

Turiel glanced in his direction, then to where the beast was looking. There was motion just visible on the dim horizon. Troops from both sides were not more than a few minutes away, and they were moving in her direction. She gathered her staff and used it to climb back to her feet.

"Yes, yes, Mott," she said, dusting off her hands. "The soldiers will come. Of course they will come. It doesn't matter. ... Well naturally there are a lot of them. That is why I remade the nearmen in Kenvard, but of course the adversaries had to destroy them. Honestly, they call themselves heroes, but they seem so eager to destroy things. ... It won't take but a few minutes, Mott. I can feel the power flowing into me. The spirits here aren't as lively. They died with the hot blood of war in their veins. Most went to rest content in the knowledge they died for what they believed in. Not much strength to acquire from a spirit at peace. But there are *so many* of them. Sipping from a thousand glasses will slake your thirst just as surely as a tall, cool goblet all your own. ... I've *told* you. Just a few minutes. ... Well if you aren't sure you can hold them off, then I'll just give you some help!"

Again Turiel drove the tip of her staff into the soil. She rubbed her hands together eagerly and then cupped them around the gem as if warming them. The glow from within intensified.

"Mmm... It seems those from both sides make it a habit to collect their dead. A pity," she grinned. "But in one hundred years of war, a few bodies are bound to be overlooked... And sometimes a battlefield grave is better than none at all..."

Her ever-present filaments of magic uncoiled and threaded their way into the soil, spreading out and blackening the ground for dozens of paces in all directions. Here and there they looped upward, then drove themselves down. In those places, the earth began to quake. It split and spread, shapes churning it up from beneath. Then came the troops. Some wore shreds of blue armor, others battered remnants of red. Most were little more than skeletons, and many of them were incomplete. They were warriors from both sides, lost to the generations of war and forgotten, some for over a century.

All told fifty or so skeletal troops emerged, with another clawing to the surface every few moments. Her black ribbons and threads wound across their bodies, holding loose bones in place and weaving into replacements for things missing or too badly damaged to do their job. When each was free of the ground and standing on its feet, the revenant would then march before her and stand at attention.

"There," Turiel said, opening her eyes to the resurrected troops. "An adequate force, don't you think?"

Mott looked at her doubtfully, then chittered and glanced to the west. There were easily a hundred Northern soldiers, and likely twice as many Tresson soldiers.

"You really must learn to be more confident in your capabilities, Mott. I made you, have some faith in me!"

He grumbled, then glanced to the sky.

Turiel craned her neck and followed his gaze. Myn was emerging from the clouds. "Oh, very well then. If you are *that* concerned, I'll conscript some sturdier soldiers."

She peered to the south. They were less than a mile from the nearest village, a settlement to the southwest called Crestview. Even at this distance it was clear the place was rather recently rebuilt, no doubt established as a way to hastily gain a foothold during a peace no one expected to last. It was barely across the border to Tressor, its northern wall perhaps half a mile from the row of wooden stakes that divided the lands. A cluster of Tresson soldiers had taken up positions just south of that border. Likely the Tresson troops were there to protect it from attack from their Alliance counterparts stationed a short distance across the border, who were in turn only there to keep an eye on the Tresson soldiers.

"There. Men…" Turiel said, addressing the troops. She tipped her head in deference to one specific skeleton. "And you, madam. To bolster our numbers, head to yonder village and see if the people there wouldn't mind terribly donating their bodies and souls to my defense. Feel free to make the same request of any soldiers who resist you. I promise their service to me will be brief. Mott, you stay here and keep the dragon busy. Let Mommy focus on her task."

The army she raised set off, Mott curled his body protectively around her, and Turiel opened her mind and soul to the power around her. It was glorious, like being immersed in a warm, nurturing bath. Thousands of lives over the years, each leaving a piece of itself behind. The soil was rich with their sacrifice. For one so tightly attuned to death, there was nothing to do but allow the power to flow into her.

In a few seconds she could feel more strength flood her soul than she'd managed to gather on her own in years. The strength came at a price, of course. Each spirit added its voice to her mind. As she steeped in the crackling, humming power of the place, the final thoughts of each soldier and civilian who had spilled his or her blood here rang out in her head. For a normal person, even another necromancer, it would have pushed a steady mind to madness. But for Turiel, who had marched that road for much of the last few centuries, it was no more bothersome than the buzzing of flies. For a madwoman, an unholy chorus of screams from beyond the grave is hardly a matter for concern.

It wasn't until the ground shook and Mott slithered forward to better guard Turiel that she finally opened her eyes again to survey the situation. She turned to the north to find Myranda standing, her staff ready. Myn was heaving exhausted breaths. Both heroes wore looks of iron-hard determination tempered with bone-deep fatigue.

"Turiel—" Myranda began.

"Really now, Myranda!" Turiel interrupted. "You've argued your side, I've argued mine. We've found our differences irreconcilable and come to blows. In the end, I have emerged as strong and healthy as I've ever been, and you are at death's door. What more is to be gained from more tiresome words? Perhaps you should ask yourself which one of us is truly mad."

"There must be *some* scrap of reason left in you! Some part of you that realizes what you are doing *must not be done!*"

"Well of *course* there is, dear. Even as we speak I can hear the voice of reason in me, screaming to set aside my task before further blood is pointlessly shed. But one doesn't last long as a necromancer without learning to ignore errant voices in one's head. I'm afraid all that remains is for one of us to kill the other. And forgive me for saying, but I think I have a greater capacity for such things than you."

"You—"

"Uh-uh-uh! You've got three tasks, my dear. You must stop me, you must stop Mott, and you must stop the troops I've sent across the border. None of them can be achieved by chitchat." She grinned, raising her staff. "To arms!"

Like an executioner dropping an ax, she brought the staff down, spreading her will through the thread-riddled ground and launching a vicious blast of raw energy at the same time. The attack was intended to end the battle before it began, ensnaring Myranda in ebony bonds to keep her from avoiding the attack.

Instead, Myranda swiped her own staff, an arc of her own pure energy severing the creeping strands and dispersing the bolt of magic.

In response, Turiel raised her eyebrow. This might be more interesting than she'd anticipated.

#

Grustim stood at the mouth of the cave, eyes set upon Deacon. The Dragon Rider had an awareness of magic. Elements of his training had been focused on defending against it. His armor and weapons had been designed to deflect and disperse black magic. All of his life he had felt that wizards were not *true* warriors. They toyed with forces that made them powerful in a way that did not pay proper respect to the training and discipline of even the lowest soldier. It felt unfair that they had been given a tool that put them in a position of power they did not deserve.

Watching Deacon work had begun to give him a new appreciation. This… *keyhole* was monstrous. Even without a drop of genuine mystic training, he could feel the fearsome forces at work. There was the sense that Deacon was doing battle with a wild animal with only his mind to defend him. And yet he worked with unshaking hands and slow, calm breaths. With a sword dangling over him by the thinnest of threads, he showed no hint of fear or concern.

One of his hands gripped his gem tightly, and the other was plunged deep into the churning knot of lights. Between his hands was a sliver of metal drifting and slowly rotating. He hadn't placed it there; it had simply appeared, accumulating from thin air.

Garr rumbled a warning and Grustim turned.

"What is it?" Deacon asked, not willing to turn away from his workings.

"The soldiers have held their position several hundred paces due north. A second and third group has met and combined ranks, but they are not advancing."

"That is good news."

"No. It is very, very bad."

"Why?"

"Because it confirms what I had already suspected. They are coordinating. That implies they were well aware that what they would find here would be a threat. And a significant one. How much longer will it take you to finish?"

"Impossible to tell. Several minutes more at least. Possibly an hour. And when we are through, we'll simply be left with the same quantity of power condensed. To be certain Turiel can't put it to use again, we'll have to keep it from her."

"Then keep working. *When* they arrive, I cannot conceive of any outcome that will preserve our peace, and very few that will preserve our lives. I will speak to them. If they do not like what they hear, they will attack. If I attempt to fend them off, it will be treason. If you do, it will be war."

"Can you release Garr from his oath again?"

"I should not have done that once, but I will not do it again. It would only ease my conscience in any case, because if any of these men die while you are near, those who wish for a reason for war will have all that they need to justify it."

"But—"

"Focus on your work. This stone has been set in motion. No amount of questioning will keep it from the bottom of the mountain."

#

Myranda's mind burned and her soul wavered. She'd begun the battle with little strength, and the tasks at hand were many. Turiel was relentless, levying attacks of devastating intensity. Myranda absorbed, deflected, and countered all she could, no stranger to battling a foe who massively outclassed her, but every passing moment only made her opponent stronger.

Joseph R. Lallo

Worse, Myranda had to split her attentions between the necromancer and the troops she had raised, who now marched relentlessly toward Crestview. The skeletons were fragile, no sturdier than the bones that composed them, but striking them down was only a delay. As soon as one fell, Turiel restored it, and as the battle crept closer to the village, more of the battlefront came under Turiel's expanding influence, and thus more of the skeletons rose.

"You put forth a noble effort, Myranda," Turiel said, her voice booming with the power that was still building within her. "If I do manage to kill you, I look forward to the chats we'll have afterward."

An earsplitting howl pierced the air, drawing both Myranda's and Turiel's attention. Myn's battle with Mott had been truly savage. Myranda had never seen the dragon more driven to defeat a foe. She'd clamped her jaws about the back of Mott's neck and blasted a breath of fire. It didn't incinerate Mott, but it was clearly more damage or pain than the beast could shrug off.

"Mott!" Turiel said, her voice scolding. "Honestly. I made you better than that. I'm beginning to think you weren't ready for the additional size. If you can't use it properly, I'll take it from you."

She raised her staff and snapped her fingers. Mott's form shuddered and shifted to black. The details dropped away and began to unravel into a nest of threads that wove into the ground. A tiny bundle of the threads separated from the rest, and after a moment of struggle, Mott's original form broke free.

Myn shook her head and recovered from the sudden disappearance of her opponent, then locked Mott's tiny scuttling form in her gaze.

Showing a remarkable amount of logic and awareness for so bizarre a creature, Mott chose to retreat rather than tangle with a still furious dragon that was now dozens of times his size. Working with the undersized vulture wings he'd started with, he alternately fluttered and scrambled off to the north. Myn turned to follow.

"Myn, no! See to the city! Make sure the people are safe!" Myranda ordered.

The wizard rushed toward Turiel, her staff braced between her hands.

Turiel turned to her and smirked, raising her staff to summon a shield. Myranda gathered her weakening will into her crystal and thrust if forward. It was enough to shatter the shield, just barely, but with no power left for a proper attack. Turiel seemed aware of it, the beginnings of a grin flashing on her face.

A moment later the grin was wiped away as Myranda continued her forward charge. If there was no time and little magic to spare for a mystic attack, there were other options. Her time in Entwell had largely been focused on sculpting her mystic aptitude into its present level of mastery, but she'd learned other lessons as well. Much as she'd resisted, she'd been required to take instruction in combat, too. Though she was loath to put it to use, times like these made it clear why her instructors had insisted she learn. She drove her shoulder hard into Turiel's chest, throwing her off balance. Before she could regain her feet, Myranda hooked the tip of her staff behind Turiel's foot and pulled it out from under her.

The necromancer struck the ground, startled and confused. She drew in a breath, but before she could release it as a threat or a spell, Myranda planted a boot on her throat and thrust the head of her staff between Turiel's eyes.

"Drop your staff and end this madness," Myranda demanded.

"You'll... have to kill me," Turiel croaked.

Myranda pulled her mind to a new task. From the start there'd been no hope of overpowering the necromancer, but now that she was so close, and she'd interrupted the woman's focus for even a moment, there was the chance to keep it from returning. She set her will against Turiel's, wrapping her own mind and spirit around the dark wizard's, walling her off from the churning spirits that surrounded her. It wasn't a matter of being stronger. It was a matter of keeping Turiel's will from her power. Tiny shoves and prods of her mind, constantly shifting, kept the necromancer off balance mentally in the same way she'd been knocked off balance physically.

"My, my, my..." Turiel breathed, trying and failing to break through Myranda's confounding influence. "I'd not expected such savagery. Brute physical force?"

"I will do what I must. *That* much I learned from your beloved D'Karon," Myranda said.

"Then kill me. It is as simple as that."

"You are a necromancer. I very much doubt killing you would do much good, and I don't kill for no reason."

Turiel rolled her eyes. "I'm no Epidime... but I *have* been curious how simple it would be to work my skills from the wrong side of the grave." She drew in a breath, struggling. "This is taking all of your mental agility. How long do you suppose you can keep me down?"

"Long enough," she said, sweat trickling down her face. At the border it was not as warm as at the heart of Tressor, but the sweat had nothing to do with the temperature. "Perhaps long enough to convince you to—"

"Fah! No more of that!" Turiel said.

"You are betraying your world for the sake of the memory of your sister!" Myranda growled.

"What better reason to betray a world than family?" Turiel asked.

Myranda felt a vicious, potent rush of strength, Turiel making an earnest and very nearly successful attempt to break the stalemate.

"Tell me, Myranda," she said. "What side of the border are we on? And what is that delightful, rhythmic sound?"

Myranda cast a precious glance aside. Myn was running herself ragged keeping the scattered skeletons from advancing, but for now the situation was in hand. The troops of both sides were only a few hundred paces away. The battle had drifted well south of the border between the kingdoms. They were on Tresson land. The Tresson soldiers were looking upon a dragon, two wizards, and a cluster of the shambling dead doing battle dangerously close to a settlement. The Tressons were within their rights and their duties to defend their people. Worse, Myn was a common sight at the border. The Alliance soldiers had certainly recognized her, and they were within their duty to come to her aid. And so they had. It was by any measure an invasion, Alliance soldiers rushing across the border with weapons in hand and the intention to use them.

Her realization was soon followed by a sharp, dizzying pain in the side of her head. The distraction had freed Turiel enough to deliver a punishing blow with her staff. Myranda had no sooner struck the ground than she could feel the necromancer's power surge like a torch flaring to life. Instinctively she rolled aside. A line of black filaments erupted from the ground, and every last skeleton Myn had shattered rose again, bound and bolstered by more of the unending black threads.

Myranda climbed to her feet and turned to Turiel. The necromancer was standing and wringing her hands.

"Direct physical violence. It seems so beneath a spell caster. I'm not certain if I should admire or pity a person such as you who willingly resorts to it," Turiel said. "I'd much prefer to leave it in the hands of the specialists."

She looked to the soldiers, who were aligning themselves into ranks, now approaching the raging battle between Myn and the skeletons with caution. Their eyes flitted from the undead assailants to their counterparts from the other land and back again, clearly viewing them as equal threats.

Myranda tried to rush toward Turiel again, slashing at the threads the necromancer conjured. She made little progress, Turiel having no trouble keeping her distance with a few lazy steps backward. Myranda had simply pushed herself too far. Days with barely any sleep, massive expenditures of energy—her spirit had been wrung out, drained. If the battle persisted for much longer, there would be no chance for her to even defend herself, let alone defeat a woman who was growing stronger by the moment.

Myn was having similar trouble. It took little more than a single swat of her claws or a curl of her tail to bash the skeletons apart, but they rose as quickly as they fell, and there were so many of them. Bony fingers and scattered, timeworn weapons scratched and gouged at her. Thick, potent blood was seeping from a dozen minor wounds, and she was huffing great exhausted breaths as she continued her assault.

"It's been so long since I folded in a dose of energy to the keyhole. I feel shamefully lax in my responsibilities. But I suspect a bit of fresh bloodshed will be the last scrap I need," Turiel mused.

Myranda shook her head and stumbled back. As surely as she needed to stop Turiel, she knew it was still more important to stop her people and the people of Tressor from tearing each other apart. It might already be too late to keep Turiel from getting what she needed to finish her spell. Likewise, the consequences of the actions she and others had been forced to take could well have already broken this fragile peace beyond repair. In the end, though, everything she'd ever done was to stop further bloodshed. If nothing else, Myranda knew she had to keep these troops from each other. To keep them focused on whom she knew to be their common enemy.

The leading soldiers were less than a dozen paces apart now. In seconds they would meet. Myranda ran to them, ignoring the slashing attacks of the lingering threads she was leaving behind. She poured a bit of magic into her voice, allowing it to rise above the din of battle, and addressed the troops.

"Listen to me! I am Myranda, Duchess of Kenvard and Guardian of the Realm. All Alliance troops, you are ordered to defend Crestview from the undead. Until I say otherwise, we are in a truce, and Tressor is an ally. Defend that village as you would defend your own home! Myn! Come here!"

The faithful dragon thrust herself into the air, a spring of her powerful legs and a flap of her massive wings bringing her to Myranda's side in a single bound. Myranda climbed onto her back, and allowed a precious dose of her flagging mystic reserves to trickle into her friend and seal the worst of her wounds. She did not speak, offering not so much as a single command to Myn. The two knew each other well enough that such was not necessary. Another wing-assisted leap brought the pair to the narrowing strip of land between the foremost troops of Turiel's army and the flimsy walls of the settlement.

Tresson soldiers had only just reached the village walls and scattered warily at Myranda's arrival. They too had been stationed at the front and had come to know Myranda and Myn by sight, but the circumstances would have been trying for even a well-earned trust. Myranda wouldn't waste her time or breath trying to steady their fears. Actions spoke louder than words. As the nearest of the skeletons stepped into range, Myn pulverized them. The bony troops spread, and soon the threat of the skeletons was a far greater one than the dragon and wizard.

The southern troops put their weapons to work, hacking and bashing at bone that was all-too eager to repair and resume its march. Between Myranda, Myn, and the troops, the skeletal march was outnumbered and overpowered, but the endless flow of magic kept their numbers from diminishing. The Alliance troops carved their way in from the back, bashing skeletons to pieces and trampling them under foot.

Then the moment came. Battling soldiers from both sides shattered through the wall of bone and corroded armor and came face to face, red to the south, blue to the north. Their weapons were raised, their blood already racing from the intensity of combat. The war had ended only months before. Each of these men and women had seen battle, perhaps even against one another. And now they stood on the battlefield.

Bones clattered and fresh threads coalesced. The fallen enemies at their feet clattered and tugged, drawing together piece by piece and assembling on the nearest patches of ground large enough to accommodate them. A man in blue looked to the Tresson soldier before him, then to the restoring army. He turned, putting his back to the Tresson soldier and raising his weapon in the former foe's defense. One by one the other Alliance soldiers did the same.

"Really now. Am I to believe we can't even trust *soldiers* to spill a little blood?" Turiel said. "Well, I'm through waiting. I'm quite sure I have enough, and if I don't, it'll just be a quick jaunt there and back again to get what I need."

She waved her staff, and the familiar point and window of a portal began to form before her…

#

Grustim stared down at the troops at Garr's feet. When the time came to intimidate, there was much to be said for requiring another soldier to look up to address you. This was particularly true when that soldier was on horseback. And he would need all of the intimidation he could muster. All told, the troops who had been gathering at a safe distance didn't approach until there were nearly fifty of them. A dragon was a formidable foe, and a dragon with a Rider was, if anything, more so, but even Garr would be hard-pressed to take on so substantial a force.

"Stand aside, honored Dragon Rider. We have orders from a trustworthy source that Northern aggressors are lurking within this cave."

"You do not have the authority to order me aside, and if there was anything for the military to concern itself with, I would have seen to it myself."

"I have my orders," the soldier replied.

"And I have mine," Grustim said.

Hands tightened about lances and bows. Horses, fearful of the massive predator looming before them, shuffled and fidgeted. For a moment there was a stalemate, neither Grustim nor the soldiers willing to make the first move in what would be a battle that would not only spill blood, but blacken the honor of one or all of those to do battle.

"I will not ask again," said the spokesman, a man with the same markings of commander that Brustuum had worn.

He was a match for Grustim's rank and he knew it. The Dragon Rider could not countermand his orders. Proper training suggested the resolution was to defer to the commander with more recent orders. A Dragon Rider could credibly make a claim that he'd been more recently informed, but there was no way to be certain. It came down to the judgment of the troop commander, and from the set of his jaw and the hardness of his gaze, there was little doubt which he believed to be true. Muscles tensed and breathing quickened across the whole of the troop complement. Each knew the decision had been made. There would be combat between Tressons. All that remained was the order.

Arrows nearly flew and swords nearly swung when the next voice rang out, but it was a soldier, not a commander who spoke.

"Commander!" called an alert mounted soldier deep within the ranks.

The commander turned.

"Sorcery! Take cover! Safe distance!" the commander barked, pointing his lance in the direction of the threat.

The soldiers scattered, pulling back in an almost chaotic retreat. A swirling black point grew into a circle, the exit of Turiel's portal. The window to the border revealed the cool and collected figure of the necromancer. She stepped gingerly through, careful to keep her hem from the swirling edge, then turned back to call into the icy portal.

"Mott! Where have you gotten off to? Bah. The rascal will turn up. Best not to waste time," she said.

"Hold! Northerner, you are trespassing on Tresson land!" called the commander.

Turiel turned, noticing for the first time the dozens of soldiers gathered about her portal. Her eyes widened in shock, but not the sort of shock that comes from fear or surprise. She seemed aghast, offended to find anyone in this place.

"I... *I* am trespassing? I'm quite certain I can stake a far older claim to this cave than you. Just what are you doing here?"

"This is the Kingdom of Tressor. No Northerner may—" the commander repeated, but his words choked off in his throat.

"That isn't an answer," Turiel said, her staff thrust toward him, and stout, thorny threads piercing his throat. "And honestly, I'm no longer interested. Be gone, all of you, there is work to be done."

Color drained from the commander's face, and he pitched to the side. Before his body had struck the ground, the rest of the accumulated soldiers burst into the chaos of battle, each seeking to be the first to strike the sorceress who had injured their commander. Turiel paid them little mind, walking with purpose toward the mouth of the cave. She waved a hand irritably, as if swatting a fly, and her staff began to crackle with energy. Bolts of purple and blue hissed forth and seared any who came near her. The air filled with the stench of charred flesh and howls of pain.

"Soldiers, back!" Grustim barked. In the same breath he coughed a sharp, simple order to Garr.

The soldiers who were still fortunate enough to be mobile barely had time to roll aside before the green dragon belched a column of intense, sustained flame. Dragon breath rushed around the dark sorceress, completely wiping her from sight. The blinding flames broiled the earth beneath her and blistered the friendly troops who hadn't retreated far enough, but Garr did not relent. His jaws thrown wide and his eyes wild with fury, he continued to heave the white-hot flames over the spell caster. So thick and bright were they that no one could see so much as a shadow of the woman who served as their target.

Then, from deep within the core of the blast, a thick bundle of black ribbons spiraled out. It speared into Garr's throat and coiled tight around his upper and lower jaws, pulling them shut and causing the flames to splash aside, scalding a few more friendly soldiers before cutting off entirely. The lingering flames flickered away, leaving a glassy, crackly patch of sandy soil. For a moment, it looked as though Turiel had been charred by the attack, but slowly the sooty and mildly smoldering surface of her body peeled away. She'd managed to cocoon herself with tendrils. Beneath them her skin had been reddened here or blackened there but was otherwise whole and untouched. From the tip of her outstretched staff, the bundle of darkness that had muzzled the dragon began to thicken and flex. The bands sizzled at the iron mask he wore, bending and buckling it before slicing through and hissing against his scales.

"That is *quite* enough," she growled, her voice rough.

A swipe of her staff traveled down the length of the bundle like the crack of a whip, throwing Garr viciously and effortlessly aside. Grustim held tight to the dragon as he was thrown. The bulk of the dragon came down hard upon his leg. Despite the remarkable armor he wore, the impact was enough to shatter the bone. Grustim didn't even cry out, unwilling to waste the time and breath to do so. Instead, he shouted a warning.

"Deacon! She is through!"

Soldiers charged Turiel, but she turned and caught the throat of the first man to reach her. He didn't even manage a howl of pain before the life was gone from his eyes, his body shriveling under her grasp.

"Defend me," she said simply.

He pivoted and raised his weapon against his own brethren, motions jerky and unnatural. Three more soldiers reached her, each getting the same treatment, before she finally disappeared into the mouth of the cave. The subverted Tresson soldiers closed ranks, blocking off the way forward.

\#

Deacon was breathing quickly, his fingers curled around a swirling mass of light that was now barely the size of a marble. He watched over his shoulder as Turiel marched closer.

"What are you doing?" she shrieked, the cool demeanor gone as she saw him tinkering with the very thing she'd come to complete.

"Necromancer Turiel," he said breathlessly, "the proper question to ask…" the last of the light swirled into his fingers, "is what have I done?"

Twisting before him was a sliver of odd-shaped metal. It didn't have any rhyme or reason. There was no design. If anything, it resembled the twisting, rounded, fluid shape of what might result from dropping molten iron into a pool of ice water, except its surface gleamed like silver. It was small, not more than one could hold comfortably in a single palm, and yet the way it shone in the darkness of the cave spoke volumes of the power it contained.

"Where is the keyhole!?" she demanded, leveling her staff at him.

"The keyhole is no more, Turiel," he said, wiping sweat from his brow with the back of his gem-wielding hand and snatching the curl of metal with the other. "What remains of the power you used to create it is here."

"No... no!" she growled, thrusting down her staff. The tip dug into the stone of the cave floor and split it, sending a fault running up the walls and across the ceiling. "You couldn't have managed such a feat! No one could!"

"I have no doubt you were one of the greatest sorceresses of your day, Turiel, but time has marched on. There are those who know far more now." He held up the sliver of metal. "This is the least of the things we have learned. I know that you seek the D'Karon for what they could teach you. In light of what you've seen here, and what you've seen Myranda and the other Chosen do, perhaps—"

In a flicker of motion too swift to see, let alone react to, Turiel jabbed her staff forward, driving its jagged head into Deacon's belly. The anger-fueled and mystically empowered force of the attack was such that it dug deep into his flesh. Blood flowed from the wound when she pulled the staff free, and Deacon stumbled backward, clutching his gem to the injury.

"I suppose physical violence *does* have its usefulness," she growled.

Deacon stumbled back, coughing. A spattering of red flecked his lips. She grasped the wrist of the hand holding the sliver of metal and pulled him forward, but he locked his fingers around the artifact, hiding it from view.

"Please..." Deacon said.

"Don't beg. It cheapens both of us. And don't try to reason with me. As Myranda has refused to acknowledge, I have no reason left. Just give me the magic and give in to death. The other side of the veil is not a place to be feared."

"If... I must..." Deacon said.

He opened his fingers and the artifact slipped free, plummeting toward the ground. Turiel released him and snatched it from the air.

"Now, tell me how to unlock the power," she demanded, holding it to his face.

Deacon slumped against the wall and slid down, his face ghostly white.

"You do *not* have my permission to die!" she barked, raising her staff and readying a spell to weave into his mind and body.

The magic spilled forth, but had no effect on the waning figure before her. Turiel's expression hardened. She looked at the item in her hand and watched as it seemed to dissolve, separating into points of light that drifted apart.

"I apologize for the deception," Deacon said, his voice distant and growing more so as similar light trailed away from his extremities. "Such dishonesty does not come easily to me."

Joseph R. Lallo

The rest of his form wavered away into a galaxy of flickering lights, and Turiel whipped around to the sound of quickening footsteps. The true Deacon, not the illusion he'd conjured to distract her, was sprinting out of the cave. The usurped soldiers were lying lifeless on the ground, her influence banished from them, and the astonished and reeling members of the Tresson force were still trying to work what to do about this new and unknown threat.

Turiel dashed toward him.

"Keep back from him! Let him escape!" cried Grustim, his voice pained.

Deacon ran for the closing portal. His arms were crossed in front of him and his head was down, ready to defend the precious items he held from any who would seek to stop him. In a diving leap, he slipped through the nearly shut portal to the north.

"No!" Turiel screeched, holding out her staff and working a hasty bit of D'Karon magic.

Energy poured into the portal, and it widened massively, back to its full size and stretching further, until its bottom dug deep into the Tresson soil and it yawned wide enough for a whole company of soldiers to march through. The breeze of the north mixed with the air of the Southern Wastes. On the other side, the battle she'd left behind still raged, Tresson troops fighting alongside Alliance troops as her skeletons continued to march toward the village.

She turned to the soldiers around her, who were just recovering enough to advance upon her again.

"Haven't you had enough!" she cried, thrusting her staff into the earth.

A shock wave of raw energy rippled out from where it struck, knocking the soldiers from their feet. When they hit the ground, black bands burst forth to secure them there. Then she cast her staff forward and sent a coiling rope of black strands forward. It lanced through the portal and ensnared Deacon's ankle. She began to drag him back, but a blur of red and gold roared through the portal and struck her with the force of a landslide.

It was Myn, taking full advantage of the enlarged portal and eager to take out her fury on the necromancer. The pair slid back along the ground, Myn squeezing Turiel tight in one claw. She opened her jaws and made ready to snap them shut around Turiel with force enough to snap her in half. Turiel cried out viciously, and a blast of power erupted from her, hurling Myn off and sending the dragon onward to bash painfully into the face of the cave.

Turiel climbed to her feet, body twitching with pain and fury. Her youth and power were beginning to wane with the sheer quantity of magic she was using, but she didn't care anymore. Deep lines etched her face, gray threaded her hair, but she stalked forward, ready and willing to squander all she had if it meant achieving her goal. Myranda and Deacon were both rushing away, their minds and wills dedicated to keeping the artifact away from Turiel. She snarled and churned the air with her staff. A portal snapped open in front of the retreating heroes. Then another, and another. The portals formed edge to edge, flicking open until they created a solid dome around them. Each portal on the north side produced a matching one on the south side, all opening around Turiel. Myranda and Deacon stopped and surveyed their surroundings, but every direction was blocked by a portal that led right back to their foe.

"It is over…" Turiel breathed, her voice suddenly gnarled and croaking, yet reverberating with mystic power. "The only way forward is back. Give me the power you've stolen. Let me call the D'Karon."

Myranda turned, looking back through the main portal, and began to step toward it. "How many more people have to die for your sister, Turiel?"

"As many as it takes!"

"And for what? So you can find a beast that doesn't exist and avenge the memory of a woman known only to you! Someone gone for so long that few who live today can even know exactly how many years have passed. Do *you* even know how long ago the twentieth year of Queen Marrow the Fierce was?"

"It doesn't matter how long ago it was," Turiel said furiously.

"It was four hundred twenty-six years ago…" Deacon said, his voice low and his eyes wide. "The twentieth year of Queen Marrow is the year Entwell was founded."

Myranda's face dawned with realization. "Turiel…"

"Enough words!" the necromancer screeched, launching another bundle of threads toward them.

Myranda raised a feeble mystic shield with her waning strength. Almost immediately it began to buckle, but Deacon stepped beside her and lent his will to hers, bolstering it.

"Turiel, was your sister's name Azriel?" Myranda called.

"Don't you *dare* speak that name! You don't *deserve* to speak that name!" Turiel shrieked, more threads joining the attack.

"She's still alive! Turiel, your sister wasn't killed! She made it through the Cave of the Beast! She's the *founder* of a place called Entwell."

"Lies! I would have felt her presence if it was so!"

"You didn't feel her presence among the dead because she wasn't dead. And you didn't feel it among the living because the mountains around Entwell are almost impenetrable to magic."

"You would say anything to stop me from contacting the D'Karon!"

"Turiel, you linked your mind with Ivy to learn what she knew," Myranda said, stepping through the portal, pushing the curling, clutching threads of magic ahead of her. "Do the same for me. I've spoken with Azriel. I've matched wits with her. You'll—"

"I won't lower my guard, Myranda. Now give me the artifact! If you don't, I promise you I will keep you both here until the portals close. What do you suppose will happen if that blast strikes the power you've stolen? Or the soldiers defending the village? Or the village itself?"

"Then what will it take to convince you?" Myranda called. "What will it take for you to believe that Azriel is alive?"

"I must hear it from her own lips..."

"Then let us take you to her. I can show you the way through the cave."

"No, *now!* I'm through waiting!"

"But we can't—" Myranda began, but she stopped when Deacon touched her shoulder with his fingers.

She turned to see the sliver of metal in his palm, then looked into his eyes.

"I think I can do it..." Deacon said.

"Is it safe?" Myranda asked.

"I don't know that we have any other options." He turned to Turiel. "Listen! I am going to use the portals you've created, combine them. And between your power and mine, I believe we can pierce the influence of the mountains around Entwell. I did it once before, though not without cost."

"Do not speak to me of cost! If you can do so, *do so!* But if this is another deception, it will be the last!"

Deacon nodded and, like a man handling a venomous snake, carefully placed his gem atop the artifact he'd created, clutching them both in his left hand. Making sure he and Myranda were on the Northern side of the main portal, he began to cast his influence out over the field of flickering images. One by one the window to the south at the core of each of them flicked shut, leaving only the churning, dark circle. They pulled toward each other, layering one atop the other, crackling with intensified energy. Each portal, when joined with the last, made the darkness within seem deeper. It was a hole in the air, leading nowhere, yet stretching like a tunnel.

Turiel's expression changed, fury dropping slowly away. One could see in her eyes that she felt something from long ago, something in her past. Whatever the sensation was, it brought a warmth and serenity to her expression. She looked to be coping with a flash of almost painful memories, as if someone smelling baking bread suddenly thinking of the home left behind long ago.

"... I... I can feel her," Turiel said, crossing from the Tresson side of a portal to the Northern side.

Deacon shut his eyes in concentration. Deep within the portal he was crafting... far, far away... a light began to shine. It showed a meadow, green and rolling with grass. At the center of the meadow was a pleasant cottage, thatched roof and painted walls making it the very picture of wholesome.

Tears ran down the necromancer's face. "That's... our cottage. From when we were girls. It was right at the border. I remember it so vividly..."

She stepped through the portal, her feet sinking slightly into the churning black mists of the tunnel as she continued forward.

Deacon's hands were shaking, sweat pouring from his brow. "I... don't know if I can hold it open much longer... The scattering of the mountains... the influence of the crystal arena... it's more than the spell can overcome. The energy of the D'Karon portals is running out. I can't add anymore, the risk of doing it improperly is too great…"

"Turiel! Surely you're convinced! You've got to get out of there! The portal is about to shut!" Myranda called.

"I won't! Not when I've come so close!"

The necromancer quickened to a run, desperate to reach the idyllic image before her and the promise of finally reuniting with her sister.

"I can't… I can't…" Deacon said, dropping to a single knee. His eyes snapped open. "No!"

But it was too late, the power was gone, his concentration lost. At the end of the tunnel, the meadow vanished, the exit of the portal snapping shut. Turiel turned back, now a single recognizable form in a roiling abyss of black energy.

"What did you do? Open it! *Now!*" she shrieked.

The entrance to the tunnel was shrinking now, its power entirely expended.

"Please… leave the portal. I don't know what will…" Deacon said, his voice wavering.

Turiel ran to the entrance of the dark tunnel. "You *will* open that portal again! You *will* take me to my sister!"

"I… don't have the strength… You must—"

"I must take it for myself!" Turiel hissed.

She reached through the steadily shrinking portal and closed her fingers around Deacon's extended, gem-bearing left hand. Her fingers touched his and he screamed in pain, searing bolts of power shooting up his arm and down hers. Each bolt left behind skin rendered gray and lifeless. The power flowed into her, and from her to the portal, but it merely slowed the portal's decrease.

"Let go of him! We will help you find her, there are other ways!" Myranda called out, leveling her staff at Turiel. "But if you do not release Deacon—"

"I am through waiting! Centuries I have waited. I will not wait a *minute* longer," Turiel growled.

The necromancer squeezed tighter, Deacon screamed in agony, and the flow of energy intensified. The portal very slowly began to grow again.

"You should be pleased, Myranda. This is what you want. If I find my sister, I shall have no need for the D'Karon. If this one man must die, that is a small price for us each to achieve our goals. Wouldn't you agree?"

Myranda gritted her teeth and squeezed her staff tight. When she spoke, it was with certainty, and not a whisper of hesitation.

"No."

She unleashed a blast of raw, crackling black magic. It was a vicious spell, one designed to cause pain above all else. Yet when it struck Turiel, it was not pain but surprise that painted her expression. The dark sorceress stumbled back, waves of churning magic washing over her body. Her fingers slipped from Deacon's. Deacon fell to the ground, clutching his afflicted hand.

Without any will or power flowing into the portal, it shrank swiftly. Turiel recovered and rushed for the opening, rage and desperation in her eyes, but it was too late. The portal slid shut behind her, and she was gone.

Drained of all of its power, the portal did not release its shock wave as the others had. It simply whisked away in a curl of black energy, taking any trace of Turiel with it.

Myranda helped Deacon to his feet, the color returning to his flesh as Turiel's attack eased away. Once on his feet, he stood beside her and stared silently at the point in space formerly occupied by the portal. The pair looked around, watching the skeleton army slowly fall to pieces, broken and lifeless once more. The soldiers defending the village lowered their weapons.

"I don't… I don't know where she is now… She was… between two points in the same world…" Deacon said, horror in his voice.

"If it is an end, it is an end she chose for herself," Myranda said.

She pointed a finger at the main portal, the one to the south. It was the only one remaining, and without Turiel's influence it was quickly closing.

"We've got to do something about that," she said. "It was massive, and it was opened from this side. When it closes…"

"I know… it could level the village," Deacon said. He shook his head, trying to restore his focus, and looked to the terrible sight on the other side of the portal. "They need help there, too," he said.

"I'll go," Myranda said, stepping toward the portal.

"Wait," he said. He held out the sliver of metal. "Here. Take the artifact. Turiel altered this portal, dumped power into it in a way the D'Karon hadn't intended. The southern side is the safe side. I don't want to risk a wave of unguided energy hitting this." He pressed it into her hand. "Keep it safe. Put it to good use if you can."

"If you aren't sure you can close it safely—"

"Myranda, one way or another I'll keep this village and these soldiers safe, but we both know I'm the only one who might be able to tame this portal, and you're the only other one who we can trust to handle the artifact wisely. Just go… I'll see you in Kenvard when you return."

Myranda nodded, stepping forward to throw an arm around him in a tight embrace. She kissed him on the lips, then pressed her cheek to his. "Be safe."

With that, they parted ways, each with their own tasks. Deacon watched as Myranda passed through the portal into Tressor, stepping cautiously forward as the restraints that held the Tresson troops to the ground loosened and vanished. He knew that she would have her hands full dealing with the chaos Turiel had left behind, but more importantly he knew that Myranda was more than capable of handling it. The same might not be true for him.

He experimentally reached out with his mind, hoping to perhaps shift the portal's location. If he could move it far from the village, there would be little threat. The instant he wrapped his will about the work of D'Karon magic, he knew moving it was not an option. Turiel's trick of restoring it, enlarging it, had been reckless and hasty. It had worked, but now the enchantment that composed the structure of the portal was fragile and unstable. If he were to attempt anything substantial, he could very well cause it to collapse, resulting in a blast even larger than the one that would result if it closed on its own. There were no two ways about it. He would have to allow the portal to close and somehow protect the village from the resulting blast.

"Everyone! This portal is very dangerous!" Deacon called to the troops. "I need you all to move to the other side of the village. Be ready to help any who may be injured."

"What have you done?" demanded one of the higher-ranking Tresson soldiers. "What is this, and why have you brought it to our land, to threaten our people?"

"You will not address the duke in that manner!" barked an Alliance soldier in return.

The soldiers, now lacking a common enemy, swiftly began to recall their animosity toward each other.

"Now everyone…" Deacon said, trying to calm the growing unrest.

"You get back on your side of the border before we do what we should have done the moment you arrived," growled a soldier.

"I assure you, as soon as it is safe—" Deacon attempted.

The hostility grew sharply, and Deacon found himself somewhat at a loss. He'd always found it rather simple to address a crowd that was open to reason, and with a bit if effort he'd always been able to get his point across even to someone hostile if it was one on one. With little choice, he was forced to alter the situation to suit his strengths, because there wasn't much time to waste.

He held his crystal tight and drew his mind to a simple and quite familiar spell. The air between the increasingly agitated factions blurred and coalesced into a veritable army of illusionary copies of Deacon. The sudden and unexplained appearance of several dozen identical duplicates of someone who was formerly an easily ignored individual shocked the soldiers into at least a brief silence.

"It is exceptionally important that we set our differences aside for just a few minutes longer," the chorus of voices said, each one stepping up to a member of one army or the other. "That portal, when it closes, will do so with a very powerful energy release, which can and will cause massive damage to the village if something is not done. I advise that Tresson soldiers quickly evacuate the near side of the village. Alliance soldiers should retreat no less than four hundred paces. I will do my very best to shield the city, but for the sake of safety I must insist all soldiers and civilians be moved from harm's way."

Each soldier, staring his or her own duplicate of Deacon in the eye, was at the very least motivated to hold his or her tongue. The first to act were the

Alliance soldiers, peeling reluctantly away and heading for new positions at a safer distance. As each left, Deacon let the associated illusion fade. The Tresson troops, though wary, held their ground.

"We don't have much time left," Deacon said, indicating the portal again. "I assure you, the evacuation will be very brief and—"

"How do we know this isn't Alliance treachery? How do we know this isn't the nameless empire trying to take our land as they have for generations!?" countered the same soldier who had first spoken out.

"Because if it was my intention to destroy this village, I could do so with far less effort through any number of different methods. I certainly wouldn't leave it to an unstable portal."

Deacon had spoken the words simply, the crystal clear logic of them seeming to him to be a fine way to settle the argument. In the ears of soldiers interested only in the defense of their people, the words were not taken in the spirit in which they were intended.

"Do you hear him? He admits to having plans for such things! Ready your arms men, before his troops can return!"

The spirited spokesman of the force raised his weapon. A few of his more hotheaded compatriots did the same, but the worst they had done was whisk a blade pointlessly through one of the remaining illusions when a peculiar sound served as a badly needed distraction.

All eyes turned to the sky. A brilliant golden light was rapidly approaching from the north, streaking through the air like a falling star. Accompanying the arrival was a spirited and complex violin performance. When it was near enough, the light revealed itself to be some manner of winged beast, looking like a griffin but burning with the brilliant light of a phoenix. Seated on its back, glowing all the more gloriously, was Ivy. Her violin bow was dancing across the strings, and her face was lost in an expression of pure, soul-deep bliss.

The griffin touched down, turning its flight into a run, and skidded to a stop before Deacon. The suddenness of the landing caused Ivy to hit a sour note, snapping her out of her reverie. Her yellow aura faded considerably as the influence of the music dropped away.

"Oh, we're here!" Ivy said, hopping down.

The instant she was clear, the griffin flashed to flame and faded again, leaving behind Ether's human form. She scanned the surroundings like a hungry predator. Her fierce gaze and effortless acts of magic were not lost on the assembled Tresson troops, who suddenly found themselves somewhat less enthusiastic about the idea of violence.

"Where is she? Where is the necromancer?" Ether demanded.

She had a spirit to her voice and a piercing intensity to her gaze that seemed utterly unnatural for the often cold and calculating shapeshifter.

"There isn't time to explain, but for now at least, she's gone to a place where she cannot threaten us. Ivy, Ether, quickly, I need your help," Deacon said.

Ivy opened her mouth to ask how she could help, but a glance at the massive but rapidly shrinking portal barely a stone's throw from the town made the threat clear.

She covered her mouth and gasped. "We've got to get these people to safety!"

Without delay, Ivy bounded gracefully past the assembled soldiers and vaulted over the wall before they could bring themselves to react.

"Everyone, quickly! Quickly this way," she called amid much banging on doors.

The Tresson soldiers were stricken with indecision, some looking anxiously to the city and Ivy's presence therein, others looking to Ether and Deacon, wary of their evident threat. Most were eying the portal, which was now barely half the size it had been. As it reduced in size, the edge crackled and sparked with a menacing indigo light.

Ether, clearly displeased to have failed to find Turiel, looked to the portal, then to Deacon.

"Do you have the strength for a proper shield?" she asked, willing to set aside her ire for the more pressing task, even if it was a bothersome one.

"I can do my best, but this portal was much larger. I'm not certain if I have strength enough to protect the village."

"Then I shall aid you. But I shall require these soldiers to clear this stretch of land," Ether said.

"I've attempted to convince them of the danger, but they have proved quite cautious."

The shapeshifter snapped her head toward the soldiers. "Have you been given orders by this human?" she demanded. When an answer was not forthcoming, she barked, "*Answer me!*"

"Yes!" came the scattered reply.

"Then I suggest you follow them, because if you do not, *I* will be forced to conduct any further negotiations," she said, adding darkly, "And I have had my fill of diplomacy."

As she spoke, the air around her literally smoldered. The rapid-fire instances of absurdity combined with raw mystic power finally passed the tipping point, and the soldiers marched quickly into the city to continue the evacuation that Ivy had begun.

Deacon gave Ether a nod. "Well handled."

Ether nodded once in reply. "I suggest you place yourself with your back to the wall, and erect the shield as near the village as possible. I shall bolster the defenses between your shield and the portal."

"Agreed."

329

#

On the other side of the portal, Myranda was by Myn's side. With the rush of battle through, her dear friend was suddenly left with nothing to distract her from the accumulated injuries she'd endured. Turiel's last attack had badly dazed her, and she was only now beginning to climb to her feet.

"Myn," Myranda said, pulling the dragon's head close. "Thank the heavens you aren't hurt badly. Does it hurt to stand?"

The dragon shut her eyes and pressed her head lovingly against Myranda, releasing a hiss of discomfort and rumbling with relief and satisfaction as Myranda scratched affectionately at her brow.

Myranda gave her a final pat and pulled away, prompting a sharp look from Myn that effectively communicated her feelings that Myranda had cut their moment unforgivably short. Around them, the Tresson soldiers were in terrible disarray. Many of them were injured, several were killed. Those who were still healthy enough to stand and perhaps fight were, for the moment, holding their ground. They were still getting their bearings after a battle that had been far more than any had been prepared to face, and it remained to be seen what sort of horrors this woman and her dragon had in store. She stepped toward them, but they pulled back, weapons tight in hand.

She looked down. Clutched between her staff and her palm was the artifact Deacon had created. He didn't tell her how to use it, but he didn't need to. It was warm to the touch, almost humming with the energy it contained. The D'Karon gems, when fully charged, often offered up their energy in this way to those who knew the proper magic, but this was different. There, it felt like a bargain with a demon, energy given only with the promise that the gem would once again be fed on the strength of others. This artifact gave its energy freely, like the sun on a summer's day. In her mind and against her spirit, it felt like a gentle heat, belying its profound power. It was like a well, its opening small, but virtually bottomless in depth. As she let it flow into her, soothing her taxed spirit and revitalizing her, she tried to work out the proper way to begin healing the damage that had been done here. A sudden motion beside her made her decision for her.

Myn rushed over to the wall beside the cave's mouth, limping painfully but paying her injuries no mind. Her eyes were set on Garr and Grustim. The Dragon Rider had barely moved since he and his mount had been thrown. The most obvious of the injuries was his twisted leg, but as Myranda swept her mind over him, she found a dozen places both in and outside of him that were badly broken. Without a healer's touch he *might* survive, but he would never recover. Then Myranda set her focus on Garr. The dragon wasn't moving. Thick blood dripped from his mouth, so dark it was almost black, and sizzled where it struck the ground. The inside of his maw was slashed and gouged with the attack Turiel had used to throw him. All over his head and neck, deep black lines had been etched into his scales, and his head was twisted in a painful and unnatural way. His breaths were shallow and reedy, his chest barely rising. As the white magic she'd learned delved deeper, what she found made the severity of the situation even more worrisome. The injuries went far deeper than what the eye could see. Turiel's attacks had a grim efficiency, and she'd held nothing back when she struck out against Garr.

Garr tried to make a sound, but shuddered at the attempt. Myn uttered a deep, forlorn wail and settled down beside him, draping a wing across him and nestling her head near his.

Myranda looked to the Dragon Rider.

"Grustim, Garr is badly hurt. I—"

"Heal him. Save him if you can," Grustim wheezed.

She nodded once and shut her eyes. If Myranda had not been familiar with the needs of dragons from her many treatments of Myn, she would have been shocked at the sheer energy required to make any impact at all on Garr's injuries. It was a matter of scale. The number and severity of wounds required to render a dragon so near death would be enough to kill a dozen men, and therefore it took all of Myranda's considerable experience and skill to mend the worst of them. Garr was quite far gone, his lungs practically shredded, internal injuries pouring blood. As she wove her mind through his body, coaxing tissues to mend and bones to knit, she was dully aware of motion around her. The soldiers were approaching, emboldened by her apparent distraction. She would have turned to them, addressed them, but this was a healing act that must be finished once it was begun, or else she could do more harm than good. But she did wrestle back enough of her mind to listen to what was being said.

"Back, all of you... Let the woman work," Grustim wheezed in Tresson.

"This woman is an invader. Look what her people have done here!" growled a soldier.

"This woman is a defender. She cares for others. *All* others. I do not agree with her ways at times, but every mistake she has made she has made in the earnest attempt to heal this world. I have seen this woman do more for Tresson soldiers than even their own commanders. The Alliance has done terrible things, inexcusable things. But if there is even one woman like Myranda in a land, then that land is redeemable, and she deserves at least the same consideration from us as she has given us," Grustim said.

The soldiers advanced a bit closer, but Myranda kept to her task. Myn rumbled a warning, and when they continued to advance, she hauled herself to her feet, bared her teeth, and shook the earth with an ominous growl.

"An enemy dragon must not—" a soldier began to warn.

"Do not quote your duties to me! No one has devoted his life to the defense of this land more dutifully than a Dragon Rider, and there comes a time when what must be done and what must not be done transcends duty to a crown or king! That this dragon hasn't unleashed her breath or put her claws to work on each of you speaks more of her restraint than can be said of my own. This woman is saving the life of a soldier who has fought for and served this kingdom since before your fathers were born. You *will* leave her to her work. When she is through I am sure you shall all feel her healing touch if you require it. But if you interrupt her and cause this noble creature to be lost, then oath's be damned I shall see to it that each of you pays for it in blood."

Myranda clicked the final and most devastating of fractures back into place, causing Garr to shudder and roar in pain. He coughed, sending blobs of his potent blood spattering across the row of soldiers, stinging them terribly, then drew in a deep breath for the first time since he'd been struck. Slowly, shakily, he released the breath, and Myranda eased him into a deep healing sleep. When he drew another breath, it was calm, steady, and strong.

"There," Myranda said, standing and placing a hand on Garr's head. "It will be a few days before he can stand, but he is through the worst of it. I thank you for your patience. If you will allow me, I will see to each of you in turn, or I will submit myself to your custody. The choice is entirely yours. This is your land, and I am at this point an uninvited guest, if not far worse."

The soldiers stood their ground, their decision stalemated between her offer of treatment and the unspoken but clearly understood threat of injury that hung in Myn's gaze. Finally, the lead soldier spoke, addressing his men.

"Gather those with the most dire injuries. Let the woman work…"

They quickly did as they were told. Myranda cast a glimpse at the closing portal, then turned her attentions as always to those things that could do the greatest good now, trusting that her friends could handle the tasks left to them.

#

Deacon stood with his back to the village walls, watching what he could see of the portal as it gradually closed. A shield spell of the sort that might actually protect the village was a massive undertaking. He had the strength for it, but only just. To give himself and the village the best possible chance, he knew the wisest thing was to wait until the last moment, so that he could devote his full strength to the shield itself rather than squandering strength maintaining it prior to the blast. Ether, on the other hand, had been quite busy. Shortly after the soldiers had cleared the way, she'd shifted to stone and crouched, driving her fingers into the soil and working her influence deep into the ground beneath them. Piece by piece, rising in stout columns and toothlike spires, a stone wall assembled itself. She'd not rested for a moment, fortifying and strengthening every inch of the wall.

"Deacon, Ether… whoa…" Ivy said, pacing around the side of the village's own meager wall and seeing Ether's handiwork for the first time.

"What is it?" Ether asked, her voice strained as she hauled up a final pillar of stone, blocking up the small sliver of an opening that had offered Deacon his view. This last piece in place, she climbed atop the wall to view the portal directly.

"The villagers have been moved to the other side of the far wall," Ivy said. "The soldiers are keeping order. And no one tried to kill me while I was helping." She cleared her throat. "Not very hard, anyway. So… it won't be long now…"

"No. Perhaps another minute. You should get to safety with the others. No sense you risking your life," Deacon said.

Ivy shook her head. "We're a team. We stick together. … What do you think will happen if we fail? If the village is destroyed?"

"I hesitate to think of the consequences. It is almost a relief to know that if such a thing happens, I quite likely won't live to see the aftermath."

"A few moments more," Ether said. "Prepare yourself."

The shapeshifter dropped down from the wall and pressed her stone palms against it. The pillars and spires shifted, pressing together more firmly, as though the whole of the wall was bracing itself for impact. Deacon held out his crystal and dropped to one knee, muttering a quiet incantation to strengthen the shimmering gold wall that spread forth from the heart of the gem. With nothing else to do, Ivy held her breath and covered her ears, watching though squinted eyes as the last of the portal's ragged edge dropped below the top of Ether's wall.

Time seemed to slow to a standstill, each pounding heartbeat an eternity. The air was for a moment alive with energy, crackling with a power that made Ivy's hair stand on end. Then came the blast. The sound was terrifying, robbing Deacon and Ivy of their hearing and replacing it with a dull hiss. The shock of it rattled their bones and shook the very timbers of the village. Cracks riddled the stone wall, but Ether redoubled her efforts to keep the wall intact. Fragments were knocked away, clashing with Deacon's shield. In all, the blast lasted perhaps three seconds, a brief time that was nonetheless far longer than both Deacon and Ether had anticipated. Vicious winds kicked up pulverized rock and soil, scouring the wall and shield and consuming the city in a choking gray cloud of dust. Then, as quickly as it had come, the blast ended.

For nearly a minute the dust hung in the air, hiding the village from view. Deacon stumbled aside, bumping into Ivy, who caught and steadied him. He touched his fingers to his ears, willing a bit of healing magic into them to restore his hearing before doing the same for Ivy. All they could hear was the clatter of falling stone and the creak of abused wood. Deacon squinted, looking forward. At the base of where his shield had been erected was a row of shattered stone, likely what had been blown free from—or perhaps all that was left of—the wall Ether had summoned. A larger than average cluster of stones just ahead of him began to shift, and the pieces pulled together into Ether's fractured form. When she was relatively whole she opened her eyes, peering around. Rather than squint though the dust any longer, she shifted to wind and summoned a gale, whisking it away.

Before them was the tattered ruin of Ether's wall, still standing in places, but mostly reduced to gravel. Behind them was the village. Its own wall had more than a few splintered holes, but it was still standing.

Deacon breathed a sigh of relief, then nearly fell to the ground as Ivy tackled him in an enthusiastic hug.

"We did it! We did it, everyone!" she trilled, squeezing Deacon tight.

He nodded. "Yes… we should see to the soldiers and the people, treat any injuries they may have." He looked over their surroundings, eying the massive crater left by the blast, the torn up, bone-scattered field, and the line of Alliance troops waiting anxiously in the distance… and still well south of the border. "And then we should head north. We've done enough…"

Epilogue

The aftermath of Turiel's actions was far-reaching. For four tense weeks troops stood at the ready on both sides of the border. Harsh words were spoken, vicious accusations made. Rather than allowing them to soar through their skies, Myranda and Myn were escorted back to the border on foot, avoiding cities. Grustim was recalled to Ifrur, the home of the Dragon Riders. He was replaced by two other Riders, each forbidden from even speaking to the Northern noble or dragon. Those Tresson dignitaries still within the north were hastily recalled as well, sent south to meet with their leaders and share what they had learned.

Heated debates and discussions continued, Queen Caya and her wisest advisers meeting with any who would hear them. The outlook was grim. Stories of Northern atrocities flooded the ears of Tresson leaders. Many, even *most*, were apocryphal. Imagined evils dreamed up by Tressons eager to see the borders close and remain so. But among those vicious tales, others began to emerge. Tales of kindness. Tales of boldness. Soldiers spoke with respect of the things they had seen. They told of Myranda's compassion, even when it was a liability to her cause. Truth was separated from fiction, and some of Tressor's own misdeeds came to light. Brustuum was found. Through him and those who served him it was learned what he'd known, when he'd known it, and what he'd sought to do with that information.

After all of the evidence had been weighed and all with a voice had spoken, the decision was made. The ceasefire would continue, the fragile peace would be spared. To affirm the dedication to a lasting partnership between the lands, it was decided that a massive hall was to be built at the border, a joint effort between north and south to replace the temporary hall at Five Point. To celebrate the breaking of the land on this historic structure, Queen Caya proposed a grand banquet.

When the day of the banquet finally came, Myranda and Deacon stood in attendance. They were outside, standing with all of the other prominent figures of the north along the Alliance side of the border while their counterparts stood patiently on the Tresson side. The air was pleasant, the seasons finally warming the border region. This made the many layers of formal clothing that such occasions required somewhat more of a burden than in prior talks. Croyden Lumineblade who among his many other duties served as the queen's herald, was nearing the end of a short speech. For some at least, the speech was evidently not short enough.

"Myn, stop fidgeting," Myranda whispered, touching her friend on the leg.

The young dragon stood faithfully beside Myranda, dressed in her own version of formal attire. This meant that the broadest of her scales had all been polished to a high gloss, and around her neck she wore a blue sash that the wind had wrapped around her like a scarf. From the moment they had arrived, Myn had been highly distracted, constantly shifting her weight from foot to foot and keeping her eyes locked on one of the representatives to the south. In honor of his role in the events that had transpired, Grustim had been invited to attend. That much didn't matter to Myn in the least. What mattered was that he, of course, had brought along Garr. Not once had Myn let him out of her sight since she'd arrived.

"You can say hello after the groundbreaking," Myranda added.

"Isn't it adorable?" Ivy cooed, leaning forward to speak to Myranda from her place on the other side of the dragon. "Myn's got a suitor!"

For her part, Ivy had once again donned her glamorous gown in its three shades of blue. There had, notably, been a few alterations to the design since last she'd worn it. The hole she'd cut for her tail was now an embroidered and accented part of the dress, and rather than the slippers that had initially been paired, she wore a sturdier, but still elegant, class of shoe. In what was likely done without the seamstress's permission, the fingers of the full-length gloves had been removed. It was a modification Ivy had made a habit of applying to all of her gloves, the better to play her instruments without removing them.

"I'm so glad she found a friend," Ivy said, turning to Ether beside her and clutching her arm.

The shapeshifter gently pulled herself from Ivy's grasp.

"I imagine it must be a pleasant for her," Ether said evenly, straightening the sleeve of a gown crafted with calculated elegance.

For another person such an act would seem rude, but Ivy grinned. It said a lot that Ether had been gentle, and that she'd not sneered as she did so. After remaining so cold and distant for so long, that Ether was even present for this occasion spoke volumes of her growth over the past few months.

"… And so, it is with great honor that I raise the ceremonial pick for Her Royal and Imperial Majesty, Queen Caya, to break ground on the Alliance side of this grand enterprise on her behalf," Croyden concluded.

He took a polished copper pick in hand as his Tresson counterpart across the border did the same, but the queen stepped forward and stopped him with a tap to his arm. She was dressed, appropriately for her role, in a gown more exquisite than any other on display. This had briefly not been the case, as Ether had made it a point to arrive with a gown of such intricate beauty that it was quite likely impossible for any seamstress to create, but a few quiet words from the other Chosen had convinced her to tone it down to mere magnificence.

"Croyden, I think perhaps *I* should have this honor personally," she said, smiling broadly.

Lumineblade released a flustered sigh, replying in a whisper, "Your Majesty, tradition and protocol dictate…"

She tugged the pick from his grasp.

"I would think by now you'd know my attitudes regarding tradition and protocol," she said, hefting the tool appreciatively. She reached a satin-gloved hand up and plucked the crown from her head, handing it to him. "Hold this. We wouldn't want a repeat of the *last* groundbreaking."

Croyden nodded in resignation and took the crown.

Caya nodded across the border. "Esteemed Ambassador."

"Your Majesty," said the distinguished older Tresson man standing opposite her, one of at least a dozen royal advisers who had represented the Tresson king during the various talks.

In unison, each noble struck his or her blow. The Tresson ambassador's strike was a feeble one, a symbolic swing for a symbolic ceremony. Caya's, on the other hand, showed practiced form that suggested this was far from her first time with a pick. She hoisted the tool up and swung it home, burying it nearly the full depth of the head into the soil. The deed done, she stepped forward and extended her hand across the border, placing it on the shoulder of the ambassador and receiving one in kind, the traditional Tresson salutation. She then stepped back and offered her hand for a firm shake.

"There! An important job well started," Caya said. "You are all welcome in my land. Let our renewed dedication to peace begin today!"

The rows of attendees began to break, crossing the border and approaching their counterparts. Seeing the motion, Myn looked insistently to Myranda and nearly pranced in place.

"Go ahead," Myranda said softly.

Myn trotted eagerly forward, parting the crowd the way only a dragon could, and made her way to Garr. The normally stoic military dragon, who perhaps in honor of the ceremony had forgone his helmet, let telltale happiness flicker across his expression. The two lightly butted their heads together in greeting.

Smiling warmly at the sight, Myranda turned to Caya, who was approaching with Croyden beside her. When she was near enough to be heard, she whispered low, a sly grin on her face.

"Did you see how much deeper I drove my pick?" she said proudly, taking back her crown and positioning it on the tight bun of her hair.

"It was not a competition, Your Majesty," Croyden said.

"Oh nonsense, everything is a competition," she said dismissively. "And don't think I haven't noticed that Tressor's king still hasn't seen fit to attend any of our joint ceremonies personally."

"It is rare for the King of Tressor to leave the capital," Croyden stated.

"So I've noticed. What's the point of being a leader if you never let your people *see* you? I cannot imagine anyone being so disengaged from his people."

"Your predecessor followed a similar policy," Croyden reminded her.

"Yes, and look how well *he* turned out." She cleared her throat and looked up. "Myranda, Deacon! As ever I am thrilled to have you close at hand again. And where, might I ask, is Greydon?"

"There was a personal matter in New Kenvard. A family matter. Tomorrow is… a very important day for us," Myranda said quietly.

"Oh… oh yes…" Caya said, her voice suddenly solemn. "When the work is done, do send word. It is certainly worthy of a royal visit. However, as for the matters at hand, I'll be heading inside the temporary Five Point Hall shortly. Once you've had enough time to mingle and be personable, please come see me. I'd like to have a word with you."

"Of course," Myranda said.

"Take the time to be a proper diplomat, but don't dawdle."

"Absolutely," agreed Deacon.

"Caya!" Ivy said, stepping forward and throwing her arms around the queen in a friendly hug. "Thanks for inviting me to another party!"

Caya returned the hug and stepped back. "Ivy, you're a Guardian of the Realm. You'll *always* be invited. In fact, it is your duty to attend."

"It's still nice," Ivy said. She gave a turn, flaring her skirt as she did. "It gives me a chance to wear this pretty dress again. And… um… maybe I could have some wine again?"

"If you're expecting me to deny a fellow warrior a good strong drink, you don't know me very well." She turned to Ether. As she did, she just barely failed to hide a hardening of her expression. "And you… Guardian Ether. In most circumstances what I have to say is the sort of thing to be put delicately and in private, but considering your general attitude, I don't imagine social decorum is really called for or expected."

"I see little to be gained from such things."

"Good, then I'll be blunt. Is it true that you demanded a child from Croyden?"

Lumineblade coughed and turned away.

"I did," Ether said, no hint of shame or embarrassment on her face.

"Care to defend that sort of behavior?" she asked, crossing her arms.

"There is nothing to defend. I was in a crisis. My emotions were getting the better of me and my purpose in the world was unclear. He suggested a family would restore focus and perspective, and he seemed as good a man as any to provide it."

Caya turned to Croyden. "Anything to add?"

He cleared his throat. "I politely declined."

Caya narrowed her eyes. "Wise decision." She turned back to Ether. "I'll make this simple for you, Ether. There are any number of reasons why it is unwise and unreasonable to make a demand such as yours, but the one you should keep in mind is this one: Croyden Lumineblade is the queen's consort. While I admire your taste in mates, look elsewhere for yours. I'll see the rest of you inside."

The queen took Croyden rather possessively by the hand and marched toward the temporary hall. Ether, for her part, did not appear to be at all bothered by the exchange. Myranda decided it was best to leave well enough alone.

Ivy did not.

After doing her very best to contain herself, the malthrope snorted and burst out laughing. A deep golden aura spilled out from her.

"Did you… did you *really* do that?" she said, wiping a tear from her eye.

"I see no source of humor in the matter. It seemed the proper course of action at the time," Ether said.

"You learned to care, you learned to feel. I guess a sense of humor will come eventually," she said, giggling.

"I'm sorry, am I interrupting something?" said a female voice.

Ivy turned and tried to restore her composure. "Oh. Ahem. I'm so sorry." She gave a curtsy. "It's wonderful to see you again, Ambassador Krettis."

It was indeed the woman with whom Ivy had shared her rather ill-fated ambassadorial debut. Beside her once again was her aide, Marraata.

"And Marraata! You came too, that's *wonderful*."

"I won't take much of your time, Ivy. Though I appreciate the sentiment of inviting me and the other dignitaries to this event, I very much doubt either of us has fond memories of the other. I am, however, mature enough to admit that any unpleasantness was largely my doing."

"No, really, I…" Ivy began.

Krettis silenced her with a gently raised hand. "I came to you having already judged you. That is a terrible crime and an inexcusable one for an ambassador to commit. I had judged your race, your homeland, and you as an individual. I was wrong on all counts. To make amends, I brought something for you."

Marraata held out a large wooden case and slowly opened the lid.

"Ambassador, you didn't have to…"

This time Ivy was silenced by what she saw. Within the case was an exquisite piece of craftsmanship. It was a lute, not so different in function from the one that Ivy had played during their journey. In form and quality, however, there was no comparison. This instrument was gleaming with polish. The deep red wood of the body was inlaid with designs cut from a wood that seemed almost purple. It was a work of art, yet something about the care and craftsmanship suggested that an equal amount of care had been taken to ensure it sounded as good as it looked.

"My great-grandfather was a luthier. This is one of three lutes he handed down through the generations. I cannot say I've ever taken up the art myself, but you played so beautifully. An instrument like this is meant to be played. Please. Take it."

Ivy reverently took the instrument from the case and cradled it, plucking a string and shutting her eyes as the pristine note rang out.

"It's… it's beautiful."

"All I ask is that you play 'Ascension to the Stars' for me once more."

"Of course I will! Come on, let's find a place in the hall for the performance!"

She led the others away. Appearing behind as though he'd been waiting in line, was Ambassador Maka. Myranda smiled and extended her hand in the Tresson fashion, but Maka held his hand instead for a shake.

"We are on *your* side of the border, Duchess. Allow me to greet you as a friend. I am Ambassador Maka."

"Yes, of course. Ether has spoken of you," Myranda said, shaking his hand.

"She has! Well then I am truly honored. In our time, she spoke of each of you as well. Guardian Ether, it is a great pleasure to greet you once more."

"Welcome, Maka," she said.

She spoke with the air of formality, as though the words were as mechanical and obligatory as a ceremonial bow. And yet, somewhere deep within her tone and expression, there was something more. The tiniest dash of respect. In another it would have been easily dismissed, but for Ether it was so out of place, Myranda couldn't help but raise an eyebrow.

"When we last spoke, you were out of sorts. Your spirit seems lighter now. I wonder, has my advice helped?"

"Some. Time has been short, and there has been much to do. I have not… spoken to all I had hoped to."

"I understand, of course. It is a trying time. But take it from a man," he grinned, "for whom death is *near*. Do not take for granted that there will always be time to do so. When things are important, we must *make* time. If you will excuse me, I believe I am wanted inside."

"Of course. I am sure we will speak more as the night progresses," Myranda said.

"Perhaps we should head inside," Deacon said. "Caya sounded as though she had something important to discuss."

"Agreed. You go ahead. I'll make sure Myn will be well enough without us."

Deacon and Myranda looked to the border. Garr had not moved, though Grustim had dismounted. Myn, on the other hand, had scampered off toward where the carriages of supplies were stationed. There she had quite impatiently been waiting to be noticed. The very moment Myranda glanced in her direction, she ducked her head into the back of a wagon and pulled it back out with a bulging sack clutched delicately between her teeth.

Myranda smiled. "Go ahead, Myn. But just one!"

The dragon leaped over the wagons, sack firmly in her grip, and pranced to the border. With all the enthusiasm of a puppy with a new toy, she set the sack down on the ground at Garr's feet, nosing it forward and looking expectantly at him.

As Myranda paced over, Garr sniffed at the sack and raised his head again, disinterested.

"Grustim. I'm pleased to see you," Myranda said.

The Dragon Rider turned in their direction. He was perhaps the only person in attendance who hadn't dressed for the occasion, wearing instead his usual armor, which aside from light mending of the worst damage still proudly displayed the scars it had earned during their trials in Tressor. He nodded in greeting.

"Duchess," he said.

"I trust things have been well for you and Garr. We never got the chance to express our gratitude for all you did for us."

"There is no need. I did as the mission required."

"Have there been any consequences?"

"My superiors were less than pleased with some of my decisions. There were reprimands, but as of a few weeks ago my debts are paid."

"And Garr is well?"

"Your treatment was exceptional. He has recovered fully. Though…"

"Is there something wrong? Something I can help with?"

He shook his head. "Nothing *you* can help with."

"Oh?"

He motioned to the pair of dragons with his head. Myn had torn the bag open, revealing some fine, fat potatoes. Garr settled to the ground and sniffed again. He flicked one into his mouth with his tongue, shuddering with distaste at the flavor. Myn twisted her head in confusion, then plopped down on the ground beside him, leaning against him and happily munching on the remains of the unwanted gift.

"Oh…" Myranda said.

"He is faithful to his duty. Does what is required of him as well as he ever has. Others notice no change. But when there is no task to be done, his mind is ever on her."

"I think it is the same for Myn," Myranda said.

"It is not a simple problem. A dragon mount may not choose his mate. Most do not earn a mate, and those who do are matched with one of the breeding mothers to produce the strongest clutch."

"The Dragon Riders have a long history, don't they? Surely this has happened before. There must be a solution."

Joseph R. Lallo

"There is, but as I've said. It isn't a simple one."

Myranda sighed and gazed at the dragons. Myn had finished the potatoes and laid her head contentedly upon the ground. Garr draped a wing over her.

Myranda smiled warmly. "Love is seldom simple. Will you be joining us inside?"

"In a moment."

"Excellent."

She paced inside Old Five Point, the strangely named temporary hall that this new hall would replace. It was a hastily built replacement for a structure destroyed in the early days of the war, and it showed; much of its structure was rough-cut timbers and thin planks. The main room was large enough to accommodate the tables set up for the feast, and two smaller rooms off the main one offered privacy for such matters that required it. At the door to one of these rooms stood Croyden. He motioned for Myranda, leaning low to whisper in her ear when she arrived.

"Duke Deacon and Queen Caya are already inside," he said.

Myranda nodded and stepped through the door. He shut it tight behind.

Deacon and the queen were seated at a small table. Caya was filling a goblet from a wine bottle, likely not for the first time.

"Ah, Myranda, lovely. I'll make this brief, as there is a fine meal and good company waiting for us outside, and we are quite likely to be missed if we linger. The woman responsible for this mess… Turiel…"

Myranda shook her head slowly. "We've searched. Sent scouts to places she might have gone, scoured the Alliance mystically and physically. We've not found a trace. I suppose that you've asked means that the Tressons haven't found her either."

"If only. Some of them are doubtful she ever existed. What precisely happened to her?"

"I don't know," Deacon said. "I've pored over the workings of the spell and the ways it might have combined with the D'Karon aspects. The place… that… tunnel that formed between the portals. It shouldn't have been there. The purpose of the spell…"

Caya raised a hand. "We haven't got the time for you to attempt to explain. Myranda, perhaps you could summarize?"

"The spell should have made two places one for few moments. When both sides of the portal shut, the portion between them simply ceased to be. At least, to the best of our knowledge."

"She *may* have been destroyed," Deacon offered.

"Mmm. 'May have been.' Not words I like to hear in reference to an enemy such as her. This may be a lingering bit of my Undermine instincts, but I prefer to have a corpse. If nothing else, it's a fine bit of closure." She sighed. "Keep searching. Keep researching. The sooner we can be certain of where she is or where she isn't, the better we shall all sleep at night." She drained her glass.

342

"Now, before we venture out, there are one or two matters of state that should be discussed…"

#

Ether stood quietly in the corner of the main hall, arms crossed and eyes distant. Food was being set out, and off in one corner a few apple crates were being stacked into a stage of sorts under Ivy's supervision. As she watched, lost in thought, a servant stepped up to her, bowing low.

"Guardian Ether," said the servant, a young man.

She didn't answer, merely shifting her gaze to him.

"I was told to inform you when your guest arrived."

"Good. Show her in."

He stepped quickly to the task, slipping outside and entering again guiding an older woman by the hand. She was dressed neatly, her outfit a faded and ancient blue, the gown of a woman who had set it aside for special occasions and had had little use of it for far too long. Her eyes were wide with wonder, sweeping the room and gaping at dignitaries and warriors she'd never dreamed she'd see. Then her eyes met Ether's and instantly became misty.

Ether stepped forward and took her hand, dismissing the servant and leading her to the private corner in which she'd been standing.

"Guardian Ether," she said, offering a reverent curtsy. "I… I don't know what to say. How do I thank you for summoning me here? This sight, so many great people in one place… it is far too grand a sight for these old eyes."

"Celia, you need not say anything," Ether said. She paused, for a rare moment uncertain of how to properly voice her thoughts. "I… it has been said, by those I have learned are quite wise, that when our minds are not as they should be, when our hearts are heavy and the way forward is unclear, there is value in having someone in which to confide. Family. There are those I would call my allies. I am certain they would hear my words and offer their thoughts but… there are matters I would prefer not to share with those whom I would fight beside.

"I know that you feel a connection to me because the face I've come to call my own once belonged to someone dear to you. Though it is not truly a thing of blood, through this connection you are the nearest thing to true family I have."

Celia reached out, intending to place a hand on Ether's shoulder, but she held back, uncertain if doing so was proper for someone in so exalted a position.

"Guardian Ether, if ever there is anything you need to say, I could think of no greater honor than to be the one you confide in."

Ether tipped her head. "You have my thanks." She glanced up to see that Myranda was leaving the back room. "One moment." She raised her voice and called, "Myranda, come here for a moment."

Myranda obliged.

"Myranda, this is Celia."

Joseph R. Lallo

Celia again curtsied. When she spoke, her voice was hushed. "The Duchess of Kenvard. It is an honor so far beyond me to have the privilege of meeting you."

"Please, stand. There is no need for that," Myranda said.

"It is my understanding," Ether said. "That for favors of the sort I have requested, it is customary to compensate."

"Oh, you needn't—" Celia began.

"And to properly perform the service I have requested of you, only one reward seemed appropriate. I have little skill as a healer. In my existence I have seldom had the need. But Myranda is quite able in that regard. She has agreed to pay my debt to you with this gift."

"I don't understand…" Celia said. "I am not ill, not injured."

"Just hold still. You shall understand in a moment," Myranda said.

Myranda placed her hands to Celia's temples. At first she offered no reaction, but when it came, it came in waves. Her eyes darted about, tears streaming down her cheeks. She sobbed once, then gasped, putting her hands to her ears.

"I trust this compensation will be sufficient," Ether said.

At the sound of the shapeshifter's voice, Celia looked at her, stricken with emotion. Without warning she threw herself forward, embracing Ether and sobbing openly.

"I… I never thought I would hear her voice again…" she said, squeezing tight. "Thank you. Thank you…"

Ether looked to Myranda, uncertain and uncomfortable. Myranda gave her a hard look. Slowly the shapeshifter returned the embrace, the gesture wooden and awkward.

"Yes… You are welcome. … And thank you…"

For a time there was only the din of the dining call, but a few moments later a voice cut through it all.

"Excuse me!" Ivy called. "Before we enjoy the delicious meal that has been prepared, I've been asked to perform a short song that has deep meaning to our friends from Tressor. I hope you all enjoy it."

Celia, unwilling to release Ether from her embrace, simply held her tight as, for the first time in years, she heard music lilt through the air.

#

The feast lasted long into the night. It wasn't until the first rays of sun were coloring the sky that Myranda and Deacon were finally able to get on their way. Myn bid a reluctant goodbye to Garr, then carried the wizards off.

It was only a short distance from Five Point to New Kenvard, at least by dragon-back. The trio arrived as the noon bells chimed. Myn, tired from the trip, quickly plodded off to rest. Myranda and Deacon entered their home, eager to see Greydon, but they didn't find him there. In truth, they hadn't

344

expected to. Without words, they walked to the edge of town, out through the gates.

There, stretching along the southern section of the city wall, was a sequence of marble slabs. Each slab had dozens of names carved into it, the names of each man, woman, and child who had fallen with the city. The victims of the Kenvard Massacre. Before one of the slabs stood Celeste, his hands folded and his eyes cast toward the monument.

Myranda took her place beside him and turned to the stone as well. Carved into the marble, one name among many, was Lucia Celeste. Had the city not fallen, the family would have at this moment been celebrating her birthday.

She reached aside and took her father's hand, lacing her fingers with his. Deacon clutched her other hand. There were words that could have been said, solemn hymns that could have been spoken, and deep truths shared. Instead, they stood in reverent silence. In some moments, family and togetherness are all that is required.

#

In a forest on the eastern edge of the Northern Alliance, just beside the mouth of a cave littered with faded warnings, the bushes shuddered and twitched. From between them trudged a beast crafted from the remains of many. His motions were sluggish, skittering, spidery legs faltering with every few steps. Nonetheless he raised his head, peering into the darkness of the cave, and released a low chitter. Taking a breath and gathering his strength, he pressed on, into the darkness of the Cave of the Beast...

#

Elsewhere, in a place without a name, there was only darkness. After a silent eternity in the inky void, a voice rang out, echoing through the endless expanse, speaking strong and clear.

"Sister... dear sister... what *have* you done..."

###

Joseph R. Lallo

From The Author

Thank you for reading this story. *The D'Karon Apprentice* is the first true continuation of *The Book of Deacon Series*. It would never have been written if not for the fans who showed such interest and enthusiasm for the series. Whether you liked my work or not, I would love to hear what you think, so please leave a review. It will help me to improve the things that you didn't like, and to give you more of the things you did. And finally, if you'd like to hear about my latest projects, please sign up for my newsletter.

Discover other titles by Joseph R. Lallo:

The Book of Deacon Saga:
Book 1: *The Book of Deacon*
Book 2: *The Great Convergence*
Book 3: *The Battle of Verril*
Book 4: *The D'Karon Apprentice*

Book of Deacon Side Stories:
Jade
The Rise of the Red Shadow

The Big Sigma Series:
Book 1: *Bypass Gemini*
Book 2: *Unstable Prototypes*
Book 3: *Artificial Evolution*
Book 4: *Temporal Contingency*

NaNoWriMo Experiments:
The Other Eight
Free-Wrench
Skykeep

Connect with Joseph R. Lallo

Website: www.bookofdeacon.com
Twitter: @jrlallo
Tumblr: jrlallo.tumblr.com

Made in the USA
Middletown, DE
02 September 2022

73063197R00199